THE KEEPER

THE KEEPER

John G. Ives

Bohème PUBLISHING

Provincetown, Massachusetts

First Edition by Bohème Publishing, Provincetown MA, June 2013
www.bohemepublishing.com

Copyright © 2013 by John G. Ives

Cover Art and Illustrations Copyright © 2013 by Justine A. Ives (Og)

Book design by Justine A. Ives (Og)

Map of Cape Cod and Vicinity, 1909, Published by Walker Lith. & Pub. Co., Boston
Courtesy of the Norman B. Leventhal Map Center at the Boston Public Library

Illustrations of Life-Saving equipment courtesy of Annual Report of the United States Life-Saving Service, 1900, and other public domain sources.

This book was set in Minion Pro by Country Press, Lakeville MA

10 9 8 7 6 5 4 3 2 1

ISBN 978-0-9894542-0-9
ISBN 978-0-9894542-1-6 (e-book)

Library of Congress Control Number: 2013909547

This book is dedicated to my wife Kina and my daughters, Justine and Camille.

PART ONE

THE CAPE

And from that time on I bathed in the Poem
Of the Sea, star-infused and churned into milk,
Devouring the green azures; where, entranced in pallid flotsam,
A dreaming drowned man sometimes goes down...

—Arthur Rimbaud, *Le Bateau Ivre*

CHAPTER ONE

On a cold night as winter faded, Lucy Macomber Duell walked alone down a wind-strafed wharf in Boston. Patches of snow still lingered on the pier's heavy timbers. She mounted the gangplank and, lifting her heavy wool skirt, stepped over the transom to board the Santa Marie, a three-masted merchant schooner bound for New York. The year was 1899. A shivering seaman in a faded pea coat accepted her ticket. Carrying her leather satchel, she nodded at him then made her way to her cabin. Lucy was weary beyond expression, physically and mentally, but she was finally going home. Just three weeks earlier she had buried her eldest son, Adam, then gone to visit her sister, Catherine, in Boston. She had promised her husband and younger son, Joshua, she would be back before Easter, the tenth of April, but bad weather had delayed the ship's departure and she would not make it. As the ship pulled slowly out of Boston harbor, the walls in the small cabin creaked with the rising and falling sea and she felt terribly alone.

The daylight lifted her spirits. By late morning, the schooner was fifteen miles north of Provincetown, headed southeast past the back shores of Cape Cod, through Long Island Sound to New York harbor, a trip of two days at most. The wind stiffened and dark clouds loomed to the north and east. Lucy sat in a folding chaise, writing a letter. She was a strong, good-looking woman of forty-three, elegant and proud; despite the weather, she appeared composed in a stylish traveling dress, heavy coat and indigo silk scarf. She had always loved to travel by sea; she inhaled the briny musk and watched the birds following the ship on currents of air. The rolling ocean was a dark, grayish green, the deck's angle sharply skewed, the sky the color of damp ash.

She was thinking about Easter, and smiled to herself, remembering a dinner six or seven years earlier, a room full of laughing people. Lucy had cooked a lavish ham delivered from a farm in Pennsylvania and insisted on carrying it herself to the table, as if bearing a sacred offering to her family and friends. She'd tripped on the rug, but caught herself, giggled, and held the platter aloft, as everyone cheered.

Lucy looked up at the blackening sky and reflexively touched two fingers to the lapis and silver brooch pinned to her dress. It was a talisman of sorts; it had been her mother's and she always wore it when she traveled. She turned to the page and wrote:

My Dearest Joshua,
 The seas grow rough, but at least we are finally underway and I shall be with you soon.

The sea has kept your father from me often, but I grew up by it and love its deep mysteries. I miss you both terribly and am so sorry to have missed spending Easter with you.

It feels silly to write a letter to someone I shall see a day or two hence. But my darling boy, there are some things, important things, that are easier to write than to say face-to-face. I have wanted to tell you this, and my heart won't let me stay silent any longer. I know you blame yourself for Adam's death, but you should not, you must not. You're a good boy, the very best, you are strong—in your own way as strong as your father and brother, perhaps more so—and I am and forever shall be enormously proud of you.

With deepest love,
Mother

She folded the leather portfolio with the letter inside, closed her eyes and floated with the rocking motion of the ship. None of the other sixteen passengers were on deck. Lucy slept a while, wrapped in a heavy blanket.

By afternoon, the sea had risen and the ride became quite bumpy. Lucy was awakened by a fellow passenger, who shook her gently.

"Sorry, Ma'am," he said, "but the captain has announced we should all assemble in the salon." There was a sound of distress in his voice.

Lucy nodded and went inside, where the crew was issuing everyone life vests as a precaution. As they passed the barely visible shores of Truro, the clouds hovering overhead grew more threatening and the waves turned into ominous rolling hills. Icy raindrops pelted the glass. Lucy sat on a wooden bench in the salon, feeling awkward in the bulky cork vest. Several passengers were drinking and talking but she had no desire to join them.

The storm moved in and the temperature dropped. Large, wet snowflakes struck the teak deck boards and stuck to the portholes. The wind continued to build, the waves grew still larger, the air colder, the snow increased in intensity. Soon icy drifts piled along the sloping deck. The captain had furled the jibs, topsails and staysails, but even with reefed mainsail and foresail they were moving at a good clip. Lucy made her way to her cabin and lay down, wearing the vest. She closed her eyes, trying to sleep, but the boat's motion had grown too erratic and she lay in the dark staring at the ceiling.

As the cabin tossed and rolled violently, Lucy stumbled over to look out the porthole. The light was fading and the sea outside was wild. She could hear breakers somewhere in the distance.

Suddenly the ship struck something, hitting hard. The thought flashed into Lucy's mind that they'd struck a sandbar. The ship veered to port and the waves breaking by the bar began their dreadful work, pounding against the heavy wooden hull with a booming rage. A rogue wave hit from the opposite direction, slamming the ship hard to starboard. Lucy heard the shrill, drawn out cracking as the mainmast splintered and ripped away from its base, bouncing against the deck before flipping over the side. She heard the fading scream of a crewman being carried with it into the frigid water.

She felt a flash of fear, like ice water down her neck. She rushed to scramble out of the cabin, to safety or to her death, she could not know, but she knew she must try to escape. Blasted by the wind and waves, the old schooner began to break apart, and Lucy could feel the very timbers trembling. Then the keel slipped and the ship listed further to starboard, hurling her against the bulkhead. She felt an astonishingly sharp pain, and she was certain her arm and shoulder, maybe a rib, had been broken. A feeling of panic seized her, as she suddenly understood she might never again see her husband and son. Determined not to die, she struggled to her feet and dragged herself up the narrow stairs, pummeled and tossed by the flailing ship. When she reached the deck, she was stunned by the clamorous thunder of the ocean and the strength of the wind. Through the blinding spray she could make out two men, one of whom appeared to be the captain, struggling with a tangle of rope. In an instant, both men disappeared over the side.

Lucy could see no other passengers, no one at all. The daylight was fading. She slumped against the last remaining mast, her face and bonnet encrusted with ice. Alone in the wicked storm, she knew she was doomed. Her heart beat fast and tears streamed down her cheeks. The portfolio was tucked inside her coat under the vest. Her mind drifted and she remembered a day when as a little girl she ran along the cliffs by the ocean, watching a distant sailboat against the sun-speckled blue. Faces passed in quick succession: her mother, her sister, Gideon strolling with her by the Portsmouth shore, Adam as he squirmed through his first bath, and Joshua, Joshua, her golden boy.

She smiled and opened her eyes. Through the driving sleet, she watched the forecastle split from the rest of the ship and float away. It floated toward what looked like the light of a small boat. In a last burst of hope, Lucy pulled herself to her feet and struggled across the slippery tilted deck to the remains of the railing. She screamed out, "Help! Help!" She heard, as if from afar, the desperation in her own voice. She might be saved.

CHAPTER TWO

The train jolted Joshua awake. He had dozed in the visceral heat of the ancient, rattling car—his third train in two days—as if smothered in a musty blanket. He sat up, unsure for a moment where he was, then struggled to his feet and made his way down the aisle, trying to keep his balance, in search of some air. His tweed jacket, which he'd outgrown long ago but still loved, made him sweat more profusely. The car lurched and he nearly fell into the lap of a man in a bowler reading a newspaper. His face pressed against the page, he could barely make out the headline, which seemed to announce the Red Sox's Cy Young had struck out Jimmy Barrett at Huntington Avenue Park and beat the Tigers. Joshua got to his feet, apologizing for the intrusion, glad to know the real world was still somewhere out there. A canvas rucksack in one hand, a ragged-eared book in the other, he searched for a window that might open, then slumped into a creaky seat, reached over and grasped the window clasps. It refused to budge, but he kept at it and finally the thing opened. The gush of fresh sea breeze was like manna from heaven.

He was twenty, tall and too thin, gangly and awkward in his gait, with a handsome face and large eyes—plagued by self-doubt, but brimming with eagerness, with a belief that all roads still lay open to him. Sometimes he could be dark and brooding, as if off in another universe—he had been to war and suffered loss, and there was a fear, an anger there. When he wasn't brooding, his smile glowed as if lit by a brilliant fire, innocent and infectious.

The train rounded a bend and there opened up an ebullient bay glistening with sunlight and white sails gliding across. The breeze blew his hair and he breathed in the pungency of the sea. It made him think of a day long ago, sailing with his mother across Long Island Sound. He could still hear her laughter filling the space of the weather-beaten sloop, the swishing parting waters and the luffing sail, seagulls with their poignant shrieks. She had been smiling at him as she perched on the side bench, in the way, at least as he imagined it, that she smiled only at him. Her laughter had been the clay that held the family together, his father and brother, all of them— her loss had been unimaginable.

It had been a year now since he and Adam had left for Cuba, young marines, following in their father's footsteps. Joshua remembered how consumed with fear he had been, while his brother had pretended not to be at all. Adam could have used a little more of that fear, Joshua thought. How could time have gone by so quickly? So many things gone wrong in such a short time. After his brother's death, the family had traveled to Washington to bury him. They had shared a doleful train ride home afterward, each of them speechless with grief, but when they reached New York, Lucy had made the sudden decision to continue to Boston to visit her sister. Gideon, his father, objected; he was worried about her after what she'd been through, but Lucy insisted she would be fine. She wasn't.

Joshua and his father had returned home without her to the old house on Sixty-Third Street, which echoed with memories. With absence. Like a room once lovely and brilliant whose life has been sucked out of it by fire, leaving only bones and scorched pages. When the news finally came of her shipwreck, they had been left bereft and barely able to communicate with one another. In some ways, that emptiness and silence had been the hardest part of all. Joshua could have gone back to Harvard, which he'd left to join the war, but though his father was incessantly cruel and foul-tempered, he didn't wish to leave him alone. His father's love, even in the best of times veiled by a curtain of distance and pragmatism, was now and would ever be blanched by bitterness.

Tragic wrecks like the one that had taken his mother were not uncommon. There was a Life-Saving station in Wellfleet, not far from where Lucy's ship had gone down. The Life-Savers manned stations along the coast and patrolled the beaches to look for potential shipwrecks, but no one had seen this one in time. When the ship was finally boarded, it was derelict and Lucy's body had not been found. All of Gideon's years at sea assured him that whatever had befallen his wife, it had been final and tragic: she had gone in the ocean and nothing was left to find or identify. ·

It had been a long winter, but one morning in May, Joshua had awakened to the sound through the open window of two cardinals calling to one another. It was as if a heavy curtain had parted: the time had come to put all the darkness behind him. But first, he had to learn what had happened. That night he went drinking at a tavern in Greenwich Village with several Harvard classmates who'd just graduated. He was glad to see them, happy for them, and acted jovially, tossing back beers and whiskeys and cheering with the others. But inside he still felt mournful and adrift. He told them his mother had drowned off Cape Cod. One of the boys said he'd once visited a magical little fishing village at the peninsula's tip called Provincetown. That was enough. Joshua made up his mind to leave in two days. He had no idea what he might discover: an answer perhaps, a way to find his bearings. But he would go to this place, on the far-flung peninsula where his mother's life had ended, and learn what he could.

Gideon thought it was idiotic. "There's no one going to remember what happened. Everyone on the ship was lost. I wish you'd stop dreaming and get on with your life." Well, that was how his father always talked. It didn't mean much, and so Joshua went.

They slowed to stop at the South Truro station, a narrow platform surrounded by sand. How marvelous this country is, he thought, so open, the sand running wild and free over the peninsula, rolling green hills spotted with beach grasses, here and there a solitary tree, farmhouses perched within the floating sea-speckled openness. Enormous dunes loomed over them as they rocked past a narrow lake. A wide bay appeared on his left, sailing ships moving elegantly in the bright sun. Joshua could see the very tip of the land in the distance, a finger of sand with a low-slung lighthouse.

A tap on his shoulder interrupted his thoughts. It startled him and he spun around brusquely. A girl who'd gotten on in

Chatham, sitting immediately behind Joshua, had leaned forward, but surprised by his violent reaction, quickly retreated. Joshua noticed a man across the aisle smiling. He smiled, too, embarrassed, and turned round to face her.

The girl managed to regain her pluck. "You have a nice smile when you show it," she said. "You going to Provincetown?"

Joshua now felt self-conscious and simply nodded, but the girl grew excited.

"Are you an artist?"

Joshua shook his head. "No, I'm afraid not. Why, are you?"

"No." She blushed slightly. "I'm not… I grew up here." She giggled. "A local girl."

"Really? What was that like?"

"Well, it was quite wonderful," she said. "You'll see, it's a very special place. There are a lot of artists starting to come here. It's the light, I think. Where are you staying?"

"I've no idea," he answered.

"Try the Union House. Nice little hotel right in town, not too expensive."

"Thanks, I will," Joshua said.

"And stop by the New Central House some evening if you like. Best after eight."

"Will you be there?" Joshua asked. "Tucked in among the artists?"

The girl smiled and sat back in her seat. "Perhaps," she said.

He turned back to look out at the busy port, wooden schooners and iron steamships hauling cargo and rows and rows of wharves. Two tall barques and a three-masted schooner sailed out toward the mouth of a perfect harbor, sheltered by the graceful arc of the coast. The fragrance of the sea was powerful now. The train moved inland briefly, and then emerged between two dunes covered with low shrub pines. Joshua's stomach churned with anticipation. They had arrived.

He could see the town was built along a narrow strip that followed the curve of the bay. The clapboarded and shingled buildings, capes and barns, grain houses, stables, hotels and stores—all were bleached by salt and ocean spray. The train slowed to a crawl and crossed a road of packed sand, bristling with carriages and freight wagons, with mobs of people crammed together in the hot sun. Joshua watched, fascinated: burly men hauling large bundles on their shoulders, housewives hurrying their children, fishermen clomping along in heavy foul weather gear, boys in shorts and caps and girls in flowery jumpers chasing raucously through the crowds, tourists in linen suits and long cotton dresses dodging the traffic. A clamorous din drifted through the open windows, voices calling out, boat horns blowing, the locomotive hissing steam and blasting its whistle. They rolled onto a broad wharf, boats tied two and three deep bobbing alongside. A large schooner unloaded its cargo of fish in a swirl of swarming, screeching gulls. Joshua felt excited as he took it all in. The little train's bells clanged as it slid to a halt in a cloud of steam. The conductor swung down from the front car and called out loudly, "PROVINCETOWN! END OF THE LINE!"

Joshua stepped off the train and hoisted his duffel on his shoulder. The late morning sun shone brightly, a few high clouds hung decoratively over the shimmering harbor; southerly breezes shook the riggings of sailboats tied along the pier and ruffled the brightly colored flags strung over the boardwalk as he made his way down the wharf.

The street smelled of sugar candies and roasting meats, cigarettes and sweat, fish and seaweed. The people pressed tightly together, mingling fearlessly with horses, carts and wagons. He passed a dry goods shop selling souvenirs and fishing gear, a tavern where a band played John Philips Sousa songs as customers sang along stridently, hoisting glasses of beer to the sky. There was a chaotic energy about this place—like a carnival, impious, lawless, yet joyful and amazingly human. Joshua could feel the oppression of the past months, the war, his brother's death, his mother's, all of it slipping away, supplanted by a buoyancy he barely could remember having experienced before. He felt suddenly, meticulously alive—as if he had stepped from the mouth of a cave into a glorious light. It was a revelation.

The Union House was down a small side street. A craggy old lady in a housedress gave Joshua a key and with a grunt pointed the way up a stairway almost too narrow for his duffel. He entered a tiny, slant-ceilinged room. It was cramped and hot, but he felt relieved to have finally arrived. He opened the window, the sea-soaked air quickly drowning out the room's musty smell. The sounds of the town and the sensation of the light itself seemed to galvanize him. He quickly changed his shirt and headed out again to explore.

He walked west along a sidewalk of shaky wood boards, to where the streets were narrower and dotted with quaint cottages. Looking over the harbor from this viewpoint, he could make out the movement of ships and murmur of human traffic from the distant wharves, but the dominant sound was of the gentle wind. He followed the open land northward along a sand path into the dunes. There was no one to be seen.

Joshua began to climb a massive hill of blazing sand. It was higher than it appeared, the slope steep and hard going, but when he reached the top, winded and sweating, the view took his breath away. A moonscape of incandescent sand mountains stretched before him, splattered with waving grass and bleached shrubs, and far beyond, the dark blue sea rippled with gentle whitecaps. It seemed to be beckoning him. He trekked across a hot sand valley splattered with patches of marsh, then up another dune. At the top he could see the water below and hear the low persistent roar of the waves, coiling as they reeled toward shore, breaking and rolling forward, recoiling and breaking again, smacking against the sloped beach, a muffled timpani, water rushing over pebbles in a hissing foam.

He stretched his arms and ran down the other side, tripping and tumbling, whooping like a young boy. At the bottom, on the edge of the beach, he began to undress, struggling to remove his boots, flinging aside one item of clothing after the next, in a great hurry as if his very existence depended on stripping completely naked. The breeze cooled his skin; he ran down and dove into a breaking wave, then emerged screeching at the cold. He had always been a strong swimmer, and he stroked hard to cut through the waves, which had surprising power, the current pulling beneath him. Swimming in the ocean like this was so incredibly liberating, the prickly water rushing over his entire body, that his soul felt suddenly unbound. He swam to a sandbar and lay back on the sand, basking in the soothing sunlight. A pack of gulls on the wet sand, spotting him, began to move in a single rhythm, first one, then several, then all, rolling forward and taking flight in a beautiful balletic pattern. Then he heard voices, and looking up, saw a group of women with parasols walking toward him along the beach, pointing at the waves and the gulls. He didn't think they saw him, and he dove back in the water and swam to shore. He stood and faced them a moment, the sun and tender breeze drying his body. He grabbed his clothes and ran the opposite way until he was far enough to safely dress.

Now Joshua looked around him. There was debris strewn along the beach, strips of wood and remnants of furniture, clothing, broken glass, a crate with a rotten orange wedged in its slats, a clock, an empty picture frame, part of a magazine, its pages crinkled and shredded. Stepping carefully he found more debris, flotsam and jetsam; ahead, screeching gulls circled around something in the sand, landing then shooting into the air. The gulls fluttered and shrieked but did not fly away until he was quite close. Then he saw the object of their attention.

A body lay in the sand, or rather a part of a body, the head and torso badly decomposed, the skin pallid and loose, peppered with holes like old cheese. The skin remaining on the face was slack and the skull showed through. The arm and leg on one side had been torn off; the remaining limbs had been partially eaten away by birds and insects. The corpse had been there for some time. The smell of the thing was shocking, putrid and nauseating. Joshua's heart beat wildly, his mouth was dry and his legs trembled. He leaned over in the sand and vomited. This was a shipwreck.

CHAPTER THREE

Joshua lifted his head from the rough oak bar, feeling disoriented. Someone was speaking, but he couldn't quite understand what the person was saying. He had fled the beach and, still nauseous, out of breath, knees weak, he had made his way back over the dunes and into the little town. It was less crowded in early evening. A sign above a set of broad painted steps had read "New Central House", and remembering what the girl on the train had said, he'd mounted the steps. "Provincetown's Only Beachfront Hotel," the sign boasted—a sprawling place, its lobby fashionably decorated with red wallpaper, people sitting demurely on tufted circular sofas. Still in his traveling clothes, he felt out of place and queasy. A gas-lit hallway led back to a large salon, crowded and smoke-filled, perched above the beach facing the harbor. The noise and thick air was unsettling, but Joshua had gone straight to the bar and ordered a beer. As he drank it down, he realized his hand was shaking. He ordered another, trying to flush the nightmare still blazing in his mind, the fetid decayed body on the beach. When he took a sip of his third beer his head swooned—suddenly he felt immensely tired. His head nodded and he rested it on his arm, drifting off into a half sleep.

"You all right, pahd?" the voice repeated.

The man standing next to him was a wizened Portuguese fisherman in canvas pants and a shredded Irish sweater. He spoke loudly, in an accent Joshua had never heard. Joshua turned and looked at him, trying to focus.

"Yeah, I'm fine," he said unconvincingly.

The man held out his hand. He was dark, swarthy, a short man, stout and strong looking, his hand calloused and powerful. "Pinky Sousa," he said.

Joshua wasn't sure if this was a name or some odd kind of statement, but he took the man's hand. "Joshua Duell."

"Not from around here, I wager," the man said. His voice was booming yet at the same time intimate, as if they'd known each other a long time.

Joshua looked at him, then around the room. A boisterous crowd—fishermen, working men, ingénues in long dresses, businessmen in suits and bowlers. The men smoked cigars, many of the women cigarettes. In the corner a small man, all bones and jaw, played rags on an upright piano, his fingers dancing smoothly over the keys, the rapid melodies filling the room with their tinkling laughter. The lights of the room reflected on the lapping water outside and a three quarter moon sprinkled a million tiny lights like a broken mirror over the bay.

Joshua told the man he had just arrived that afternoon, and described what he'd found on the beach.

"Ay, pahd, that was one of them missing bodies off the Jersey Princess."

Joshua looked questioningly at him, then signaled the barkeeper to bring two more ales.

"Yes sir," Pinky continued. "A four master what was run aground off Wood End, musta been near six seven weeks now. Nasty storm. Lotta folks died that night."

Joshua pictured the mangled corpse on the beach. "What happened?"

"What happened, you ask? The ship come up from Boston, rounded the Cape headed for Providence. A dozen passengers an' the crew. Late in the year for a storm of that sort. But there it was, blew up outta nowheres, quite a squall. Captain drifted too close, got hung up on one a' them bars out there—you seen 'em, ain't ya, pahd, them shiftin' devils? One day the sea lane is clear, the next there's a load a' sand's been moved by the current and hidin' there 'neath the waves. The Life-Savers spotted her and got the boat in the water, but she was an old ship and the big waves broke her in two pretty fast. Most of them folks went in the ocean, and it was still cold, y'know." He paused, took a sip of his ale and looked at Joshua with great severity. "Don't take long sometimes. Depends on the wind and the waves. Seen a ship hang in there fer days, crew hung on the riggin' freezing to death. Other times it happens quick and everyone's a-gone."

Joshua stared at the row of bottles sparkling among a dozen candles on the mirrored shelf behind the bar, refracting light and figures moving about the room. "Do you remember a wreck Easter day, off the town of Wellfleet?"

Pinky Sousa stopped and scratched his chin. "We had a few bad ones this past year," he said, pronouncing the last word 'yee-ahh'. "I remember hearin' sumthin' about a wreck where the Life-Savers was too late to save anybody…"

Joshua nodded. "That's the one. You know anyone who saw it?"

Pinky Sousa shook his head. "Nah, don't know too many folks down there."

There was an outburst of laughter at a nearby table, the kind of laughter that sounds too forced to fully believe. A man's voice lilted sonorously above the music. Joshua looked toward the table. A man was speaking to two women. One of them was the girl he'd seen on the train who, spotting Joshua, stood and came over.

She looked very different, striking really, if somewhat fantastically dressed in a white silk skirt and brocaded vest over a bright yellow blouse.

"So you came," she said in a bubbly voice. She reached out her hand to shake his. "I'm so glad."

Joshua took her hand. "Hello," he said. It seemed to him he must be mumbling.

"I'm Emily."

"Joshua…"

He was interrupted by another loud outburst. At Emily's table, the man whose back was to the bar spoke loudly to the other woman. He had shoulder-length hair breaking over a velvet jacket and a whiskey in one hand, which he waved around as he spoke.

"Of course I have," the man was saying. "I've been all over Europe."

The other woman giggled. "Really? Where for example?"

Emily took Joshua's hand. "Come meet my friends."

Joshua, still feeling a bit dazed, was hesitant, but she

seemed to pull him along. Meanwhile the loud conversation continued.

"Oh, Paris… Munich," the man said. "Italy, of course. It's a different world over there, believe me."

The other woman said wistfully, "I've never been. It must be very romantic."

"Hardly romantic," he replied. "The people over there have hard lives. Many of them are fighting for their freedom."

"Freedom from what?" the woman asked.

"From persecution and from government."

The woman frowned. "From government? Oh, what rot."

Joshua and Emily walked over to the table.

"You have to understand," the long-haired man proclaimed, "all governments are built on violence. They exist for the protection of economic interests, of a social order that rests on materialism and the suppression of the working classes. Governments promote violence, against their own people and against other nations, to protect their economies, and there are people in this world willing to fight for what they believe is…"

There was something familiar about the man's voice and tone. Then he turned his head. He and Joshua recognized each other instantly.

"Buddy? Is that you? Jesus, what are you—?"

Buddy leaped to his feet, grasped Joshua's shoulders with both hands and kissed each cheek like a European general. "Joshua! I can't bloody believe it! You're looking great… just great!"

Joshua's heart was pounding. It seemed so incongruous to see him here. They'd known each other a long time, since their teens, but he hadn't seen Buddy since the day he left for the war. Was he glad to see him? He was struck instantly by the realization that he wasn't sure if he was. It was like a jarring return to a time before everything in his life had changed—as if Marley's ghost had materialized and transported him back to the past.

The two women exchanged glances. Emily sat down. Buddy scurried off, grabbed an empty chair and dragged it over.

"Here, sit, sit down," he said to Joshua. He turned to the two women, pronouncing triumphantly, "Ladies, this is a very dear old friend of mine, Joshua Duell."

"How do you two know each other?" the second woman asked. She wore a dress nearly as theatrical as Emily's, but she seemed less confident.

"Why, from Harvard, of course!" Buddy exclaimed, at the same moment that Joshua, too, said in a much lower key, "Harvard…"

They both laughed awkwardly. They had been roommates there and in prep school in Connecticut. Buddy's real name was Robert Anschluss, from Cleveland; his father had given him the nickname to make him feel better when the neighborhood boys had teased him. He had always been handsome, with long hair and a rugged face, bright and quick-witted, athletic, exuding charm, and the girls had always loved him. Yet as hard as he'd tried, he'd never been popular with other boys. He and Joshua had helped each other out of a few scrapes over the years.

"We had some adventures together, didn't we, sport?" He turned to the two women. "We haven't seen each other for ages."

Joshua stifled a laugh. Buddy hadn't changed much—if anything he seemed more intense. He had matured, filled out, and still looked like a leading man. "Where've you been, Buddy?" he asked.

"Oh my lord, so many places," Buddy said with a sigh—as if the weight of all those memories were too much to bear. "We haven't seen each other since…"

Joshua cut him off, something stirring inside him, an undefined misgiving. "The day I left. For the war."

Buddy nodded. "Yes, that's right."

"Why are you here, Buddy?"

"Oh, man, have you seen this place? It's gorgeous!" He gestured excitedly, though it was unclear whether he meant the town or the women. "And you?" he asked Joshua.

Before Joshua could respond Buddy turned his chair around and leaned over the back, facing Joshua and the two women. "May I buy you ladies another drink? What would you like?" he asked cheerfully. He quickly turned to Joshua. "Oh, forgive me, this is Emily and… sorry, what is it?"

The second woman answered, "Larissa."

"Right, sorry," he repeated, then called out to a passing waiter with a magisterial gesture, "We'd like to order some more spirits."

The waiter approached suspiciously. The women ordered glasses of ale. Buddy asked for a whiskey. He looked over at Joshua, who shook his head.

"Two whiskeys," Buddy said and turned to the girls. "So, tell me, ladies, is this the first time you've visited Cape Cod?" he asked, winking at Joshua.

"I'm from here," Emily said.

"This is my first time," Larissa said quickly.

"Larissa's a writer," Emily said. "We know each other from school, too."

Joshua turned to Larissa. "What do you write?"

She seemed thrilled to be asked. "Oh, you know, stories, poems…"

Emily was nodding in agreement, but Buddy, no longer the central part of the conversation, interjected.

"The pilgrims landed here. Did you know that?"

"I thought they landed in Plymouth," Larissa said. Emily laughed.

"No. They came later to Plymouth," Buddy said proudly. "They landed in Provincetown first and explored Truro, the next town over. Then they sailed across the bay to Plymouth."

Joshua smiled. He'd always found Buddy's antics amusing. "I never knew that."

"Well, it's true," Buddy said defensively.

"He's right," Emily said.

Buddy grinned proudly. But Joshua detected something uneasy about him, an uncertainty, a fear. Buddy lifted his glass, facing the two women with a grand gesture.

"Here's to the ladies!" Buddy exclaimed. "To summertime! The sun, the water, and the lovely ladies." He took a sip.

Three men appeared in the doorway, scrutinizing the room. Something about them caught Joshua's attention. The man in front was thin but solid, medium height, and carried a heavy walking stick. He moved with a swagger—even standing still he seemed to swagger—and he had a disturbing, unhealthy look about him. His face might have been considered attractive, but at certain angles he appeared quite ugly. He had black hair, piercing grey eyes, and long arms that extended beyond the sleeves of his black coat. A curved dagger, rather Asian-looking with an intricately carved wood handle, hung from the front of his belt.

The other two men followed slightly behind. One was stout and swarthy, in a rumpled shirt whose sleeves were rolled up, a bright red tattoo of a whale on the inside of his left arm. The other was tall and bony, nearly emaciated, with dark circles under his narrow eyes and deep hollows in his cheeks. His skin was the color of caramel and he looked vaguely African, his charcoal hair in clusters of tight knots. The three men sauntered over to the bar.

The leader spoke in what sounded like a Russian accent. "Give me a whiskey, friend."

The bartender seemed to know him. He poured him a glass and slid it over. "Hey, Gogol," he said warmly, "I thought Russians drank vodka."

The Russian picked up the glass and drank it down. "I'm an American now." He laughed loudly.

The other two ordered ales. The stout fellow took tobacco from a weather-beaten pouch and began to hand roll a cigarette. The tall one draped himself across the bar and began puffing on a raggedy pipe.

Buddy saw Joshua watching the men and paused. Then he turned to Larissa, who seemed intimidated by him, and began again.

"Have you read Nietzsche?" he asked.

She shook her head, puzzled by the question. She had tight blonde curls that bounced upon her shoulders when she spoke. "No. Who is he?"

"He's a German philosopher. All the rage in Europe these days." Buddy looked over at Joshua. "It's human nature—and therefore the nature of the state—to strive for power. This is what Nietzsche talks about. Any living being will try to grow, to spread, to seize, to become predominant, not from any morality or immorality but simply because it's alive. It's a basic organic function." He paused, and looked earnestly at the ingénue. "Like love. Yes. Very similar to love, but…"

Buddy took a long sip of beer, a gleam in his eye. Joshua shook his head incredulously. What a charmer, he thought, what a way to seduce women. Buddy had always been smart, a clown sometimes, but his interest in the world was authentic.

The Russian was watching Buddy, but seemed to be flashing his eyes at the two young women. He ambled over and the other two followed, holding their beers.

"Hello, young ladies," he said, ignoring Joshua and Buddy. "Allow me to introduce myself…"

Buddy stiffened. "We're talking here. Do you mind?"

The Russian continued to ignore him. "My name is Vassily Kirov. My good friends call me Gogol, I don't know why. These are my friends, Tucker and William."

Buddy tried to pick up where he'd left off. "Where was I? It's the responsibility of the people, through the exercise of their own determination, to control the state's will to power. Through force, if necessary. The state is controlled by the rich, and the rich seek power and more riches, always…"—he pounded his fist into his hand—"at the expense of the man in the street. The people must rise up, as they've done in Germany and Russia, in France and Ireland, to put a barrier before the state and its soldiers."

The two girls appeared lost. But Tucker, the stout one, with a rolled cigarette burning between his lips which distorted his already distasteful expression, moved closer to Buddy, dropped his cigarette to the floor and began to roll another.

"What shit yer talkin," he said with an Irish brogue. "Where in fuckin' Ireland are they puttin' a goddamn barrier before the state?"

Buddy looked at him, sizing the man up. "Well, they will, you'll see. The people there are oppressed."

"Oppressed?" Tucker answered. "Yeah, by the bloody English. Should kill the whole fuckin' lot of them."

Buddy interpreted this as supporting his theories and nodded enthusiastically. "The people have to take control of their destinies," he said, grinning at Larissa.

Larissa tried to look as if she were following all of this, and smiled back, then seemed to retreat as William stepped closer, wraithlike as the light from the bar shone through his plaited hair. He took a puff on his pipe, turned to Tucker and sneered, "This guy is full of it."

Buddy looked stung; Joshua could see the blood rushing to his face. Buddy began to stand, but Kirov put his hand on his shoulder, keeping him in his seat.

"Now there's no need for anyone to get themselves worked up here," Kirov said, grinning broadly. He had a surprisingly caressing voice despite the accent, but there was an undercurrent of tautness, as if he were holding himself back. Joshua looked closely at him for the first time. A sudden glint drew his eye to the man's vest inside his coat: a silvery piece of jewelry, which caught the light of the bar.

Buddy pushed the man's hand brusquely off his shoulder and jumped up. Looking directly at Kirov, he said, "That's not polite, sir."

The three men burst into laughter.

Emily leaned toward Buddy and whispered, "You should be careful of them."

Ignoring her, Buddy addressed Kirov. "I was just explaining Nietzsche's political theories to these young ladies here."

"Pile a' crap," Kirov said, and spat on the floor.

The men laughed again. Kirov looked at Emily, his lip curling. "Was you talkin' about us, darling?"

"No... no I wasn't," Emily said, trying to remain defiant.

"Leave her alone," Buddy said.

Kirov's expression darkened. He turned again to Buddy, turned back his coat and placed one hand on the handle of his dagger. With his other hand he poked the end of his stick against Buddy's chest. "Or what?"

Joshua was pretty sure what was coming next. He'd seen it in school, in the Marines—wherever men came together, he thought. He put his hand on Kirov's arm. "Let's back this down, sir. No one's looking for any trouble."

Kirov shook his arm free and turned to face Joshua. His large eyes illuminated and bore into Joshua's. "Who asked you? Go back in your hole."

Joshua could now clearly see the jeweled trinket pinned to Kirov's vest. It looked familiar, very much like his mother's brooch, the one she always wore when she traveled.

Buddy stepped forward. "I'm warning you, sir, please don't push me any further—"

"Ya little piece of shit," Kirov growled. He turned his staff and pushed it against Buddy's chest, heaving him into the couch on top of the two women.

Buddy was up in an instant. "Sorry, ladies," he said.

He lunged at Kirov, knocking him off balance. The other two men rushed in. Joshua stepped toward them and pulled the scraggly-haired one by his shirt. The man reeled then threw a punch, connecting with a sideward blow to the nose. Joshua could feel the room start to spin. He tumbled against a lamp, which crashed to the floor.

A crowd gathered and men were jeering. The music stopped. Kirov stood up straight and hit Buddy squarely in the chest. Buddy gasped, losing his breath, but stood his ground.

"Hold him up," Kirov commanded. They moved toward Buddy.

"That will do nicely now, Mr. Kirov!"

The voice came from a man dressed in a sailor's coat and captain's hat, puffing a pipe. He appeared to be in his sixties, medium height, thickset, with powerful shoulders. He had a weathered face and a white mustache that hung thick and long on either side of his mouth. His expression was stern, but there was a warmth in his eyes. The man looked around the room. People seemed to be tentatively going back to what they had been doing.

Kirov glared at the man, who glared back.

"Evening, Cap'n," Kirov said tersely.

"Mr. Kirov, I think you should be taking your boys out of here now," the man said.

"I didn't know you was the police around here," Kirov replied, but he straightened and brushed himself off. "Well, have it as you will." He glared at Buddy. "I'll see you again soon, my friend," he growled, picked up his stick, turned and swaggered out the door. The other two followed.

"Wait, you!" Joshua called to him. "What's that pin you've got on your vest?"

Kirov stepped toward Joshua, held back the edge of his coat and pushed the vest forward. "You mean this?"

"Yeah, that."

"It's nothing," Kirov smirked. He started to turn.

Joshua lunged after him. "Where'd you get it?"

The older man grabbed Joshua by the shoulder and held

him back. "Let it rest, son."

Joshua could feel the rage churning inside him, but he stopped and watched Kirov leave the room. Then he turned and looked at the man.

"Why'd you stop me?"

The man turned to Emily. "You all right, young lady?"

She seemed to know him, and she nodded and smiled, embarrassed by what had taken place. The crowd dispersed and the skinny piano player started playing again, quickly getting back up to speed. Glasses clinked and the murmur of the crowd revived.

Joshua tried to clear his brain. The side of his head ached; his nose didn't seem broken, but it hurt as if it were. It had been a while since anyone had hit him like that, and he didn't like it any better now than any other time. And what about the brooch? Who was this Russian fellow?

The older man turned back to Joshua, his expression softened. "You know why, son." Then he looked at Buddy. "I don't know what you said to him, but you should watch yourself." He looked back at Joshua. "Those fellas are dangerous."

Joshua nodded. The man held out his hand.

"John MacDonald," he said.

"Joshua Duell. This here's Buddy."

The man nodded at them. "New in town?"

"Yes, sir. Seems like a pretty interesting place," Joshua said, nodding in the direction of the retreating Russian.

"That it is, that it is," MacDonald said. "Wonder how interesting you'd find it in winter time, though."

"What do you mean?" Buddy asked.

"We get some wild weather out this way. Bad storms. And there's not much work when the tourists leave."

Joshua was curious. "What about working on the boats?"

"Well," MacDonald answered, "the fishermen can't work much past Christmas, 'cept those out in Helltown, and no one goes there much anymore. Not a lot of other boat work in these parts when the air gets cold and the sea gets rough. 'Course it's beautiful here, but not an easy life."

Buddy grinned. "We're not afraid of hard work." He looked over at Joshua, as if they were a team. "Anyway," he added, "we're only here on vacation."

"I see," said MacDonald. He puffed his pipe. "Well, you young men enjoy your vacation, then. Stay away from those other fellas, I'd say." He headed for the door, then stopped and looked at Joshua. "If you decide you might want to stick around, you come see me. I'm looking for men. Come find me. I'm the Keeper." He turned again and walked out.

Buddy burst into laughter. "The Keeper? What the hell does that mean?"

Joshua. "Damned if I know."

A man nearby said, "That's Captain MacDonald, the Keeper at Peaked Hill Bars." He pronounced "Peaked" as two syllables, accentuating the first.

"What's that?" Buddy asked.

"The Life-Saving Station, out beyond the dunes," the man answered. "The Keeper runs the station. Hell of a good man. Courageous man."

"The Life-Saving Station?" Joshua asked.

"What do they do there?" Buddy asked.

The man answered reverently, "They save lives."

They all left the hotel together; the two women seemed to have lost their taste for the nightlife, and said goodbye.

Buddy watched them go, disappointed. The night was warm, peppered with the mixed scents of beer and seaweed, carried on a steady breeze. Joshua turned the other way and they walked together down the street.

"Damn! I could really have…"

Joshua interrupted, smiling. "You could have what, exactly?"

"I don't know…" The restiveness fell away from Buddy's expression and he returned the smile. "Pretty amazing, you and me in the same place, isn't it?"

Joshua nodded.

Buddy continued. "I mean, what are the chances of running into you here?"

Joshua looked at him. "What happened to you, Buddy?"

Buddy seemed surprised by the question. "What do you mean?"

"The war. I mean the war. Did you go?"

Buddy shook his head. "No. But you did."

"Yes." Joshua walked along silently. "What did you do?"

"Went to Europe," Buddy said. "There was no way I was going to fight in that stupid war. I told you that…"

"I see."

"You thought it was wrong, too."

"Yes. I did."

Buddy looked at Joshua's nose, which was swelling at the top. He reached over to touch it. "You all right?"

Joshua knocked his hand away, surprised to find himself feeling a little irritated with Buddy and not knowing why. "I'll live," he said. "Where are you staying?"

"A boarding house in the west end. Nothing much. You?"

"The Union House."

"Yeah, I know it. Maybe I should move there," Buddy said.

Joshua looked at him. "Suit yourself."

"What was all that about the pin?" Buddy asked.

"Nothing," Joshua said. "Something familiar about it, that's all."

CHAPTER FOUR

Buddy arrived at the Union House the next day. A bigger room with two beds was available, and they saved money by moving in together. Joshua had a funny feeling about it, but couldn't seem to figure out exactly why.

He awakened in the middle of the night and couldn't fall back asleep. He got up and walked to the bay. The stars shone crystal clear and it was low tide. Twice a day the tide receded some fourteen feet, leaving a quarter mile or more of moist sand and tidal pools, as if someone had pulled the stopper out of a bathtub. He walked out on the flats in the darkness and looked back at the few twinkling lights in houses on the shore. There was an overwhelming sense of the sea in this place, as if it were the soul of the harbor and the people who lived here. Joshua could feel an unknown force working on his spirit. He thought about his mother's shipwreck, that no one had seen it and no rescue had been attempted. He needed to discover why. Maybe the Keeper could help him figure it out.

He returned to the room, sat down on Buddy's bed and stared at his sleeping friend until he stirred and opened his eyes.

"I want to go and see the Keeper," Joshua said.

Buddy's eyes were barely open. He sat up. "What about?"

"He said he needs men."

"For what?"

"For the Life-Savers, I assume," Joshua said.

"You're out of your mind," Buddy said, irritated. "You think I came here to the Cape in summertime, with warm sun and pretty women, to work for the goddamned United States government? What a stupid idea."

"I don't know if it is or isn't. All I know is I want to go talk to the Keeper and see what he wants. You coming with me?"

Buddy stood up and splashed water from a pitcher over his face into the washbowl. He looked at Joshua with a scowl. "Look, you saved my ass that day at college. You watched over me. I owe you something for that—"

Joshua interrupted. "No, Buddy. You don't owe me a thing."

They stared at each other.

"I... I want to be your friend. But I don't like this idea," Buddy said.

"I know," Joshua smiled.

Mid-morning they followed the same path toward the dunes Joshua had taken before. Joshua stopped and asked an old salt how to find Peaked Hill Bars.

"Well, first off, young fellas, you're at the wrong end of town. You've got to head back the other end, north out on Snail Road, and cross the dunes there. You'll find the station if you keep straight to the ocean. Going to see the Captain, are ya?"

Joshua marveled at how everyone in a small town seemed to know what everyone else was about. "Yes, sir, we are."

"Well, you boys watch yourselves now. It's a long journey out, but a longer one back." And the old man continued on his way.

"What the hell did he mean by that?" Buddy asked.

"Damned if I know," Joshua said.

"These people are a little nuts, I'd say."

They walked to the east end, past old wharves with sagging, weathered shacks and houses with rows of codfish covered with salt drying in the front yards, creating a pungent odor that permeated the streets. At a poorly lettered sign stuck in the sand that read "Snail Road," they turned north. The sand grew deeper, the road disappeared, and beyond the railroad tracks they reached the base of the dunes and set out to cross them.

At the far end they came to the long, deserted beach. They walked for a while, rounded a bend, and there nestled into a dune was a large house, painted red, with a tall square tower, its windows heavily etched by sand. Two sets of wide barn doors were open to the beach with broad ramps sloping downward. Inside one was a large white dory on a cart. The odd-shaped red house seemed completely incongruous in such a wild setting.

"This is it," said Joshua. "The Keeper must be around somewhere."

Except for the hissing waves and soft wind, it was completely silent.

"Hello!" Buddy called out.

There was no reply.

"Hello! Anyone here?" Buddy called again. "Maybe he's sleeping."

"I doubt it. Let's go in."

Buddy followed Joshua up the ramp. Inside the barn-like room the air was cool and still. Ropes and pikes, rubberized coats, oilskin slickers and hats were neatly arranged on hooks on the wall, and another set of hooks held cork lifejackets. The room was filled with equipment, all stowed in perfect order. Joshua knocked on a door. Silence. He knocked more firmly then pushed the door open. In the center of the room was a rectangular table, with eight chairs around it, and at one end a large cast iron stove. An adjacent room held a smaller table, an icebox with its door ajar and neatly stacked storage crates.

Buddy called out again. They walked through yet another door and there, at a roll top desk, sat John MacDonald, puffing on a pipe and writing, with great concentration, a quill pen moving swiftly across a sheet of linen paper. He didn't look up, but kept on writing.

"I heard you," he said. "Just a moment."

Joshua and Buddy waited uncomfortably, hands clasped, watching the man. His powerful shoulders were hunched as he wrote, his strong right arm reaching across to the inkwell. Suddenly he lay down his pen and turned, looking sternly at them.

"Yes, how may I help you boys?"

"We... we met you a couple of nights ago," Joshua answered, a bit taken aback.

MacDonald suddenly smiled. "Ah yes, the pugilists. You've come a long way. Perhaps you'd like a drink of water."

Joshua and Buddy looked at each other, taken by the man's intense manner.

"Cat got your tongues? Would you like some water to drink, or would you not?'

Buddy stepped forward slightly. "Y-yes sir, we'd love some water," he stammered.

"Well," said MacDonald, "there's a crock in the corner, and a ladle on a hook above it. Help yourselves."

They each dipped the ladle in the pot and drank.

"And what can I do for you?" MacDonald boomed, startling them.

Joshua put down the ladle. "You said to come see you, so here we are."

"Ah, yes, so I did." He turned and looked at Buddy. "And why are you here?"

Buddy answered nervously, "I'm here with him."

"Here with him, eh? Do you always go everywhere he does?"

"No," Joshua said, "he doesn't."

"But we're good friends," Buddy said.

MacDonald looked at each of them in turn. "I see." He picked up his pen and wrote a few more lines, as if worried he might forget something. Then he looked up again. "Do you know what this place is?"

"It's a Life-Saving station, sir. Peaked Hill Bars." Joshua felt strangely awkward.

"Yes," MacDonald replied. "All right. Imagine this..." He looked at them intently. "You are a midshipman on a sailing ship, a fine old lady that has served its captain and crew well, heavily laden with cargo, riding low in the water. You're headed for Boston, where you and the rest of the crew hope to receive bonuses. It begins to snow, the waves grow larger. The ship's course takes you near the Cape, though you can see no land.

The captain calls to come about. You hear breakers pounding, far off you think. You see white caps, but nothing else in the blackness. Now you see the waves. The watch in the rigging calls out, 'There's a bar, Cap'n!', and the next instant the ship hits the bottom with a powerful jolt. You are thrown off your feet. You hear a cry as one of your shipmates goes overboard. There is a loud crack. The ship is breaking up. The captain calls out to abandon ship. The very thought of it chills your bones. There is no turning back. The deck begins to split. You and your friend are hurled into the sea. You are dressed in your wool coats and watch caps, but in the water these are a deadly burden. You are stunned by the cold of the water, racing up your legs and along your arms, taking away your very breath. You each try desperately to remove your heavy coat. One of you..."— he looked sharply at Buddy—"is caught by an enveloping wave as you attempt to slip your arm out of the sleeve. The wave swallows you, you gasp for breath, the water rushes into your throat and eyes and lungs, and in moments you slip into the depths. Then you..."—he looked at Joshua as if hurling daggers with his eyes—"you understand there is nothing in the universe but survival. You are frozen with cold and fear; your friend is dead, the ship breaking apart. You have but one chance, and that is to make the shore. You slip out of your coat, even colder now, and beat your arms against the surf. The sea is wild, random flying fortresses of thrashing surf. You can barely breathe, you are certain you will die any moment, but you are determined and swim harder. A wave breaks and carries you with it, over the top, then smashes you under. You fight for the surface. Your feet touch bottom, though standing in this current is impossible. You are in shallow water, in the pitch dark, all you can see is white foam and black ocean, but the land is there and you crawl up the beach." MacDonald paused and looked at them. "And now what?"

"What do you mean, sir?" Joshua asked, transfixed.

"I mean, young sir, it is January amidst a bitter cold nor' easter, you are in the dark, the only one of your crew who has survived, you have no coat, you are near frozen to death, with no idea where you are. The only thing you know is if you do not find shelter soon, you will die out here. Of that you are dead certain. What do you do?"

"Build a fire," Buddy said.

MacDonald looked at him. "Out of what? I repeat, you are drenched and frozen, alone, without any coat, equipment or resources, you cannot see more than two feet ahead of you, the sound of the ocean is like dynamite exploding. How will you build a fire?"

"You won't," Joshua said.

"Correct," MacDonald replied. "You will stagger blindly in the dark, and finally, exhausted, fall to the sand and sleep. You have made it ashore, but your fate is sealed."

The Keeper stopped speaking. The silence was corporeal. Joshua and Buddy looked at him, their faces filled with fear and anticipation.

"This, gentlemen, is the scenario that caused many a seaman and citizen to stop and ponder. The answer was developed right here. The Massachusetts Humane Society was formed, and what they did was quite simple. They built little wooden huts along the beach, where blankets and food were stored, and firewood, and a fire could be made in an iron stove. And they told the sailors sailing these waters about these huts, so if a man were to wash ashore as I have described, he would know if he pressed on a bit further he could find the shelter he so badly needed, and survive. This was the origin of the Life-Saving Service."

Joshua and Buddy each let out a deep breath, as if they'd experienced the disaster first hand.

"But, what does that have to do with this place?" Buddy asked.

"It was not enough," MacDonald answered. "Thousands of people still died on these shoals every year. Some sailors, who knew what to look for, did find the shelters. But it was an insufficient solution. So the Humane Society began taking volunteers to patrol the beaches."

He stopped and puffed on his pipe. Joshua and Buddy watched him, spellbound.

"Again, the idea was a simple one. Patrol the beaches, and if you see a wreck, get some help. Ah, but remember the circumstances. These are beaches literally engulfed by the tides. No beach, just breaking waves. The sea is ice water. The air is bitter cold. The wind takes your breath away. You cannot see your own nose, it is so dark. Who can survive such a conditions? Who would be mad enough to go out on a night like that? Well, there were quite a few brave volunteers who did go, but still it was not enough." MacDonald stopped and gestured with both arms. "That was where we came in. The Life-Saving Service, created as part of the Revenue Service, run and supplied by the government. Once the rescuers were made part of a service, a military service if you will, there was sufficient strength and will power. And it has saved thousands of lives…"—he looked at them more keenly with his large brown eyes—"lives that would otherwise have been lost."

"You said you needed men, sir," Joshua said, his throat a

bit choked.

Buddy looked over at Joshua, seeming to want to hold him back.

"Part of my task as keeper is to recruit men to serve at the station," MacDonald. "There are eight, myself and seven surfmen. We could have eight, if needed, but seven has been sufficient. Two of my men died last year in service. They were temporarily replaced by men from town, who have not renewed their positions."

Buddy looked grimly at the Keeper. "Sounds like a dangerous job."

"It is that, son," MacDonald said. "Many men have been lost, but most have not—and you have good mates to watch your back."

"Where are the others?" Buddy asked.

"Surfmen are employed for ten months. We start August first and finish June first. The storm watch is necessary beginning in September and runs through the winter. August is for training."

Joshua glanced at Buddy. "What would we have to do to become surfmen?"

Buddy shook his head in disbelief.

"To start, you'd take a written examination. Once that has been successfully completed, you would undergo a test of your health and agility. If you were to pass muster and still wished to proceed, it would be up to me to decide whether you'd be suitable. If so, you'd be given the opportunity to sign up. The contract is for ten months, and you must be committed to that time period. The pay is seventy five dollars a month."

"That much, eh?" Buddy asked.

"It is enough to live comfortably during the year. The

Service provides living quarters and all meals, uniforms and equipment. You are allowed one day each week to visit relatives in town. That's about it."

Joshua didn't know what he was going to do, but he felt a beating in his chest, an elation that seemed to catch hold of him. "I'm prepared to take the examination immediately," he heard himself say. He looked over at Buddy. "Speaking for myself, of course."

Buddy was speechless.

MacDonald scrutinized them, first one, then the other, as if judging them for their pedigree, bearing and strength. "Very well. Return day after tomorrow first thing in the morning, I shall have the exams ready for you. I wish you luck. Good day, gentlemen."

And with that, he returned to his writing, and did not look up as Joshua and Buddy, dismissed, turned and went out.

Outside the building it was hot and still, though ripples of wind skirted the water's edge. Buddy removed his shirt and shoes and walked through the surf.

Joshua felt elated. "What a fascinating man!"

"What an odd turkey," Buddy answered. "And you... are you out of your mind?"

"What do you mean?"

"Ten months in a little shack by the ocean? You're nuts," Buddy said. "Not for me... Working for the government is the last thing a free man wants to do."

They turned up a sharp slope to walk back over the dunes. Visible waves of heat emanated from the stark surface. Their feet sank in the sand and they were quickly out of breath, but at the top the ocean breeze cooled them. They stood side by side, the grand dunes stretched before them, a harsh but magical world.

Without turning his head, Joshua spoke. "I was thinking about the brooch. On the Russian's vest. I could swear it was my mother's."

"How could that be?" Buddy asked. "Did the house in New York get robbed?"

"My mother died this spring," Joshua said.

Buddy was shocked. "How?"

"A shipwreck, off of Wellfleet, not twenty miles from here. No one knows what happened exactly or how she died. Her body was never found."

"Jesus," Buddy said, clearly stunned. "So you think—"

"I don't know. But she always wore that pin when she traveled. It was her mother's, and she wore it for good luck."

After a few moments, Buddy said quietly, "I guess it didn't work."

Joshua shook his head.

"I'm sorry," Buddy said.

Joshua nodded. "You see, I feel like the Keeper can help me figure this thing out, you know? If anyone can…"

"That doesn't mean you have to join the Service," Buddy said.

"I know. Maybe I won't at all. But something feels right about all this."

"Well, I wish you luck," Buddy said. "Definitely not for me."

They walked quietly down the side of a dune, slipping as they went.

"What was it like?" Buddy asked when they got to the bottom.

"What was what like?"

"Cuba. The war. Last time I saw you was when you were

about to leave school. You went to New York, didn't you?"

"I had to go. My brother and father were going. I didn't want to, but I felt I had no choice in the matter."

"Was it bad?" Buddy asked.

Joshua closed his eyes. He could feel the sweet breeze on his skin. It made him feel tired to think of it all again—tears were welling in his eyes. "I don't want to talk about it."

When he was fourteen, with Gideon always in Washington and Lucy running a charity and two arts groups, he had been sent to a prep school in Connecticut, the same one his father and uncle had attended and from which his brother had just graduated. Joshua never really liked the place, but it was a family tradition. He was tall and athletic, and got along with the other boys. His second year, Buddy had come from Ohio. He got in on scholarship, and though he, too, was good looking and athletic, the boys disliked him. They thought he talked too much, they looked down on him—no one from Ohio could possibly be as smart or sophisticated as a boy from a good east coast family. Buddy always felt he had to prove himself there. Joshua thought he was cleverer than he was given credit for, and he could always make Joshua laugh, especially once he started drinking. Their roles became fixed—even when they both made it in to Harvard, where they became roommates. Joshua would stick up for Buddy, Buddy would cling to him like a shadow, and neither of them was ever quite comfortable with the arrangement.

The day Joshua got to Harvard a group of boys at the registration office had decided to play a trick on Buddy, and misdirected him to an office across campus. He missed signing up for two classes he'd wanted. When he discovered he'd been tricked he came steaming back and found the boys in the students lounge. One of them, a priggish Rhode Island fellow, pushed Buddy hard and he stumbled, then leapt to his feet and slapped the boy hard on both sides of his face. Standing nearby, Joshua was shocked to see a fight break out, but quickly understood Buddy deliberately hadn't hurt the fellow. Deciding to teach the Ohio upstart a lesson, the boy and his friends held him and took turns punching him. Buddy fought hard and made a lot of noise. Joshua thought it was an unfair fight, and came to his rescue. He pulled the Rhode Island fellow off by the collar and flung him to the ground; his height and tenacity made the other bullies back off.

"I had it under control, but thanks anyway," Buddy had said.

By the second year they were roommates at the old vine-covered dormitory, along with Sam Endicott from Philadelphia. Buddy's father had come from Cologne and become a pharmacist; he believed in hard work and a simple, ethical life. Buddy's mother was from Connecticut, and taught history at a local grammar school, but she was never happy in Ohio. Buddy would talk about how his parents' differences kept them at each other's throats—she disapproved of her husband's lack of curiosity, he of her snobbishness. Buddy had two older sisters, who teased and fawned over him. After Joshua got to know him, he understood Buddy had built inside himself a feeling of mistrust, as if the world would be safer for him if he kept his own counsel and didn't reveal himself. Joshua liked Buddy, though; he admired him for his street smarts, his ease with girls, and also for a zest for life other people never seemed to notice—Buddy was insatiably curious and ravenous for new influences and people.

They didn't talk the rest of the way home, but when they reached the hotel Joshua stopped. "Look," he said, "I know you would never join up. It's not your style. But just for the hell of it will you take the test with me? I hate to trudge all the way out there by myself."

Buddy laughed and agreed. And that was that.

CHAPTER FIVE

The first of August burst forth in splendor, a hot, near perfect day.

"Let's go to the beach," Buddy joked nervously when he awoke.

Joshua knew he was only half joking: this was the day they had to report to the Life-Saving station. They had passed their written tests, which were basic compared to exams at Harvard; they'd returned for a morning of physical tests which included swimming, running, climbing, and towing a wagon—they'd both performed these with ease; then the Keeper had invited them to join. At first Buddy had refused, but eventually he agreed.

Before he did, they had sat together, legs dangling, on a pier near the beach across from the hotel.

"You really want to do this?" Buddy had asked.

Joshua nodded. "I do. I feel like I have to."

"That's what you said about the marines."

"That was different. I had no choice that time. I do now."

"Yes, you do."

"So do you," Joshua said, looking at Buddy intently.

"You should have taken me with you then, you know."

Joshua was taken aback. "What? You've always said you would never have gone."

"I didn't believe in that war. It was a wrong war." Buddy thought a moment. "But you left me behind."

Joshua laughed. "I'm not sure I'll ever understand you, you crazy bastard." He looked at Buddy. "Well, now's your chance."

A look of fear washed quickly over Buddy's face. "Promise me if it's not right we'll quit."

"Sure we will," Joshua said. "Of course we will." But he knew once they went it would be much harder, if not impossible, to leave.

After they joined up, the placid summer days had passed like wispy clouds strung together. They swam and sailed, their bodies became tanned, and at night they would go out, drinking and flirting with young women. They spent several evenings with Emily and Larissa—a convenient arrangement for all of them, but never anything more. Joshua had visited nearly every one of the piers in town, asking fishermen and sailors if they knew anything about the wreck of the Santa Marie, feeling each time like a cross between Sherlock Holmes and a Confederate spy—but as Gideon had predicted, no one remembered a thing. It was as if the tragedy had never happened.

The night before they were due at the station they had one more date with the girls, who prepared a picnic dinner to share on the beach. The sun formed a gigantic globe of the deepest orange that seemed to sizzle as it dissolved magically into the rippling sea, the moon waiting its turn then emerging blazing and full. They built a fire and sat talking and drinking wine. After a while Buddy and Larissa slipped off into the darkness, and Joshua sat with Emily. She told him of her childhood in Provincetown—her father, a bank clerk who'd always dreamed of a more adventurous life, had married the daughter of a Portuguese fisherman.

"In my father's mind, that was the end."

"He was always unhappy?" Joshua had asked.

"No, I wouldn't say so. He loved having a family. But he always seemed to feel he had missed out on something."

Joshua nodded, and they sat silently under the bright moon, each in their own thoughts—until the other two stumbled back, smiling and disheveled.

Despite their agreement, Buddy had said often how much he dreaded this moment. Now it had arrived. Joshua accepted that Buddy would come with him and had not pushed deeper to understand this concession or their respective motivations. He wanted Buddy with him. He secretly harbored his own doubts, wondering if he would have anything in common with the other Life-Savers, if he could live up to the physical demands, if he could be patient enough to learn what he had to and brave enough to succeed at this mission he'd undertaken—and foisted upon Buddy. Joshua also hoped somehow he'd be able to solve the mystery of his mother's death, though, in truth, he doubted he ever would. His father was probably right about that.

They walked together, carrying their duffels on their shoulders, to the train depot, where Captain MacDonald had arranged for a wagon to carry some of the surfmen over the dunes. They stopped to look at the flawless bay. Plumes of smoke rose in the air from the ice houses and shipyards. Men in white suits with their pants rolled up and women in linen dresses, the hems dipping into the water, picked their way barefoot among tide pools and clam beds in the sun-splattered morning.

Two other men stood waiting at the train station, smoking cigarettes. They sported handlebar mustaches and wore summer uniforms of heavy white duck trousers and jumpers, with white linen caps outlined in black silk ribbon marked with the words,

U.S. LIFE-SAVING SERVICE.

Joshua approached them and held out his hand. "Joshua Duell. We're new."

The two men looked at each other and laughed.

"We can see that," one said. He spoke with a strong Portuguese accent, and a slight sneer on his jagged face.

The other was tall and thin, with long blonde hair and fair skin. He took Joshua's hand. "Peter Abbot. I'm Number Four. This here's Punchy Costa. He's Number Two. Don't mind him, he's got no manners."

Punchy Costa was smaller, stocky and solid. He reached out his hand, which was large, coarse and strong. Buddy came over and shook his hand, as well.

"Who's this?" Punchy asked.

"I'm Buddy. Pleased to meet you."

"I'll bet you are," Punchy said with a grin.

Peter Abbot shook Buddy's hand. "You're the new boys?"

"Yep," Buddy said. "Can't wait to start." His sarcasm was lost on the two surfmen.

Punchy looked at Peter Abbot, shaking his head. "Fresh fish."

Buddy looked offended, but to Joshua's relief, he restrained himself.

"Fresh fish," Joshua chuckled. "I like that."

An old buckboard arrived, pulled by a sway-backed nag and driven by an elderly black man in a sailor hat with a cob pipe in the corner of his mouth. He reined in the horse. "You the boys goin' to Peaked Hill?"

They nodded.

"Well, get in then. It's a long ride."

"Yeah, we know," Buddy said.

They tossed their duffels in the shallow wagon bed, which offered little in the way of handholds, and climbed in. The driver clucked and the old horse moved forward. The air was clear and the sun warm as they plodded roughly along a sand track. Climbing the dune face the buckboard tilted precariously. Punchy sat on one side, smoking a cigarette, unfazed by the lurching. They passed through a gap in a tall dune, descended to the wild, empty beach, and finally stopped as the square red tower came into view.

The other three surfmen were already there, and men from town were unloading provisions from wagons. Above the wide ramps the doors were all open, and the two life carts and various other equipment had been dragged out onto the sand. The Keeper was not in sight, but a tall man with broad shoulders and a bushy red beard came over.

"Greetings!" he exclaimed. "Abbot, show these new men the living quarters." Then, to Joshua and Buddy, "Stow your gear and report back here."

"Aye, sir," Peter Abbot responded.

They went up a narrow flight of stairs. The main sleeping room felt cramped because of the steep slope of the eaves, but was the width of the building, with four cots on each side. Four windows filled the wall near the stairs, and at the other end was a door.

"What's in there?" Buddy asked.

"Another sleeping room. We call it the guest room," Peter Abbot said.

"You have guests here?" Joshua asked.

"We do. Sometimes too many." He opened the door for Joshua and Buddy. The room was smaller, but essentially the same, with two rows of three cots and a window at the end. "This is where shipwreck victims are brought, to rest and recover, to die, or until they can be moved to better facilities off-cape."

"Sounds cheery," Buddy said.

"Hardly that, my friend," Peter Abbot said. "You'll see." He gestured to the last two beds in the first room. "Leave your duffels and let's go down."

All the men gathered outside. They did not stand at attention in neat lines, as Joshua had done in the Marines, but there was a sense of discipline and a deference to rank. The large Scotsman stepped out to address the others.

"Welcome back, men. For you newcomers, I'm Scotty Pendleton, Number One." He spoke with a bit of a burr. "You will be measured for uniforms and storm gear, which will be sent over within the week. In the meantime, you are expected to be neat and to pay attention. The other men know the drill. We'll begin training right away, and we will work hard. All men must be in tip-top shape within the month. Nightly patrols will begin immediately and go to full schedule the first of September. One man will be on watch in the tower or out here at all times."

Incredibly, Buddy laughed. They all turned.

"What's so funny, Bairn?"

"My name's Buddy."

"What's so funny, Bairn?" Pendleton repeated.

"What exactly are we watching for? Sunbathers?"

Pendleton turned back to the others. "There's a strict regime here. Mondays we put the station in order. Tuesdays we drill launching the boat. Wednesdays we practice signal codes. Thursdays we drill with the beach apparatus and breeches buoy." He faced Joshua and Buddy. "You'll learn what those are soon enough. Friday we practice rescue techniques and medical procedures. Today is Saturday, which is normally wash day. But we'll begin working with the boat this afternoon. Sundays you are free to go to town to worship…"

Buddy's face broke into a grin in spite of himself.

"As I was saying," Pendleton continued, "to worship or visit with loved ones. You may do as you please on Sunday, but you must return by sundown to report for duty." He turned and looked at Buddy. "And that means sober, Bairn."

The Keeper emerged and walked down the ramp. "Good morning, men," he boomed. "Welcome to Peaked Hill Bars. As most of you know, I'm Captain John MacDonald. I've been Keeper here for eighteen years now. Folks say this is the most dangerous passage on the east coast, with more shipwrecks than any other place in America. Regardless, we have a challenging year ahead of us, but I know you men will distinguish yourselves. To ensure that, we shall begin training immediately after lunch. We shall train hard all month and you will all be the better for it. Speaking of lunch, Mr. Pendleton will organize the mess. Each of you shall take his turn for one week preparing the meals." He smiled. "And I, for one, expect meals that are pleasing to the palate. This is not a fancy life we lead here, but you will be well-clothed and well-fed, and we'll try our damnedest to keep you dry."

The old-timers all laughed. Joshua liked this man. There was something reassuring about his folksy authoritativeness. Joshua felt he could be trusted.

"That's all for now, men. Welcome aboard." He turned and walked back up the ramp.

Pendleton took his place again. "You are expected to be in uniform at all times. When you go to town, you may wear your civilian clothes or your uniform, but never a mixture of the two. Your uniform is to be kept in perfect condition, as is all equipment at the station. A great many people's lives depend on your competence, your bravery and your discipline."

He turned as if speaking to Buddy directly. "And as the men who have been here know quite well, my Bairn, the reputation and dignity of the LSS are of the utmost priority. For the next ten months, this will be the creed by which you will live." He looked up, now smiling. "That is all, men. Get your gear stored. We shall reassemble after lunch."

Pendleton, too, walked up the ramp. The others began to disperse, talking among themselves. Each of them cast a glance at Buddy and Joshua.

"What the hell is a bairn?" Buddy asked.

"It's a Scottish word," Peter Abbot said. "It means 'child.'"

Joshua burst into laughter.

"Very funny," Buddy said.

Punchy and Peter Abbot prepared lunch: fish stew, bread,

water and fruit. They ate in the mess room. The talk was mostly about fishing, of fish caught off the back shore or on small sailboats by the men during the summer break. One of them, Jurgen Kline, said he had caught a fifty-eight-pound striped bass at Race Point just last week. Jurgen, whose rank was Number Three, was stocky, medium height, with prominent arm muscles, a summer tan, and an angular face. Billy "the Whale" Carneiros, from a long line of Portuguese fishermen, expressed skepticism at Jurgen's claim, but Punchy insisted his uncle Manuel had caught a sixty-three-pounder from a sloop off Wood End.

After lunch the crew assembled in loose formation in front of the station, some of them smoking. Pendleton stood before them, hands on his hips.

"All right, men, we begin. We're off schedule today, but the calendar ain't our invention, it's God's or someone else's higher up than us. Since we're all here on a fine summer day, let's start practicing our surfboat drill. You fellas who've done this before know what to do, but we're gonna start from fresh as if no one knows a thing, and we'll work hard on these drills the next month until you can do them in your sleep."

"Or at least in the middle of the night when you'd like ta be asleep," Punchy said.

Pendleton walked over to the surfboat, which rested on a long cart, and put his hand on the gunwale. "This here's a twenty-six foot Beebe-McLellan surfboat. She's a beauty, and yer life depends on knowing how to handle her. She's self-bailing, up to a point, and she's got a water ballast system and a centerboard which help get her aright if she capsizes and yer in the drink. We're gonna practice that trick. I'm expectin' by the first of September you'll be able to do the capsize drill in twenty-five seconds, and I'd like to see ten seconds faster than that. In the cold water, you'll bless every second ya can save."

"That's the truth," Jurgen said.

a. Lifeboat on its cart.

Pendleton continued. "Some of the stations has horses to pull the carts. We've heard rumors for two years we might get a horse, but we ain't got one now, so we do the luggin'. Punchy and Jurgen will tell ya how easy that can be in a gale wind at high tide."

"Doesn't look so bad," Buddy said.

"We'll see how you feel soon, Bairn." He looked up at the men. "First, everyone grab a life vest."

b. Life-Savers pulling a lifeboat on its cart.

They ran up the ramp to the gear room and each man took one of the bulky vests from its hook. They were made of panels of thick cork woven together with canvas straps and buckles at their ends. The vests smelled musty and were hard to put on and uncomfortable to wear. Joshua tightened the straps tight in their clasps as the other men did. They reassembled, looking like a tribe of misshapen turtles.

Pendleton walked to the front of the cart. "To pull the cart takes at least four men, two on each side." He tapped the hardware along the tongue. "There are brass grips to catch a hold of. The cart with surfboat and gear weighs close to eight hundred pounds, and haulin' the thing over sand makes it heavier. It can also be towed by rope, and if we're all available, we tow it together." He smiled mischievously. "Now let's give it a try, shall we? Punchy and Jurgen, Joshua and Bairn… let's get this cart to the edge of the water."

The four men took their positions. Without warning, Pendleton blew into a silver whistle that hung by a lanyard on his neck. The men strained to move the cart, its large wooden wheels, each wrapped in a band of steel, moving sluggishly.

"Don't worry, lads, yer muscles is weak from too much layin' about. In a month you'll be strong as oxen and it won't seem so heavy," Pendleton said.

The hot sand parted and the long cart moved toward the shore. Small birds skittered out of the way. Joshua sweated as he strained with one hand through the brass grip, the other holding his wrist for support. The men puffed and grunted. Joshua looked over at Buddy, arms straining, face muscles taut, struggling to keep a cheerful expression.

"All right, now," Pendleton said loudly, "walk her right into the water."

The tide was rising but it was still a calm day. It felt strange to wade into the water fully dressed. Joshua's soaked trousers felt cool clinging to his legs, his feet heavy in shoes filled with seawater. They rolled the cart twelve feet out, until the water supported the seaward end of the surfboat.

"That's good, lads, now, Punchy and Jurgen, come pull the cart out while Joshua and the Bairn slide the craft off it."

"I wish he'd stop calling me that," Buddy muttered to Joshua.

"He will," Joshua said.

Struggling to grasp the boat's gunwales above them, Buddy and Joshua moved the boat off its cradle into the water. The vests were awkward and blocked their reach. As the craft became buoyant it slipped more easily off the cart—but its bobbing made it harder to hold steady and water splashed over their shoulders. The men on the beach laughed as the rookies struggled.

"Don't let the boat drag you out to sea, lads. Now ease her back till the stern rests on the sand, so's the other men can jump in while you hold her."

The four others grasped the gunwales, vaulted themselves into the craft, and each man took a seat and lifted an oar.

"Now you two climb in and take yer places." Pendleton stepped in and stood at the stern, lifted the long steering oar, and inserted it into its holder, tilting the handle down to raise the paddle. "The Keeper will usually take the helm in a rescue. If he can't, then I will."

Buddy and Joshua tried to clamber in but the sides were high. Joshua grabbed hold of the gunwales with both hands and, straining his arms, hoisted himself up. The boat rolled toward him; the weight of the men acted as a counterbalance, but the gunwale dipped close to the lapping waves.

"In rougher waters, you'll have to get yourself up hard and fast so's not to swamp the boat. Best if each gets in on the opposite side."

Joshua tried to flop over the gunwale, but was stuck on the bulky vest, rocking like a sea tortoise on its back, until he slid over and landed awkwardly on the boat's floor. Buddy flopped over the other side, soaking everyone. They lay in the bottom while the others jeered.

"When the waves are wilder, you'll not be able to avoid gettin' some water in the boat, but try to get in as cleanly and quickly as possible. Now fast, lads, take yer seats."

Joshua and Buddy took the last empty plank and picked up their oars.

"Oars in place, men," Pendleton barked briskly. "Now pull!" The big Scotsman's face turned red as he repeated, "Pull! Pull for all yer worth!"

Facing the stern the men began to row, in unison except for Buddy and Joshua, who could barely keep the oars in their oarlocks and felt awkward in their vests. Jurgen flipped a clasp on Buddy's oarlock, securing the oar.

"Like that," Jurgen said.

"Thanks," Buddy replied.

Rowing against the incoming waves was hard, the boat heavy and slow moving, but after a bit the rookies began to pull with the others. Joshua gripped his oar with both hands, imitating the others.

"Put yer back into it, Joshua!" Pendleton called out. Then to the whole group, "Together, now men, pull HARD!"

The men began to row together. Punchy yelled "Pull!" at each backward stroke, building a tempo. The surfboat cut unevenly through the waves, bouncing over small breakers.

Joshua, out of breath, got into the cadence of the thing. He looked up to see Pendleton, holding the steering oar steady with great focus. What the hell is this like in a storm? He felt a shiver of fear.

"Here comes a bigger one," Pendleton called out.

Joshua turned to see.

"Never do that," Pendleton snapped. "This is about concentration. You've got to trust yer helmsman to be yer eyes and guide you. Your job is to haul that oar as hard as ya can, work those oars fer dear life, and keep the boat movin' forward and not rollin' over."

A larger wave hit, breaking to a point with a spray of wet salt. The bow lifted out of the water, but the forward motion kept the surfboat going and it cut through the breaker. Water rushed over the men's shoulders and into the boat. The bow smacked down behind the wave, slamming Joshua's vest into his chin.

"Good," Pendleton cried out. "Now faster!"

They picked up their pace and the surfboat moved swiftly. At two hundred yards out, the ocean was a rich blue, glittering and rolling in the hazy sun.

"The water's lighter here, you see, boys?" Pendleton said. "The color of sand." His voice grew sober. "That's the bars, two rows of them, sandbars that shift around, get smaller and larger, drift toward shore a hundred yards, then out again, to the north, to the south. These are why we're here. These are the enemy." He paused. "A captain knows the bars is there, he's read the reports and heard the tales. He tries to stay offshore and away from 'em but the current works on them, slamming and driving the tiny hills so's they move without no one knowing. In a heavy sea, the wind or current'll push a ship right into 'em."

Buddy interrupted. "Sorry, sir, I don't understand. What's so damn dangerous? Aren't they only sand?"

All the men guffawed, even Pendleton.

"Ah, ya poor, naïve lad. Just a little pile a' sand, you'd think? Well you'd be dead wrong. A ship of two hundred ton, loaded with bricks or coal, lumber, barrels of wine, whatever it is, moving at ten fifteen knots in a wild sea—that ship come roaring into the side a' one of them bars, and these boats is strong, even the old ones whose timbers've been slammed and tugged for half a century, and the new steel hulls as well, sail or steam, they come a' crashin' into the bar and is stuck fast. The waves and wind batter the ship from all directions, grind it into the bottom and knock out its rigging. In a good gale, most any ship'll begin to break up soon enough."

The older men grumbled their assent. They resumed rowing, past the bar, until Pendleton held up his hand and let go of his steering oar.

"All right, now," Pendleton shouted. "We're gonna flip her."

Buddy looked astonished. "Flip her?"

"When you're fightin' a heavy sea, a rogue wave'll flip yer boat right over. And ya go in the drink, no warning. And what is it we notice most then, boys?" Pendleton taunted.

"It's fuckin' cold!" Punchy said.

"Ay, that's right," Pendleton said. "Colder'n you've ever felt, Bairn, and ya want to get outa there fast as ya can afore ya drown. In a January sea, water temperature can go down to thirty-four. A man can live but a few minutes in that, then the blood freezes and the heat goes out of your body and you're done for. So if the boat flips, ya got to get it aright fast. The iron centerboard makes it easier, but she needs help. That's the drill."

Buddy and Joshua looked at each other, unsure about this.

Pendleton glared at the men. "We'll concentrate the weight on the port side, so move over."

Three men slid over, squeezing between the seats. The boat tilted sharply starboard.

"See how the weighted centerboard works against the pressure of yer weight to hold her steady? Now reach across the boat, anchoring yer feet on the port ribs and grasping the pulling ropes on the starb'd gunwales."

Joshua noticed the sets of ropes hanging loose and coiled under the seats.

"Shift yer weight, get a good grip on the rope and roll back while ya pull toward you." He cracked a smile. "Ya might find this a wee bit disagreeable."

Joshua felt as though he'd been asked to walk a tightrope, but they all seemed uncomfortable, stretched, suspended, across the boat, grasping the lengths of rope. The boat rocked gently, its weight centered, waves slapping its hull. A gull flew over and seemed to laugh at them. The moment lingered.

"Now—drag them ropes toward yerselves with all yer might!" Pendleton boomed.

The older hands knew the move well enough, though no one liked it. Joshua and Buddy had no idea what they were doing. The men pulled together, the starboard side sliding upwards and rolling like some wheeled circus contraption, the port gunwale closer to the surface—but the force was not sufficient, and she flopped back, smashing the men downwards as the surfboat hit the water.

Pendleton called out. "Joshua and the Bairn, work it harder! All right, try it again!"

They repeated the move, the boat rolled upwards, the port gunwale dipped below the surface this time, but the force was still not enough. She slapped back down.

"Third time's the charm," Pendleton cried. "Pull hard!"

The men stretched and groaned and Joshua felt the rolling motion as the starboard rolled toward the sky. The port gunwale dipped in the water, further and further, until the water rushed into the boat, aiding the men's efforts.

"Here we go!" Pendleton cried.

The boat's entire equilibrium shifted as the starboard side rolled over the vertical axis of the port. In fractions of a second, the force of the heavy craft turning flung all of them into the water in a crashing chaos. Daylight disappeared, the water enveloped them, and the smell of the boat and the musty life vests filled their noses. Joshua was trapped under the boat by his vest. A loose oar hit the side of his head. He was confused, struggling in the darkness, surprised he was still breathing. Then strong hands grasped his legs and he went under completely, emerging on the other side gasping for breath.

His head began to clear. Held up by the vest, he looked around at the others treading water. The overturned boat bobbed nearby like a gloating whale.

"Good, men," Pendleton said. "Now comes the hard part."

They moved clumsily toward the boat. Buddy was out of breath. Joshua fingered a bruise on his forehead.

"Now we're going to flip her back over," Pendleton shouted. "It's not as hard as it looks. But it takes coordination—and remember, you'll be doin' this in the dark and cold, waves tossin' you about."

Joshua tried to picture this, but it seemed too fantastic.

"Now lift yerselves up on the bottom, as fast as possible, find the ropes hanging from the far gunwale and grab hold of 'em."

Punchy and Jurgen mounted the overturned hull first, followed by the others. Climbing up the keel in the bulky vests was awkward. Finally, they draped across the upturned craft and scrambled for the loose leads.

"You'll be holding on as hard as you can," Pendleton shouted. "On my word, pull the ropes hard and fast up and toward you. Use all your weight. She'll resist, but pull hard! GO!"

Like mythical beasts on a wave-battered rock, six men spread around the upturned centerboard grasped the ropes in unison. The far side of the boat lifted from the water: up it came, the creature turning, but again the force wasn't enough and she crashed back down, slamming the men against the bottom.

"Good lord, you men are out of shape," Pendleton said. "Try her again. Go!"

Again they found the ropes and pulled, groaning. The gunwale lifted, the boat began to roll toward them, the weighted keel added momentum, and in a flash the surfboat flipped and landed upright with great force, flinging them all back in the water. They scrambled back in the boat, Joshua and Buddy flopping again into the bottom, and took their places.

Pendleton resumed his position at the stern, grasped the steering oar, and said with a mischievous grin, "Good, men, let's try it again!"

It was late afternoon when they finally rowed ashore, tired and sore, their vests heavy with seawater. The men jumped over the side, and Punchy and Jurgen held the boat while Peter Abbot and Billy retrieved the cart and got it down into the water. Buddy and Joshua helped ease the craft into place on the rails. A line fitted with a brass hook attached to a ring in the prow of the boat. Peter Abbot cranked the handle of a winch on the cart, which creaked as it carried the craft up. When it rested on its berth, the men emerged from the water. Joshua felt as if his legs would give out beneath him. Buddy dropped onto the sand.

"Get up, Bairn," Pendleton said. "We're not done yet. You and Joshua haul the cart back up to the station."

Buddy, incredulous, looked as if he'd been asked to leap off a high cliff. "What, sir?"

"You heard me, Bairn. Get yer butt up and let's get this cart back to where it belongs. Then it needs to be washed down."

Joshua felt too weak to argue. He walked to the heavy cart, his knees still shaking. "Come on, Buddy, let's get it over with."

"Aye, that's the spirit," Pendleton said. "The Bairn has a lot to learn."

Buddy leaped to his feet and faced Pendleton. "That's enough of the 'bairn' crap!" he shouted. "You've been on my ass all day, and I don't like it."

Pendleton shrugged, as if to just let it go, then walked casually over to Buddy. "Now listen to me, Bairn," he said, his face inches away. "This is not a bar full of fellas showin' off fer the ladies, nor is it a democracy. Ya do what yer told and with all the strength and fervor ya can muster, or I'll have you on yer ass so fast you won't know what hit ya."

Buddy held his ground, his wrinkled eyes and pursed lips the only indication of his trepidation. "I'm warning you, sir, do not push me too hard."

Joshua whispered to Buddy, "C'mon, let it go!"

Buddy ignored him, his eyes now glaring.

Pendleton laughed and turned toward the other men. "He's warning me. You hear that?" He looked at Joshua, as if challenging him to defend his friend, then back to Buddy. "You'll not be warning me again, lad." He grabbed hold of Buddy's wrists and pressed inwards with an astonishingly powerful grip, twisting the wrists back and forcing him to his knees on the sand, yelping in pain.

"All right, that's enough," came a firm voice from behind. There was MacDonald, a pipe in one hand, its smoke curling wispily into the warm air.

Pendleton released Buddy and stood up straight.

MacDonald walked over to Buddy, still on his knees. "Get up, son."

Buddy got to his feet, his face bent with anger.

"What's the trouble here?" MacDonald asked.

Buddy began to answer. "He said we should carry the cart ourselves, and we just—"

"Nothing is wrong, sir," Joshua interrupted. "We're all just fine. Right, Buddy?"

Buddy got himself together. "Yes. Right. That's right, no trouble at all, sir."

MacDonald smiled. "Very good, then. Carry on, Mr. Pendleton."

"Aye, sir," Pendleton replied.

He put his pipe back in his mouth and walked back to the station.

Pendleton looked at Buddy with a gentler expression. "Very good, lad." Then he looked at Joshua. "Now let's get this cart back into place. Punchy and Jurgen, give these lads a hand.

Smartly now!" And Pendleton, too, turned and walked up the sloped beach.

That night they sat by the beach in the moonlight. Buddy nursed his bruised ego and Joshua massaged his sore leg muscles. He was stiff everywhere. Punchy sat in the half dark, his stocky legs crossed in the sand; Jurgen carved a wooden pipe with a pocket knife. Joshua wondered if Buddy had been right—but no, they could make this work.

Punchy looked over at Joshua and Buddy, in possession of some deep secret they were too ignorant to comprehend. "You fresh fish'll get to feelin' better after you've been doin' this a while. First couple of weeks is the hardest, that's for sure." Punchy winked at Jurgen. "Ain't that right?"

Jurgen just nodded.

"You'd best stay clear of Pendleton," Punchy said, pointing his finger and squat chin in Buddy's direction.

Buddy looked at him. "Yeah, why's that?"

Jurgen stopped carving. "Because he'll whip your ass if you push him hard enough. Don't think for a minute he won't, neither." Then before Buddy could get his dander up, he added, "And 'cause he's a good man, strong, and a man to be trusted when your neck is in a sling out there. Remember that, next time you mouth off at him."

Buddy started to protest. "I wasn't…"

"Let it be," Joshua said.

The next day, Sunday, they drilled again with the boat, then after lunch a couple of the men went into town. Jurgen showed Joshua and Buddy around the equipment room. After a quiet supper, Punchy made a fire on the beach and the men sat smoking and watched the sun go down and the moon rise. They turned in early. The first night Joshua had fallen asleep instantly; now he sat in the dark, listening to two men snore. He slept fitfully and awoke again in the middle of the night in a black mood, surprisingly the blackest since he'd left New York—he felt untethered and unsure. Had he committed the biggest blunder of his life by coming to this place? Would it answer any questions or simply lead him further toward the void?

The following morning, Monday, Joshua felt more self-assured and, anyway, had little time to feel otherwise. The frenetic energy of the place overcame whatever blackness might linger. Even Buddy seemed chipper at breakfast. This was the day for putting the station in order. It had been unoccupied for two months and Pendleton assigned the men to undertake a complete cleaning of the building and an over-haul of the equipment. Joshua and Buddy learned that day the immense importance the Life-Savers placed on keeping their gear in the best possible shape at all times. They worked past sunset, with only a short break for lunch. But it was their introduction to the complex tools the Life-Savers used.

They began with the faking box, companion piece to the Lyle gun, named after its inventor: a short, blunt bronze cannon, smooth bored, one hundred eighty-five pounds, which

c. faking box.

fired an eighteen-pound projectile from its mouth. At the end of the projectile shank was an eye through which was fastened a tightly braided linen thread a quarter of an inch thick, two hundred yards in length. The line was kept coiled inside the wooden faking box in a pattern of overlapping W's around tall pins.

d. Lyle gun

Punchy explained the faking box would be lifted off the equipment cart, the Lyle gun placed on the sand, the line attached to the projectile, and the pins removed so the line could pay out freely. When the gun was filled with powder and set off, usually by the Keeper, the projectile would shoot over the water, the object being to snag the line in the rigging of a foundering ship. The little cannon was surprisingly accurate if handled by an experienced shooter—but it was a hard shot to make in a heavy storm. The cart contained spare projectiles and several faking boxes. The shooter would aim to the windward, so if he missed, the projectile might carry, with luck, toward the hands of one of the stranded crew. Punchy showed them how to lay the line into the faking box. It had to be placed perfectly or it would tangle.

"If we think we can make it out there through the surf," Punchy said, pointing out to where the waves were breaking,

e. Setting the crotch pole to carry the breeches buoy

"we'll try to launch the surfboat. If it's too far or too rough, that's when we'll fire the Lyle gun and get the breeches buoy out there."

Joshua, a bit baffled, said, "The breeches buoy?"

"You'll see. It sounds complicated, but…"

Peter Abbot interrupted. "If Punchy can figure it out, I'm sure you will, too."

"Go fuck yerself," Punchy snarled.

If the shot line reached the ship, a crew member would pull it in to find a stronger rope attached, known as a whip line, a circular loop; on it was a tail block to be tied off on the

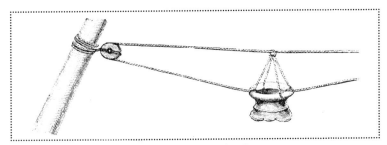

f. Breeches buoy rigged to hawser.

foundering ship and used to manipulate the line from shore. Attached ahead of the block was a tally board, which contained instructions in English and French: *Make the tail of this block fast to the lower mast well up. If the masts are gone then to the best place you can find. Cast off shot line. See that the rope in the block runs free and show signal to shore.*

The hawser, a much heavier rope, was sent out on the whip line and tied off above the tail block; a pulley on the hawser would hold the breeches buoy, a circular seat on which a sailor or passenger would sit and be carried to shore. The other end of the whip was attached to one of several reels of line on the equipment cart back on the beach, and the Life-Savers on shore used the whip line to move the breeches buoy along the hawser. Tension was maintained on the hawser using a double block and tackle system, known as the fall. The fall was connected to the sand anchor, made of two wooden planks the men buried in the sand.

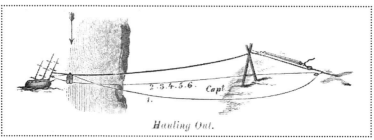

Hauling Out.

g. Diagram of the breeches buoy set-up.

The double block of the fall allowed the surfmen to pull the whip line and hawser with a four-to-one ratio, giving five surf-men the power of twenty against the potent force of wind and sea. The final component was called a crotch pole, made of two eight-foot boards crossed like a pair of scissors. The ends of the boards were cut out so when the short ends were drawn near each other, a round channel was formed through which the hawser rope would run. After the men put tension on the hawser by pulling on the fall, they would lift the crotch pole into position to keep the hawser raised high, keeping victims being transported to shore safely above the roiling surf.

"Like a clothesline," Peter Abbot said, "'Cept instead of unmentionables dryin' in the sun, you're bringing in a half-dead human danglin' in a little canvas seat over a nasty sea."

Peter and Punchy snickered. Joshua and Buddy looked utterly confused.

h. Man in breeches buoy.

At the end of the day, the station was sparkling clean and the equipment ready to be put into service. The men relaxed and Joshua sank to the sand looking at the sky, thinking about sleep. But Pendleton came over, grinning: Joshua would get the first patrol.

"There are no wrecks this early, and the seas are calm, but the Captain wants us to start patrols now so everyone's accustomed to the routine."

"I see," Joshua said.

"Once the season starts in earnest, we'll send out two patrols at once, one in each direction, but, for now, we're just practicing. It's not too bad, particularly this time of year. You just go for a stroll along the beach." Pendleton looked at the sky, streaked with purple and orange. The half moon was a quarter way up over the horizon, sending its wide, glittering beam toward shore. "Beautiful night for it."

Joshua was to walk south along the beach, carrying a lantern and a Coston signal, a tube attached to his belt which, when ignited, produced a bright red flare to alert a stranded ship it had been spotted and to warn the other men at the station there was a wreck. Three and a half miles to a small shack, known as a halfway house, then back again.

"Normally, you'd meet another fellow there from High Head station and exchange checks—little medallions—which proves you've gone the whole way. Those slouches up to High Head don't start patrol till mid-August, so's we'll have to trust ya tonight."

"I'm honored," Joshua said.

"You'll make the run from eight to midnight, then your Buddy'll take over. Peter Abbot'll do the last shift, four to eight. In winter, there'll be four shifts, starting at four in the afternoon. During daytime, if there's no storm, we keep watch from the tower. From now until the first of June, this seven mile stretch of beach is ours to watch."

After downing a plate of beef hash and a glass of ale, Joshua went with Punchy to the gear room. It was an uncommonly warm night, so there was no need for outerwear. Joshua strapped on the belt with the Coston flare, lit the lantern, and headed over the sand.

"Have fun out there," Punchy called after him. "Don't get swallowed by no whales."

A hundred yards out, he rounded a bend and the station was no longer in sight. The night lit up and surrounded him with its stark, astounding beauty. Hidden from all manmade light, the sky clear as an infinite pool of black water, the stars hung brilliantly, pulsing toward him in three dimensions out of the unthinkable distance. The crests of the waves, as luminous as stars, rolled and broke and washed ashore with a gentle crackle, and the wind carried the summery smell of seaweed, cotton and oranges. He moved sluggishly through the soft sand in his heavy boots, trying to keep the lantern from knocking against his leg. He didn't need it on a bright night like this. The lantern, its flame turned low, cast only a small yellow sphere on the sand.

He came to the tiny wood shack, not much taller than him, nestled in the base of the dune. Grey battered shingles hung off the frame, a crooked smokestack protruded from a roof in need of repair. A small warped door faced away from the sea. In one corner rested a rusty pot-bellied stove, wood matches, a stack of firewood and a large water crock. A crude shelf held a stack of blankets and a rusted tin filled with hard-tack. These were the original rescue shacks MacDonald had described. It was frightening to think this had once been the only hope for ships wrecking on the bars. He secured the door and began his walk back.

Tuesday was designated for working with the surfboat. This time MacDonald participated, but otherwise the procedure was the same: hauling the boat to the water, rowing against the breakers, practicing the capsizing drill, rowing back, hauling the boat onto the cart, then beginning again. By day's end, Joshua and Buddy were both exhausted.

Wednesday's task was to learn and practice the International and General Signal Codes, communicated through the use of flags set up on the beach to signal ships. Using what were known as Wigwag signals, a captain could receive detailed information from a half mile offshore, if he could see that far.

Wigwag signals. Sitting on the beach half-listening to Pendleton's lecture, an image, frighteningly real, popped into Joshua's mind, a memory of Cuba. Joshua, his brother Adam, a squadron of men dug in on a hill over Guantanamo, in complete darkness, the explosive sounds of heavy fire filling their ears. A lone signalman ventured out and stood on a box to signal a ship in the bay. He used Wigwag signals, swinging one lantern over another, to direct fire toward the enemy. Joshua could see in his mind the yellow light reflected upon the signalman's face, a clear target for the Spanish in the bushes below. How the man found the courage Joshua could never understand.

Pendleton explained how the lighthouses functioned, five at this end of the Cape: the one at Long Point which Joshua had seen from the shore in Provincetown, Wood End Light, Race Point Light, Highland Light, and many miles further down the beach, Nauset Light. The lighthouses and life-saving stations were connected by telephone with lines laid into the dunes. And he told them the legend of the mooncussers, gangs of men who used false lights along the beach to trick faltering ships into running aground, to salvage the cargo from the wrecked ship. They were called mooncussers because the moon was their worst enemy, providing enough light for a ship offshore to find its way, spoiling the trap. The pirates, it was said, would cuss at the moon for stealing their prey.

"But there are no actual mooncussers on Cape Cod," he maintained.

Thursday they drilled with the beach apparatus, which included the Lyle gun and projectiles, the breeches buoy, sand anchor and crotch, faking box, shot lines, whip lines, hawsers, blocks and tackle, tally boards, and hawser cutter— all mounted on the equipment cart, which weighed close to a ton when fully loaded and required six men to drive it along the beach.

A pole was set in the sand down the beach, like a ship's mast with a small crow's nest. This was their target. The men had to pull the cart down the beach, fire the Lyle gun to snare the line on the pole, and set up the equipment to work the breeches buoy.

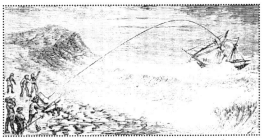

i. Shooting a lyle gun at a foundering ship.

"We'll try to get you men to where you can accomplish the

entire exercise in two and a half minutes," Pendleton said. "And I tell you this: if after six weeks of training you cannot do it in five minutes, we will all have failed."

The exercise was carefully choreographed, each man with an assigned task. As Pendleton and Punchy set the Lyle gun, Jurgen, Number Three, laid out the apparatus from the cart, while Peter Abbot and Billy, Numbers Four and Five, showed the newcomers how to dig a deep hole in the sand and bury the anchor.

"Just to remind you lubbers," Pendleton said, "there's three lines here. The shot line is the lightest, fired by the gun to connect with the ship. Next comes the whip line, then the hawser, which does the heavy lifting. The whip is used to carry the hawser out, and to work the breeches buoy." He looked up with a sneaky smile. "Any of you stinkers remember this?"

All the old timers mumbled, "Aye, sir."

Punchy put a charge in the mouth of the gun, tamped it down, and inserted the projectile, while Pendleton reeled out some line and tied it to the projectile's loop. They located the gun in the sand facing the practice pole. Using a flint, Pendleton lit the fuse and set it off. The gun exploded with a loud bang that made Joshua jump.

"It's just a bloody cannon, boy," Punchy yelled. "In a good gale you'll hardly hear it."

The charge had sent the projectile flying through the air, over the arm of the practice pole, perfectly on target so the line rested on the crosstrees. The men cheered.

"Good shot, Scotty," Jurgen cried.

"Not bad," Pendleton agreed.

"Try and make that shot in a blizzard with the wind at seventy knots and the goddamn target bobbing and tossing out where you can't hardly see it," Punchy said.

"That's the fuckin' truth," said Billy, who'd never tried it himself.

Pendleton attached the block of the whip line to the end of the shot line. Punchy ran to the wreck pole, clambered up to pull in the shot, secured the whip block to the mast, then ran back. He told Joshua to take his place on the pole. Pendleton tied the hawser to the whip on the leeward side and Punchy took hold of the windward side.

"Always make sure you know the direction of the wind," Pendleton said. "We all haul together from the leeward going out, and from windward going in."

The sand anchor was buried, and Peter Abbot and Billy showed Buddy how to assemble the crotch pole and attach the fall.

Pendleton called to Joshua, "We're sending ya the hawser. Secure her to the mast above the whip. A good double clove hitch. Know how to do that?"

"Aye, sir."

Punchy pulled on the line and the hawser snaked to the pole. The whip block lifted it where Joshua could reach the heavier rope and tie it off.

"Ready, sir," he called out.

Pendleton nodded. "All right, lift the crotch. Billy, you and the Bairn man the fall."

Punchy, Pendleton, Jurgen and Peter Abbot together lifted the scissor-like mechanism, Billy pulled in on the fall's block and tackle to tighten the hawser, the crotch pole rose slowly and slid into place, the hawser slipped into its guide hole, and Billy and Buddy strained to make it snug. Pendleton took the breeches buoy from the cart. It was small, like a life ring with a canvas bucket with leg holes hanging from its sides. It hung from a brass ring attached by four lines to a sturdy wood and iron pulley. Pendleton slipped the pulley over the hawser and clipped it in place, testing that the mechanism could slide easily. He tied the two ends of the whip to the pulley ring.

"Man the line to leeward," said Pendleton, and while Punchy held his end of the whip line, the other men joined Pendleton on the other side. Pendleton called to Joshua, "Ready?" The bucket slithered along the line and dangled above Joshua's feet.

"Get in the bugger, will ya dammit?" Pendleton shouted.

Joshua grappled with the ropes and the dancing ring, swung himself off and wiggled his feet into the bucket, then lowered himself in. He heard Pendleton yell—"Now pull! Pull hard!"—and the bucket began to slide rapidly along the hawser, flying about wildly. He felt ridiculous and couldn't imagine dangling like this over a wintry sea.

They reeled him in and cheered as the breeches buoy neared the end. Like a hero who has singlehandedly stopped the enemy entirely by accident, Joshua stepped out of the ring and promptly tripped, falling head first into the sand. The men whistled and whooped.

j. Breeches buoy rescue.

Over lunch of cold herring and bread, Pendleton addressed them gravely. "That was excellent work, lads. The entire exercise took seventeen and a half minutes. That's only twelve minutes and thirty seconds longer than what is minimally acceptable. You'd be a sad lot with long faces mourning the loss of an entire ship's crew at that rate."

The men looked down at their tin plates. Then Pendleton laughed.

"But hell, this is only the first day!"

Friday's task was the resuscitation of victims. Captain MacDonald explained the newly coined skill called first aid, becoming popular for use by soldiers, policemen, firemen, nurses and physicians—procedures to stop a profusely bleeding wound, prevent burned skin from peeling away completely, and restore breathing to victims whose air passages were blocked or filled with water.

That night they ate fresh sea bass a townsman had brought by, and Captain MacDonald served an English ale he'd been saving. He tapped the keg and ceremoniously poured himself the first glass, then raised it to toast his surfmen on a successful first week.

"We've much to learn, even for you old-timers, and a long road ahead. But I'm heartened by the seriousness of your work. It bodes well for us. Help yourselves to some ale, men."

MacDonald drank his glass in one long swallow and the men cheered. They each took a glass from the cupboard and lined up, bumping into one another, to help themselves to the brew.

Saturday was cleaning day and the men reorganized the equipment. Before dinner, Pendleton told them they were free to go into town. Peter Abbot and Billy stayed behind; they were on first and second watch, starting at eight since the evening light remained in the sky until well past that time. Joshua was due back at four a.m. for third watch.

Joshua and Buddy headed across the dunes. It was a crystalline night, the sand swirling gently, the stars like wildflowers stretching to infinity. Trudging up and down the slippery sand peaks, they saw ahead the glow of the town in the sky. The moon was a flat distant persimmon adorned with slivers of cloud, a welcoming beacon.

The outer streets were tranquil, an occasional carriage rolling past, a couple strolling down the half dark street, sudden laughter through an open doorway.

"My God, what a night this is!" Buddy said. "This is our night! We're free, released from that prison, humans again, free men on the earth!"

"What the hell are you raving about?" Joshua said, though he was excited, too.

Gaslights on the street flickered in the blue dark and houses were ablaze with electric light as they neared the town's center.

"Can't you feel the energy here?" Buddy asked. "This town is so alive!"

He was practically dancing and his giddiness was contagious. They sped up as they got closer to the center. The street was busy now, carriages moving in a slow line, horses fidgeting, people jostling. They passed tiny crowded shops, young men at a café smoking and watching, and softly lit restaurants, candles on each table casting a sweet yellow glow on the diners. Inside the music halls, crowds sang dancehall songs. They walked up the steps of the New Central House.

"Feels like a year or two since we've been back here,"

Buddy said.

"It's only been a week," Joshua said.

"Seems like a bloody lifetime."

"Definitely a long week," Joshua agreed.

The bar felt warm and familiar, the room abuzz with the eager expectancy of a Saturday night anywhere. Sailors in their blue jackets, striped shirts and neck scarves, fishermen in dark canvas guzzling their beers, city men with bowlers and shoes marred by sand and dung, smoking skinny cigars which filled the room with green clouds of smoke, women in bright summer dresses of linen and cotton, sipping champagne and laughing too loudly at each other's jokes or the men's boasting. Some held cigarettes self-consciously between their fingertips, coughing between puffs.

Buddy ordered glasses of ale. "To our freedom and the freedom of man!" he cried.

They clinked their glasses and drank. He rolled a cigarette, struck a wood match and lit it, then looked gravely into Joshua's eyes.

"We've spent a week out there now, my friend."

"I know. And?"

"And I'm too young for this shit."

Joshua laughed, though when Buddy got like this it often led to trouble.

"We're getting pushed around by a bunch of Portagee idiots."

"Why don't you quit, then?" Joshua asked sardonically.

"You know I can't quit. You wouldn't quit." He paused and looked at Joshua to confirm this. "Anyway, that's just what they want."

"Why would they want you to quit? You just got there."

"They want to prove they're right about me."

"Well, are they?" Joshua grinned, although he immediately regretted the remark.

"What the hell do you mean by that?" Buddy demanded.

"Nothing, Buddy."

"You think you're better than me, don't you?"

"Don't be ridiculous."

"Anyway they're not after you like they are me."

Joshua took a sip of ale. "Maybe it's your attitude."

Buddy looked stung. "My attitude? I work just as hard as you do."

"Yeah, but you seem to be making fun of the whole thing. Maybe they feel you think they're silly."

"Well I do," Buddy said. "The whole thing is silly. They're all so damned serious. I hate it." He took a long puff of his cigarette, looking over the water. "I really do." He picked up his glass. "Like I said, I'm too young for this shit."

They moved to a table and ate fish and potatoes. After several hours and a few drinks Joshua found himself laughing hard at Buddy's jokes and quips. It felt good, like Harvard before the war.

When they finally left the hotel, the street was less crowded. The tourists had thinned out. They began to walk toward the east end to head home. As they passed a tavern, Buddy spotted the three men they'd tangled with that first night, lounging on a corner smoking and passing a bottle around. William and Tucker were laughing loudly and hurling insults at passersby. William saw Buddy and Joshua coming and elbowed Kirov, whose shoulders suddenly spread like the wings of a bat. He ambled over in their direction.

Joshua felt a sinking sensation. It didn't matter where you

were in the world, fellows like this would always behave the same. It made him angry.

"Hey, I remember you two," Kirov said in his Slavic accent, friendly as can be. He looked at Buddy. "I think you still owe me an apology, mister." He grinned broadly through his handsome mustache.

"I don't think so," Buddy said defiantly.

"Oh, but you do," he said. "You were very unpleasant to me and my friends here."

"You're full of shit," Buddy said.

With a nod from the Russian, William and Tucker moved toward Buddy. Joshua felt a surge of rage and stepped in front of them.

"Leave him alone," he said.

Tucker pushed him in the chest and Joshua swung and punched Tucker in the jaw. He felt a sharp pain in his hand.

William rushed in, dipped his shoulder and ploughed into Joshua's gut, knocking the wind out of him. Joshua staggered then pulled himself up, gasping for breath. Kirov moved toward him lifting his heavy walking stick to strike at Joshua. In a flash, Buddy leapt on Kirov and yanked him backwards, stopping the blow and pulling him on top of him as they fell together to the street. Kirov, red faced, shook free and stood, swinging his cane and hitting Joshua in the ribs. Buddy found his feet and lunged at Kirov again. William and Tucker grabbed him from behind and Kirov struck Buddy with his stick on the side of his face, drawing blood. Almost as an afterthought, he slugged him in the stomach.

Joshua moved toward Kirov, but the Russian simply held up his stick.

"That's enough for now," he said, and the other men let

Buddy slump to the ground. "Just wanted you to know I don't forget a face."

He brushed off his clothes. The other two laughed, and they all walked away.

Buddy let out a moan. "Bastards. Gonna kill 'em."

Joshua, out of breath, helped him to his feet. "I don't think you're killing anyone tonight. Though it would feel good, wouldn't it?"

"Fuckin' bastards," Buddy said.

Blood was running down his face. Joshua handed him his hand-kerchief.

"You all right?"

"I think so," Buddy said. "You?"

Joshua felt his rib cage. Sore but nothing broken. "I'll live." He smiled. "Thank you for stepping in there."

Buddy held the cloth against his face, and managed a smile. "Can't say it was my pleasure."

"Let's get out of here," Joshua said.

"Don't think I can get very far," Buddy said. "Let's get a drink and sit for a bit."

"I have third watch, Buddy. Time to head back."

"No. I need a drink first then I can do it. Come on."

Buddy walked shakily down the street, and Joshua had no choice but to follow. They went back to the Mermaid Tavern, the one they'd passed earlier, through a broken screen door into a long dark room filled with sailors and hard-drinking men. The air was thick and smelled of cheap cigars and whiskey. At the back was a pocket billiards table, a dim electric light swinging above it. Buddy ordered two whiskeys. The warm liquid felt good going down. They had another round. It felt even better.

Two hours later, they staggered out, bodies aching and quite drunk. The street was quiet, only a few stragglers walking down the planked sidewalk and an occasional carriage swishing by. Joshua looked squint-eyed at his pocket watch.

"Damn you, Buddy, I'm screwed now."

"Why damn me? Damn you!" Buddy said, his voice slurred.

"It's two thirty and a long walk home, and I feel like shit," Joshua said. "Come on, let's head back."

When they reached the station, it was nearly half past four. MacDonald sat on the porch.

"You missed your watch, Duell. And you're drunk. Pendleton sent one of the others. This'll not happen twice. Now go to bed."

They made their way up the stairs and slept in their clothes.

CHAPTER SIX

T he next weeks passed quickly. August turned to September. Joshua, unofficially on probation, worked hard and kept to himself. The men gave him the cold shoulder at first—shirking duty was not an option for a Life-Saver—then they teased him, and finally they took him back into the fold. Buddy also worked hard, but remained aloof and was treated stiffly by the other men. Each day they practiced the drills and each night they patrolled the beach. The late summer ocean light was stunning, the weather remained good, and the long empty beach and rolling waves seemed like paradise. They grew leaner, their muscles stronger; they swam two hours each day. In their free time at the station, Joshua and Buddy were always together. For Joshua, the times of silence, when no one spoke and there were only the sounds of nature, of the sea and the air, were like discovered treasure.

Giant humpback and right whales swam past, sometimes in pods of six or seven, sometimes alone, following the schools of baitfish and plankton. It was always Billy who spotted them first, and he would drag the others out to see them, jumping up and down as the whales spouted, condensed air shooting out of their blowholes like fountains. "Will you look at that?" he would cry. Billy loved the whales and knew about their history and behavior. The others mocked him affectionately when he started his rants about the beauty of these creatures. He believed it was a sin to hunt them, as they had been, nearly to extinction—like the buffalo, he would add—and he said this to anyone who would listen.

Seals cruised the beach from afar. Thousands of gulls, terns, plovers and other species built their nests and hatched their young in the tall beach grass. From time to time, a massive school of bluefish would swarm just offshore, and the men of the station would rush to haul nets into the water. Dinners were raucous affairs, filled with stories and laughter, as the Life-Savers settled into their daily existence. They would exchange gossip with the men from other stations at the halfway houses.

Joshua was happy to bask in the beauty and tranquility of the seashore and felt no need to go elsewhere, even to Provincetown—as if the weight of the past year were being lifted from him, out here by the sea day and night. He focused on his duties as a Life-Saver and for now it was enough. Buddy did not feel the same way, of course. He didn't seem particularly miserable, rather he was constantly restless, as if kineticism were somehow the answer. This was especially true on Saturday.

"You coming with me this time?" Buddy asked.

Joshua shook his head.

"You didn't come last week either. I don't want to go alone."

"Go with one of the other guys," Joshua suggested.

Buddy's face darkened. "You know that won't happen. They all hate me."

"That's not true."

"It is," Buddy insisted. "And you know it."

"Maybe it would get better if you tried to be friends with one or two of them."

"I don't think so. It's as if we're from different planets."

Joshua laughed.

"No, it's true," Buddy said. "Even worse than at Harvard. You're my friend—you come with me."

"But I don't feel like it, Buddy. Why don't you stay here? I like talking with you."

"Well, you can talk with me walking into town, and back if you don't drink too much…" Buddy laughed.

"If I…? Oh, I see." Joshua laughed, too. But he did not go.

Joshua did value Buddy's friendship. But Buddy's failure to acclimate to the life they'd signed on for worried Joshua, and as time passed became more of an impediment. Buddy continued to joke and complain during the drills, and the men continued to give him a cold shoulder. So he stayed as close to Joshua as he could. Yet without anything specific to point to, Joshua sensed a void growing between them.

One afternoon, the sky clouded over; a storm was brewing. By late in the day the clouds turned a striking silver, reflecting back like mirrors hanging above the deepening green of the sea. Vast charcoal smudges of clouds, driven by high altitude winds, chased across the sky. The light changed rapidly, now shining and electric, now luminescent and deepening grey, while streaks of bright blue still peeked through above. The wind picked up and the gulls rode the thermal currents over the water's edge.

MacDonald sat on the porch, smoking his pipe and watching the sky. The afternoon drills were done, and Joshua wandered over. MacDonald did not shift his gaze.

"Wind is shifting round to the east," he said. "Could be some weather heading our way."

Joshua looked at the darkening sea.

"I think you're ready, boy," MacDonald said.

Joshua wasn't sure, but he nodded. He'd been about to ask the Keeper about his mother's shipwreck; he thought of it often, but he and MacDonald rarely had any opportunity to speak and there never seemed to be a good time to bring it up. The dinner bell clanged.

The talk as they ate was of the weather.

"No doubt," Punchy said.

Jurgen, cutting a slice of meat, nodded. "Early for a storm."

"Remember the nor'easter three years ago? October, I think," said Peter Abbot.

MacDonald seemed unusually pensive. He looked at Pendleton. "Tell them, Scotty."

Pendleton took a sip of ale. "Had a call from Highland Lighthouse. Telegram from a lighthouse on the Outer Banks said there's a big system, might be a hurricane, way southeast of here, movin' up the coast. They was getting heavy rain and wind down there."

"Hurricanes come up this far?" Joshua asked.

The men laughed.

"Not too many," Pendleton said. "But they do come."

"What do we do if one comes here?" Buddy asked.

There was silence. Pendleton answered. "It'll not get here until at least tomorrow night. May not be a hurricane by then... but if it comes, you'll see, Bairn."

The increasing wind whistled through the shutters all night, and despite his normal fatigue the rushing sound of the breakers kept Joshua awake. In the morning, the sky was dark, the air heavy, and the sea tossed about more strongly. The men drilled in the morning. After lunch, MacDonald announced they would commence beach patrols immediately, the first time in daylight that year. Joshua headed down the beach with Billy, while Buddy and Peter Abbot went the other direction. All wore full gear with Coston flares on their belts. The wind whipped the sand into swirling eddies. It was hard to look straight ahead with sand blowing into his eyes, but Joshua squinted and kept walking.

"Not too often we walk in the day," Billy said. "Only when they're worried about the weather."

"You worried?" Joshua asked.

"Nope. Least it ain't cold."

They plodded along, unable to hear each other in the wind. The sea churned as far out as the eye could see, all white foam with waves seven or eight feet high. Occasionally a fish jumped from the foam. Despite the potential consequences, Joshua found it exhilarating, even beautiful. They reached the hut, stopped for water and biscuits, which they shared with one of the High Head men, then turned back.

Billy shouted in Joshua's ear. "The wind'll shift around so's it comes from the other end of the beach, then it'll pick up. You'll see."

They got to the station and each had a cup of tea, then

went back out. By the time they reached the hut and headed home, the light was fading and the sky darkening. It was raining now, and Billy had been right: the wind had shifted. As they walked back, a mixture of driving rain and sharp sand blew at them from sideways and behind. They were well soaked when they returned to the station. Punchy and Jurgen immediately set out down the beach in opposite directions, dressed in nor'easter gear: long black slicker and sou'wester hat, canvas over-pants and high rubber boots, which made walking even harder. The rest of the crew ate supper. The electric lights flickered and Billy lit lanterns.

"You've all got to be sharp tonight, fellows," MacDonald told them. "Very sharp. We've got Billy on the telephone, Mr. Pendleton in the tower, and we'll keep walking all night, though it may be tough going. Keep your eyes peeled and watch for ships a' foundering."

"The sea keeps building like this, if there is a ship she'll break up pretty fast," Pendleton said.

MacDonald nodded. Joshua felt a sense of foreboding and anticipation. It was how he'd felt when he arrived in Cuba.

Joshua set out after midnight to make his round. While Pendleton helped him with his gear, Peter Abbot headed the other way. There'd been a call an hour earlier from Chatham Bars saying they'd seen a ship heading north northeast around the elbow of the Cape. This was not a good sign, MacDonald said. Any ship out in this sea was looking for trouble.

"If you see a ship, shoot the flare immediately and run back fast as you can to get us," Pendleton said.

"Aye, sir," Joshua said. "I know the drill."

"I hope so, lad."

The wind was gusting to sixty knots, and between the dark

and the driving sand, Joshua could hardly see to walk. He kept the sound of the waves on his left as he pushed down the beach against the wind, the lantern knocking against his knee. The rain drummed against his slicker, while the wind pushed him in frightening bursts of force. It was mid-tide, but waves washed clear up to the edge of the dunes. More than once he lost his footing entirely. He squinted and tried to study the sea for signs of ships. After a while, his eyes adjusted, and he could faintly see the white churning foam, but mostly he saw nothing. He was afraid he might imagine something and set off a chain of events for no reason. The temperature was dropping, but Joshua felt secure inside his heavy slicker.

After much difficult plodding, Joshua reached the little hut, where his counterpart from High Head station was waiting, a fire burning in the stove. Joshua nearly fell through the door, his legs like rubber.

"Where you been, Duell?" asked the other.

"Why, how long you been here?"

"Good twenty minutes. Quite a night, eh?"

"Yeah," Joshua said, still out of breath. He took a metal cup from a shelf and poured himself water from a bottle.

"Your first storm, is it?"

Joshua nodded. The man got up and fastened his slicker and the chin strap of his sou'wester. He handed Joshua the little brass beach check.

Reminded, Joshua took his own from his pocket and handed it to the other man.

"Good luck then," the man said and pushed open the door.

It was almost silent in the hut, the wind and surf like ghostly distant voices. Joshua felt a knot in his stomach. What if there was a wreck? His greatest fear was to act in a way that might cost the lives of others. He stood resolutely, fastened his gear and headed out.

Half a mile from the hut, he thought he saw a light in the distance. The land curved here, and he couldn't tell if he were looking at the beach or the sea. The roar of the wind seemed louder and the surf rushed up the shore. It became harder to walk. He stared in the direction of the waves, scanning what he hoped was the horizon—but he could see nothing. He pushed on, looking right and fighting the wind. He thought he saw a tiny flicker. He stopped and was nearly blown over by a gust. Darkness. A flash of white foam. Then darkness. Finally, he saw it again: a pinpoint of light, flying about wildly and quite a distance away. He paused and watched, and sure enough, there it was. Through the wind, he thought he heard a bell. Barely there at all, but steady now, a delicate clanging. Joshua's heart beat faster. He was sweating beneath the oilskin. He felt afraid to act and afraid not to. He peered and squinted, trying to see the ship—if it was a ship— more clearly. All he could see was the faint light that came and went like a dream. He thought he heard a cry, a voice high pitched and distant, fractured by the wind and rain. It sounded—although Joshua really couldn't be sure—like a cry for help.

He stared out and listened. The light seemed to grow brighter, as if it were coming closer, though still flying around wildly. If he signaled his fellow surfmen and there was no ship in danger, he'd be a laughingstock. But if he ignored the light and the sound and a ship was in trouble, people would die. Joshua made his decision. He reached for his belt, the tails of the long slicker flapping, and fumbled until he set free the Coston flare. Holding the tube in one hand, he popped open the end and used the striker to ignite it. It burst into red flame and heavy, swirling smoke, making him cough violently.

The flare was blindingly bright, casting the beach and surf in an eerie red hue. Joshua could see more clearly now, waves crashing out to the horizon, and the ship, still indistinct, moving closer to the shore with tattered sails. Then she turned in an odd direction and came to a halt. Through the whipping wind and rain and sea mist, he saw now that the ship had struck a bar and run aground, and with what sail remained, must have been struggling to break free.

Joshua stuck the flare in a patch of dry sand, turned toward the station and broke into a run, or as close to a run as he could muster in his heavy clothes. He hoped the Life-Savers could see the flare and that they would be ready. He fell clumsily and a wave washed over him, chilly water seeping through the canvas of his pants. He got to his feet and kept running. He was sweating and out of breath. But mostly he was aware of a sense of fear, not for himself but for the men and women on that ship, that whatever action he was taking might be too late. He pushed on until finally he could see the silhouette of the station ahead.

Feeling both relief and panic, he stumbled again, and as he struggled to his feet, there were the rest of the men, wrestling the two carts through the sand. Buddy, Billy and Captain MacDonald were pulling the surfboat cart; Pendleton, Jurgen, Punchy and Peter Abbot manned the equipment cart.

MacDonald waved at Joshua. "How far out is she?"

Joshua wasn't sure. "At least a quarter mile, maybe more. Pretty far."

"Is she whole or broken up?"

"Looked like the sails were torn, but she was whole when I last saw her."

MacDonald made his decision. "Take the surfboat, leave the other," he barked.

In an instant the crew on the equipment cart helped take hold of the surfboat cart. Joshua joined in, and they sprinted as best they could, moving the cart with its tall wheels through the wet sand. The wind and breaking waves roared in the night. In the distance the flare still colored the sky.

They rounded a bend and spotted the red flame in the sand. They picked up the pace and soon reached it. MacDonald shaded his eyes and peered out. The fog had thinned and the ship was more clearly visible. She was a three-masted schooner, but two masts were already broken and hung dolefully, shredded sails flailing.

"She's breaking up," Pendleton said.

"Launch the boat," said MacDonald.

"Aye, sir," Pendleton replied, then called to the men. "Launch her. Smartly now!"

Pendleton, Punchy, and Jurgen plunged into the water, while Peter Abbot and Billy slid the boat off its cradle into the waves. All five men worked to keep the lifeboat steady. "In the boat now!" Pendleton cried. Joshua and Buddy scrambled in and took the middle seats, followed by Peter Abbot and Billy. They looked at each other apprehensively. This was the moment they had trained for, yet feared.

MacDonald stepped in effortlessly and took his place at the stern. Jurgen came over the gunwale smoothly, dripping wet, and took his seat. Pendleton and Punchy slid the boat further into the water, then flipped over the gunwales and made their way to their seats. The bow listed slightly to port and a large breaker smashed into the starboard side, nearly tipping the boat. "Move her forward, men," MacDonald said, unfazed by the motion, "now ROW HARD!" The men settled in their seats and grasped the long oars.

The pressure of the waves against them was astounding. The long boat moved forward into the breakers. Joshua rowed with all his strength and hoped he could overcome his fear and the implacable barrier of water now facing them. The noise of the surf this close was like cannon fire.

The boat cut through a large wave, its bow tilting sharply upwards, then slicing through the top of the breaker and sliding over. The men found their rhythm and rowed together. MacDonald held the long steering oar—Joshua marveled at the strength the man must have to do that—and kept his eyes forward, trying to locate the ship and steer toward her. The waves were wild and disorganized, breakers forming with curling crowns of foam like the pointed helmets of a marauding army. The boat rocked and tossed and seemed from moment to moment about to capsize, but somehow they plunged ahead, leaping into breakers, nearly leaving the surface, then crashing back into the white roiling water. Joshua and Buddy strained against the ocean's overpowering force.

"Jesus Christ!" Buddy said. "This is hard!"

Joshua nodded, unable to respond. He looked up for a moment at MacDonald, who was squinting to see where they were going.

"I see her," he shouted above the din. "Two points to starboard." He leaned hard against the oar to move the boat around.

At that moment, a rogue wave slapped into the port side and tipped the boat far enough over to take on water. She did not flip, and MacDonald shouted to keep pulling. They were up to their knees in chilly ocean water, but the boat was self-bailing and the water began to empty out.

Grunting with each stroke, Buddy managed to laugh nervously. "Now that's a nice trick."

Joshua looked over at Buddy. He felt his right shoulder cramping and his stomach churning like the water around them. Suddenly, his insides seemed to explode and he vomited, leaning as best he could over the side, but splattering everyone nonetheless.

Pendleton laughed loudly, like a bark, breaking the tension. "Don't worry," he shouted. "Everyone does it at least once. Now row!"

MacDonald, struggling to keep upright with the intense rocking, straightened suddenly. "There she is!" Several of the men, including Joshua and Buddy, turned to see. "Don't look! Her hull's a' splittin' up. No time to waste."

They passed through the worst of the breakers and the boat moved faster. As they reached the shallower water around the sand bar, the breakers again grew fiercer. They could now hear the loud clanging of the ship's bell nailed to what was left of the mainmast and voices, fearful and desperate voices. Unable to stop himself, Joshua turned to see.

She was thirty yards away. Two of her three masts hung, broken near the deck, splintered and tangled in ripped sail and rigging. The center mast remained erect, though it was broken near the crow's nest, her square rigging half furled and dangling. Four sailors hugged the mast, which dipped and pitched wildly. There seemed to be a woman, shrouded in dark clothes, hanging from the ratlines, calling for help in a tired voice. Another two men, a sailor and a civilian, clung to what was left of the ship's railing. When the people on board saw the lifeboat, they reached out their arms, beseeching the Life-Savers to rescue them. They represented salvation yet their task seemed impossible. The Life-Savers would have to steer the lifeboat close enough to the ship in the violently tossing waves so the people could be transferred, but there were too many of them to rescue all at once.

MacDonald straightened his steering oar, pausing momentarily. The men held their oars steady and the boat slowed, rocking in the surf. MacDonald quickly made his decision. "We'll come at her from the port amidships," he called to Pendleton. "Get a line to one of their men."

"Aye, sir," Pendleton shouted.

MacDonald leaned into the steering oar as the men rowed and the surfboat turned and moved closer. Pendleton took a coiled rope from beneath the bow seat, and tied off the end on a cleat on the starboard side. At the other end was a heaving stick with a smaller line attached to the main one. Holding the coil in his left hand and the handle of the heaving stick in his right, he called to one of the sailors holding on to the lower part of the mast, now thirty feet away.

"You there! Sailor," Pendleton's voice boomed. "I'll toss you this line—make it fast!"

The sailor leaned out, holding onto a dangling line with one hand and reaching with his other. Pendleton turned then rebounded sharply, letting loose the stick. It flew through the wind and spray and clattered onto the ship's deck, but it fell short and slipped off.

"Gotta get closer, sir!" Pendleton boomed as he retrieved the rope and coiled it again.

The men rowed closer. Joshua could not see how this would succeed. The ship was rolling intensely, waves crashing against her sides, rising and falling dangerously. The lifeboat tossed wildly, too. It seemed sure they would crash into the ship.

"Try her again," MacDonald said.

Pendleton once more flung the heaving stick. They were not fifteen feet from the sailor, who stretched out as far as he could. The stick flew toward him, but just as he went to close his fist around it, the ship shifted as its keel slipped several feet, nearly dislodging the sailor. The rope fell into the sea.

"Damn!" Pendleton cursed.

Once more, he gathered the rope and flung the stick out into the spray. This time the sailor caught the end and secured the line to the mast. The Life-Savers cheered. Pendleton pulled the boat closer and MacDonald called to the sailor.

"Any more of your people below?"

"Should be a woman down there with her baby," the sailor answered. "Hard to know if she's alive, sir. Some men are missing."

"Captain?" MacDonald asked.

The sailor shook his head. "A wave caught him. He went over twenty minutes ago."

MacDonald looked at Jurgen. "Take Joshua and go get the woman below."

"Aye, sir." Jurgen turned to Joshua. "Let's go."

Joshua began to move in the tossing boat, but fear struck, spreading like a sudden fever. He thought he might be sick again. An image popped into his mind, both memory and dream, of the palm grove in Cuba: Adam firing, bullets flying, noise. Just a split second, and the pounding surf brought him back. There could be no debate, no hesitation. He found his feet and moved shakily toward the gunwale, stepping over one of the men, clumsy but no longer wavering.

MacDonald called out to the woman on the ratline. "You all right, Miss?"

She hesitated, frozen in fear, but finally called back. "I think so, sir. Can you get us off?"

"We shall do our best, Miss. Try to climb down and move toward us. Keep a hold of anything you can."

Jurgen and Joshua struggled to keep their balance in the pitching boat. As Pendleton tugged on the line to bring them almost touching the vessel, Jurgen climbed onto the starboard gunwale and jumped for a piece of rigging hanging off the ship's railing. Joshua doubted he would be capable of such a feat, but Jurgen caught the rigging line and pulled himself up onto the deck. He turned and reached his arm out to Joshua. There was no choice. Joshua stepped onto the gunwale and leaped. He caught the same rigging and Jurgen's hand and clambered onto the deck.

"Help that woman down from the ratline," MacDonald commanded.

They made their way across the deck, stumbling at every step as the ship swung side to side and geysers of foam broke over them. The woman had come most of the way down and her feet were on the railing. A large wave hit the ship's starboard side, and the keel slipped in the sand, tilting more sharply to port toward the lifeboat. The woman slipped off the rail, screaming as her legs went in the sea. Joshua grabbed her about the waist, pulling her toward him as he grasped the railing.

"Sorry, ma'am," he said.

The woman was in too much of a panic to speak, but made a feeble effort to smile. Jurgen took her hands and together they guided her to the edge of the rail. The lifeboat tossed below.

"I... I can't do this," she whispered, her voice weak with fear.

"Yes you can, ma'am," Jurgen assured her. "You must. Or you'll die here for sure."

The woman nodded and Jurgen and Joshua helped her over the side. Pendleton held the boat as tight as he could to the ship, while Punchy and Buddy took hold of her legs and eased her toward them. She did not have much strength and the boat kept moving, but somehow they managed to get her over. She slumped onto one of the seats.

"You'll be all right, Miss," MacDonald said and turned to Jurgen. "Now the other one!"

"Aye, sir," Jurgen answered.

As Joshua and Jurgen lurched across the deck to the hatch leading below, the four sailors descended from the mast and made their way toward the port rail. At the same time, the sailor and civilian clinging to the deteriorating railing worked their way up the slanting deck. The sailors from the mast reached the rail and began to climb over.

"Not yet, lads," MacDonald warned them firmly. "We'll get all of you, but you'll wait for the other woman."

The panicked sailors didn't listen. Two of them continued to clamber over the side.

"Stop, I said!" MacDonald roared. He took a revolver from inside his coat. The sailors looked at him as if he was the devil himself, but they stopped.

With great effort, Jurgen and Joshua slid back the hatch and descended the steps to the cabin below. It was pitch black and eerie; doors slammed open and shut, dishes and pots and bits of glass slid back and forth along the floor. The wood frame of the ship creaked and cracked around them. There was the smell of spilled food mixed with a more pungent odor. Joshua tripped over a form on the floor. It was a body; he could feel the wet wool of the clothing and the stickiness of blood.

Jurgen called out. "Anyone here?"

There was no reply.

He called again more loudly. "Anyone alive here? We've come to rescue you!"

Again, no reply.

"Let's go," Jurgen said.

"Wait," Joshua said. "Let me try." In his loudest voice, he called out into the darkness. "Ma'am, if you can hear me, we are Life-Savers, come to help you and your baby get ashore. We can't see in the dark. If you can hear me, please make a sound so we may find you."

Joshua listened in the dark silence, filled with the smell of death, the creaking wood, and the noise of the storm just beyond the fragile wood walls. Then there was a whimper, like a wounded dog, a weak voice in the blackness.

"Help me. Please, help me."

They moved toward the voice, stumbling over objects and more bodies. They felt their way along the cabin wall to an opening where a door seemed to be flapping.

"You in here, ma'am?" Jurgen asked.

"Yes."

As they made their way through the narrow opening, Jurgen asked, "Can you stand?"

"I think so," said the voice.

"And your baby?" Joshua asked.

"He's hurt. But alive, thank God."

"We'll help you," Joshua said.

They moved through the dark to the voice and found the

woman holding an infant clutched to her breast.

"Take my hand," Jurgen said.

The woman put her hand in Jurgen's. Joshua reached around her back, and together they guided her through the little door and across the cabin.

They managed to find the steps and make their way up to the deck. They were struck full force by the fury of the storm and the comparative brightness of the night. They could see the woman now: perhaps thirty, dressed in black wool, a soaked and tattered cloak over her, partly wrapped around a baby whose tiny head bore a bleeding wound.

Joshua reached for the child. "Let me take him."

The woman resisted. "No," she said, as firmly as she could muster.

"I'll get him into the boat," Joshua said.

She looked at him. He had the strange sensation, one he would come to recognize, that he was her only hope. She yielded the baby to him. He held the little body close against his chest, while Jurgen took the woman by the arm and helped her to the railing. They looked over. The boat still rose and fell in crazy leaps. The five sailors clung to the rail, along with the civilian, a man in his forties who appeared sturdy but terrified. They all glared at MacDonald, who kept them at bay with his gun.

"Look here," pleaded the civilian, "you can't keep us on the ship."

"Sir," MacDonald replied, "it is not my intention to do so. The boat will only take four extra people, or it will swamp in these seas."

When they saw the woman and Joshua holding the baby, compassion overcame fear and they made room for them to pass.

The woman was terrified, but Jurgen helped her to climb over the rail and down the ship's side. Punchy and Peter Abbot grabbed her arms as she stepped toward the boat, and despite the wild tossing she landed on her feet. She glanced at the other woman, who sat staring ahead in shock.

Joshua climbed over the rail, clutching the baby against him and taking hold of a rope with the other hand. He leaned out toward Pendleton, who reached up.

"Okay, son, hand me the baby."

Joshua hesitated, but stretched as far as he could and guided the child into Pendleton's strong hands. Pendleton handed it to its mother, who broke into sobs.

Suddenly, a piece of the mainsail caught a gust of wind, and a timber from the cross arms broke free and fell from the mainmast. It struck Joshua on the shoulder and knocked him over. Stumbling and confused, he fell and his head hit the railing.

The other Life-Savers were on their feet, shouting.

"Get him out of there," MacDonald commanded.

Joshua lay on the tossing deck, aware of the activity around him, but floating in a half-daze of noise and shouts. Through blurred vision he saw Pendleton, Billy and Buddy leap for the ship's rail and land near him. As they did so, two of the sailors took advantage of the confusion and made a dive for the lifeboat, landing with a crash on its floor and causing it to rock alarmingly.

MacDonald glowered at them. Motioning with his gun, he said, "You stay seated right there and don't fuckin' move or I'll blow you away and throw you in the sea, I swear it." The men sat rigidly in the bottom of the boat.

Joshua saw Pendleton hovering over him, then felt himself lifted up. Pendleton draped him over his shoulder as Billy and Buddy helped to lower him and Peter Abbott and Punchy reached out to guide him into the boat.

"He'll be all right," he heard Billy say.

The boat was crowded now, sitting low in the water, and they were short one rower.

MacDonald looked up at the four men on the deck. Joshua, only half conscious, saw the strain in the Keeper's face. His first responsibility was to protect the lives of the people in the boat, those they had rescued and his own men. If he took these others, there was a strong chance they would all die.

"Cut us free," he commanded Pendleton, who took a knife from his pocket and cut the line holding the lifeboat to the ship. The waves carried them off rapidly.

"We shall come back for you," MacDonald called to the four men. "You have my word."

The Life-Savers took their places and began to row hard as MacDonald took up the steering oar. All those aboard the boat were somber. Lives had already been lost that night; they had just abandoned four men and the boat, low in the water and surrounded by crashing waves, seemed a tenuous hope at best. The woman holding her baby, on the floor of the boat next to Joshua, was crying.

MacDonald looked at the two sailors. Pointing at Joshua's seat next to Buddy, he said, "One of you men, sit up here and take the oar." Both sailors scrambled for the spot, but the shorter of the two won out, and he took hold of Joshua's oar. MacDonald looked at Joshua, who was slumped against the bulwark, his head bleeding. "Don't you worry, son, we'll get you home." Joshua closed his eyes and nodded. Then Mac-

Donald turned to the men. "Now ROW you bastards!"

The boat moved forward. It was a different motion this time; the battle was not to pull against the waves so much as to avoid tipping over as they rode over the crest of a wave into its trough. This required a steady, fast pace and perfect steering on MacDonald's part to keep them ahead of the backwash of the following waves. At times they moved quite swiftly. A wave hit them from the starboard side, throwing water over the gunwale and nearly flipping them, but they had enough speed to pass through it and the water drained away. They moved toward the beach. Joshua had the sensation of flying as the boat sped along. He got himself up to a sitting position.

"There's the lad," Pendleton said. The other men smiled.

Joshua felt a throbbing pain and the warm trickle of blood through the chilly spray. He touched his head. There was a rough spot on his left temple. He could not move his shoulder or arm. He sat back and took the ride.

The breakers near the shore were as strong as any they had encountered; it was nearly high tide and the last set of waves, some near ten foot, crashed directly onto the sand. It would be a neat trick to ride over this last ridge and get the boat successfully ashore without scuttling it and tossing its passengers into the sea. The men rowed for all they were worth and MacDonald held firmly to the steering oar as they mounted the wave. The boat felt tiny and powerless as the ocean flung it over the churning ridge and slammed the bow into the sand. Water poured in from both sides, and the lifeboat came to a dead stop. Pendleton, Billy, Jurgen, and Punchy leaped into the water and drew the boat as far up the sand as they could.

MacDonald stepped out, cool as ever, barking orders. "Billy, you get up to the station and use the telephone to call the doctor. We need him out here as fast as he can ride. Say we have an injured baby, maybe several Life-Savers and sailors." He looked at the men. "The rest of you get the women and Joshua to the station, then back here as fast as you can run. We've got to go back for those others."

"Aye, sir," they cried out.

The flare was still burning, and the reddish glow shone weirdly on the crew and the tattered survivors as they made it onto the beach. One of the sailors fell to his knees and prayed, sobbing loudly. The men helped the two women, the one clutching her baby, out of the boat. Then they reached for Joshua and helped him out. His head was bleeding and he staggered as his feet touched the sand. Jurgen reached his arm under Joshua's and helped him walk.

"I'm all right," Joshua insisted. He felt dizzy and weak.

"You're not. Now help me."

Joshua turned for a moment to look out over the sea. Although the beach was a churning mass of foam all the way to the dune's edge, the wind made it difficult to stay upright, let alone walk, and the blowing sand was bitter and stinging— still, it was an astounding relief to be on solid ground once again. The sea was a stew of white water and vicious, dark waves. The battered ship hung at an angle like a dying animal. Joshua knew those men out there were scared to death, but now he could do nothing for them. Jurgen helped him up the beach.

It took fifteen minutes to get back to the station. Billy had removed his heavy coat and sprinted up the beach to call the doctor. He met them as they neared the porch.

"I reached the doc's office. Someone is on the way," he sputtered. He ran back toward the wreck.

Jurgen helped Joshua up the stairs to the sleeping quarters, got him out of his heavy coat and onto his cot. He removed the heavy rubber boots and laid a blanket over him.

"Got to go back. Doc'll be here soon. Hang in there, you'll be all right, I'm betting."

Joshua nodded. "Thanks. Get those men back here."

"We'll try. Get some sleep."

Joshua could hear Jurgen's heavy boots descending the stairs. Then more steps, as Punchy and Peter Abbot helped the two women up. They passed by Joshua and went into the guest room. The baby whimpered mutedly. His mother, smeared with blood and grime, looked sick with anguish, and Joshua fell asleep to the sound of the baby's moans.

Sometime later he became aware of a commotion nearby. He was unsure where he was, and his mind's eye was distracted by shotgun images of wounded soldiers, flopping fish, women crying, dirt and sand and water flying through the air. He opened his eyes, squinting against the light. The wind howled through the edges of the window. Inside it was warm and sheltered. He felt dizzy and had a brutal headache.

A woman stood over him. He could not see her clearly, but she was tall, with a serious face and friendly eyes. She wore a dark dress and a heavy cloak. She removed the cloak and sat on the edge of the bed.

"What's your name?" she asked.

He told her.

"Do you remember what happened to you?"

"Yes, I think so. We were in the lifeboat… no, I was on the ship. I slipped. No, something hit me, I think. I… fell."

"You've hit your head. Can you sit up?"

Joshua tried to raise himself. The movement caused a bolt

of pain to shoot through his shoulder, and he grimaced.

"What's that?" she asked.

"My shoulder. It's… sore."

"I'll look at it."

"The baby…" Joshua said.

She nodded. "I'll be back."

The woman disappeared into the next room, and was gone a long time. Joshua felt better with his eyes closed, although the pounding in his head seemed to keep time with the pounding of the surf beyond the window. He felt despondent to be here while his crewmates risked their lives on the lifeboat. Still, it was comfortable in his bed, safe and warm, like when he was a child, so long ago… he faded again into sleep.

Once more the woman awakened him. She was pretty, but not in the usual delicate way women had. There were no frills on her dress, and her facial expression suggested she would brook no nonsense. Yet her smile was reassuring.

"How do you feel?" she asked.

"I expect I'll be all right."

"That's not what I asked."

"I know," he answered. "My head hurts. Are the men back?"

"No. Are you still dizzy?"

"Yes, a little." He looked at her and managed a smile. "I can see you clearly."

"How nice for you," she replied a bit tartly.

She opened a small black bag, and laid out several items on the bed. "Let's look at that head wound." She moved closer, leaning over him, and began to dab at the cut on his head with a ball of cotton.

"Who are you?" Joshua asked.

She opened a bottle of disinfectant, poured some on a clean

rag, and swabbed the wound. She paused to take a splinter from his head and placed it on the bed. He winced. Her face was inches from his and he could feel her breath.

"I'm a doctor," she said. "My name is Julia Masefield."

She pulled out another splinter and laid it next to the first one. Then she poured more disinfectant and cleaned the wound again.

"How... how can you be a doctor? You're... a woman."

She picked up a roll of gauze and neatly wrapped it around his head, then picked up a scissor, cut the gauze, and tucked it perfectly.

"I admire a man who is observant. Now let's look at the shoulder."

She walked around the bed and lifted him so he was sitting straight, then opened his shirt to look at his shoulder. She was strong, moving him without regard to any pain she was causing. Then she took hold of his shoulder and yanked it rather hard.

Joshua yelped. "That hurt," he said.

"I realize that. It's only bruised. There's no dislocation. It will feel better soon."

"But..."

"You know, Mr.— what is it?"

"Duell. Joshua Duell."

"Yes, well, Mr. Duell, somehow you don't strike me as the stammering sort."

"Sorry, I've just never heard of a woman doctor."

"We are a rare breed," the Doctor said. "I realize that." She sighed. "But there will be more of us. I attended medical school at Johns Hopkins University, and I am working here for Dr. Meads." She paused and looked at him almost coyly. "I hope you don't mind."

"Mind? No, ma'am, I don't mind…"

"Please, Mr. Duell, whatever you do, please don't call me ma'am, I beg of you."

Joshua smiled and leaned back against his pillow. "All right, I won't."

"You have a mild concussion," she said. "In fact, you and that baby in there have quite similar conditions. There is no particular treatment other than a bit of rest. You should be fine in a few days, perhaps less. I'd suggest you take it easy until the dizziness is completely gone. You may find your memory of tonight's events is a bit blurry, but for better or worse, it shall return." She put on her cloak. "I must go back to town. Unfortunately, there's plenty of activity tonight with the storm. When the other men return, they can call for me again if I am needed. And please, come see me when you feel better, and I'll check your head wound."

" I will," Joshua said. "I will do that."

"Good. Good night, Mr. Duell."

"Doctor," Joshua called out.

She stopped and turned toward him. "Yes?"

"Aren't you afraid of the storm?"

She simply laughed and headed down the steps.

CHAPTER SEVEN

The sun beat down on the beach the next day as if nothing had occurred and the waves, still churning but only slightly, trundled innocently over iridescent fissures of light. Joshua awoke with a piercing headache, and sat up to gaze on the sea. He could barely believe his eyes; the day could not have been more different from the night before.

He tried to stand, but immediately felt dizzy. The others had risen long before and he was alone. He heard the baby in the adjoining room and forced himself to get up and peer in the doorway. The young mother, still wrapped in tattered clothing, held a naked little boy in the air, giggling despite the large bandage on his small head.

"Good morning," Joshua said.

"Good morning," the woman replied languidly.

"How are you feeling?"

She smiled. "Grateful to be alive."

Joshua nodded. "Have you been attended to this morning?"

"Oh, yes, quite nicely," she said. She noticed Joshua looking at her clothes. "They sent for some new clothing for me."

Joshua felt the room spinning and grabbed the doorway. "That's good. I'm afraid I have to sit now."

The woman nodded.

"What's his name?" Joshua asked.

"Gabriel."

Joshua nodded and staggered clumsily toward his bed.

Just before he faded again, he heard the woman call to him, "Thank you."

Later, Buddy and Jurgen came to check on him. Buddy brought a bowl of porridge and a cup of tea.

Jurgen sat on the edge of the bed. "How you feeling?"

"I'm fine," Joshua said. "Well, my head hurts a bit."

"You got quite a clunk there. We was all worried about you."

"Uh… thanks," Joshua said. He didn't like the idea that the other men worried about him when they were risking their own lives to rescue the stranded sailors. He looked at Buddy. "How'd it go last night?"

"It ended well," Buddy said. "We got three men off the ship, no trouble."

Jurgen shot Buddy a quick glance.

"I thought there were four," Joshua said.

"No, three—" Buddy said.

Jurgen interrupted him. "It was four. One that you saw didn't make it out. He was dead when we got back. But another who had been knocked unconscious in the hold managed to get up top when he heard us."

"Then… what happened to the other sailor?"

Jurgen looked again at Buddy.

Buddy spoke. "It was the civilian fellow. He slipped getting into the boat."

"He slipped?" Joshua asked.

"I was helping him off the ship. He jumped, I had his hand, but… I lost him."

"You lost him." Joshua looked at Jurgen, whose face was stolid.

"The water was wild! You saw it. He fell in and I tried to grab him, but the surf carried him away."

"Why didn't you go after him?"

"What, you mean jump in and swim?" Buddy asked, anguished.

"No. I guess not. But no one tried to save him?"

"The man went under," Jurgen said. "Twice. Second time, he did not come back up."

Joshua was silent. What a sad ending, to come so close to being rescued. Jurgen was glowering at Buddy, who turned his face away. Joshua lay back and closed his eyes.

"Get some sleep," Jurgen said.

Without opening his eyes, Joshua asked, "But all the others were all right?"

Buddy and Jurgen were on their way out the door. "Those what lived, yes," Jurgen replied.

Joshua awakened feeling disoriented. Buddy walked in with another cup of tea, helped Joshua sit up and handed it to him.

"Thanks," Joshua said. He took a sip. "Good."

Buddy pulled up a chair. His face looked strained.

"What's the matter?" Joshua asked.

"Nothing," Buddy said, a bit sharply. Then his voice softened. "I've been worried about you, is all."

Joshua smiled. His head still felt like a split plank. "I think

I'm going to be okay. Nice of you to worry, though."

"What're friends for?"

"Here we are, roommates again."

Buddy nodded. "And of all places, this one—who could have imagined?"

Joshua's smile vanished. "What happened last night?"

"We lost a man."

"Was it your fault? Seemed like Jurgen thought…"

"Shit, of course he does. I don't stand a chance around here, you know that."

"I don't think that's true, Buddy."

"They don't like me and I don't like them."

"What are you saying? You're going to leave?"

Buddy looked at him. Then he shook his head. "No, sport, I'm not going to abandon you to these fools, particularly with a busted head."

Joshua laughed. "That's good." He closed his eyes.

Sometime in the afternoon, Joshua awoke and got out of bed. His head was still pounding. He went downstairs. Pendleton was at the galley table.

"Doc said you're not to get up," Pendleton said.

"I know. I had to stretch my legs."

"Quite a doctor you drew there."

Joshua wasn't entirely sure she hadn't been some figment of his imagination after the blow to his head. "Have you ever seen her before?"

"Never," Pendleton said. "Not bad looking, though."

"No. But I'd wager she'd be a handful if you tried to mess with her."

"Aye, lad, she might."

Joshua went outside. The sun was intensely bright. The sea

was calming but the sand was still wet clear up to the dune line, covered with seaweed and debris. The beach had been eaten away, leaving a steep three-foot wall of sand where there had been a gradual slope. Pieces of ship railing, splinters of spars, twists of rope tangled with brass hardware and clumps of dried grains lay scattered over the beach. The hulk of the ship sat like a twisted lump two hundred yards out, still pounded by the waves, timbers prying loose. The deteriorating hull sent ghostly creaking sounds across the water. Only a piece of the center mast remained. Curls of rigging hung from the sides. Joshua decided to walk. The distance to the site seemed much shorter. He could see crates and planks washing up at the water's edge, and more scattered debris. A dozen or more men and women from town sifted through the wreckage. Three men in a cart hauled away a load of lumber.

Joshua picked up a piece of bracelet of polished red stones. He held the stones between his fingers and thought of his mother's brooch, the one he thought he recognized on Kirov's vest. If only the Life-Savers had been there. The beach smelled of spoiling produce and rotting flesh. Two dogs picked at something in the sand at the base of the dune, snarling and snapping—a human arm, still wrapped in the white canvas of a sailor's shirt. The smell of it was powerful. Joshua gagged and turned away.

Three riders moved rapidly toward the wreckage. His vision was blurry and he could not make out their faces until they were quite close. It was Kirov, who rode like a cavalry officer onto the field of battle, with his two sidekicks. They slowed their horses to a walk and surveyed the area. Kirov pointed to the remains of the ship languishing in the surf. The other two nodded then they took off again at a gallop in the direction from which they had come.

Joshua walked back to the station. The rest of the crew was drilling on the beach. MacDonald sat in his chair watching them from afar.

"How you feeling, lad?" he asked.

"Not too bad," Joshua replied. "I was lucky, I guess."

"Getting hit on the head by a falling timber isn't lucky. But you appear to have survived and are recovering. I'm glad of that. Come here." He made Joshua lean down so he could look at his head. "Nasty bang you got. It's discolored and a bit swollen. You should go in town in the morning and have the doc look at it again."

"All right, sir, I will." Joshua looked out over the beach. "Do they always do that?"

"Pick through the wreckage? Yes, always. It's part of the procedure, I guess."

"Doesn't it bother you, sir?"

"At first it did," MacDonald said. "But these folks are pretty poor. Free goods wash up on the beach, they figure it's theirs to take unless someone claims it."

"What about those others?"

"The wreckers? Your friend, Kirov?" He laughed. "They're part of it, too. There are crews up and down the coast, some more savory than others. The ship owners use them to salvage their ships and cargo, if they can." He paused and looked at Joshua more intently. "I'm not saying it's right, but it's like any other cycle. There's life and there's death."

"Yes, sir." Joshua paused. "I wonder, Captain... I've wanted to ask you something since I got here. May I now?"

"Of course."

"Sir, I don't believe I ever mentioned it, but my mother died in a wreck this past spring."

"Really? Where?"

"Off of Wellfleet. Easter day."

MacDonald nodded and looked at Joshua with sympathy. "I'm sorry, son. You never said anything, I didn't realize…"

"Yes, sir. I'm sorry, too." Joshua paused. "But there was no rescue. Her body was never found. I think there were Life-Savers who eventually made it to the ship, but no one aboard survived and the exact nature of the event was never officially determined. You don't happen to know anything about it, do you, sir?"

"I heard about it," he said. "Always talk when there's a wreck."

"Yes, sir. But how come there was no rescue? What happened that night, do you know?"

MacDonald looked at him intently. "I don't, son, no. It was mentioned to me by a friend as an odd thing, but I guess the fellows at Cahoons Hollow didn't see it in time. Happens sometimes, you know."

"I suppose it must," Joshua said. "Do you know those folks?"

"No, I don't know anyone down there. I knew the fellow who was keeper before this one—good man, but he died of cancer a few years back." MacDonald lifted his head and looked at Joshua. "Wish I could tell you more."

"Yes, sir. Thank you." Joshua turned to go.

"Joshua," MacDonald said.

"Yes, sir?"

"I'm a bit worried about your friend."

"Buddy?"

"That's right. You heard about the second rescue?"

Joshua nodded.

"It's not good, you know, what happened."

"I wasn't there, sir…"

"I know that, lad. I'm just letting you know there's concern over his behavior."

"But I thought it was an accident. What could he have done differently? No one else went after the man…"

"It's more the approach, you understand? It was too dangerous for anyone to dive in and try to save the poor fellow at that point. The lifeboat was filled to the brim and might have tipped. But his attitude is not that of a Life-Saver. It could one day be a danger to one of the others."

"I see, sir. What would you like me to do?" Joshua asked.

"Nothing, son, I doubt there is anything you could do. We are all born with the tools God has given us to work with. Your friend will have to figure out his own way. Just don't let him bring you down with him." MacDonald turned his face to the sea and resumed puffing his pipe.

"Aye, sir," Joshua said. He turned and walked to the station.

In the morning, Joshua rode into Provincetown on the supply wagon that came twice a week. The driver, a crusty old Portuguese named Sam, offered Joshua a ride in and back out again later that day. Joshua's headache was not improved by sitting up on the wagon as it bounced and rolled. But he found himself looking forward to seeing the doctor again.

The medical offices of Herbert Meads were located in a new Cape house with a surrounding porch on Bradford Street. The reception room was bright and cheery. A pleasant looking older woman sat at a desk writing in a ledger. She looked up at him.

"Good morning, ma'am," Joshua said. "I'm here to see Dr.

Masefield."

The woman looked him over. "Are you a patient?" she asked, with a hint of irony.

'Yes, ma'am. I'm one of the Life-Savers. Dr. Masefield treated me night before last, during the storm."

"Oh, yes, of course," she said. "I'll let her know you're here."

She disappeared through a door. Joshua hung his coat and cap and sat on a bench by the window. The street, which ran parallel to Commercial Street but further inland, was busy with carriages and delivery wagons. The sun shone through a large window. The little room felt sheltered and peaceful.

The door opened and the woman reappeared. "She will see you now. This way, please." She gestured with her head to the door.

Joshua went through it. He felt dizzy—and suddenly anxious, his heart beating rapidly. He began to sweat. Inside was a large central room with doors open to two small offices off to one side, and two more closed doors on the other side. The main room had two examination tables and glass cabinets against the walls filled with medicines and supplies. The faint smell of alcohol hung in the air. Julia Masefield stepped forward, offering her hand and smiling cheerily.

"Good morning, Mr. Duell. Lovely to see you up and about. How are you feeling?"

"I feel fine, ma'am... I mean, Doctor," Joshua said. He felt ill at ease, stumbling over his words.

"You feel fine?" asked the doctor.

"Well, um, no, not fine."

"What, then?"

"I feel... my, ah, head still aches and I'm a bit dizzy."

She smiled again. She had an intriguing smile. "Yes, I can

see that. Why don't you sit down, Mr. Duell?" She gestured toward a wooden chair.

Joshua sat and found himself fidgeting with his hands. The doctor took his left hand in hers and felt his pulse.

"Please take off your shirt, Mr. Duell," she said.

If the doctor were a man he would have thought nothing of this, but the doctor was not a man. Still, he did as he was asked. Dr. Masefield took a stethoscope from around her neck and pressed its cold steel cup to various spots on his chest and back. She asked him to take a few deep breaths.

"What do you hear through those things?" Joshua asked.

"I'm listening to your heart and lungs."

"How do my heart and lungs sound?"

"Just superb, Mr. Duell, I assure you. Stand up for a moment, please."

He did, feeling ever more uncomfortable.

"Can you bend over and touch your toes?"

"Pardon me?"

"It was a simple question, Mr. Duell. I've heard tell the Life-Savers do a lot of exercise. This is a fairly simple one."

"Yes, I suppose it is…" Joshua said.

He felt entirely foolish. He stretched his arms above his head, aware of his bare chest, then lowered his arms to touch the tips of his boots. His head filled with blood and began to spin. He nearly fell over, but the doctor caught his arm. As she helped him straighten up and slide into the chair, he noticed again how strong she was.

"Sorry, Mr. Duell, that was a test."

"Which I apparently failed."

"That depends upon your perspective," Dr. Masefield said. "Your body reacted the way I supposed it might, so in a sense you succeeded."

Joshua smiled. "I see."

The doctor opened a drawer in one of the cabinets and took out a mercury-in-glass thermometer. "Please open your mouth and put this under your tongue."

Joshua did as he was told, feeling even more awkward with the instrument protruding from his mouth. The doctor went to the corner to look over several papers on a counter. She wore a long yellow skirt of wool, which flared above her ankles, pretty but functional, with a white, lace-embroidered blouse and a fitted navy jacket. Her boots were black with buttons. She turned and caught him looking at her. He tried to mumble something. She came over and removed the thermometer.

"What's that, Mr. Duell?"

"Thank you. I… was simply asking what made you decide to attend medical school?"

"Ah. Thank you for asking." She popped the instrument back into his mouth. "My mother was from Baltimore. We grew up in Connecticut, where she occasionally wrote articles for newspapers. She once had an article published in Harper's Magazine."

"Wudadout," Joshua mumbled.

"About the right to vote."

"Wibbn?"

"Yes, Mr. Duell, women."

She laughed. He liked her laugh—it was sincere and a bit boyish.

"My mother was a strong woman and taught me that women can be strong…"

"Mos wibbn eyefv kno awr stwn," Joshua said.

"Perhaps she taught me that women could do more than

is normally acceptable in a world run by men. But I also liked helping people… and animals… anything, really. I once nursed a sick beetle." She laughed again. "I did well in school, and my mother heard that Hopkins was entertaining applications from a few women, so I applied."

Joshua's mumble suggested sympathy.

"Yes, it had its difficult moments. But you see? I survived." She looked at the clock on the wall. "I think it's been long enough."

She stepped over and withdrew the instrument from Joshua's mouth. His lips ached from six and a half minutes of holding them stiffly. She looked carefully at the thermometer, tilting it in the light.

"Well, Mr. Duell—"

He looked suddenly alarmed.

"You have no fever. You are going to live."

Joshua smiled.

"How is the shoulder feeling?"

He rolled his shoulder. It made a creaking sound and he winced slightly. "I think it's fine," he said.

"Very good. You may put back your shirt. The examination is over."

"Thank you, Doctor," Joshua said.

"You seem to be getting better, Mr. Duell. You had quite a blow, but you have a hard head. Your concussion will not cause any permanent damage, though I suspect your head may continue to ache and spin for at least another week."

"Can I go back to work?"

"As soon as you feel up to it. I'd say give it another day."

"All right. Thank you, Doctor."

"You're welcome, Mr. Duell. Come and visit again, will

you?"

He looked at her. The sun cast a glow upon her yellow skirt. "I shall."

At dinner that night, Joshua was the brunt of a flurry of jokes by the ebullient crew.

"How's the doctor?" Punchy asked with an exaggerated, childish grin.

The men snickered and hooted.

"We heard ya got you a gurrlll doctor!" Jurgen jeered.

"Did she examine ya?" asked Billy, torn between teasing and lascivious envy.

"Yep—all over!"

The men hooted even more loudly. Even Pendleton laughed. MacDonald sat at the head of the table, puffing his pipe wisely.

"Can't say as I've ever heard a' no lady doctor," Pendleton said with the weight of great expertise.

MacDonald sighed. "Doc Meads needed another physician. He'd gotten a letter from a woman doctor who lived in Boston. He asked the Medical Society there about her, and Miss Mase-field came all the way down here to see him. I heard he was very impressed with her. She had the top grades in that school she went to…"

"Johns Hopkins…" Joshua said.

"Right. Hopkins. Damn fine school, I'm told. She took good care of you, did she?"

"Yes, sir, she did," Joshua said. "Very professional, seems to know what she's doing."

At this the hooting started again and continued until Mac-Donald stood up.

"All right, lads, enough hootin' and hollerin'. Leave the

poor boy alone. Let's get some sleep and get an early start in the morning. Lifeboats!" He left the room in a puff of white smoke. "G'night, lads!"

"Good night, sir!" they answered.

For the next month the men drilled hard, working from early morning until sundown. As the days grew shorter, the nights of lonely patrols along the beach seemed longer and colder, and the wind sharpened as the temperature dropped and they moved through October. By mid-month the nights were frosty and the wind downright biting, sand whisking along the beach and into their eyes. Joshua's headaches were gone. He and Buddy had grown stronger from drilling and rowing, their arms and hands gaining muscles, their endurance increasing. They ate and slept well, and Joshua loved nearly every moment spent at the ocean's edge. Even Buddy seemed to fall into the rhythm of the place, though his troubles with the men continued unabated. But at night, on patrol, the memories of the first rescue would return to haunt Joshua, the bodies below deck and the desperation of the sailors. He was proud he'd taken part in a rescue and they had saved lives. That was what they were here to do—it was why he was here, to do some good. No one could dispute that fact. He thought of his father, that if he knew what he was doing here it might make things better between them. He decided to write him a letter.

Sitting on the porch with a pen and a few sheets of paper laid upon a book, Joshua thought about what to say. He'd written Gideon once, after he arrived in Provincetown, to say he was safe, and received a telegram: "Glad you are well. GD". He wrote again after he had been accepted in the Life-

Savers. Once again, he received a telegram: "Good news. Wish you luck. GD". He knew his father could be cold, withdrawn, abrupt—maybe it was his way of saying he didn't really approve of how Joshua was spending his time. Still, he felt badly for his father, alone in the house, though Gideon would surely insist he was fine. Joshua knew otherwise. He began to write. The pen scratched along the paper, but it was all wrong; he crumpled the sheet and started on another. Then he stopped and looked out over the ocean.

He remembered the night he'd returned home in his second year at Harvard. He'd received a telegram from his father saying the USS Maine had been sunk in Havana harbor and he must come home immediately. For months there had been talk of war with Spain. The Maine had been sent to Havana as a conciliatory gesture, but the mysterious explosion killed two hundred American sailors and suddenly across the country there was a clamor for war. On the train home Joshua had felt anxious and afraid. His father was an Annapolis graduate, a Civil War veteran, and had just been given command of a new battleship, the Indiana. He was an admirer of Teddy Roosevelt, who was Secretary of the Navy and one of the most zealous crusaders for the war. Joshua knew his father would most certainly support it—but what would it mean for Adam, and for him?

His parents were hosting friends for dinner, and Joshua and Adam joined them, as was the custom. That night his parents had an argument over the looming conflict, a rare public quarrel. They'd just sat down when one of Gideon's friends boomed out, "Looks as if you might see some action, old fellow!"

Gideon laughed. "I hope so," he said. Several other men

laughed, too.

Lucy threw down her fork, startling the guests. "It's not funny, not a bit. This war of yours," she said, pointedly directing her comments at her husband, "is going to get a lot of people killed."

There was more laughter. "Isn't that what happens in wars?" one man shouted.

Lucy glared at them, and particularly at Gideon. "Spain is old," she said slowly, being deliberately provocative, "worn out like an old strumpet. She is no threat to us. But all you old fellows who haven't seen action since you were your sons' ages think it would be fun to go out and win a little war. Make America great, as TR keeps saying. I say it's pure hooey. Dangerous hooey, at that."

Joshua and Adam looked at each other with alarm. Adam hitched up his courage and spoke. "I think the war will be good for us. It will make us greater, increase our standing..."

"Oh, for God's sake, Adam," Lucy interrupted, "you don't know a damn thing."

"That'll do now," Gideon had said sternly. "If we do go to war, the boys will make their own choices. Now please, my dear, do settle down."

Joshua smiled remembering his mother's boldness, and the little grin she'd flashed him as she stormed out of the room.

Adam worshipped his father and from an early age talked of joining the military as his father had done. Adam and Gideon would visit sailing vessels together along the lower Manhattan waterfront, and Adam had a treasured collection of model ships, which he and his father would tinker with when Gideon was not in the capital or off at sea. Joshua found his brother's interests grating—or maybe in truth it was his closeness to their father. Joshua was more like his mother: he was athletic, enjoying games of Lacrosse, rugby and lawn tennis, and he loved to read.

A few days later at dinner, Gideon had announced he'd been assigned to the waters off Cuba. Lucy was about to protest when Adam stood and clanked his water glass.

"I have an announcement, too." He was smiling proudly.

They all looked at him.

"I've joined the Marines, just this afternoon," Adam said.

Lucy stared at her husband. Gideon shrugged, though there was a twinkle in his eye. Joshua could not recall ever before seeing her so strained and anxious.

His mind jumped to a different scene, half a year later, not long before his brother passed away. Joshua and Lucy were at Adam's bedside. Adam was asleep in a ward with half a dozen other wounded soldiers, all suffering, some recovering, others not. Sometimes he and Adam would speak, but his brother had grown weaker and slept much of the time. It was a strain on them both to visit there each day, a mix of anguish and a heavy, languishing tedium—but Lucy's spirit was indomitable and Joshua felt he had to help her however he could.

They'd heard footsteps in the corridor outside the big room. Lucy ran to the door. Joshua couldn't see her face, but her body seemed to elevate as if lifted by some unseen force. Then she cried out, "Oh, Gideon!" His father had finally come home from the war. She rushed to him and threw herself into his arms. Joshua stood watching, she crying and he comforting her. Joshua caught a glimpse of his father's face, stolid and grim, the heavy mustache and jowls—yet he held his wife firmly in his arms and seemed relieved to see her. They remained like that a long time. Then, slowly, they relaxed their grip on one another and walked toward Joshua. His father reached out his arms and Joshua embraced him. "Joshua, my boy," Gideon said solemnly. Joshua was afraid of what would happen when he saw Adam. They went together to his brother's bed, and he could see the deep furrowed lines on his father's face. It was a look of despair.

He began to write again.

> *Dear Father:*
> *I hope you are well. I'm sure it is lonely in the house, though you must be busy with your work. I, too, am busy. My work for the Life-Savers is very engaging. It is challenging, sometimes even thrilling! We rescued a ship foundering on a sandbar and saved the lives of several people. I felt good about being a part of this. I felt you might be proud of me.*
>
> *I miss you as much as I know we each miss the others. I hope to see you soon, but please know that I am well.*
> *Joshua*

The next day he re-read the letter. It seemed woefully inadequate, but he gave it to be posted.

Joshua had grown more comfortable spending time with the other men. They were unsophisticated, without much education, wild in a sense, all of them living and working together on the exposed beach, but he liked their company,

sharing their thoughts, their mariner's humor. The only problem was Buddy.

They all ate together each evening after the arduous days
of training. One week in mid-October it was Joshua's turn
to cook. Joshua had very little experience with cooking, so
Buddy offered to help, and the first night they decided to
prepare potatoes and fish in a Portuguese-style stew.
Buddy was cutting vegetables and putting them in the pot
when Punchy came in and stopped him.

"That's all wrong," he said. "You cut 'em like this."

He pushed Buddy aside, took the knife from his hand and
began slicing the carrots, leeks and potatoes into larger pieces
than Buddy had.

"What's the difference?" Buddy demanded.

"Ah, you're just a novice," Punchy said.

Buddy got moody. "I've cooked plenty," he said.

"Well, it don't show in your technique."

Joshua stepped between them. He asked Buddy to get the
bucket of cleaned fish from the porch. Buddy grumbled. When
he returned Joshua was working side by side with Punchy, but
Buddy pushed his way back in and began to cut the fish, a
twinkle in his eye.

Joshua hated to admit it, but he felt torn by their friendship. The other men continued to be hard on Buddy. They
didn't laugh at his jokes, they didn't understand his wry
humor or his remarks about unjust governments or the
oppression of the working class. For these men life was simple
and Buddy was full of twists and turns no one cared to un-
ravel. No one sat down with him for a man-to-man talk,
which they sometimes did with Joshua—though the conversations were never any deeper than missing their homes or

what it was like at sea or in the military, or how to cut up a fish or hunt for deer. Buddy's wide-ranging curiosity and longing for far off cultured shores seemed immaterial to the tasks at hand. Buddy was jealous of Joshua's ability to have these conversations, and imagined them more intimate and weighty than they were. Feeling excluded, he would sit off by himself, and Joshua would hate seeing him that way, lonely and dejected. Joshua would push him to participate, but he knew it was hard for Buddy to break through the wall that had been erected. Buddy would always bounce back with a cavalier joke or prank, which could break the ice with the men or make things worse. Buddy was ever loyal to Joshua, who accepted his devotion and perhaps had begun to depend upon it, but he came to realize he did not return Buddy's loyalty. When the men teased him or criticized his actions, Joshua would try to divert their attention, but he never stood up for him, never took his side in an argument. He would chalk it up to how difficult he knew Buddy could be. But Joshua found himself feeling irritated with Buddy rather than with whomever was picking a fight with him. Joshua wanted to fit in here, and he believed Buddy neither cared about fitting in nor was capable of it. Fortunately, neither Pendleton nor Captain MacDonald had much tolerance for sniping or complaints. As far as they were concerned, everyone had to pull their own weight, and if they did, they were part of the team. This made each discordant moment easier to shrug off—and despite his problems with the other men, Buddy always did pull his own weight when it came to his duties. He was strong and fearless and rushed to help the others in every situation. Joshua thought he might be trying to make up for the man who was lost during the first shipwreck, but still he marveled at his tenacity.

After dinner they would all sit together, outside when it was warm enough, otherwise around the big table, drinking ale and telling stories. No one got too drunk. Some of the men liked to smoke. Buddy sat with them and laughed at most of the jokes, although Joshua suspected his joviality was forced.

One night Punchy sat perched outside the station on an old barrel with rusted hoops, puffing his pipe, and began to tell a tale, a favorite pastime among Portuguese boatmen. Punchy and Billy both came from Portuguese fishing families. Punchy's father had been what was called a Brava, from the Cape Verde islands, whose population, known as mestiços, was a rich stew of Portuguese settlers, West African slaves, Jewish refugees, Moroccans and Sudanese. As the whaling industry grew, New England sea captains stopped at the islands to recruit sailors. The Cape Verdeans made good money at whaling, and were called the Bravas by the Americans because of their courage at sea. Later, with their earnings, many settled in Provincetown and other New England fishing towns. Portuguese also came from the Azores, islands west of Portugal, and from the mainland. By the late 1890s, they dominated the fishing industry on the Cape and in New Bedford. Joshua was starting to appreciate them: they were tough from life lived by the sea and built with their own hands; they had sharp tongues and quick tempers, but they were ethical and generous, with wry senses of humor. Jurgen and Peter Abbot loved Punchy's stories, and Billy wandered over and stood whittling a piece of wood with his knife.

Punchy looked up at him. "Hey, Billy. Ya remember Capn' Madeiros, had the trawlin' schooner, Mary Jo?"

Billy said, "You mean the one lost in the big gale few

years back?"

"That's the one. Capn' lost his left leg whalin' off New Zealand when he was young, had himself made a beautiful wooden one, and he kept it that way. Always carried around a scrap a' sandpaper an' he'd a sit there with his wood leg on a stool sandin' away. Had a devoted wife, Mary, it was for her Frank named his boat, and she loved that man more'n most do, and that's a lot.

"He was out in his trawler that late November night—your father was out that night, too, Billy."

"Sad to say. Lost two good men that night, nearly lost Pa, too. He ain't fished since."

Punchy nodded sympathetically then turned to Joshua. "Damn storm tore up half the town. They're still fixin' them wharves."

The other men all mumbled in agreement.

Punchy continued. "The night of the gale, Frank stood firm at the wheel, tryin' ta keep her steady. All but one a' the crew was lost, and later that one said Frank took a hold a' that wheel and wouldn't let her go, till a big wave come and swept him out onto the deck and over the side. They found most a' the crew washed up over the next few days, but never found the Capn'. They did find his ole leg, though, up near the Race, sittin' on the sand like a piece a' driftwood. So they brought the leg to Mary, and she was broke up, lemme tell ya, broke up real bad. She took the leg and cleaned it up real good and set it on the mantel of the big stone fireplace in the house Frank'd bought from a whaling captain years before.

"Well, one night she's a-home alone, the kids, they had eight, I think, was all growed and moved on, 'cept for little Enis who died on a wreck when he was only twelve, but that's another story. She's upstairs in her bed, half sleepin', thinkin' of Frank, and she hears bangin' downstairs, like someone comin' inside. She's scared half ta death now, and don't want to move. She swore after that ole Frank come a-walkin' up the steps, wearin' his ole leg, and stopped in the doorway an' he smiles at her, he had kind of a crooked smile, as if to say it's all okay, then the next minute he was gone. When she went down in the morning, the leg was back on the mantel.

"Mary was quite shook up by this, though she was glad to see her Frank. The next night, she took the leg down and laid it on the bench in front of the fire, as if to welcome him to come in and get it anytime he felt the urge, and she swears he came back three or four times over that winter, said hello and left again.

"One night, there's another nor'easter, late March I think it was, an' she hears the same bangin'. Frank appears in her doorway again, smiles, says 'Goodbye, Mary', and turns around. She hears him walkin' down the steps, crossin' the parlor, and the door slammin'. She fell asleep."

Punchy looked around at all the men watching him intensely. "Next mornin'," he said, "she goes downstairs, and the ole leg was gone. She never saw it, nor ole Capn' Frank, again."

All the men raised their glasses and cheered. For a long while, they drank and laughed and cheered some more. Joshua looked over at Buddy. He was only half listening, his eyes wandering around the room while the others enjoyed the moment. It made the experience feel less precious. Joshua knew this could not last.

Twice a week, a wagon would arrive over the dunes with

supplies for the station. Pendleton was in charge of provision-
ing, and arranged for local townspeople to come out. Sometimes, when something special was needed from town, he
would send one of the men.

Billy caught a virus of some sort, and, soon after, Pendleton had it, too. For a few days the two men slept in the guest
room to protect the others. Pendleton spoke by phone with
Doc Meads, who prescribed some medicine and an herbal
concoction, and Joshua was sent to town to get it.

He was annoyed at first to leave the beach mid-week and
miss the drills. He'd grown used to the daily exercise and
the primitiveness of the surroundings, and apart from the
occasional trip to town on a Saturday night he had no interest in leaving. But as he crossed the dunes, he found himself
relieved to get away, even if for a short time, and to see the
town without Buddy. He arrived at the east end and walked
along the plank sidewalk to the center. It was a clear, late
October day, a few trees still bearing their leaves, including
the big willow near the town hall. Joshua remembered his
father saying willows were the first to grow their leaves and
the last to lose them. He felt like a boy kept home from
school, privileged to be allowed outside the routine.

He reached Doc Meads' cottage. He expected to see Mrs.
Meads, but no one was at the front desk. He called out for
the doctor and his wife, but there was no response. Finally, he
opened the door to the inner chamber and called out, "Hello!
Doctor Meads?"

There still was no response. He stood at the doorway
wondering what he should do. Suddenly, Julia Masefield came
out of her office.

"Yes, what is it?" she asked. Then she recognized Joshua.

"Ah, Mr. Duell. What brings you here? Are you ill?"

As had happened the last time, Joshua became tongue-tied in her presence. "Um, no."

She stood looking at him, expecting some response. When none was forthcoming, she asked, "Well, why are you here?"

Joshua laughed, suddenly embarrassed. "Oh, yes, sorry," he stammered. "I'm here to pick up medicines for the station."

"Ah," the young doctor said. "Why didn't you say so?" She went to the front desk to look for the package.

Joshua stood there in the big room, surrounded by tables and medical instruments, feeling self-conscious. The doctor returned quickly and handed him a small package in brown paper.

"I think this is the one," she said. She watched him a moment and seemed to be smiling at him. "Would you like a glass of water before your return journey?"

"That would be nice," Joshua said.

"Sit down. I'll get it."

He looked around and found a chair near an examination table. The doctor came back with a glass of water and handed it to him. He drank it down quickly.

"You were thirsty," she said.

"Yes, Doctor. It's still hot crossing the dunes."

"Tell me, do you like what you're doing out there?" Dr. Masefield asked. "I mean, aside from getting hit on the head by falling spars."

Joshua felt the tension momentarily lifting. "Yes, I do. Very much so. The beach, the ocean…"

The doctor nodded.

Joshua felt his discomfort sneaking back. "Of course it was tragic… I mean the shipwreck."

She nodded again. "Yes, it always is."

"Have you seen many?" Joshua asked.

"A few. Unfortunately."

"But, as a doctor, you must see a lot of…"

She interrupted. "Much too much suffering, yes. It's part of the job."

"It doesn't bother you?"

"Of course it does. How could it not? But you've seen a shipwreck—is it your first?"

Joshua nodded.

"Well, still, you see how it works. It's hard but you do it… because somehow you must. It drives you forward, doesn't it?"

Joshua looked at her. "I never thought of it that way, but yes. It does." He considered a moment then continued. "How did you end up in this far off place?"

The doctor laughed, a hearty, throaty laugh. "Well, it's not that far off. Besides, you're here, aren't you?"

Joshua laughed with her.

"My father was a physician, and when I was a girl I always wanted to be one, too. He tried to talk me out of it, of course, but when I pushed him he helped me get accepted at Hopkins. There were three women in my class. I thought I'd find work in a big hospital, in New York or Philadelphia or somewhere—that's what I hoped, anyway."

"But you didn't?" Joshua asked.

"No. For the most part, people aren't yet ready for women doctors."

"But they are here?"

She laughed again, a bit nervously, he thought.

"After Dr. Meads made the leap and hired me, people had a lot of trouble with the notion. Especially the men. The only women who examine most men, besides their mothers, are their wives and prostitutes."

Joshua looked up.

"Well, it's true," Julia said. "Even today most men think women incapable of learning the skills needed to perform operations, for example."

"Really?" Joshua asked, though in truth he wasn't surprised.

"Yes. So for a while I was like a glorified nurse. I helped out Dr. Meads and people treated me politely."

"Then what changed?"

"Elizabeth Sousa's wild child, Cristina. She was three. Some little boy took her ball and she chased the poor kid down the street out onto a pier. Cristina was running and fell off the end. It was half tide and she hit some timbers below and broke her arm. Three women came in with Betty Sue—that's what her friends call her—carrying her screaming daughter. Well, she was in pain, but she also had a flair for the dramatic. Still does." She grinned. "Dr. Meads was out in Truro attending to a sick woman. I had no choice but to take care of the child. I set her arm, made a cast, and removed some painful splinters. Somehow I managed to calm the little girl, and the women relaxed. They told other women in town, and after a while I had a real medical practice." She looked at Joshua. "Amazing, isn't it?"

Joshua was transfixed. He shook his head. "I think it makes perfect sense." Suddenly he felt awkward again. "Excuse me for asking, Doctor Masefield, I don't mean to be rude, but..."

"What is it, Mr. Duell?"

He cleared his throat, now feeling completely ridiculous. "Are you married?"

"You are something, Mr. Duell, I must say. I'm not sure this question isn't a bit forward of you."

"I'm sorry—" he stammered.

She interrupted him. "But that's all right. I was married. Before I came to the Cape. To a very nice man who, unfortunately, decided California might be more appealing than Boston."

"He left you?"

"Please, Mr. Duell…"

"The man was obviously a fool."

She seemed surprised at his answer and laughed again.

Joshua began to fidget. "I only mean…"

"Yes, Mr. Duell? What do you mean?"

He cleared his throat. "I don't really mean anything. I, uh… I suppose I have to be on my way, Doctor."

"Yes, I'm sure you do." She smiled. "It was lovely to see you again, Mr. Duell."

"It was?" Joshua stammered. "I mean, yes, it was."

"Do I make you nervous, Mr. Duell?"

Joshua blushed. "Yes, I suppose you do."

"Well, we can't have that. I'll tell you what. May I ask you one little thing?"

"Certainly. Anything."

"Would you please consider calling me Julia?"

"Um, yes, of course, that would be fine," Joshua said. Then he had a thought. "But if I'm to call you that, you must call me Joshua. Every time you say 'Mr. Duell' I wonder who you mean."

She laughed the same hearty laugh. "It was nice to see you, Mr. Duell. Perhaps we can do this again some time."

He looked into her eyes. She didn't appear to be mocking him. He liked her frankness, her easy hilarity, and that she took herself seriously. "I hope so, um... Julia. Thank you." He took her hand and shook it, not too hard, feeling silly doing it, then took the package and went out the door.

"Goodbye, Joshua," the young doctor called after him.

One cool night, Joshua and Buddy took patrol together. Normally the men went out alone, but during severe storms, when one might not be sufficient, or when the weather was mild and the demands on them light, MacDonald let them double up.

Joshua carried the lantern. Buddy talked randomly, stringing together various gripes and slanders, and analyzing famous political blunders—one of his favorite pastimes. Who else would he ever know in his life, Joshua wondered, with such eclectic interests? Yet Joshua found himself thinking again about Buddy's problems with the other men. Buddy asked a question, but he didn't answer. As had happened more often lately, he found himself feeling annoyed, though Buddy had done nothing wrong. Neither spoke for a time. Then Joshua stopped. The dim lantern light flickered over their faces in the darkness.

"Why did you let that man go during the rescue?" he asked.

Buddy stopped, too, and turned to Joshua. "What the hell is wrong with you?"

"Are you sure you couldn't have tried harder to save him?"

Buddy shouted angrily, "Yes, goddamn it, I'm sure. What's eating you, anyway?" Suddenly he rushed at Joshua and pushed him in the chest, knocking him down. "Why do you always take their side against me?" he demanded.

Joshua looked up at him. "I don't," he said, uncertainly. He got to his feet.

Buddy pushed him again. "I think you do. You're supposed to be my friend."

Joshua was backing away, not wanting to fight but unable to restrain his verbal attack. "Are you sure, Buddy? Did you do all you could?"

Once more Buddy pushed his friend, shouting at him in an anguished voice, "Son of a bitch! You always do this! I thought we're in this thing together. Why do you think it was my fault?"

Joshua brushed himself off. "I don't know, Buddy. Maybe it was the way Jurgen looked at you that day. Even the Keeper said…"

Buddy threw up his hands, shouting. "I'll bet other people have died here! Without my help."

Joshua looked over the ocean. "Yes, they have." He turned and took Buddy by the shoulders. "I'm sorry, Buddy. I'm sorry I let you drive me crazy…"

"I don't…"

"You do. I don't know why, but you do."

Buddy suddenly turned and glared at him. "You know, you're always mister righteous, aren't you? But you don't fool me. I'm your friend and I know you better. Why won't you tell me what happened in Cuba, anyway? Must have been pretty awful."

Joshua was glad it was dark and Buddy couldn't see the tears in his eyes. "I told you it was awful."

"Yes, but you never told me what happened."

"I just can't talk about it yet. That's it."

Buddy grunted, not happy with his answer. They walked for a bit then Joshua stopped.

"What about you, Buddy? What happened to you while I was in Cuba?"

"I told you. I went to Europe."

"Where?"

"Munich," Buddy answered softly, then added, "and Italy."

"What did you do?"

Buddy didn't answer. They walked along quietly.

"See, you won't tell me either."

"You go first," Buddy said.

"Oh for God's sake, Buddy. You can be such a child."

Buddy laughed. "I'm a child?"

"Remember the night of the march at Harvard?" Joshua asked.

"Yeah, I do. You kept me from getting my head cracked."

This time Joshua laughed, a warm laugh of genuine affection—the way pain that smolders deep in the memory can suddenly take on an unexpected sweetness in retrospect.

After Adam left for training at the Marine camp, Joshua had returned to Harvard to find the campus in pandemonium. He was shocked at how worked up everyone had become over the impending war. The explosion on the USS Maine in February had divided the country, and Harvard, many of whose students came from influential families, was suddenly in the thick of it. People were singing "There'll be a hot time in the old town tonight"—later the war's anthem—and shouting "Remember The Maine!" Joshua's roommate, Sam, studied nearly all the time, more than Joshua ever did, but now he couldn't stop talking about enlisting. Buddy, fascinated by history and politics, had come to like studying, too; he was vigorously opposed to the war with Spain.

They were sitting in the student lounge one night, drinking whiskey and smoking cigarettes, as sophisticated college boys like to do, when Sam began one of his spouts about the great moment of history waiting around the corner.

"Did you see Roosevelt's piece in the Herald? He says this is our chance to take our place on the world stage."

"What a crock," Buddy replied. "He wants the United States to become an imperialist power like France and Britain with colonies around the world."

"France and Britain are powerful. So are Spain and Portugal," said a boy named Philip.

Buddy snickered. "Spain has nothing left but the Philippines and a few spots in South America. The Cubans are ready to throw them out. They aren't a threat to us and we should not be starting a war over nothing. War is serious."

"This is serious," Sam said. "The Spanish were brutal with the so-called Cuban rebels. These people just wanted liberty—and they were hauled away to 'Re-Concentration Camps', as the Spanish call them. Thousands of 'em never escaped."

"So what then?" Buddy demanded. "You don't think the other powers do the same to the people they colonize? We've done the same damn thing to the Indians, haven't we?"

The boys all nodded and mumbled their agreement.

"TR says the Spanish blew up the Maine and we need to punish them," Buddy said. "But no one knows who did it. Maybe someone lit a cigarette in the boiler room, for God's sake…"

"Come on, Buddy," Joshua said.

"No, really. All the papers are worked up about the Spaniards, but I don't see any justification for declaring war on them."

"All the Cubans want is freedom from oppression. We ought to help them—like the French helped us in our revolution," Sam said.

"I like what Professor James said yesterday," Joshua said. Professor William James' philosophy class was one of his favorites.

"What was that?" Buddy asked.

"He looked at us sternly, wagged his finger, and said, 'Don't yelp with the pack!'"

"Yes, exactly," Buddy said. "Don't."

"What will you do if there is a war?" Sam asked Buddy.

"I'm not going off to fight, I'll tell you that much," Buddy said. "I don't believe in it."

"What about you, Joshua?" Philip asked.

Joshua was thinking about his parents' skirmish at the dinner party. But in all honesty, he didn't know what he should do. He was feeling the pressure of the war fever all around him.

Two days later, a group of boys Joshua knew assembled in Harvard Square in the late afternoon to voice their dissent against the war. Fueled by a certain amount of beer, the students tromped en masse to the main quadrangle, yelling slogans. Joshua followed. The students formed a circle, observed by curious faculty and students, and lit a bonfire on the great lawn. Several of the boys gave spirited speeches against the war, while many other students standing in groups around them tried to shout them down.

Suddenly, there was Buddy, standing up on a rock. He began to rail loudly against the government. Joshua knew Buddy had been spending time with a few of the more radical organizers of the protest and it seemed he had latched onto some of their ideas. He ranted about the virtues of socialism and the greed of the rich Americans running the country, about the corruption of the military and how one day the people would rise up. Joshua had never heard anything quite like it. Where did Buddy come up with these ideas, he wondered? He had to admit the anarchic spirit of the whole scene fascinated him, but he also found himself embarrassed hearing his roommate spout such vitriolic rhetoric. One of the opponents threw a stone at Buddy, which hit his chest with considerable force. Joshua became concerned. The bonfire blazed and the crowd on both sides grew more agitated—some seriously engaged, others just whipped up by the circus atmosphere. At this moment, the president of Harvard, John Taylor, came out. He seemed truly shocked to see such a rowdy outburst on his campus, and the presence of several Boston journalists and photographers who had appeared out of nowhere didn't help. President Taylor tried to shout above the noise and appeal for calm, asking everyone to disperse and return to their dormitories.

Finally, he asked an assistant to fetch the police. A coterie of uniformed Cambridge policemen soon appeared at the edge of the quadrangle, wielding clubs, nervous and unaccustomed to dealing with students, whom they considered members of the elite. President Taylor again demanded the crowd disperse, and when no one budged, he signaled the police to move in. Joshua's first instinct was to stand with his fellow students, his brain buzzing with passion and outrage that the police would dare attack—but then he saw them moving forward from two sides of the fire-lit square, clubs held high, and Buddy, fists raised, shouting, ready to defend the honor of his convictions no matter what. It had to end badly. The police came on quickly and began to attack the line of students, flailing with their clubs at the future leaders of the nation. Students fell to the ground, heads bloodied. Joshua understood the futility of the situation and the serious danger Buddy faced. He rushed toward his friend, and wrapping his arms around Buddy's chest, dragged him out of the way of the charging police line. Buddy, his fervor peaking, incensed at this abrupt interference, swung at Joshua and knocked him to the ground. Joshua jumped to his feet and, grabbing Buddy by the shirt with both hands, wrenched him away from the crowd. Only when they had moved away from the melee, into the darkness, did Buddy stop struggling. He leaned over, grasping his knees and gasping for breath. Joshua was bleeding from a cut on his cheek, and he was angry—at Buddy, at himself, at the students, at the foolishness of the moment and the stupidity of human behavior in general. Satisfied Buddy was out of harm's way, he turned and walked angrily away.

Buddy caught up with him two blocks later, still out of breath and laughing.

"What the hell's so funny?" Joshua snapped.

Buddy bent over, catching his breath again. "That was fun!" he exclaimed.

Joshua shot him a dirty look. Buddy understood immediately.

"Sorry," he said. "And thank you."

Joshua stood looking at his friend.

"No, really," Buddy said. "I mean it."

Two days later, Joshua left Harvard for New York and then for the war. It was a bittersweet memory.

They walked further, neither saying anything. Joshua stopped again and looked at Buddy by the dim light of the lantern. "Listen to me now. Are we in this together? Really?"

Buddy was still angry. "I thought so. Aren't we?"

"Yes. We are," Joshua said. He was already feeling regret about the conversation, maybe somehow he was mistreating his friend—and about dragging him into all this in the first place. But looking deep into Buddy's eyes, he added, "The next time I want one hundred percent of you there, no matter what happens. Every ounce of strength you have to give. Understand?"

"Shit," was all Buddy said.

CHAPTER EIGHT

On the first day of November, it snowed heavily. It was a wet snow with a frigid east wind that swirled down from Canada. MacDonald added day patrols, but the ocean remained fairly calm and there were no incidents. As the snow tapered off, Joshua walked along the beach. It had a different feel now, crusted lightly with ice, the air a moist dismal grey, the sea but a few shades darker. The monotonic quality, the stillness, the air, all had their own form of beauty, heavier and darker but just as striking as before. A seal swam parallel to him, bobbing its head, a deep brownish globe, out of the water to watch him. Yet Joshua felt the gloom stealing up on him. The further toward winter they got, the more disaster became inevitable. He had gotten no closer to solving the riddle of his mother's death. Was this really where he belonged? Would saving people's lives alleviate the pain of his mother's or Adam's death? One thing was sure: it wouldn't bring either of them back.

Despite the increasing cold, the Life-Savers continued their daily drills just as before, a near-religious ritual. Rowing in the ever colder sea and dragging heavy equipment through the damp sand on the wind-whipped beach became increasingly taxing, though there was a comforting familiarity in the replication of duties and the physical demands of this life lived almost entirely out of doors. The very nature of their work was defined by the ocean's awful power to reap destruction on men and their fragile ships, yet day to day, the changing light and complexion of the sea grew ever more alluring, like an enigmatic lover.

As Joshua's strength and stamina continued to increase, the rowing and lifting became easier, the cold seemed less biting, his hands grew calloused and his muscles firmer. Buddy saw the same changes in himself, although he never missed the chance to question the value of what they were doing. Even if Joshua sometimes felt the same doubts, he reacted to Buddy's complaints with renewed insistence on staying positive and working harder. The insularity of their life brought all the men closer, even Buddy—only Punchy seemed never to accept him. To MacDonald, developing an immutable trust among his men was as important as physical training. Joshua worried whether the tension over Buddy would lessen that trust. But he had other matters on his mind.

Joshua went into Provincetown on a Sunday, his first afternoon off in several weeks. For once the sun was shining, if hazily. He went to Dr. Mead's office to inquire after Julia. The office was closed, but he knocked on the door, and after some time Dr. Meads himself opened it. He was a tall man with long graying hair, so tall he stood hunched over and still towered over Joshua.

"Yes?" he asked.

"Hello, sir," Joshua said. "My name is Joshua Duell. I am one of Dr. Masefield's patients."

Dr. Meads harrumphed a bit. "Yes, well, it's Sunday. The office is closed this afternoon, lad," he said. "Are you ill?"

Joshua felt slightly embarrassed. "Uh, no, sir. I was hoping to find Dr. Masefield."

"Well you won't find her here today, son. I'm sorry. Come back in the morning." Meads started to close the door.

Joshua stepped forward ever so slightly. "Yes, I'm sorry to trouble you, Doctor, but perhaps you might let me know where I might find her?"

Dr. Meads looked Joshua over. "And why should I do that, son?"

"Sir, I realize this may be a bit forward of me..."

"Yes, I'd say so," Dr. Meads said.

"Yes, sir. But I am one of the Life-Savers, and do not get into town often, and I was hoping to say hello to Dr. Masefield this afternoon. You understand..."

Dr. Meads nodded. "Yes, I do." He hesitated a moment. "Well, perhaps there's no harm. You can find the good doctor on Dyer Street, number 49. Please let her know if you see her that I wish her a pleasant afternoon."

"I shall do that, sir. Thank you," Joshua said, suppressing the elation in his voice. He turned and ran down the road like a schoolboy. When it came to Julia, his feelings were impossible to describe, confusing and inexorable.

He arrived at a small Cape with a white picket fence and a painted blue door that was peeling and chipped. He went through the gate and knocked tentatively on the door. There was no sound from inside. Annoyed at himself for his timidity, he waited a few moments, shifting nervously on his feet, then knocked again, this time more loudly. The hazy sun cast a dim glow on the door. There was still no response. He knocked once more, waited two minutes, and swept by a flood of disillusionment, turned to go. But as he unlatched the gate, he heard the door open behind him. There was Julia in the doorway, dressed in a simple peasant dress, a scarf tied about her head like Portuguese women often did.

"Yes?" She looked out, unsure who she was looking at. She recognized him. "Joshua. What a surprise," she said tentatively.

"Yes, well, um, hello. I, uh, I had the afternoon off, and didn't know how to reach you, so I—":

"How did you find me?" she asked.

"I asked Doc Meads."

Julia laughed. "You've got nerve," she said. "Why don't you come in?"

"Well," Joshua said, "I'm not… I don't wish to bother you."

"Oh, Joshua, you're not bothering me. It's good to see you. Come in."

"Yes, ma'am… uh, Julia," he said. Joshua chuckled at himself and went inside.

The parlor was small, with low-beamed ceilings in the old Cape manner and a broad brick fireplace filling an entire wall. A dusty pink sofa faced the fireplace with a table beside it. Books were piled everywhere.

"You read a lot," Joshua observed. He still felt nervous, but he was glad she turned out to be home.

"Yes," Julia said. "These are mostly medical texts. But I do like to read. Don't you?"

"I do, yes, very much."

"Would you like some tea?"

"That would be nice."

"Have a seat, please," she said, pointing to the one sofa.

Joshua sat down, holding his cap. "You live here alone?"

"Yes, I do."

"Wonderful," he said, nodding.

In one corner was a small coal stove next to a pump over an iron sink. She filled the kettle and put it on the stove. Joshua noticed how graceful her hands were with long fingers and clean fingernails, yet strong and muscular like her arms. He watched as she prepared tea in a china pot. The room smelled of citrus and wood smoke.

"You have the day off?" Julia asked.

"Yes. Haven't had one in a while. Have to be back tonight."

"What do you fellows do out there? When you're not working or rescuing people?"

Joshua felt his nervousness easing. "Well, it's a peaceful existence. We read, do some fishing, eat our meals. A couple of the men like to make music. I walk along the shore. I like that particularly well."

"Do you?" Julia asked, looking up at him. "I do, too. I enjoy that a great deal. I'd say it's the best thing I've found about this place."

"Yes," Joshua agreed. "The shore here is thrilling, isn't it?"

"Yes, and so very mysterious," Julia said. "Sometimes I just look out there, imagining far away places, and ships traveling long distances."

"Yes, I know what you mean," Joshua said.

"No more wrecks recently?" Julia said.

"No, fortunately. But I guess you'd know if there were."

"I suppose so." She looked over at him, seeming to stare for a moment. The kettle came to a boil and she poured the water.

"I was thinking," Joshua said.

"Yes?" Julia poured tea into a cup and handed it to him.

"When I was here last summer, I would sometimes hire a horse at the stable on Shankpainter Road and ride out to the beach. Would you like to do that?"

Julia looked surprised. "Well, yes, that sounds nice. We must do that sometime…"

"No, I mean today. Now."

"My, but you are impetuous, Mr. Duell." But the tone in her voice was warm.

"I'm sorry, I don't mean to be too forward, only… I thought you might enjoy—"

She interrupted him. "I think it's a splendid idea. Why don't you finish your tea, and I'll go and change."

Joshua seemed taken aback that she accepted his offer so readily. "All right, that sounds good. I'll wait here."

"Yes," Julia said, "I think you should." She turned and went through a low door into an adjoining room. The door hung slightly open.

Joshua looked around. Photographs of Julia, her mother and father, and a boy who looked like her brother, sat on the mantel above the fireplace. Two of the pictures were taken on a field overlooking a wide bay. Her father and brother were tall, rugged men and her mother quite beautiful.

"Did you ever go to sea?" he called out.

"Yes, I sailed with my family to England when I was sixteen. In late autumn."

"Now that's cold."

"Yes, it was. Very. We had one storm. Nothing like the one last month, though, thank the Lord for that. But it was lovely.

A quite elegant ship, a steamer, solid and fairly fast."

"Sounds nice."

Joshua picked up another photograph. It was of Julia, perhaps twelve, kneeling with her arms around a big, fluffy retriever. The door opened and she emerged in a long wool dress and high boots.

"That's my dog, Ulysses."

"He's a handsome fellow."

"Yes, he was. We lost him in a hunting accident. My little sister was very upset."

"Are you close?"

Julia frowned. "No. We were when we were little. She had polio, not too bad but she has a limp. It was hard on her."

"Probably on all of you," Joshua said.

She nodded. "Particularly my father. As a doctor he understood the risk. But now she lives in San Francisco. I worry about her, so far away." She looked up at Joshua. "How about you? Have you traveled much?"

"No. I was in the Marines, though. Went to Cuba."

"That must have been exciting…"

"Well, no, not exactly." Joshua frowned for a moment.

"Yes," she said. "I see. Sorry."

Julia put on a heavy cloak, a scarf and a wool hat, which she tied under her chin. Joshua opened the door for her and they went out into the blustery wind. The clouds were winning the battle with the sun. They walked to the stable, not saying much. Joshua tried to think of something to talk about, but soon they arrived.

He turned to her. "Are you sure you're up for this? It gets chilly by the shore."

"Yes. I come from hardy stock."

They went inside. The stable owner, a Portuguese named Charlie Barros, was delighted to see customers. He recognized Joshua, but didn't know his name.

"Can I help you?" he asked.

"We'd like to hire two horses," Joshua said. "I used to take a horse from you last summer. Do you have two good ones we can ride out to the back beach?"

"Not a pleasant day for that," Barros said, looking at Julia. She smiled and gestured toward Joshua. "It's all right, he's a Life-Saver."

"Oh, I see. All right, then, I'll get 'em ready and bring 'em out in a few minutes."

Barros headed back inside. A stable boy was half asleep on a rickety chair; Barros kicked it and the boy jumped up. Julia and Joshua paced at the entry. It smelled of hay and manure.

"I like that smell," Julia said.

"You do?"

"Yes, always have. I find it comforting."

"Comforting. Horse manure. I see."

Ten minutes later, Barros and the boy came out leading the horses. Julia took a white mare with a red spot on its side and a reddish mane. Barros led the horse next to a box, and Julia stepped up and mounted easily. Joshua's was a chestnut stallion. He stepped into the stirrup and swung up, and they turned their horses out the door.

"You be careful now!" Barros called after them.

"Thanks, we will," Julia called back.

They trotted along the sandy road and headed west out the end of Bradford Street to an area known by the locals as the moors, a plain of beach grass and marshes dotted with small sand dunes. At high tide the moors filled with water, but at low tide it was passable. They steered their horses down an embankment and headed across the plain, through puddles of seawater and brine, clumps of mussels and seaweed, broken clam shells dropped by the gulls, skate egg cases and razor-like sea clams. They rode lazily across the marsh, enjoying the pungent sea odor. They turned the horses into the soft sand of a slight hill and climbed to where they looked down on the ocean.

The wind blew stiffly and strands of Julia's hair fluttered over her face. Thousands of birds mingled on the wide beach in the low tide—petrels, curlews, sandpipers, Northern Gannets, Kittiwakes, Herring Gulls, Shearwaters and Great Black-backed gulls. The smaller ones skittered along the edge, avoiding the incoming waves, while the gulls and larger birds perched there peering out to sea, then looping in the air to ride the currents, screeching to one another, and settling back in the sand. No other signs of human life were evident, and the dour faced gulls did not approve of their transgression.

Julia looked at Joshua. "It is truly magnificent, this sea of yours."

Joshua smiled and nodded. "Yes, it is. Magnificent. It's hardly mine, though. I'm a newcomer."

"You seem to be adjusting well."

He was feeling more at ease. "I love being near the ocean. It's been... how do I say this? Life transforming."

"Indeed! Well, it suits you," Julia said, then snapped her heels against her horse's belly and rode down the other side.

She kicked her horse to a canter and rode along the water's edge, and Joshua quickly caught up to her. The steady wind, fresh sea smell and rolling gait of the horses in the sticky sand made them feel delirious. They picked up the pace, chasing birds and dipping into the foamy waves. Then they slowed to a walk and rode a half-mile down the beach.

Round a bend, tucked into the base of a low dune, sat the remains of a small shed-like cabin, its bleached and cracked wood nestled into a sandy hollow.

"What is it?" Julia asked.

"An old rescue shed," Joshua said, "where shipwrecked sailors could get out of a storm."

"How on earth would a shipwrecked sailor find this thing?"

"It wouldn't have been easy on a dark night in the freezing cold. But I guess some people did. There used to be a lot of these."

"Fascinating. Have you been in this one?" Julia asked.

"No. I've seen others."

"Let's have a look."

She dismounted easily and led her horse by the reins toward the cabin. Joshua rode over, jumped down and wrapped his reins around an enormous driftwood tree, bleached pure white, resting regally on the sand. He took Julia's horse and did the same. The horses whinnied and stomped their hooves, and Joshua patted their necks.

The cabin sat half buried in the sand hollow, its roof of broken shingles lower than their shoulders, a rusted iron stovepipe protruding from the roof. The thick door sagged in the sand on rusted hinges, leaving a gap below the door's lintel. Julia leaned down to pull at the handle of the door but it seemed stuck. She tried harder, and it moved slightly.

"Let me try," Joshua said.

He knelt and yanked hard on the handle. The door gave way, the hinges creaking in protest. Julia bent and stepped in to the pitch-black interior.

"Careful," Joshua said.

Julia had to practically crawl through the narrow doorway. There was no floor, only sand. She pushed open the hinged square of wood that covered the hut's little window, letting in grey light. A tiny pot-bellied stove sat in one corner with a stack of wood and a faded box of matches, a battered metal cup on the shelf. There was no water. She sat in the sand against one wall, adjusting her skirt.

"This is so... adorable, comfy—kind of primitive!"

Joshua bent and entered. Apart from the breeze coming through the window, the interior was completely sheltered. He sat next to her. The sand was not warm, nor particularly cold, just soft and enveloping. He removed his cap and leaned against the wall.

He looked at her, saying nothing at first, then spoke. "It is awfully nice in here."

"Yes, quite remarkable."

"I'm not sure I'd like stumbling in here half frozen to death in a shipwreck."

"Me neither," Julia said. "That would be truly terrifying. Still, there's something womb-like about it."

"Womb-like. I like that."

"It's the doctor in me. Can't help it, always thinking of anatomy."

"You like being a doctor, don't you?"

"I do. I love it, really. It's helping people in a way that's critically important to each person, but I think what I like best is becoming a part of their lives. Being inside with them, so to speak."

"Part of the family."

"Yes, very much so. You'd be amazed at the things I hear.

Sitting at their kitchen tables. The women here love to talk."

"About what?" Joshua asked.

"About what people do and say, about their children, their relationships, about love starting and ending. But it wouldn't be fair to reveal their secrets, would it now? You wouldn't want me to reveal yours, would you?"

"Do I have secrets?"

"We all have secrets."

Joshua was fascinated by her, how she spoke, her very presence. "What are your secrets?"

"Oh, no. It's not that easy."

"Why not?"

She looked at him, rather deeply, he thought. "No, it's not."

He took her hand. "I'd like to know your secrets. Someday. If you'd let me."

"Well," Julia answered slowly, "we'll see, won't we?"

They sat with their backs against the wall, listening to the hushed sound of the sea.

"It's so silent in here," she said.

He nodded. "A real shelter."

"I like our little shelter," she said.

He turned toward her. "Me, too." And he leaned over and kissed her cheek.

Julia turned her head and looked into his eyes. He moved closer, leaned in and kissed her on the lips, softly at first. He could feel her weight shifting toward him. She kissed him back, their lips pressing together more fervently. He could smell the freshness of her skin and feel her breath on his cheek. She pulled back, resting against the wall.

"My, my, Mr. Duell."

"Yes?"

"You kiss rather nicely."

"Are you an expert?"

She smiled. "Hardly. But still…"

He leaned his head back, smiling as well. "You too."

They rested there, each thinking of the other and all the things that might or might not be, and the wind outside and the beach and the birds and the terrible, beautiful sea. Time seemed to merge into itself, endless yet but a flashing moment, two humans in a silent old shack at the edge of the continent, outside and beyond the rest of the world.

After some time, Julia straightened. She turned to him. "We should get back."

"I suppose so, yes," Joshua said.

"This shall be our little place."

"Yes. Just ours and no one else's."

Joshua got up, crouching under the low ceiling, took her hand and helped her up. They went out the little door. The air was bright, but the sun was gone and it felt like rain. The wind had picked up again and the tide was coming in. Joshua pushed the door shut as tightly as he could. The horses waited impatiently, snorting and stamping their feet. They untied the reins, not speaking. Julia lifted the reins over her horse's head, grasped the edge of the saddle and catapulted herself up. Joshua did the same and they cantered back along the beach.

They reached the stable and returned the horses, feeling a bit melancholy as the afternoon faded. Joshua walked her home. At the door, she took his hand.

"Joshua," she said.

"Yes?"

"You be careful out there."

"I will."

The winter came in quickly after that. For two weeks, the Cape was plagued with unremitting rain, stiff wind and temperatures hovering just above freezing. The Life-Savers continued their patrols and their drills, and Joshua and Buddy learned how uncomfortable this life for which they had volunteered could become. Buddy complained, but then they all did. The beach was cold, the water frigid, all their gear and clothing were damp. Wet clothes never really dried. Dampness caused heavy wool clothing to smell badly and itch terribly. They caught fresh fish less frequently, and more meals consisted of stored foods such as potatoes and rice. The men patrolled the beach each night wrapped in thick wool sweaters and pants, large boots and heavy wool coats. The wind would burn their faces and bring water to their eyes.

Thanksgiving dinner was an important tradition for the Life-Savers. Each year one of the five outer stations, Race Point, Peaked Hill Bars, High Head, Highland, or Pamet, would host the feast. This year it was at High Head, the next station to the south. The weather was relatively warm, for once, and the sun had broken through. When they arrived at the High Head station, a large fire was burning on the beach, with a half dozen wild turkeys roasting on a long spit.

When the turkeys were ready, each man was given a metal plate of succulent meat dripping with juices and fat, the skins crisp and dark, with roasted potatoes and corn and a glass of ale from several tapped kegs. When they'd finished and the sun was setting, Captain MacDonald stood on a large driftwood log and addressed the throng.

"Men, we're all grateful to the High Head Station for this

excellent meal. I hope you've all eaten plenty and not drunk too much."

The men hooted and cheered. MacDonald continued.

"I want to make note of some other things we've got to be grateful for here tonight. This great country of ours, which pays our salaries."

More cheering.

"The sea in all her glory and power, a force of great beauty and, as we all know too well, a lady with a terrific temper. So then, our thanks to all of you men who have battled her and saved many lives, and our prayers and thanks to those that gave their own lives in duty so we might live to fight again. And may the coming months not be too rough on all of us and may they pass quickly."

He lifted his glass of beer high in the air. All the men in turn lifted theirs.

"To the sea!" MacDonald declared.

"To the sea!" the men replied.

A chorus of cries rang out, as a large flock of seagulls down the beach took to the sky in a sweeping procession, calling out with their screeching voices. Joshua and Buddy walked home silently. The sky was darkening with mountainous grey clouds tipped with silver and shaded beneath by the rich pink orange glow of the setting sun. Peter Abbot caught up to them.

"If you ask me, " he said, sniffing the air, "there's a storm a' comin.'"

Just after supper two nights later the telephone rang. The person on the other end of the line was a superintendent of a lighthouse outside Boston harbor. He asked to speak to the Keeper. There might be a major weather system on its way and the Life-Saving stations were being informed to go on high alert. As had happened in the past, and would happen again, a confluence of two storms would create a higher risk than usual.

MacDonald called the men to the galley table. One of the things he had taught them in their Friday sessions was how to read the weather. It was a complex subject, one that was just beginning to be understood. MacDonald insisted the creation of the National Weather Service by President Grant had already saved lives and would save many more as the young science improved.

"We're in for a big one, I'm afraid," he said. "I've received telegrams from the NWS about a nasty storm dumping snow on Chicago and torrential rains and a cold snap moving up the coast from Florida into Georgia and the Carolinas. The so-called "experts" are saying the two storms'll meet south of Cape Cod, somewhere between Montauk and the Rhode Island coast, then move north and east. This would mean snow, bitter cold, and strong wind—your classic winter nor'easter."

"Do you believe 'em, Cap'n?" Jurgen asked.

"I do," MacDonald answered. "Or let's say I've no reason not to and we need to be ready. It won't be the first for most of you, but there are always uncertainties and usually the results aren't good, no matter how hard we try to do our part. We've drilled and drilled, and been through one disaster already this year, and I'm confident you men are ready for whatever Mother Nature and her friend Neptune can throw at us." He paused a moment, puffing his pipe, and gave a half-grin that betrayed the concern underlying it. "You boys know well the motto of this organization is 'You have to go out, but you do not have to come back.' Well, I don't believe in that motto. We all have to go out—it is our sworn duty, no matter how terrible it gets out there—but I want to see all of you sitting here with me on the next sunny day."

"Hear, hear!" they all cried.

It took a day and a half for the two fronts to reach New England, and another half day for the storm to reorganize itself, but the forecasts were right this time. By the middle of the third day, the 5th of December, it was snowing heavily, but the flakes were still large and wet. The beach was clammy and cold and the waves grew wilder. The Life-Savers were on full watch round the clock, each man taking two patrols, a two-hour rest, then beginning again. At mid-tide, as daylight faded, the surf already reached halfway up the beach.

Joshua took his patrol, heading south toward High Head. He wore high rubber boots over wool pants, a heavy sweater and oilskin slicker, cork life vest, wool watch cap and sou' wester. Walking on the wet sand in all this gear made him feel prickly and uncomfortable. Except for the sand stinging his eyes and the wind slicing through his skin wherever it was exposed, he felt relatively protected in his stiff cocoon, though he wondered how on earth he'd be able to perform as he was expected to encased in this get-up. The temperature was dropping quickly and the snowflakes grew drier and sharper, driving at him relentlessly and obscuring his vision. With the sound of the crashing waves in his ears, he marveled that he was finally experiencing the real thing, nature at her wildest and most magnificent. He was calf-deep in the surf washing up the sand when a large wave broke and swept twenty yards higher up the beach than any before. Now up to his waist in wild water, he felt the undertow pulling him forcefully into the sea. He fought it and moved toward the base of the dune. Holding the kerosene lantern in his left hand, he tried to keep his balance while scanning the obscured horizon—in vain, he thought—for signs of ships.

Joshua exchanged beach checks at the halfway house and made his way back through the gale to the station. He went inside for a cup of coffee. The wind was gusting above fifty knots and still picking up speed. It whistled through the windows and doors of the station like a shrieking demon. Punchy and Peter Abbot sat at the galley table.

"Helluva night, eh, pahd?" Punchy said.

"Yeah, pretty wild!" Joshua agreed. The hot coffee felt good.

"Abbot was tellin' me he was near swamped comin' up from the Race a while ago."

Peter Abbot nodded. "Larger waves are comin', boy, you watch yourself out there. Buddy just went the other way. I told him the same thing."

"Thank you. I'll do my best," Joshua said.

He put his coat, hat and life vest back on and went out again. By ten o'clock the men were already tired. Captain Mac-Donald doubled up the patrols for safety. Buddy and Jurgen went toward Race Point, Joshua and Peter Abbot the other way toward High Head. The wind was a steady fifty-five knots with gusts as high as eighty—it was near impossible to stand—and the snow flew at them in a full blizzard. Temperatures were in the twenties. The sea, now past high tide, covered the entire beach in a stew of swirling foam. They mostly stuck to the tops of the dunes, where the wind was more intense but the waves could not reach them. Joshua shielded his face against the blizzard—snow, sea water, sand and wind coming at him like razors. He could not fathom heading into the sea in these conditions—or being trapped on a foundering ship.

They reached a wider section of beach, where the surf

wasn't licking at the dunes, and descended, hoping for a better view of the ocean. As their eyes adjusted, they could see perhaps fifty yards out, but saw nothing except wild, threatening foam, and beyond that waves as high as twenty feet. The roar of the ocean was louder than Joshua could ever have imagined.

Peter Abbot tripped over a log floating in the brine. He fought to regain his feet. Joshua rushed to help him and together they managed to get upright. Another log rushed at them, then two from the other side. Within seconds they were surrounded by thrashing logs, cut trees sawn in the same lengths, a load of lumber from a ship. The logs crashed and tossed around them perilously. One hit Joshua in the ankle. He went down, but painfully dragged himself up again. Each man fell, stood, fell again, going under the icy foam and ducking the dark projectiles. The logs thinned out and they tried to make their way back to the dunes.

Suddenly Peter Abbot grabbed Joshua's coat near the throat and shouted into his ear. "Jesus! Joshua, watch out!"

Fear shot through Joshua's veins. He turned to see the steel prow of a steamship shoot up the beach. The enormous boat headed straight toward them. It was badly skewed, moving diagonally, half keeled over, slicing violently through the sand and churning tide as if through a wildfire. The ship came to a sudden halt just ten feet from them. On the bow was her name, "SS Lydia".

Joshua felt his heart leap into his throat as they stared in awe at the steel mammoth that had nearly devoured them. They scrambled around the starboard side. They could hear screams from the deck. The ship settled at a sharp angle, her large paddlewheel crushed and splintered beneath her own weight.

Peter Abbot leaned close and yelled, "I'm going back for help."

Joshua watched him go, scrambling along the base of the dune. He looked up at the Lydia, a shallow draft paddle steamer built for hauling freight along the coast. Joshua wondered why anyone would take a ship like this into such weather and how the ship's captain had managed to pass both bars and reach the beach.

Such freighters were fitted with a small number of staterooms and often carried passengers. Joshua could hear desperate cries coming from the deck above—terror and confusion muffled by the storm's roar like the pleas of ghost children in the wind. As he tried to sort out the sounds, a terrified voice cried out just above him.

"Help! Someone, help! My husband!"

Joshua looked up but could see only the ship's steel railing, which had split and hung precariously. He grabbed hold of the crushed paddle wheel and hoisted himself up the tilted hulk. The beating snow blinded him, the wind and freezing spray made it tricky to hold on to the slippery surface. He managed to heave himself over the railing.

The deck was at such a sharp angle he could barely keep his balance. He heard the voice again. Through the thick snow he could see a woman in a hat and cloak, waving her arms in a state of near delirium. He managed to reach her and grasped her shoulders. She was startled by Joshua's sudden appearance but grabbed his arm and jerked him toward the deck-house, which housed the staterooms. This part of the ship had been designed in a spirit of blind optimism, for unlike most deckhouses, the staterooms were fitted with real glass windows and handsome wooden doors—the windows were now shattered and the doors had been torn from their hinges by the gale. Joshua followed the woman into a cabin, where all the furniture, including an armoire and a heavy, carved oak bed, had slid against one wall. A man was pinned helplessly by the impressive bed, as the wind and snow and spray blew around the room. He was perhaps sixty, his long grey hair flying about and arms flailing, gasping for air, in agony as the bed pressed against him.

Joshua rushed over to grab hold of the bedstead, which had tall columns at the head and shorter ones at the foot. The bed moved slightly, but was too heavy and gravity was working against him. He looked toward the woman; despite her panic, she understood and helped him. She was stronger than her demeanor suggested, and together they managed to move the bed a bit further. Then the boat shifted in the sand and the bed slipped back, again pinning the man. Before the woman could relapse into panic, Joshua tugged at her shoulder and pointed, indicating they should go in a different direction. She nodded and together they moved the bed far enough to get behind it and free the man. The woman nearly collapsed on her husband, but he was in no condition to support her. Joshua put the man's arm over his own shoulder and they all staggered out of the slanted cabin into the onslaught outside.

Joshua heard a man's voice, solid and deep, roaring in pain. He got the husband to the railing and left him with his wife, then ran back toward the wheelhouse. The ship's captain lay on the deck; a large splinter of the fallen mast protruded through his left leg just above the knee. Blood flowed from the wound and mixed with the snow. The sharp-pointed spar was three inches thick and four feet long, and Joshua grasped it and strained with all his might to free it. The friction made the captain scream even louder. The captain touched the rim of his hat in gratitude, and Joshua helped him, too, toward the railing.

Joshua saw with great relief that his station mates had arrived. Jurgen led the way; he had told them they would not need the carts. The Life-Savers scrambled up the ship's side and helped the two wounded men down, then rushed through the ship and got the remaining crew out onto the beach. The ship was breaking into pieces, battered by the tide and the flailing logs. The logs had been lashed on deck, but had broken free, killing the first mate. The rescued sailors helped the Life-Savers carry the captain and the woman's husband. With great effort, they made their way back along the beach, leaving behind four dead crewmen on the ship and two missing in the storm.

At the station, the men helped the wounded upstairs to the guest room. Billy telephoned for the doctor. Peter Abbot had used a makeshift tourniquet to stop the bleeding on the captain's leg, but he'd passed out and remained unconscious. The woman whose husband had been pinned by the bed was named Martha. She sat down in the galley, and Buddy brought her a dry blanket while Billy gave her hot tea. She took a long sip and explained that the ship had embarked from Portland, Maine, with a load of lumber and four passengers, two besides her and her husband. Despite the cold air, it had been a pleasant journey to Boston, and the weather was still tolerable when they sailed across Cape Cod Bay to go around the Cape and drop the lumber in Providence. There they were to pick up a load of barrels and steam to New York. Her husband had questioned whether a steamer like the Lydia could make such a journey this time of year, but the captain had assured them it could. Halfway across the bay, the weather grew menacing, and by the time they passed Truro on the bay side, it was snowing.

"Why didn't you take shelter in Provincetown harbor?" Pendleton asked.

Martha didn't know; the captain had assured them they would be fine. Three hours later, they were enveloped in the blizzard and lost their way in the darkness. She said she'd been terrified at the size and strength of the waves; her husband, an experienced sailor, had attempted to calm her, but she could see he was profoundly alarmed. The ship's mast, which carried a steadying sail, cracked early on, but they soldiered on until they hit the outer bar, which damaged their rudder. The waves pounded the ship and the breakers carried them over the bars to the beach.

"I shall never set foot on a ship again," she vowed.

"Your husband will live. At least there's that," Pendleton said.

She nodded.

The telephone rang. It was Highland Station. They had seen a ship moving quickly, lights flickering, toward High Head and Peaked Hill Bars, and they were notifying both stations. MacDonald sent Buddy and Jurgen to walk the beach. The storm was raging as powerfully as before, the temperature still dropping, waves pounding, interminable snow. Though the tide was receding, the surf still covered the beach and licked at the dunes.

Doc Meads came by wagon, drenched to the skin even through heavy rain gear. Billy tied up his mule behind the station while the doctor went upstairs to tend to the wounded. Peter Abbot and Joshua were preparing to head out on patrol in the other direction, toward Race Point, when Jurgen came running in. There was a ship breaking up off the first bar a quarter mile down the beach, some ninety yards out.

"Must be the one Highland called about," MacDonald said. "Gonna be a long night, lads. Joshua, you and Billy hook up the doc's mule to the equipment cart. We need all the help we can get tonight. We'll try to get the breeches buoy out there, not that it'll be easy."

Joshua and Billy ran out the door and were blasted by the wind and sand. Billy led the mule up the ramp to the equipment room. There was an old harness for the carts still hanging on the wall. Joshua grabbed it and, hurriedly sorting out its stiff buckles and straps, attached the frightened animal, whispering in its ear to give it some comfort. Then he and Billy led the mule down the ramp to where MacDonald, Pendleton, Punchy, Jurgen and Peter Abbot were waiting. The men gathered around the cart, helping move it through the heavy sand, and headed down the beach.

She was a four-masted freight schooner of the kind and size that had become rarer in the age of steam and combustion engines, fully rigged for an ocean crossing. Stuck in the sand, the action of the waves on the wooden boat immediately began to take its toll on its structure, pounding at the steam cured planks and tar seams. The boat made strange creaking sounds in protest as she began to break apart. It is quite amazing how a vessel, hand built of heavy timbers by true craftsmen with the experience of a hundred generations of shipwrights, a ship capable of sailing around the world and sustaining its integrity through the fiercest storms on the open sea, can quickly come apart when held fast in the sand and pounded by breaking waves. Three of her masts were gone and the jagged remains of the fourth dripped with a tangled mess of shredded sails and rigging flailing wildly in the wind.

Even with the mule's help the one-ton cart was difficult to move, and it took nearly a half hour to go the quarter mile to where Buddy waited, watching the ship break up on the bar. The flapping sailcloth helped the men locate the ship through the whirling snow. Buddy was frantic. He had been there alone for three quarters of an hour, unsure what to do or if anyone would come. The tide was lower now and parts of the beach were no longer submerged; Buddy led them to a clear area at the base of the dune where they could unload the cart and set up the breeches buoy. Punchy and Jurgen lifted the heavy Lyle gun onto the sand, while Joshua and Buddy removed the faking box. The cannon was loaded with its projectile and connected to the shot line. Though they had practiced a hundred times, doing this in a nor'easter with white out snows had a decidedly different feel to it. Joshua's fingers were numb as he tied the shot line; he could barely see what he was doing, blinded by the blowing, icy sand. MacDonald and Pendleton aimed the Lyle gun, trying to calculate how the wind would skew the shot. The gun was loaded and fired. In the sea's terrible roar, the cannon boom was barely audible. Joshua remembered the first time, when the little cannon's boom had made him jump.

The men watched as the projectile flew through the air straight toward the wildly listing ship. It appeared to be a direct hit—but a wave hit the ship broadside and knocked the target out of reach. The despairing cries of the sailors aboard could be heard even over the ocean's roar.

MacDonald cursed in his deepest, most fearsome voice. "God damn it! Another box, and be quick!"

They set up the Lyle gun for a second try. MacDonald and Pendleton consulted for several minutes how to calculate the aim. The shot was fired. All the men watched, eyes squinting against the insane cold and stinging sand to see the little projectile hurtling through space. The snow was too thick to see if it reached its target, but a ragged cheer rung out over the surf. This time, the Lyle gun had hit its mark.

The Life-Savers cheered, too, then sprang into action. The whip line and block were attached, and Scotty tugged on the line. Someone on the ship knew the drill and began pulling in the whip. The block moved across the water, dipping into the leaping waves, and after it was secured, a tug came from the other end. The hawser was attached and sent to the ship. Billy and Peter Abbot buried the fall in the sand, and Jurgen and Punchy helped Joshua and Buddy lift the crotch pole into place. With the wind, it was like lifting a building. Everyone manned the whip line and together wheeled the breeches buoy out to the waiting sailors.

The first man to be carried to the beach was near death. He had been struck by the falling mast and lay on the deck freezing and bleeding until two of his mates found him. He was a young fellow, tall and solidly built, though by the time he reached the shore, he looked like an old man, frozen and shriveled. His head was swollen on one side, half his face covered with a purple bruise, his broken body covered with blood, his hair tangled with ice. Still, he had managed to get his legs through the canvas leg-holes and hang on, clinging to the rope above as he was transported half-conscious over the sea. The men helped him off the breeches buoy and he tumbled into Peter Abbot's arms.

"Help that man to the station," MacDonald bellowed. "And make sure the doc knows there's more a' comin.'"

"Aye, sir," Peter Abbot yelled back.

The breeches buoy was returned to the ship. This time its passenger was a woman. She was in a torn wool dress and wrapped in a blanket drenched with seawater and streaked with salt, her hair caked with ice, her face a mask of terror as she was hauled like a carcass through blizzard winds over snarling waves in the little bucket. She was shaking and trembling, but as she was extracted from the ring, all she could say was, "Thank you. Thank God. Thank you. Thank God."

Four more crew, the first mate and, finally, the captain were taken from the ship. The captain had almost reached the shore when the ship broke completely in two. The mast to which the line was attached fell into the sea, and so did the captain. Buddy and Joshua plunged in after him. The jolt of icy ocean water pierced Joshua's clothes like an electric shock. Its intensity produced an instant fear; any man would know such cold would quickly kill him. The choice was clear: move instantly to escape it or die. He swam as hard and fast as he could, but he felt his body slowing down. He looked around the thrashing water. Buddy was right behind him and gave him his arm. Together they reached the captain and towed him the last fifty feet to shore. Two of the men ran over; by the light of a lantern the captain's face was nearly solid blue, but he smiled weakly in gratitude.

The other men helped Buddy and Joshua drag him to the cart and put him in next to the woman. Then they all helped the frozen mule haul the cart, and somehow they reached the station.

They staggered into the warmth and light. Punchy, his hands shaking, put on a kettle. Dr. Meads came downstairs to inspect the new group. The captain collapsed into a chair and Billy got him a blanket. All of the rescued crew and the woman were suffering from exposure. The doctor ordered the men to get the captain upstairs and into a bed; he tried to resist, but had no strength.

The Life-Savers themselves were frozen and exhausted. Joshua felt as if his muscles couldn't carry him one more step, and he slumped in a chair. Captain MacDonald looked pale and shaken. He left the room, unsteady on his feet. When he came back into the galley holding a bottle of rum, Joshua jumped to his feet.

"Relax, lad. You've done well tonight," MacDonald said. He looked around the room. "You've all done unstintingly well. I'm proud of you."

The men grumbled their appreciation.

"Are you all right, sir?" Joshua asked.

"I reckon I've seen worse," he said, popping the cork from the bottle, "though not by much." He attempted a grin. "Some rum for the crew?" he demanded.

"Aye!" they all answered.

MacDonald looked at the woman. "Bit of rum, miss?"

She nodded. "Thank you, sir, I'd love some," she said in a croaking voice.

They raised their glasses and drank their shots. The dark liquid felt warm and delicious going down. Billy served them all tea, proud to be contributing some small comfort. The little room was crowded; those not sitting stood around the table and against the wall. The stove gave out much needed heat.

The men and the rescued crew stared at one another through grimy, distressed faces. It was two o'clock in the morning and the storm had not abated.

MacDonald sent four men back out on patrol and ordered Punchy and Joshua to rest for an hour. As he sank to his bed fully dressed, Joshua thought that a simple cot had never felt so good. He fell right asleep and began immediately to dream.

He was on a sailboat, a schooner with a broad deck, clean and bright. There were many people on board, none known to him. They were sailing in clear weather in a sea of glistening turquoise so lovely it strained the eyes. The wind was stiff, but Joshua leaned over the teak railing, feeling the warm wind against his skin. The prow of the ship rose and fell. All at once, there was an explosion. A cannonball struck the mainmast a third of the way up. Joshua heard a sharp crack, and the mast fell to the deck tangled in ropes and shredded sails. He heard a familiar voice call his name, and despite the chaos now surrounding him of people rushing across the deck and crying out in fear, the voice was calm and gentle. It sounded at first like his mother's voice, but soon he knew it to be Adam's, his brother's, from long ago when they were small. He understood he was to go back to the railing. He crossed the deck, aware of the sweet breeze that still rustled his hair. He looked over the rail. Adam hung by one hand from the bottom rung, blood dripping from a wound in his head. His other arm extended upwards, reaching for Joshua. The voice grew deeper and more desperate. "Help me!" it cried. Joshua reached over to grab his brother's bloody hand. But Adam slipped further away, the distance increasing as he fell. Adam's voice grew deeper still. "Please, Joshua, help me! Help me!" Joshua leaned over the rail, reaching as far as he could, afraid he would fall. Adam slipped away. Joshua cried out to him, "I can't…"

He was awakened by Punchy shaking his bed. He had slept less than an hour.

"Get up, lad," Punchy said. "We've got another one."

Billy and Jurgen had spotted an old barquentine run aground just north of the station. The ship was some sixty yards out and breaking up fast. Her square foresail still stood proudly against the battering snow, but the rest of her rigging was gone. Although the storm still raged, the waves had settled somewhat, and MacDonald called for the surfboat. Billy and Jurgen went in the frigid water to launch the boat then lifted themselves aboard. With grim determination, their bodies aching, the men began rowing the long oars against the surf.

MacDonald held the steering oar and barked his encouragement, his voice raspy. "Pull, pull, you can do it, men! You can do it! Pull harder now!"

Each of them believed in their leader's experience and in the training they had received just enough not to surrender to the will of the storm. Joshua strained to move his oar through the crashing waves. Buddy, next to him, did the same. They nodded to one another, a momentary reassurance. The surfboat leaped through the breakers, her bow pointing nearly straight toward the sky as she climbed the wave then crashing hard against the quieter water at the top. The air was astoundingly cold, but the men shared a fanatical resolve as they rowed together and got through the first set of breakers.

Their victory was short. The ship sat foundering on the outer bar, and the lower tide had created a second line of breakers. They moved toward it with great trepidation.

"Steel yourselves, lads. We shall make it," MacDonald swore.

The surfboat hit the break at a slight angle and began its climb.

"That's it, boys, that's it!" MacDonald urged.

They rowed with all the strength each man could summon. The ship rested like a ghost in the snow just at the upper edge of the waves. They could hear men screaming as they clung to the one remaining spar.

As they reached what seemed like the crest, each man felt he had achieved some form of greatness. If we can conquer this, what can't we do, each thought. It was illusory, however. The waves were wild and disorganized, and they were hit by an even larger wave from their port side. It slammed the boat and flipped it over. The men went into the sea, each and every one.

For the second time that night, Joshua felt the frigid stab of death pierce his body. It was all he could do to fight back the fear it induced. They swam for the boat, fast and hard. As they had been trained, as they had practiced so many tedious times, the men, as one straining organism, mounted the lifeboat's upturned hull, grasped the ropes attached to the gunwales and heaved with every ounce of strength each could muster. With great resistance, the boat began to turn upwards in the churning sea.

Pendleton shouted at them, as he had done so many times before. "Pull, 'ya fuckin' saps, pull with all yer fuckin' might!"

The men stretched across the bottom of the surfboat in their soaked and heavy clothes, each gripping the opposite gunwale. Suddenly, Billy lost his grip. He screamed out. Joshua saw him slide over the bottom and reached out his hand. All of them wore heavy gloves, but the gloves were full of water and half-frozen. Billy's hand found Joshua's. Punchy made his way over and reached for Billy as well. Then Billy's hand came out of his glove and he slid rapidly into the water. In seconds the raging tide carried him away from the surfboat. Joshua and Punchy jumped in. Buddy and Jurgen followed. But Billy had slipped too far. The voice of the Keeper, like a roaring god, ordered them back to the boat. Once again he commanded them to pull. And they did. The boat slowly rocked then flipped back upright, and the men, back in the water, hauled themselves up, flopping onto the wet floorboards and quickly retaking their positions. They took up their oars, which had held fast, and cold beyond their wildest dreams, rowed toward the ship.

Peter Abbot wailed, "Billy! Billy!"

But there was no sign of him. He had vanished, taken by the pitiless ocean.

The Life-Savers reached the ship, frozen, exhausted, and filled with horror at losing Billy. She was a merchant ship, on her last legs, but still seaworthy, a large load of coal in her hold. The heavy weight helped anchor her to the sandbar and speed her disintegration. The crew had numbered eight, plus the mate and captain, who had died as the mainmast fell. Two men had gone over, never to be seen again, one more fell beneath a tumbling spar, and one died of cold. That left four desperate sailors alive, clinging to the foremast rigging, ice building around their frostbitten hands, collecting on their caps, on the scarves wrapped over their faces and on the slick surfaces of their pea jackets. Some called out to God, or whoever might hear them, some moaned, some hung silently praying for any miracle that could save them. As the lifeboat came into view, they cried out in unison.

But rescuing them was a tricky proposition. The surfboat had to get close enough to the ship, which the wild ocean made extremely dangerous. MacDonald cautiously guided them nearer. He called out for someone to get a line to the closest sailor in the rigging. Buddy stood in the rocking boat and picked up the coiled line and the heaving stick. He gestured at a sailor whose legs and arms were entwined in the ratline. The sailor nodded and Buddy threw the heaving stick. It missed. The sailor reached out. His ice-encrusted watch cap flew off his head and disappeared. Buddy looked determined to succeed. He recoiled the rope and threw the stick again. The sailor caught the end, drew in the heavier line and held fast to it—but Buddy was holding the line too tight, afraid to leave too much slack and lose his man. The bobbing motion of the surfboat tightened the rope and the man was yanked from the rigging. He bounced on the deck with a thud, cursing, and was thrown by the action of the water against the remains of the railing, his head hitting a post. He was being dragged into the sea, but he braced against the railing post and held on. The rope slipped from his hand and the stick dropped in the sea. The man's face sagged, his last hope falling away.

Punchy got to his feet in the sharply rocking boat and moved next to Buddy. "Ya fuckin' asshole!" he bellowed. "Ya made it too tight, fuckin' idjot!"

Buddy just hung there a moment, stunned. Punchy grabbed the rope from him and pushed him aside, and Buddy lost his footing and fell to the bottom of the boat. Punchy recoiled the line, grasped the heaving stick and flung it at the sailor, who caught it. The man gathered himself up, triumphantly holding the rope around his wrist. The Life-Savers and the three men stranded in the rigging all cheered hoarsely.

"Make it fast!" Punchy yelled to the man.

When the line was secured, the Life-Savers helped the sailors one at a time, beginning with the one who had fallen, to leap across to the tossing lifeboat. Each man tumbled painfully into the boat. When all four were in, Pendleton cut the line and the Life-Savers hauled on their oars to make shore. As a final snub from the deities of the sea, the surfboat was flipped over the last set of breakers, tossing the men into the water. They helped each other onto the beach then hauled the lifeboat out.

Buddy looked angry and grim. Joshua walked behind him. "You all right?" he asked.

"Fuckin' son of a bitch that Punchy."

Punchy was pushing the other side and heard him. "Fuck you, Bairn."

"You'll be sorry, asshole," Buddy replied.

"Fuck your mother," Punchy said.

Buddy lunged at Punchy. Joshua saw him do it, and suddenly the night's horror caught up with him and he exploded. After what they'd been through, this last squabble, so insignificant in light of all the death and suffering they'd seen, was too much.

Joshua jumped on Buddy and they both went into the water. Joshua was screaming at him, "Fuckin' stop it! Get hold of yourself, you bastard! You never know when to stop!"

All the men stopped, their faces plastered with utter disbelief. Joshua helped Buddy up. Buddy started to take a swing at him then stopped.

"Fuck it," he said. "And fuck you, too, for taking their side." Dripping wet, disheveled, and looking like a man betrayed, Buddy stepped clear and huffed alone up the beach.

Shaking their heads, the others turned to head home,

struggling to get the cart up the beach. Joshua, out of breath and holding back tears, watched them go. Pendleton patted him on the back.

"Let it go," he said. "We're done now."

Joshua stood alone on the beach then staggered up to the station, exhausted beyond human possibility. He could see a dim grey light peering through still dark clouds in the eastern sky. At the station he spoke to no one, climbed the stairs and collapsed on his bed.

The storm continued another half a day, but there were no more wrecks. MacDonald had kept two men on patrol while others slept. Joshua took his patrol at eight in the morning. The sun came out briefly, peering through a discolored haze, but the waves still raged and the white water stretched as far as the eye could see. The two wrecks on the bars continued to break up; debris filled the surf and littered the beach. The USS Lydia was a splintered hulk on the sand. Bodies lay on the beach, dark and frozen vessels, relics of the lives they'd once held. The Life-Savers barely spoke; all were in shock at the way Billy had been lost. They looked for his body, in groups and each on his own, in their spare time.

Soon after dawn the ravaged beach had begun to fill with townspeople. Joshua came up to where Peter Abbot and Jurgen were watching a crowd of nearly fifty people scavenging on the beach, some with wagons, some on foot, whole families and groups of local men carting away timbers, chunks of coal, kegs of beer and whiskey, boxes of soap, clothing and linens from Europe, and the broken remains of the ships—railings, parts of engines, ropes, pulleys, rudders, even torn patches of sail. They stepped around the bodies. It was a somber carnival. A pair of men in black suits sent by the town morgue stepped from a cart and began collecting bodies. Suddenly Kirov rode up on horseback, followed by William and Tucker in a long wagon with two mules. Kirov shouted at them to hurry and they hooted and whistled at the animals.

They stopped next to a man with a long moustache loading sea-soaked crates of liquor onto his buckboard. His wife sat watching. William and Tucker jumped down and pushed the man aside. Kirov rode over and dismounted before his horse had come to a stop.

"These're ours," Tucker said.

"No they're not," said the man.

William stepped up. "You'd be doin' yourself some good by steppin' aside," he said.

"You lot don't scare me," the man answered. "And ya don't own the beach neither."

His wife looked nervous. "Leave it be, Sam," she urged him.

"No, I'll not," he said.

William and Tucker each hit him at the same time on opposite sides of his ribs. The man fell to his knees on the sand, the wind knocked out of him, while they grabbed two of the crates and put them on their wagon. The man pulled himself up and moved back to grab another crate. Kirov, holding his staff, pressed it into the man's chest to push him away.

Joshua turned to the others. "We've got to stop this." They nodded and walked over.

"He's right, you know," they heard Kirov say in his gently odious voice. "These two fellas won't hesitate to take what's theirs, no matter what." He took the long-bladed dagger from his belt and pointed it at the man. "And me neither, if you get my drift."

"Up to your usual, Mr. Kirov?" Joshua called out.

Kirov looked at Joshua in his uniform of wool pants, pea coat and Life-Savers hat. He twisted the knife, gripped its handle, and stuck the blade back in its sheath on his belt.

"I remember you," he said. "Quite the outfit you've got on."

"Leave these people be," Joshua said.

"What, now you're wearing a uniform you're the cop of the beach?" Kirov said with a snort. "I don't think so, my friend."

Joshua tried to stare him down. With his eyes and dark face and domineering posture, the man emanated a sense of menace that frightened Joshua—the Russian had that effect on people and took full advantage of it—but Joshua knew he had to hold his ground. And the uniform did give him an odd sense of entitlement, at least on this beach and after the night they had just suffered.

"Sorry, but I'm not your friend. Like I said, you should let these people be."

Jurgen and Peter Abbot moved closer. Kirov sized them up and sneered. With a sigh, he straightened and shrugged.

"Have it your way," he said. He spit and nodded to his cronies.

Tucker and William each lifted a crate onto the wagon. Kirov looked at Joshua, spit again and said, "Let's move on." He jumped into his saddle, kicked his horse and rode away. The other two mounted the wagon and clucked at the mules, moving down the beach. The man looked at the Life-Savers and nodded his thanks then quickly loaded the last two crates on his buckboard, and moved to the next pile.

"That Kirov fellow and his pals is up to no good," Peter Abbot said.

Joshua nodded. "Now that, my friend, is an understatement."

Joshua continued his patrol. On his return leg, he found a brass lantern from the USS Lydia, intact but for one broken pane of glass, with the name of the ship embossed on its cap. He picked it up and carried it home. He felt tired beyond anything he had ever felt before, not only from the arduous night, the intense cold and strained muscles, but also from sadness and loss. So much loss caused by the sea when she was angry. Joshua wondered if Billy the Whale had found peace. He returned to the station, placed the lantern next to his bed, and slept until evening.

The next morning, the Chief of Police, Nickerson, came out. The townspeople were back, picking through the salvage. Kirov and his pals returned, too, and a few other unsavory types with similar aspirations. Most of what remained wasn't worth the effort.

That afternoon the Life-Savers held a quiet memorial for the lost boy. As if in acknowledgment, Billy's body washed up fifty yards down the beach while the men prayed for him. It was an odd coincidence, but one all the men accepted without question. The morgue sent its wagon so Billy's family could hold a proper burial.

Joshua and Buddy went on patrol as the sun was going down. They walked along solemnly, feeling the biting wind and watching the whitecaps. Buddy suddenly stopped and looked at Joshua. "I don't want to end up like him."

"Scares you, doesn't it?" Joshua asked.

"Goddamn right. Every day I wonder what the hell I'm doing here."

They were sophomores, just fifteen, looking for girls and trouble, or not trouble so much as adventure, which often led to trouble. At parties the boys drank. Someone always knew how to obtain liquor, and they would sit in the basement recreation room of the dorm and sip from a bottle of whatever the designated procurer had procured, sometimes whiskey, sometimes gin or wine or brandy. There were maybe eight of them in Joshua's group. There was a billiards table, and the boys would take turns playing. Buddy was the new kid, and he had been put in Joshua's room with two other boys. The others made fun of him from the start, and Joshua, not liking how harsh they could be, began to stick up for him. When Buddy wasn't there his friends would ask what he saw in Buddy. "He makes me laugh," he would answer. They would sit up late together in their room, talking about the world and what it all might mean, though they were both young and could have no idea. Buddy was different around Joshua—he felt less threatened, and so didn't feel the need to be as disruptive and pretentious as he did with the others.

When it came to girls, Buddy's companionship was quite useful. Joshua was handsome, but shy. Girls didn't tend to notice him, but they would home in on Buddy from across a room and listen to his speeches with confused delight. It was chemistry. Buddy was the first boy Joshua knew to go on a date and to engage in kissing and petting with a girl. Buddy pushed Joshua to be more adventurous—and Joshua was terrified, though seduced by Buddy's assurances of success. Joshua wanted to eat the forbidden fruit. And one night, he finally did.

There was a town near the school, a quaint little place with white clapboard houses, picket fences, dirt-paved lanes with giant maples and chestnuts. It was late October, the red and yellow leaves on the curving branches falling in swirling clouds, the air growing chilled. Students were allowed to walk in groups of two or more the half-mile from the campus to a pharmacy in town center where there were a soda fountain, dime novels and candies. One blustery afternoon Buddy and Joshua went into town for a chocolate soda. Two town girls sat at the counter, sipping Sarsaparillas and chatting excitedly. When the boys entered, the taller and prettier of the two noticed Buddy immediately and caught his eye while pretending to ignore him.

They walked over and Buddy started a conversation. They bought the girls sodas and sat talking for over an hour. Buddy asked if they could all meet again and the girls said yes. Over the next two weeks, they met every other day. An hour became two hours, and twice Buddy and Joshua were reprimanded for returning late to school. Then Buddy suggested they meet after dinner one night. The taller girl, Elizabeth, who liked Buddy, thought this far too brazen, but she was fascinated by the concept and the next time he asked, she and her friend, whose name was Celia, looked at each other, giggled, then nodded their heads.

They met in a clearing in the woods. There was a nearly full moon and they found each other easily. Buddy brought a jam jar, which he'd emptied, cleaned and filled with whiskey he had stolen from the housemaster. The girls had never tasted whiskey; after several sips they began to like the sensation it produced, a kind of joyous lightheartedness that suggested freedom. After a few sips, Buddy produced cigarettes and they all smoked. The night was cold and the girls had to get home, but this illicit half hour of pleasure was too delicious and they met again several more times. The colder it got, the more they drank. The girls complained they had gotten hangovers, but it was a badge of illicit adult behavior and spurred them on.

The next time they met, the leaves had fallen and the ground crunched beneath their feet. In the light of a half moon they drank a full jar of the secret elixir. Buddy sat next to Elizabeth, Joshua next to Celia, and they held hands, staring awkwardly at the star-speckled sky. Joshua was terribly nervous and between the liquor and his skittishness, his stomach felt like it might flip over. Then Buddy turned toward Elizabeth, took her chin in his hand, and moving closer, kissed her on the lips. She closed her eyes and let him. Joshua and Celia watched, awkward but riveted. Joshua wondered if this was how love began. Elizabeth stopped to catch her breath and smiled knowingly at Celia. Joshua felt more self-conscious than at any time previously in his life, and couldn't bring himself to do it.

In a soft, dewy voice, Buddy said, "Kiss her, Joshua."

Joshua could feel his face turning red, grateful no one could see. He swallowed and leaned forward. Celia held very still and Joshua pressed his lips to hers. He remained like that, his lips pressed against hers, for several long moments until, unsure what to do next, Celia broke out laughing. Soon they were all giggling. The cold brought them down to earth and they went home separately as usual.

They saw the girls at the soda fountain a few days later. The boys bought sodas then Elizabeth announced they had something important to say. She nudged Celia, who took a deep breath and spoke. Celia's parents were going on a trip to New York City the following day. Celia had an older brother away at college. If they came over and brought the whiskey there, it would be warmer than the woods. Joshua was nervous, but

Buddy agreed immediately. They set a time for the next night.

Buddy stayed up half the night, excited and full of anticipation, refusing to let Joshua sleep; the next day in class, he kept giving Joshua secret glances.

They sneaked away from the dormitory at eight, during after-dinner study. Buddy chattered animatedly, but Joshua said nothing. They arrived at a white farmhouse, walked up to a porch of warped floorboards, and swung the brass horse head knocker. The clack made Joshua jump, but they heard the patter of feet inside. Celia opened the door, smiling bashfully, lowering her eyes like a geisha. They went in and removed their coats, and Buddy took out his jar. The girls wore white dresses, their hair plaited, and they looked striking. Joshua was very nervous. Buddy placed the magic jar on the table, the girls exchanging glances, and began a debate-worthy description of the politics of socialism that he had gleaned from a magazine in the school library. No one knew what he was talking about nor cared in the slightest. Elizabeth finally interrupted him and asked him if he wanted to pour them some whiskey in the four little cordial glasses on the table. Buddy complied. They toasted to staying young forever. The girls sipped politely, but Joshua and Buddy downed their portions in single gulps.

They drank together for a half hour, no one but Buddy speaking, then Elizabeth began to giggle, and Celia, as if they had rehearsed the whole thing, went to the piano and began to play a popular dance song. Elizabeth extended her hand to Buddy; he stood and they began to dance, gawkily at first, but soon twirling enthusiastically around the room. Joshua knew some basic dancing steps from his parents' parties, but never felt comfortable in front of others. Still, the warmth of the whiskey, the pretty, grown-up room and the string of sweet, effervescent notes on the piano made him relax.

He closed his eyes for a moment and floated with the sound until he gradually became aware the music had stopped. Celia sat next to him and took his hand. He looked at her, strong and frail, daring and terrified, beautiful and awkwardly young, and he leaned forward, put his arm around her shoulder and kissed her. She kissed him back. Buddy and Elizabeth were still dancing with only the memory of the music filling the air, moving more slowly and pressing together. Celia stood, took Joshua's hand, and led him out of the room.

Her bedroom was small and dark, but there was enough light from the street that he could see a dresser covered with dainty bottles and framed photographs, and a child's bed with silk curtains hanging open. The moment seemed to unfold around him. His heart was beating hard, his breath short—it seemed unreal what was happening even as he made it happen. They sat clumsily on the bed and he kissed her. She fell back on the bed, and they continued, terrified, and began to touch one another, exploring, and the kisses became longer and warmer and suddenly, somehow, her dress was pulled up and she didn't seem to mind. Time froze and there was nothing in the world but this one endless moment as they moved closer and closer and touched and caressed and kissed until they found themselves almost naked. They stared in the half-light into each other's eyes and knew they had crossed a threshold too soon, perhaps, but there was no turning back.

A door slammed and there were voices. Joshua heard Buddy shouting. Celia sat up, her expression changed from soft dreaminess to panic and horror, the mood broken, most likely forever. She lunged for her dress, which lay crumpled next to her. The door opened, light flooded in—a tall young man stood there, his face in shadow, his rage obvious.

"Celia!" he shouted. "What in God's name are you doing?"

Celia gasped. "My brother," she said to Joshua.

"Who the hell are you?" the brother asked.

Joshua began to stand, unsure what to do. Perhaps introduce himself? But Celia's brother, Thomas, was on him in a second, and he felt his fist plant itself across his cheek. Joshua fell to the bed then leaped up again. Two other men rushed into the tiny room, illuminated now by the light through the door. There was a strong smell of alcohol, and Joshua noticed Thomas and his friends spoke with slurred, angry voices, shouting and cursing at him. Thomas jumped on Joshua and began punching his face and chest.

"I'm gonna kill you," he shouted.

His two friends shoved him off of Joshua, he thought to rescue him, but instead they held him up by his arms so Thomas could hit him again. Then suddenly there was Buddy, bellowing in a strange tone, charging like an enraged rhinoceros. He knocked two of the men over, grabbed hold of Joshua's other arm, and dragged him out of the room. Joshua's pants were on the bed and he wore only his shorts, but Buddy had a grip on him and they bolted out the front door and into the street. The cold hit Joshua like a body blow and the ground felt like ice on his bare feet, but there was no stopping Buddy. They hurtled down the street, into the woods and back to the school.

CHAPTER NINE

The December air was uncommonly warm, oddly gentle breezes riding on colder gusts off the sea. After a week of morose silence and attending Billy's funeral at the old cemetery behind the town, the men again began to speak more openly to each other and the station returned to its routines. A new man, Sonny Silva, came out to take Billy's place, a Portuguese in his late thirties who'd been a Life-Saver before he quit for a life with his family. MacDonald had gone to town and convinced him to return, for a while at least.

It was nearly Christmas time. This had always been Joshua's favorite time of year. New York had been a joyous place, filled with lights and roaming carolers, people rushing from place to place like madcap fools, the stores gaily decorated, their windows filled with gifts. He closed his eyes and could picture it. When he'd been away at school, it had been the time of homecoming. The irony of time passing by seemed especially biting now—a year ago, she had still been with them.

At supper one night, the men talked of their own families. MacDonald had been married, but had lost his wife to cholera ten years earlier. His father had been a whaler, and he still had a brother and cousins in New Bedford, as well as a son, Stephen, a lawyer in Philadelphia, whom he missed terribly. Joshua had the impression MacDonald felt an unwanted distance between himself and his son, which touched a familiar chord. Jurgen had come from Hamburg at the age of fourteen, and was alone here—his friendships among the Life-Savers and a few of the fishermen were what he valued most. Peter Abbot's family lived in Boston and he would see them at New Years. His mother still taught history in grade school. Pendleton had a wife and two daughters in Wellfleet, but he was divorced. He confessed he had been hard on his wife when he was younger, and would not make the same mistakes now. The men teased him about his gruffness. Punchy's father had been here thirty years; Punchy was the only man in the family who had not become a fisherman. The family always had a big Christmas dinner at his father's house in Provincetown. MacDonald said some stations allowed the married men to build cabins where they could live with their families. Buddy told them about his father in Ohio, and how his grandfather had taken him ice fishing.

"What about you, Joshua?" Peter Abbot had asked.

Joshua stared ahead silently as the men all turned to hear his answer. He felt tears forming in his eyes and fought hard to repress them.

"Joshua?" Pendleton insisted.

"My father still lives in New York," Joshua replied quietly. He stood up, carried his cup to the galley sink, and walked outside.

The next day, Joshua went into Provincetown. MacDonald had given him permission when he told him he wanted to find a present for someone.

"That young doctor?" MacDonald had asked, a twinkle in his eye.

"Yes, sir, that's right."

"You go ahead."

He had no idea what to look for, or whether Julia would accept a gift from him. She seemed to like him, but then she was a good deal older and why would she pay him any attention at all? Well, she had kissed him at the old shack. Joshua laughed to himself, marveling at how unversed he was in these matters.

The shops were decorated with pine boughs and candles burning in the windows. The sun was low, reflecting warmly off the white clapboards of the old houses. He walked up and down the street, looking in windows filled with sundries and gifts and feeling a slight panic about what in the world he might find, until he came to a shop with a large paned window where a drawing on a canvas block with no frame sat on a low stand. The drawing appeared to be of the little shack he and Julia had visited. Joshua felt a warm thrill rush through him. The shop had a sweet, stuffy smell and a creaky floor, wind whistling through a space above the door. He asked the shopkeeper to take the drawing from the window, then held it up and examined it. When they had agreed on a price, Joshua asked the man to wrap it in tissue and ribbon. Then he walked back across the dunes, carrying the precious gift.

Christmas eve, Joshua was on patrol. There was an icy wind, but the sky blazed with stars. His mind wandered back to his childhood. When they were kids, he and his brother would descend the broad stairway of the silent house in their footed pajamas very early Christmas morning. Filled with exhilaration and dread, they looked for evidence that while they slept the great man in the red suit had appeared from another universe to place parcels of magic under the tree. They would creep into the parlor where the tree stood before the bay windows.

It was always a massive tree, cut down in the forest of northern New Jersey. The entire family went together each year, by ferry and train, hired a horse and sleigh, and headed out over the rolling snowy hills, huddled in blankets, the bells of the sleigh jingling as they slid bumpily over the rutted earth into the silent woods. There, deep in the forest, would be the perfect tree that called out to his father in its special voice. Gideon would reign in the horse and the sleigh would come to a halt, the horse's breath exploding in puffs of steam as it tossed its head, snorting and stomping, while his father stepped down and took the heavy axe from under the front seat. The family would descend into the deep snow. Lucy would lift her voluminous skirts, revealing a glimpse of the dark wool stockings she wore in the cold, and step down, her laced boots planted on the undisturbed ground. His mother always carried herself gracefully, although she could summon tremendous physical power, if needed. Gideon, tall and proud, with a handlebar mustache and large, furry eyebrows, would approach the tree, axe on his shoulder, and carefully walk round its base, examining the branch structure, the width at the bottom, the consistency of its shape as it narrowed to the slender peak where the porcelain angel would sit. Lucy would follow slightly behind, commenting on the layering of the branches. Then his father would stop and face the tree, holding his axe at an angle, while the rest of the family stepped back. The axe would slice into the heavy pine base, releasing fragrant eruptions of rich, wooded scent with each squishy, muffled blow of the blade. After several minutes, his father would say, "Watch out, now" and they would take a further step back as he delivered the final blow and the tree fell with a dampened thud in the snow. He would wrap the tree with rope, assiduously looping it in a crisscross until it was properly trussed. Then he would make a strong knot and attach it to the hitch at the sleigh's rear. They would climb back in, his mother commenting on what a magnificent job his father had done as they dragged their treasure the two miles back into the town. Gideon would arrange for the tree to be delivered to their house in the city, while Lucy took the children for hot cider at the little general store.

By Christmas morning, the tree would be wrapped in gold ribbons and strings of dried fruit, the blue and white porcelain angel perched on its perfect peak, the candles resting in their little holders on the edge of the magisterial branches snuffed and blackened in the grey light. At one corner of the alcove, his mother positioned the two winged leather armchairs which occupied the bay the rest of the year. Between the chairs was an ornate Italian table upon which rested a gilded lamp; under the lamp, a China plate, emblazoned at its edges with delicate pines, held the remains of several sugar-dusted cookies which his mother had placed there ceremoniously the evening before, along with a tall crystal glass now exhibiting small puddles of milk at its bottom. This was the evidence the boys were seeking. It gave Joshua a deep, rushing chill— the spirit come alive—and it meant there would be presents under the tree. Joshua and Adam would kneel down and look beneath the broad boughs at the piles of lovely, wrapped boxes.

Julia had sent a note to Joshua at the station inviting him to accompany her to Christmas dinner at the home of the Sousas, Joe and Elizabeth "Betty Sue." Joshua convinced MacDonald to let him go back to town while Jurgen and Peter Abbot kept watch. The day was calm and warm, the beach grass on the dunes turned a pale straw color, the patches of beach plum had lost their fruits and were bristly and bare, and wind-carved ripples in the sand were unsullied by animal or human.

The usual hubbub on the streets of Provincetown had been supplanted by strolling families carrying bottles of wine and whiskey and wrapped gifts and children dressed up and prancing like giddy elves.

When Joshua arrived at Julia's, she met him at the door in a burgundy dress and an embroidered shawl. She looked ravishing. He caught his breath and told her so. She kissed his cheek.

"What are all the people doing in town?" he asked.

"It's a wonderful Portuguese Christmas tradition," Julia said. "Everyone opens their homes to all who wish to visit. The women spend days cooking."

"A moving feast," Joshua said.

"That's right," she said, smiling at him, then looking up. "We should go, Mr. Duell."

"Just a moment," he said. "I have something for you." He had been holding the package behind his back, and now she could see it.

Julia blushed slightly. "For me?"

He laughed. "Well, I thought I'd give it to the first girl I met today, and that's you…"

"You're very mean," she said. "Come in."

Joshua entered the salon and handed her the package. She sat on the small sofa to open it. When she saw the drawing, she seemed stunned, but recovered her poise and smiled warmly.

"It's beautiful."

"That's our little place," he said with a grin.

"Yes, I see that," she said. "Thank you. It is quite striking. This means a lot to me, Mr. Duell."

They gazed at one another. Then Julia leaned forward and kissed him. The kiss lingered several long moments.

"Why do you call me 'Mr. Duell' when you insist upon my calling you 'Julia'?"

She smiled at him mischievously. "Because if I call you 'Joshua,' we may not get to Christmas dinner."

"Oh. I see."

Julia stood up, straightening her dress.

The Sousas were second generation Provincetown Portuguese. They lived in a Cape house facing the harbor, its shingles stained brown by the harsh winters. Inside, the home was aglow. The main room stretched from street to beach, its walls decorated with holly and pine wreaths hung on satin ribbons. An iron cooking stove and a brick oven warmed the kitchen; a rough hewn table set with a bright yellow tablecloth was covered with platters of dried cod and roasted turkey, pitchers of wine, Christmas plates, and desserts—Sopa Durado or Golden Soup, sponge cakes in sugar with custard, and Bolo-rei, a Christmas cake of dried fruit. Next to the fireplace, several children played with small porcelain figures in a presépio, or crèche, and in the corner stood a Christmas tree, a recent tradition for the Portuguese.

Julia introduced Joshua to Joe and Betty Sue, uncles, aunts, and four grandparents, including Betty Sue's father Saul Pereira,

a retired whaling man puffing on a pipe. Joshua felt nervous—
he was no longer used to social gatherings like this—and for
a moment he felt overcome with emotion at finding himself
in such an agreeable setting, simpler yet just as meticulously
layered with meaning and symbols as the Christmases of his
youth.

Saul looked at him sympathetically. "How about a glass of
whiskey, son? You look like you could use one."

Joshua nodded. "That'd be great. Thank you, sir."

Julia was greeted warmly and embraced by the women and
all the children ran to her and hugged her around the waist.
Julia turned to Saul and told him Joshua was a Life-Saver at
Peaked Hill.

"Young Billy's station," Saul said.

Joshua nodded.

"Hard work you do out there," Saul said. "Dangerous work.
Hat's off to you."

Joshua nodded his thanks as Saul handed him a glass. A
small boy ran into the room, naked and screeching, followed
by two older sisters in pretty red dresses.

"Tony, put some clothes on, right now!" Betty Sue shouted.

"I will," he answered in a squeaky, lisping voice, then pushed
open the back door and ran naked toward the beach.

"Tony!" Betty Sue looked at Julia. "Sorry. Please excuse me
a moment."

Julia laughed. "You go ahead."

Saul poked his pipe in Joshua's direction. "Ever think
about havin' kids?"

Joshua looked uncomfortable.

"Might think twice about it," Saul said.

"Why don't you show Aunt Julia your presents?" Betty Sue

said to the children as she slipped a shirt and short trousers on the rebellious Tony.

Julia had been through this ritual before and settled into a stuffed chair. Joshua leaned over her, sipping his scotch. The oldest boy, known as Little Petey even though he was a tall, gangly thirteen-year-old, stuck with the men. His sisters Jennifer and Penelope—known by all as Jenny and Penny— gathered their small piles of gifts to show Julia what Pai Natal had brought them.

Penny had a stuffed grey elephant on wooden wheels and Jenny a soft cuddly bear with a big smile; the girls were excited about showing off their presents to Julia. Joshua was fascinated to see this other side of her—she was so gentle and affectionate with the girls, almost as if they were her own. To his own amazement, he found himself wondering what Julia's children might look like.

Jenny retrieved a book from behind the sofa. "This was for Tony," she said.

Julia opened the cover. Inside she found pop-up images of soldiers in scarlet tunics and bearskin hats, pointing rifles and waving swords. "Oh, my," she said.

Betty Sue leaned toward Julia. "Don't you think he's too young to be learning about war?"

Saul interrupted. "All boys love soldiers and guns, right, Joshua?"

Joshua nodded. The only thing Adam ever wanted for Christmas was a new toy soldier; he'd amassed a huge collection of Scottish guards, Ottomans and Serbs, men on horseback with lances and fringe, generals with glowing brass helmets.

Then Saul called out, "Hey! Little Petey! Show her what

you got."

Petey scurried out and came back holding a model schooner, eighteen inches long and intricately made with wood masts and canvas sails.

"It's the first whaler I shipped on, the Dorothea," Saul said proudly. "I made her just for Petey."

They sat for dinner and Saul said Grace in Portuguese. The plates were filled with turkey and yams, fried eggplants and spicy orange sausages known as linguica, cranberries and apples in honey, and a stew of tender squid with kale and cubes of white potatoes in a heady tomato sauce.

Joshua watched Julia across the table, eating heartily. He turned to Betty Sue. "This is spectacular, ma'am."

"Why, thank you, Joshua," she said. "Your first Portuguese meal?"

"No, ma'am. A couple of boys at the station cook. Just my first good one…"

Joshua looked around at the bustling family—chatting, laughing, stuffing their mouths, the men drinking, their voices growing louder—while a part of him retreated to some space high above, picturing his family as it once had been, as if it were he, and not his mother or brother, looking down from heaven on the radiant, cantabile moment.

The sun was nearly down when they finished. The children were restless. Tony removed his clothes and ran through the house, and Petey settled on the floor with his ship. Julia told Betty Sue it was time to go.

The street was empty and quiet. They passed an overturned skiff on a bulkhead overlooking the beach.

"Let's sit a moment," Julia said.

They watched without speaking as the sun trailed brilliant traces of orange and purple across the darkening sky. The water lapped against the beach, a foghorn tolled across the harbor, the wind rattled the halyards of ships at piers whose waterlogged posts creaked against the timbers.

"It is an exquisite night, isn't it, Mr. Duell?"

"Yes, Julia…" He leaned in and kissed her cheek. "Can you call me Joshua now that we've made it through Christmas dinner?"

"I think so," she said softly then turned her face to him.

They pressed their lips together, the smell of the sea drifting through the chilling air. She pulled back.

"Where were you a year ago?" she asked, her hand lingering on his neck.

"New York. My father and I were waiting for my mother to return home from visiting my brother."

"He was away?"

"In a hospital. He was wounded in the war."

Julia nodded. "Did you have a girl in New York?"

Joshua blushed. "No. I mean, sometimes I met girls, went out. But no real girl."

"Have you never fallen in love?"

"No," Joshua said. "Not that I know of." He looked at her. So beautiful. He felt lucky to be there with her. It made him wonder why he should be so lucky. "What about you?"

Julia smiled. She seemed to be deciding something. Then she spoke. "Yes, I guess I have. Twice, in fact."

"So you're an experienced woman," Joshua said.

She laughed. "I suppose I am. My husband, Bill, William…"

"The one who left."

Julia sighed. "Yes, that one. We met while I was in medical school in Baltimore."

"Was he a doctor?"

"Oh, no. He wanted to be a lawyer like his father. He was from a proud family. When I finished school he enrolled at Harvard and I went with him. We eloped!" She giggled. "Not sure why. It seemed romantic at the time. But he started school and found it very difficult. We spent two years struggling, he with school, me with trying to prove that a woman might know something about medicine. But we had good times, too."

"I'm sure you did," Joshua said nervously.

She smiled. "But Bill was offered a position with a commodities broker in San Francisco. His father arranged it. He saw it as a way to escape."

"Escape law school?"

"Well, yes, but I think he wanted to escape me, too."

"Why? Were you so awful?"

"I don't think so. But I was ambitious. My mother says I can be intimidating, particularly to men. I think he felt that way, though I didn't understand it at the time. He was rather mean about it."

Joshua nodded. "I see."

"Do you find me intimidating?"

"No, I'm afraid I… well, maybe a little."

Julia was looking at him in the dim light. Her face seemed softer. Her hand absently caressed his neck and shoulder. "I like you, Joshua."

He smiled. "I like you, too. Was it hard when he left?"

"No, not really," she answered. "I just rolled into a ball and cried for a week. Then I was fine."

Joshua laughed. "That's all?"

"I believe my pride may have been hurt."

"Like I said, the man was an idiot."

"You're so young, Joshua," Julia said softly.

He looked at her. He wanted to kiss her again, but instead he asked, "Am I too young for you?"

"Well, I guess we'll see. So far your maturity is rather overwhelming."

"Who was the other?" Joshua asked.

"What other?"

"You said you loved two men."

"Oh, yes," Julia smiled. "My last year in medical school, a young doctor, we were both finishing our studies. He was a wild one."

"Did he leave you, too?"

"You are a mean-spirited man, Joshua Duell. No, he didn't. I broke it off. I had to. We had… how do I put this? We had a rather torrid affair, and I was afraid it would compromise my ability to earn a degree. He became careless and seemed more interested in his own career than in taking mine seriously."

"What do you mean?"

"Well…" She paused. "He didn't seem concerned about my reputation."

"So you left him."

"Yes." Then she suddenly took his hand in hers.

They sat looking at the stars, their bodies close; they did not feel the cold. There was something timeless about the moment, and he wanted it to last forever. He turned and kissed her. She put both arms around his neck, pressed herself against his chest, and kissed him back. They held each other, enjoying the coldness outside and the warmth of their intimacy, the sensation of desire but also of moving toward some unknown place. A beguiling thought. They looked in each other's eyes. Her smile reassured him; he understood, was certain, that she was feeling what he was. After looking up once more at the winter night, they rose silently and he walked her home.

The next morning Buddy was brooding. Joshua was in a good mood and determined to hang on to it as long as possible, so he said nothing to Buddy about Julia. At breakfast, the men were buzzing with funny stories and making jabs at one another. Punchy made a joke about the newcomers' first Christmas and began to sing the hymn, The First Noel. Buddy reluctantly broke a smile, then, annoyed at himself, stood and walked out of the galley. In the afternoon, Punchy and Jurgen fished off the beach. Joshua walked down and asked how they were doing. Not too well, they said. Punchy told Joshua he should look after his "pal", who was sitting atop a dune. Joshua looked up and shook his head. He was still trying to stay in good spirits; he was sick of Buddy's problems and would have much preferred to be in town with Julia.

Joshua hiked up the dune and sat next to Buddy. "What's the matter?"

Buddy sat there, stoic and silent. Then he was shaking his head. "I don't know. It's this place, those guys," he said, nodding toward the men below. "You'll laugh at me, but maybe it's Christmas, for chrissakes..." And Buddy began to giggle.

Joshua laughed, too, and patted Buddy's knee, then stood and went back down, assuming the episode was over. But in the early evening, as Joshua and Buddy set out on patrol in opposite directions, Joshua called out to Buddy to have a good walk. Buddy didn't reply.

For a few days, Buddy seemed in a better mood. Then at lunch the day before New Years, he told a raunchy joke about three mermaids and a priest. Joshua knew Buddy was nervous doing this since the men were so intolerant of him, but he soldiered through it with his innate charm and wit, and the men all laughed at the joke. In his exuberance, Buddy knocked over a bottle and it spilled on the table. The men laughed even louder, particularly Jurgen. Even Joshua was laughing. Buddy sat there, watching the liquid spread and making terrible faces, which the men interpreted as crude humor—not realizing Buddy was becoming upset. Joshua realized it, but still he joined with the men laughing and poking fun at Buddy. It all happened quickly. Punchy snapped at Buddy, "Clean it up, fer chrissakes!" The men laughed again. Buddy stood up and went to get a rag, cleaned up the mess, threw the rag down in front of Jurgen, spun on his heels and walked out.

"What's the matter with him?" Jurgen asked.

Joshua sighed, then stood and followed Buddy. He found him on the beach half a mile down.

"Hi, Buddy," he called.

Buddy didn't answer. Joshua approached and sat down next to him.

"What's going on?" he asked.

"Nothing," Buddy said.

"You've been acting awfully pissy lately. What's on your mind?"

"What the fuck do you care?"

Joshua was taken aback. "What does that mean?"

Buddy suddenly spun around. "I told you before. It means I'm sick of this place! I'm sick of these people." Buddy turned to face Joshua. "And you know what? I'm sick of you!"

"Why me? Did I do something wrong to you?"

"You? You never do anything wrong," Buddy snapped.

Joshua felt his patience wearing thin. "I don't know what your problem is, my friend," he said. "If you want to tell me, that's fine, I'll listen. If not, I don't give a damn."

"That's exactly right," Buddy said.

Joshua stood up, exasperated. "You know what, Buddy? I'm getting sick of you, too. How's that? I'm sick of your complaints, of your fights with the others, your lousy attitude. I like it here." Joshua paused and looked at Buddy for a reaction, but there was none, just his somber expression. "I'm getting to be sorry I ever found you again. You've become a real pain in the ass." Joshua walked away.

Joshua spent New Years Eve on patrol. Peter Abbot, Pendleton and Punchy were off with their families. The weather was calm. He walked the beach with his lantern, feeling the wind pick up and enjoying its briskness as he trudged along looking out at the sea. His outburst at Buddy had plagued him all day—he knew he shouldn't have said those things, and didn't really mean what he'd said. Buddy has no one here on his side, he thought, he's not popular at the station. All this was true. It would have to be hard on him. But Buddy was annoying, and he was not such a good friend, not really. Maybe Joshua would have been better off joining the Life-Savers without him.

Soon he felt a calm spread over him. The end of another year—a terrible one, but it was finally ending. He thought about all that had come to pass in the year gone by, and the one before it for that matter. It couldn't go on like that, things had to change—maybe they already were changing. At what seemed about midnight, he stopped and sat in the damp sand. In New York people would be thronging the streets, carrying torches, watching fireworks, drinking and laughing in celebration of a new century. Joshua stood alone by the ever-present ocean and spoke to the breaking waves, saying farewell to the year 1899 and praying the next year and the decades to come would bring some semblance of peace and happiness to the world. A simple prayer in the solitary night.

Punchy returned to the station around six in the morning, even though MacDonald had told him to take the morning with his family. Peter Abbot came in at eight. It was a foggy day, chillier than the last few—and unlike any other New Years Joshua had known. MacDonald asked him and Jurgen to go on patrol. When he came back, he heard shouts from the station.

He ran inside and found Punchy and Buddy in the galley, tussling on the floor, knocking over chairs, dislodging the table, and cursing bitterly. Peter Abbot stood yelling epithets at Buddy. Jurgen came in and started shouting, too. It was a terrible scene, a terrible way to start the year. Joshua rushed over and tried to pull Buddy off, but Buddy took a swing at Joshua and knocked him away. He swung viciously, wildly panicked, as if he had slipped into some other dimension. Joshua could see it in his eyes, the anger and fear. Punchy was bleeding from above his left eye; he was older and slower, but he hit Buddy hard. Joshua sprung at Buddy again, intending to stop the fight. Peter and Jurgen moved toward him. Buddy backed into the corner like a trapped animal. Punchy got up and spit blood on the floor, then rushed at Buddy and punched him in the mouth. Buddy swung around from the blow. A bottle of rum sat on the galley counter. He grabbed it, smashed the end, and went at Punchy with the jagged glass.

"Buddy! No!" Joshua yelled, as he moved in on him.

Some deep inner voice made Buddy pause, hold the broken bottle, and look around him. Punchy was staggering from the fight, though he looked ready for more. Joshua moved toward Buddy to take the broken bottle. But Buddy was all defense, all anger and hurt—he turned the bottle in Joshua's direction and lunged at him. The edge caught Joshua's arm, but Joshua twisted his body to avoid a real blow. They stood facing one another, Buddy's expression distorted, his breathing labored.

"You… of course, you, too," he stammered. "You would sell out anyone! You're only here because of your fuckin' dead mother."

Joshua felt the blood rush to his head. He jumped at Buddy, swinging hard, and hit him in the temple. Buddy lost his balance and fell to the floor. Joshua stood over him, ready to hit him again.

At this moment Pendleton rushed in, followed by Mac-Donald, both flabbergasted by what they saw—Buddy's wild expression, the mayhem in the galley, Punchy covered with bruises.

Pendleton looked at Buddy and spoke in a startling voice. "This stops now, Bairn!"

A glowering silence palpitated through the cramped room. Buddy grabbed the back of a chair and pulled himself up. He still held the broken bottle in his other hand, which hung by his side. He looked at Pendleton.

"Don't call me Bairn," he said, but he was out of steam.

MacDonald looked at the men, disappointed and hurt. "That'll do, now. This is over. Everyone back off!" He'd seen men at their best and their worst, but this—in his own galley—was beyond the pale. Everyone knew they had crossed a line.

Jurgen and Peter Abbot walked off. Pendleton spit, turned away and left also. Punchy, visibly shaken, brushed himself off, sneered at Buddy and left the room. Buddy, beaten and brought low, his face wracked with anguish, threw down the bottle and stomped out. The front door of the station opened and slammed.

To Joshua it was like an iron gate closing which might never open again. He was breathing hard and felt suddenly tired. And angry—but as he stood there in the small room facing Pendleton and MacDonald, he felt his anger shift, away from Buddy, away from the confounded little room. He, too, turned and walked out. He could feel MacDonald's stunned presence watching him go.

Outside in the damp air, Joshua felt ashamed. He had let Buddy down. He was angry with himself for letting things go so far and for not sticking up for his friend, who was there because of him. He looked up. Buddy stood on the beach looking out at the ocean. For a long time Joshua remained, watching his friend stand there, alone and abandoned, knowing he was hating the entire world, contemplating what to do next. Tentatively, he moved closer.

"You all right?" Joshua asked.

"What does it matter?"

"What the hell happened?"

Buddy stared at the ocean. He took a deep breath. "It was the rum."

"The rum? You mean you were drinking?"

"Fuck you." Buddy said. "No. I wasn't. I wanted to take the damned bottle upstairs. It's fuckin' New Years!"

"And Punchy stopped you?"

"He tried," Buddy said. "Called me 'Bairn', said it was the Keeper's rum, I should keep my fuckin' hands off. I told him to fuck himself. That son of a bitch has been on my ass for months. Like to kill him…"

"You came close," Joshua said.

Buddy turned and looked at Joshua. His face was hard. "I almost wish I had."

Joshua felt a shock run through his body. He hadn't seen this coming—but he should have. He had no idea what to do. He looked at Buddy, his eyes, hoping to break through, but it wasn't going to happen. He turned and walked to the station.

MacDonald was on the porch watching them. "Any idea who started it?"

"No, sir. They've been at each other since the first day."

"Punchy's not an easy man. But he's a good man."

"I think Buddy is too, sir."

"Maybe, but I don't think he's cut out for this work. I can't have this going on in the station. We can give it a few days, but I'm afraid he's going to have to go."

Joshua went inside.

He took his patrol at nine that evening then went to bed. Buddy was not in his bunk.

Jurgen awakened him at three. "You seen Buddy?"

Joshua sat up and rubbed his eyes. "No, why?"

"He's supposed to go on patrol, but he's nowhere around."

"Damn," Joshua muttered.

He forced himself up, put on his pants, and went downstairs. Pendleton was there.

"You ain't seen yer friend?" he asked.

Joshua shook his head. "You haven't seen him?"

"No, I ain't seen the little bastard. I'd like to wring his neck, though."

"Maybe someone did just that," Joshua said.

"Go see if his stuff's all there," Pendleton told Joshua.

"All right."

Buddy's gear was still stowed in place: sleeping roll, extra pants and sweater, a book he'd been reading. Joshua looked around. The only occupied bed was Peter Abbot's.

"His stuff is there," he told Pendleton. "Who's covering his watch?"

"Sonny."

"And Punchy?"

"He's asleep."

"No, he's not."

"He took the other patrol," Jurgen said.

"Great, they're both out there," Joshua said. "Is Punchy all right?"

"He's a big boy," Pendleton said. "A bit bruised, but he'll be fine."

"I'm going out to look for Buddy," Joshua said.

Joshua walked the beach and along the front dunes and through the wild sand hills leading toward town. He found no sign of Buddy. After a few hours he realized it was futile. Buddy was gone. Would he return? Would he be allowed to stay if he did? Joshua was tired of all of it.

It was a new year.

THE KEEPER

PART TWO

THE
WINTER
SEA

Roll on, thou deep and dark blue ocean, roll!
Ten thousand fleets sweep over thee in vain.
Man marks the earth with ruin—his control stops at the shore.

—George Gordon, Lord Byron,
    from *Childe Harold's Pilgrimage*

CHAPTER TEN

It was mid-January. Buddy was living at the Union House down the hall from the room he and Joshua had shared. The place was a mess, clothes strewn about, a whiskey bottle and glass by the bed, the odor of stale cigars hovering in the close air of the room. He felt restless and frustrated. When would he finally leave this stupid little town, and for where? Maybe he could get on a ship and work his way over to Europe, go back to Italy or the south of France for the rest of the winter. Only he didn't have much money left, and what if he couldn't find a ship that would sign him on? One thing he knew for certain—there was nothing for him here, no adventure left in staying. Then why was he still here?

He had to admit he missed Joshua. What a colossal mistake it had all been: Joshua's decision to join the Life-Savers, and that he, Buddy, had allowed himself to get talked into signing up with him. It made him angry. At Joshua. At himself. Fear never had anything to do with it. He wasn't afraid of much in life. He wanted to keep traveling and see the world while he still could. He should have distracted Joshua from that crazy idea. What a disaster it had turned out to be. He'd hated the men, their arrogance, the notion that as Life-Savers they were automatically to be considered as heroes, given special deference, allowed the greatest leeway in their personal habits and the way they acted toward others. Toward him. Cruelty and intolerance are the same under any guise, he thought. If they had understood him better, the complexities of his ideas, the things he believed in most, like freedom and loyalty. These were what mattered. Sure, it was a good thing to save lives or protect property when it could be done, but it was the bigger values that really counted. Kindness, open-mindedness. He believed in these things, truly and to the depth of his soul. Yet he had transgressed against his own values, more than once, hadn't he? He thought of Munich. For a moment, his heart turned black.

The station. It had been like a private club, with its privileges and hierarchies. Like any political system—but that's not what he'd signed on for. It was to help people, wasn't it? Or not. Maybe just to help Joshua. He was glad they'd found each other—though Joshua had become a bit strait-laced for Buddy's taste. He hadn't always been that way. All the crap he went through, the war, his brother, his mother, it had killed his spirit. Well, not exactly killed it but dampened it. They might have traveled together, around the country, even the world. Joshua was someone Buddy always felt he could have a real friendship with—the kind he'd never had, but knew was possible. Now Joshua was at the station and Buddy was out of it, snubbed and rejected. It made him angry just to think of it. And what about Joshua? What made him right and Buddy wrong? Joshua good and Buddy bad? I don't get it, he thought. I work hard when I do something I care about. I tried to get those men to like me, tried the ways I know best, through humor and intellect. But they lacked those qualities. Maybe Joshua did, too. Joshua was smart, like Buddy—but he could be terribly cruel. Selfish. He'd been welcomed at the station while Buddy had been turned into a scapegoat. Did Joshua help him? No. He dragged him there in the first place, but he never stood up for him with those men. What kind of friend is that?

Buddy rolled a cigarette and smoked it, staring out the window. The icy wind blew in round the cracks in the windows—winter in an abysmal sea town, life going nowhere. A cold shadow passed through his brain. Buddy had never told Joshua what happened after he went off to the war. Joshua had asked him once. He never told him, never wanted him to know how much it had affected him. How it had been the reason he'd come here, to this place, in flight, in retreat, looking for a new start, somehow. He took a long drag of the cigarette. Munich.

He'd left school soon after Joshua did; with his only friend and half the class leaving for the war, he had no desire to stay. He found a job unloading ships on the Boston waterfront, and one day, met an Italian named Franco who considered himself an anarchist and trade unionist; what this meant was unclear, but Buddy was fascinated. Franco had friends in Siena and they found places on a schooner to Genoa.

Buddy and Franco had spent the spring and early summer working in the fields, though not very hard, passing their evenings in the cafes. Buddy smoked cigarillos, drank Tuscan wines and anisette, and fell in love for a few weeks with a young Italian girl. Then they met a group of Austrian boys and went with them to Munich, where they discovered the great beer halls filled with young people drinking and singing. Europeans were more sophisticated about the world, more vocal about everything, especially politics and poetry. Buddy adored the place.

He was introduced to a bright man of twenty-three named Peter Griffel, who had met Bakunin, the famous anarchist, and considered himself one of his followers. Griffel and his friends would convene at the beer hall, then return to someone's apartment and spend the night drinking, smoking, and discussing politics and philosophy. The favorite topic was the repressive and violent nature of organized government. The group took Buddy in; none of them had ever known an American. They became friends with a pair of young builders, Hans and Misha, who were strong, handsome, and fanatical about collectivist anarchism, a philosophy growing in popularity that was opposed to private ownership of property. The ideas Buddy had first encountered at Harvard were now falling into perspective.

The young men and several women met often, drank heavily, and fantasized about revolutionary actions. They took themselves very seriously, and the women felt liberated from society's strictures and freely had affairs with the men. They were a commune, Griffel's disciples, a kind of extended family, accepting of each other's quirks—a family of devoted, zealous radicals. Buddy found it thrilling; these people excited him. He discovered an English bookstore and began reading translations of Friedrich Engels and Karl Marx. He knew some German from his father, and picked up more, and Griffel and some of the others knew some English.

One day, Griffel came from a seminar effusing over a little-known philosopher named Friedrich Nietzsche, who had a cult-like following. "I feel as if my eyes have been finally opened!" he said. "He talks about 'slave-morality', from when Christians and Jews were slaves in Rome, and sees this as a social illness that has overtaken Europe. He says Christianity exists in a hypocritical state—people preach love and kindness, yet condemn and punish others for doing and thinking things the slave-morality does not allow them to do or think in public. He says people should break their self-imposed chains and assert their own power, health, and vitality upon the world."

The others were silent when he had finished.

"What does it mean?" Buddy asked.

"What does it mean? You're an idiot!" said a young woman named Maria, who had spent the night with Buddy a few days earlier, but seemed to have changed her mind.

Griffel looked at him with immeasurable calm. "It means we must act."

The others murmured their agreement, then someone opened a bottle of wine.

One evening, Hans and Misha came in. Misha's face was severely bruised and Hans was fuming mad, cursing and kicking the furniture. A German bureaucrat named Franz Hargen had caught them stealing a telegraph machine out of the window of his office. He'd fallen on Hans and boxed his ears; when Misha jumped in to defend his friend, the burgher, a large man with a red face, had turned on him and beat Misha in the face and head. He might not have stopped, but a woman came along pushing her child in a carriage. Hargen was distracted and the two would-be thieves took off. Misha was embarrassed by the incident, but Hans wanted to call a "meeting" immediately. Griffel agreed. Two of the women went out for sandwiches and beer, and at ten o'clock the entire group assembled to discuss the crisis that had befallen them.

"We must take action," Hans insisted.

Maria agreed vehemently, and soon several others were calling for the burgher's head. Buddy did not understand.

"I don't see what the fuss is about," he said. "You were caught stealing."

Misha seemed to agree but Hans jumped up, incensed. "How can you say such a thing?"

Maria had a good answer. "Because he's immature."

Griffel intervened. "Hans is right. This man is a bureaucrat, a representative of the imperialist government, the same government that keeps the workers poor. He has brutally struck one of our own to protect the property of the state. This cannot stand."

"What should we do, then?" someone asked.

Griffel looked around but said nothing. Buddy felt a powerful sense of dread. The energy of the people in the room was growing collectively, like a living, breathing thing.

"Kill him," Hans said.

"Precisely," said Griffel.

Over three nights of drinking and longwinded diatribes, the group hatched a conspiracy to murder the bureaucrat. The plan was not terribly original. Maria, who was quite attractive, would go to the man's office and lure him outside. Several others would come along in a carriage, kidnap him, and take him to an abandoned farm outside the city.

"What if he resists?" Misha asked.

Hans laughed. "Of course he will resist." He took a heavy revolver from the pocket of his jacket. "And we shall overcome his resistance."

Buddy understood this was no longer a game. He was afraid—not so much of getting caught as of entering into a new realm in which he was decidedly uncomfortable. Murder was not justified, not right. A fascinating concept, perhaps—he was curious to see what would happen—but he knew it was wrong.

On a cold November evening, the group assembled at Griffel's apartment. Buddy was torn, but he felt a part of the group and in the end showed up at the appointed time. He was to ride in the coach, along with Griffel, Hans, Misha, a woman named Marguerite, and a man named Lewis, who drove the carriage. Maria got out several blocks from the municipal office and walked. It was dark and starting to rain. They waited fifteen minutes, as planned—Maria was confident of her charms—before the carriage moved out. It proceeded slowly, its passengers hushed. Buddy sat crushed among his co-conspirators, plagued by consternation and regret, but unable to prevent himself from going along.

Buddy heard Maria's laughter, loud and harsh, and the coughing of the burgher. Griffel said in a whisper, "Let's go." Maria was in the street, her arms around the burgher's neck, acting as if she were drunk and being wildly seductive. Hargen, reacting as expected, stumbled over himself with excitement. Hans struck the first blow with a baton, hitting the man in the back of the head. The burgher cried out, "What are you doing?" His head began to bleed. The others moved in, striking the man with canes and sticks. Buddy's conscience wouldn't allow him to take part in the assault, but no one noticed. Hargen, who was quite fat, fought desperately as they tried to push him through the carriage door. He swung at Misha, but slipped on the ice and fell. They helped him up and pushed him again toward the carriage. This time he rushed at Maria, as if to strike her. In a flash, Hans pulled out his revolver and fired at the man, who staggered, bleeding from his thigh. The conspirators lifted him up and jumped in after him, and the carriage took off. Inside everyone began yelling as Hargen moaned in pain and begged to be released. "I have a family," he pleaded. Buddy sat buried in sweaty bodies, the carriage filled with the steam of their breath and the smell of the suffering burgher, wondering how he could get out of this.

The revolutionaries took the man to the farmhouse. It was bitter cold, and Hargen had lost a considerable amount of blood. They put him on an old sofa and covered him with a blanket. Most of the group were terrified and Buddy was, too, though he pretended not to be. He felt deeply angry, at himself for going along with this fiasco, but more at Griffel for leading them into it and the others for bungling things so badly. They kept the man alive several days feeding him and cleaning his wounds, but it became clear he would soon die. Someone went into town and returned with a newspaper reporting the bureaucrat missing. No one knew what to do, least of all Griffel, who tried to maintain a calm detachment, as if he were an observer rather than the chief instigator. Buddy thought about fleeing, but was afraid the others would stop him, maybe kill him, too. The atmosphere grew volatile, as the comrades metastasized their fear into drinking, shouting and forced revelry, verging at times on hysteria. Buddy withdrew, deeper into himself—but for the rampant madness, someone might have noticed he was no longer with them—and grew terribly depressed.

On the fourth day, Herr Hagen died, his large, smelly body covered in blood and sores. A pall fell over the room. Misha asked innocently what was next. They took a vote and decided to bury the man, not to save his soul, but to hide his body. They took turns digging a large hole two hundred meters from the house.

"You must speak of this to no one," Griffel said as they covered the grave, attempting to sound menacing. "If any of you betrays the others, there will be hell to pay."

They all nodded. Buddy tossed a handful of dirt on the man's grave. The group was silent the rest of the night, and very early the next morning, they all returned to the city, tired and miserable. Buddy wanted desperately to sleep, but he was too afraid. He collected his things, went to the main station, and boarded the first train out of Munich.

The memory of it still gave him chills. He tossed the cigarette out the window. Got to get out of this town, he thought. He had tried to redeem himself, but somehow it had failed and here he was again, uncertain and at peril. He put on his coat and went out on the street. It was cold and deserted. He headed for the Mermaid, sat at the bar and ordered an ale, thick, dark and fine. A fire burned in a fireplace in the corner. The bar was nearly empty: a few ragged sailors with nowhere to go.

The heavy front door kicked open with a rush of wind, and Kirov came through it. He wandered over and sat next to

Buddy, then ordered a beer. William and Tucker came in soon after and sat at a table near the fire.

"The Life-Saver," Kirov said, flashing his eyes and lifting his glass in mock salute.

Buddy looked away. A fight with the Russian was the last thing he wanted.

"Speaking to you, man," Kirov said.

"Yes, I know. Why don't you just leave me in peace?"

"Hey, man, I'm not disturbin' your peace. Nor do I want to. Just sayin' hello."

"Last time you said hello, my friend and I ended up on our backs."

Kirov laughed. "Yeah, well, that happens sometimes." He looked at Buddy, then extended his hand. He had long, almost delicate fingers, yet the hand looked powerful. "Don't mean nothin' to me, though. How about I buy you a beer?"

Buddy thought better of taking the man's hand, but he nodded, saying, "Sure, I'll drink with you. Why not?"

"Why not, thatta boy, I like that." He turned to the bartender, who winked at him.

William and Tucker looked suspicious when Buddy and Kirov approached.

"What's the punk doin' here, Gogol?" William asked.

"The man's joining us for a drink. Just be polite," he said to them.

They sat down. The grimy table was covered with graffiti carved into it by generations of knives and pikes. Up close, both Tucker and William looked dissolute, their expressions blank, staring at their drinks, then away liked chided children.

Kirov sat very straight, shoulders out, head high. He grinned deviously. "So how goes the life of a Life-Saver?"

"I've left them," Buddy said, with a touch more bitterness than he had intended.

"Left? Ya mean you've run off?" William said, an edge in his voice.

Buddy shot him a dirty look, then faced Kirov. "It wasn't for me, that job. I could do it fine, but the rules, the whole military thing... no."

"I understand," Kirov said, sounding sympathetic. "Must have been hard out there."

Buddy snapped at him. "No! Not hard. Just maddening."

"Sorry. I see what you're sayin'. So what you gonna do now?"

"I'm not sure."

"Must be nice to not have to worry like that. Not sure," Tucker griped.

Buddy took a long sip of beer and slapped his glass down. "I've got to make a living just like the next guy."

"Sure you do," Kirov said.

These guys were bad news. Kirov wanted something. Buddy stood to leave. "Well, fellas, thanks for the conversation."

"Just one thing," Kirov said.

"What's that?"

"Well, if ever you're in need of a little extra income, I could use some help."

"What do you mean?" Buddy asked.

"Everyone's got his own way to make a livin', as you put it." Kirov said. "We've got ours. We finds goods and sells them, for example. And we carries goods from here up to the mainland, for another. We are facilitators of commerce, you might say."

Buddy laughed. "That's a good one. Facilitators of commerce."

"It's a good one. A clever description, no?" Kirov said.

"Kind of like gangsters," Buddy said.

Tucker and William jumped up, pushing back their chairs, ready to defend the honor of their profession.

"Settle down, settle down," Kirov said. "The man means no harm. Do you?"

"Harm? Why no, of course not. But what's all this got to do with me?"

"You're a smart guy, you been around a bit, you're strong—"

"And you was a Life-Saver, don't forget," William blurted.

Buddy looked at him disdainfully.

Kirov interceded again. "Well, yes, there's that. You know your way around the sea—and the beach, don't you?"

"I don't know where you're going with this, but I don't think I like it," Buddy said.

"I ain't goin' anywhere with anything. Just, there's real money in the salvage business. Some folks would say it's the best business around here, that and fishin'. All's I'm sayin' is think about it."

"I'll do that," Buddy said. He touched his cap, turned and walked off.

"I like his spirit, that boy," Kirov said.

That weekend, Joshua came back to Provincetown, but not to look for Buddy. Buddy had been on his mind plenty; he felt terrible about what had happened—the more so because MacDonald and the others blamed Joshua, at least partly, for Buddy's failure. Or that was how Joshua interpreted it. "Where's your friend?" they'd ask snidely. MacDonald had called him into his office and intimated that, if nothing else, Joshua should have recognized Buddy's flaws and not let him join the Service with him. Buddy probably felt the same way. Joshua never answered their accusations, nor did he pursue

Buddy to try to get him to return. He was relieved to have the pressure of Buddy not fitting in with the others disappear—and the horror of that scene in the galley.

With Billy and Buddy gone, there was an undercurrent of tension at the station, during drills, at dinner, on patrol, and, with the winter cold, it made life there that much more unpleasant. But there had been no further wrecks, no more deaths, and Joshua still felt he was doing the right thing by being there. The fellow who brought supplies told him Buddy hadn't left town and was staying at the Union House. Joshua thought about going to see him, to make sure he was all right. Joshua was angry with Buddy and angry with himself. He felt guilty, he was as much to blame as Buddy—but despite how it had ended, in his mind they were still friends and he owed him something. He just didn't know what.

But he wanted to see Julia again and that was more pressing. She inhabited a running conversation he had with himself, joy, anxiety, frustration at not being able to see her enough—he would drift into memories of the time they'd spent together, and it left him feeling unsettled.

Sunday morning he walked across the dunes under a strong sun, but with none of the heat or soft breezes of summer—the sand was hard now and blew in his face mercilessly—while his stomach tied itself into knots. He arrived at Julia's cottage and knocked on the door around noon. She opened it.

"Hello, Joshua. How are you?"

Right away he sensed a difference in the tone of her voice.

"Hi, Julia."

He leaned in to kiss her. She stepped back, then leaned forward and delicately offered her cheek. He kissed it lightly, puzzled.

"Come in," she said.

He entered the little living room and removed his coat, feeling awkward.

"Oh, sorry, give me that," she said, and took his coat. She put it on a chair. "Please, sit down."

Joshua sat on the sofa. Julia had a fire burning in the hearth. The room was warm and pleasant.

"Would you like some tea?" she asked.

"Yes, thank you. I would."

He followed her to the kitchen area. As he watched her fill the kettle and set it on the stove, then put tea in a teapot, he had the sudden sensation that she felt his presence next to her a burden.

"Is everything all right?" Joshua asked.

"Oh, yes, fine," Julia said. "Perfect. I've been… quite busy. I was just relaxing."

"Well, if this isn't a good time for you…"

"No, Joshua, sorry. It's good to see you." She smiled.

He felt a sudden relief. He returned to the sofa. Julia prepared the tea and brought him a cup. After she handed it to him, he took her wrist.

"Sit with me," he said.

She gently pulled her hand free, then poured tea for herself and sat next to him.

He bent his head to place his lips on her neck. "I've thought about you."

She moved back slightly, then smiled, but he felt—or imagined—it was a stiff smile. They were silent for what seemed a long time. He began to speak, but she cut him off.

"I've been thinking, Joshua," she said. "About us."

"Yes?"

"It's too fast." She sipped her tea, looking at him over the rim of the cup.

"What is?"

"This… thing… between us. I'm not ready, I've come to realize."

Joshua put down his cup. He felt a new knot in his stomach, this time as if he'd swallowed a potato. He put forth a strained smile. "What do you mean?" He hoped he didn't sound as panicked as he felt.

Julia's face seemed to soften and she looked in his eyes. "I like you, Joshua. I think I like you too much. I've been married. I'm not really a young girl anymore. I'm very independent."

He interrupted. "But I know these things."

"Please, Joshua, let me finish. I've thought about this a lot the last two weeks. I like you and could get involved with you. I think you have a great future, though it's too early for you to know for sure what that is. You're a bright man, caring, brave. You will make a wonderful husband some day."

Joshua grinned in spite of himself. "So far I don't sound too bad."

"Let me finish. What do you plan to do with your life? You come from an educated New York family. You could go into politics, be a lawyer or a businessman. You weren't brought up to be a Life-Saver. Will you really stay here and work with these unrefined people, rescuing sailors and fishermen from their storms? It's very dangerous, you could die anytime you go out. Or will you do this for a year, maybe two, then tire of it and move on? And to do what? Will you go back to school, or apprentice in New York? You're not ready to settle down."

"For God's sake, Julia, we've barely kissed each other."

Julia gave a short laugh, uncomfortable, but determined.

"Maybe I want more. More than a kiss. More than a few months. Maybe I don't want to fall in love with you only to lose you—to the sea or to your future."

Joshua was stunned. He'd never had a conversation like this, never even imagined one. His heart felt like a stone and he was stricken with a strange kind of panic, a sense of impotence.

"I'm terribly sorry, Joshua. I do like you. Very much. But I'm just afraid…"

"I… guess I don't really understand," he said.

"I know," she said. She looked at him tenderly.

She was too beautiful, he thought, too perfect. No one was perfect, but at this moment, to him, she was. He could say he loved her. Perhaps he did. He didn't know what it was supposed to feel like—but he felt such longing and affection and defeat. He just looked at her, into her eyes.

"I think you should go, Joshua. I need time."

He got his coat. He felt shattered and lost. "All right," he said. He opened the door and went out, carrying his coat.

Julia lingered in the doorway and watched him struggling to get his coat on as he walked away. She closed the door and leaned against it, tears in her eyes, her heart beating quickly, almost painfully. Oh God, she thought, I've hurt him. She hadn't meant to. She'd been looking forward to seeing him again, to the touch of his hand on her face, to his beatific smile. He was such a boy. He'd become physically tough working out there on the shore, and he was not afraid to put himself into danger, yet she sensed he was very vulnerable and she had no desire to wound him. She could, in fact, love him, and that was the problem. She knew she had a side that was impulsive, even reckless. Yet she'd learned from a young age, from her mother and all the women in her family, that a woman had to be smart, controlled—tough, if necessary. If they were to gain their rightful place in a world that had been almost exclusively dominated by men, they had to be shrewd and possess great patience and strength. This knowledge had served her well, and now she was a doctor, one of the few women who could say that. And yet…

She was alone. Her marriage had failed. She had worked hard and built a career, but she wanted someone with whom she could share her life. She wanted children, a man who would be strong, a good companion, someone who wouldn't be intimidated by her own strength and ambition. Joshua had the potential to be those things, and she felt herself succumbing to his seductive power, a power he seemed unaware of, because he was, after all, not much more than a boy. He'd suffered tragedy, but he hadn't really lived. The practical side of her felt she needed a man with experience, with wisdom.

Since Christmas night when they had sat together by the sea, she had wrestled with this conflict, longing to see Joshua again, yet thinking she should let him go before things went too far. She felt too strongly about him just to have an affair, and she knew if they consummated their relationship he would never understand her reticence once it came, which it inevitably would. She had not known how she would react to seeing him. When he showed up at her door, her tougher side took control and she had presented her dilemma in a cold, dispassionate manner that had driven him away. She felt as stricken as he did, and wished, against her better judgment, that she could take back all she had just said.

Ten days after their first encounter, Buddy was playing poker in the Mermaid with a group of listless fishermen. Buddy was even more miserable—with each day that he remained, he berated himself for sticking around and wondered why on earth he did. It was raining and windy outside, the town itself a bleak and dreary outpost, a prison, it seemed, even if a self-imposed one. Buddy glanced up through the greasy, misted window and saw Kirov walking toward the bar, dripping wet. Buddy wondered how the earth could harbor such a man without weeping—though he knew perfectly well it could and did.

Vassily Kirov had been born in Budapest. His father, a Ukrainian, had been a blacksmith in a small city until he got in a fight and had to leave, with cash belonging to his former employer. He had fled to the Austrian-Hungarian Empire and started over as a builder. Kirov told his friends his mother had been Italian, but her grandfather on her mother's side had been an African slave and she'd come to Budapest from northern Italy during one of the famines. Kirov's sister was worshipped by her father and doted upon by her mother, who found a way to have her trained as a governess and receive a limited education, but Vassily had always been tough and a loner. His father assumed any son of his could fend for himself. When he was fourteen, he ran away, to Vienna and then to Trieste, where he hopped a freighter bound for America. He had no papers and no desire to go through immigration, so he convinced the captain to let him off near a cove on the Rhode Island coast. He made his way to Boston, where the drifters and hooligans populating the bars and street corners were mostly Irish. Kirov picked up some English and established himself as a man to be respected; he was called the Russian, and one night he got in a card game with an English fellow who gave him the moniker Gogol, for the Russian writer, which stuck. Sometimes he took jobs on the docks of Boston. At twenty-four, he found work with a so-called salvage company, a team of roughnecks hired by wealthy Boston ship owners to track down wrecked vessels and retrieve lost cargo along the south coast and the Cape, by whatever means necessary. It was work he came to relish.

Kirov was his own man these days, but he'd been hired by a big salvage crew from Scituate to retrieve lost goods on several recent wrecks. During one of those jobs, he had heard the story of a salvage team on the Jersey coast, which went out one night in a storm and saw a ship foundering on the rocks two hundred yards offshore. They were aware a ship carrying expensive textiles from Europe was sailing toward New York harbor. When they spotted the ship in trouble, the team of four men raced out ahead of the Life-Savers and retrieved a substantial portion of the goods. The Life-Savers at Seabright Station launched their surf-boat to make the rescue, but the wreckers got out with their plunder. The two boats passed in the rough surf and the Seabright keeper fired at the wreckers, wounding one man. Nonetheless, it had been a successful venture. Kirov thought it was brilliant.

He came through the door, which hung partly open in disrepair, took off his cap and shook the water from it. He looked around, then sat at the bar and ordered a whiskey. When Buddy walked to the bar, Kirov nodded at him.

"Good to see you again," Kirov said, a bit too loudly.

"Why is that?" Buddy asked.

"And why not? We're friends, ain't we?"

"Not that I'm aware," Buddy said.

"Look, my friend, if you'll permit me to call you such," Kirov continued, "I'm planning a little operation and could use your help. Your expertise, let's say."

Buddy looked at Kirov, looked into his blue-grey eyes under heavy brows, delicate and sparkling, almost feminine, yet fearsome. Buddy found the man distasteful and didn't trust him worth a damn; he felt afraid to respond in the way one might be afraid to open a door when someone is knocking late in the night. "What kind of operation exactly?"

"It's a salvage job, a little idea I've been working on."

"Why me?"

"You've been trained as a Life-Saver, you know the beaches, the bars. I want your help to avoid running into the Life-Savers while we retrieve some merchandise."

Buddy twisted his beer glass and stared at the foam. He took a sip, put the glass on the bar, and looked at the cracks in the mahogany counter.

"We'd be happy to have you. Even shares, minus my extra ten percent for getting the information."

Buddy thought there couldn't possibly be anything legitimate about any of this. He didn't mind bending rules—he imagined himself rebellious and unafraid; for him, it was part of what defined "freedom"—but despite what he'd allowed himself to get dragged into in Munich, he didn't see himself as a criminal. Everyone knew taking goods off the beach was technically illegal.

Kirov sensed his hesitation. He tapped the bar for another whiskey, then turned to Buddy, a disturbing grin on his slick face. "You know, I've heard it said the Lord helps those that helps themselves."

"I'm not sure I'd bring the Lord into the conversation if I were you."

"Why?" Kirov asked. "Are you a religious man?"

"Hardly," Buddy said.

Kirov laughed. "Well, I'm not exactly sayin' that." He was rolling a cigarette.

"Listen, Mr. Kirov, I don't know what you're up to, but it doesn't sound good and I really don't want to get involved."

Kirov's face suddenly darkened. "Opportunity knocks but once, my friend. I won't ask again." Then he paused and lit a cigarette. He looked at Buddy with what seemed like a twinkle in his eye. "The way I see it, ya don't owe them fellas nothin'. They never treated you right, now did they? And you could make some money without hurtin' nobody. I thought you was the adventurous type."

"I'm plenty adventurous. I'm just not a robber or a gangster."

Kirov smiled at him. "Those are big words. But I can promise you no harm will come to anyone. This is just a business, like any other."

Buddy looked at him. "What is it being salvaged exactly?" "Now that's the interesting thing. I don't know yet." Kirov snickered. "How's that?"

"I have no idea what you're saying," Buddy said.

"Well, suppose a bunch of fellas was out on the beach on a night when the weather ain't too good—you done that plenty before you left, no?"

Buddy nodded.

"And suppose, as so often happens, a ship was to hit one

of them bars and get stuck."

"If the captain and crew had any luck, the Life-Savers would see them and go out and get them."

"That's right," Kirov said. "But what if they didn't?"

"Didn't?"

"Yeah, what if there were no Life-Savers there? What would happen to the ship?"

"She'd likely break apart. The sailors and passengers aboard might die."

"And what about the goods on that ship?" Kirov asked with a twisted smile.

"I don't know," Buddy said.

"Sure you do! They'd wash up and someone would find them. Ain't that what's always happened?"

Buddy was trying to stay ahead of this logic.

"All what I'm sayin' is if we was to get there first, we'd get the salvage. Could be worth a pretty penny."

"How much do you think?"

"Now how the hell do I know? Depends what's there, don't it? You could walk away with a few hundred easy, maybe a lot more."

"You're saying we just walk along the beach and hope a ship gets wrecked in front of us? Seems like pretty long odds, doesn't it?"

Kirov smiled. "I like a fellow who thinks things through. But this is what the Life-Savers do, no? What if you could improve the odds, say by hearing in advance that a ship was making its way along the coast on a night of poor weather? And what if you had a way of knowin' what is on that ship, so if she does wreck you know there's real loot to be had?"

Jesus, Buddy thought, loot. "How the hell would you

know that?"

Kirov grinned. "I have my sources. Let's just say."

Buddy stared at his beer, a sick feeling in his stomach. He'd had that feeling before—the voice of caution that had called to him in the past and to which he'd failed to listen. But Kirov was right about one thing: he didn't owe those guys at the station anything, not loyalty, not sticking to their self-righteous standards; he didn't owe anything to anybody here. He was bored and frustrated with himself; a part of him longed to do something audacious, something risky. And he could use the money.

"What if there's no ship that runs aground?"

Kirov knew he had him, and smiled. "We come back another night. Everything comes to him what waits, as they say."

"And if the Life-Savers show up?"

"We'll have to avoid them, won't we? You know how to do that."

"When?" Buddy asked.

"Weather's getting worse," Kirov said. "Tomorrow night.

For days after his disastrous visit to Julia, Joshua went through the routines of the Life-Savers as if by rote. Inside, he was half-dead. The other half felt scared and abandoned; he had a constant queasy feeling like indigestion. When he was alone, his hand would shake, and he could not stop thinking about Julia. As in some inexorable nightmare, he ran through their conversation again and again, trying to think what he had missed, what he had done wrong. Perhaps he hadn't spent enough time with her, or she was afraid he would get hurt in a rescue and was protecting herself.

Would he be thinking about her this much if she hadn't essentially said she was cutting him out of her life? Or was that even what she meant? Was she the one who was afraid? Heartsick and weary of feeling this way, he decided he'd just have to give her some time. She would come back.

The first day of February, it turned bitter cold. The wind had shifted and came out of the north from Canada. By morning the sky was grey and the air uncommonly damp. The onshore wind was twenty knots and the ocean was starting to churn.

Joshua walked down the ramp and spoke to Peter Abbot. "Looks like another storm."

"Yep, it sure does," Peter Abbot replied.

MacDonald put them on day watch. By nine in the morning, Joshua was walking the beach.

Buddy awoke with renewed resolve. He would go to New York and find a ship to sign on, a freighter headed to Europe—to anywhere. But first he would work with Kirov, make some money, and maybe even have a little fun at the expense of his friends at Peaked Hill Bars. For a brief second, a flash really, he imagined what he might say to Joshua if something went wrong. But he shut it out. These characters took salvage from the beach all winter long. All he had to do was act as a lookout, give Kirov some information about the schedules the Life-Savers followed. It didn't seem too bad, and it would be his ticket out.

They met in the west end of town at four that afternoon. The wind was blowing on the harbor and the sky grew dark as what little sun there had been disappeared and night fell. Kirov and William were on horseback, and Tucker drove a long wagon pulled by two mules. On the wagon sat a skiff, twenty feet long, with three benches and three sets of oars.

Buddy liked the skiff and told Kirov so. "Do you guys know how to row this thing?" he asked.

"Don't you worry," Kirov said. "We'll do fine."

They headed out along the moors, over the dunes, and came out on the beach past the Race Point station. The sea was rough and the air cold. They stopped the wagon, tied the horses, and made a fire.

"We'll wait here a while," Kirov said.

By around seven, the air was thick with drifting fog banks. There was no snow, but visibility was limited. The fire kept them warm enough. Kirov said they'd take turns patrolling the beach, and he sent William off on his horse, toward Peaked Hill.

Buddy had explained the Life-Savers' regimen carefully to Kirov: the patrols on foot, the equipment they carried, the signals if they spotted a ship in trouble, the two types of carts and the methods of rescue. None of this was secret information, Buddy reasoned.

By nine o'clock, the storm had settled in. It wasn't a big storm, just off and on light snow and a lot of wind and waves. And cold, of course. Kirov sent William and Tucker off by horseback in opposite directions. At quarter to ten, Tucker returned, shook his head when Kirov looked at him inquiringly, then came over to sit by the fire.

Around ten, William came thundering back from the direction of Peaked Hill. He leaped from his horse and ran over, out of breath and excited; his strange, thin face with one missing tooth and wild knotted hair looked even more bizarre through the firelight.

"Gogol," he gasped, "there's a ship. She's already passed Peaked Hill and heading this way. Looks like she might be in trouble." He gave a snaggly smile.

Kirov jumped up. "Get the wagon," he ordered Tucker.

Kirov kicked out the fire, then he and William headed back in the direction from which William had come. Buddy and Tucker followed in the wagon. Not a quarter mile down the beach, William and Kirov sat on their horses looking out at the wild sea. Buddy walked over to them. Sure enough, there was a ship out there, struggling against the wind in the breakers between the first and second bars. It was hard to see, but the sails were definitely visible among the white foam and she looked as if she was facing the wrong direction. Then one of the masts lifted and flew away. It took only seconds.

"Jesus," Buddy said.

Kirov turned to William. "The flare."

William nodded and took off again toward Peaked Hill.

"What flare?" Buddy shouted.

"You'll see," Kirov said. "Little extra protection."

Buddy started to feel uneasy.

"Let's get the boat off," Kirov said.

Tucker drew the cart closer to the water and the three men took the skiff off and dragged it to the edge of the surf. Buddy remembered the drills with the lifeboat, the embarrassment of the first few times they'd done it, Pendleton and Punchy taunting him. Fuckin' bairn.

Suddenly, there was a bright orange light down the beach—the flare. Buddy judged it to be more than a quarter mile away. William came galloping back, pulled up sharply and jumped off the horse.

"All right, let's go!" Kirov commanded.

The four men ran to the boat and pushed it into the waves and three of them climbed in. Buddy was to stay behind to watch for the Life-Savers. He and Kirov had worked out a series of signs with the signal lamp to warn the men the Life-Savers were coming, how close they were, and whether they were using the lifeboat or breeches buoy. The others would board the ship, grab what they could carry and throw as much else as they could over the side. They would be on board only a few minutes.

They scrambled to find their seats and grab their oars. Buddy pushed them off. He doubted whether three men in a twenty-foot skiff could breach the waves the way six trained Life-Savers had done in a heavier, but more seaworthy, boat. But Kirov and his men were strong and determined and managed to move the boat forward.

As they had planned, Buddy drove the cart through a gap in the dunes leading the two horses behind. He left the cart and climbed to the top to keep watch. He could see the flare burning, its eerie light distorted by the blowing sand and snow, flooding the beach. He figured they were at the far end of the stretch covered by Peaked Hill Bars Station, and a bit farther from Race Point Station, so he scanned carefully in both directions for anyone on patrol. He saw no one. He sat down at the top of the dune to continue watching, and thought about what he was doing there. It was a stupid plan, and he was stupid for letting himself be a part of it.

But then, in an agonized instant, he realized what they had done—what he had allowed to be done. The flare would draw the Life-Savers from Peaked Hill Bars, Joshua included; they would be confused as to its source, and while they puzzled over the mysterious flare, they would not notice the foundering ship further down the beach. This meant any rescue effort would be delayed. People—innocent people, whose only mistake had been to be aboard a ship in a storm—could end up dead. It might not be his fault exactly, but he'd done nothing to prevent it.

Punchy had first seen the flare go off and told MacDonald, who ran out to see. It was easily a mile and a half down the beach, maybe more.

"Who's on patrol?" he had asked Pendleton.

"No one, sir."

"What do you mean?"

"I mean Jurgen just got back from that direction."

Jurgen came down the ramp.

"Did you see anything?" Pendleton asked him.

Jurgen shook his head. "No, sir, nothing."

"Puzzling," MacDonald said. "Could be the Race Point boys, though it's not likely." He turned to Pendleton. "Have the men suit up and get the lifeboat cart. Jurgen, you telephone Race Point and see what they know."

Jurgen and Pendleton ran to the station. MacDonald looked out over the tossing waves.

The men, in full foul-weather gear, moved the cart down the ramp, ready to go. Jurgen ran back.

"What'd they say?" MacDonald asked.

"They don't know a thing."

"Very strange," MacDonald said. "Well, flares don't light themselves. We'd better head down there and see."

Kirov, William and Tucker managed to row the skiff out to the ship, although the other two complained bitterly to Kirov whenever they caught their breath. His repeated response, as he rowed hard against the waves, was "Shut the fuck up and row."

The ship was hung up on the first bar and listed to port as the wind shredded the mainsail. Waves battered the hull from all sides, but for the moment, she held together as the captain tried desperately to maneuver off the bar. The main-mast was bowed and looked ready to snap. She was an old clipper, strong and steady, and made her living hauling lumber up and down the coast. She carried no passengers, but there were half a dozen crew plus the captain and first mate. The skiff pulled alongside. The sailors, terrified of dying on the notorious bars like so many before them, held on to the rail. At first, they thought the Life-Savers had arrived. Kirov brought the skiff right to the ship's side and tossed a line to one of the sailors, who tied it to a trun-cheon. The three men scrambled up onto the deck and drew their pistols.

"What the hell?" a sailor shouted.

"Now listen to me!" Kirov hollered over the pounding water. "Just stay out of our way and we'll be gone in a few minutes. Interfere and you'll be shot."

"You ain't Life-Savers?" a sailor asked.

William treated the man to his snaggle-toothed grin. "No we ain't fuckin' Life-Savers!"

Kirov pointed his gun at the man and they moved over the deck. A stack of lumber sat securely strapped onto the deck amidships. Kirov examined it for a moment and looked over the rail to check where the skiff was, then cut the straps with his dagger. The lumber began to slip off its stack and bounced clumsily over the rail into the sea. The sailors looked on in astonishment.

The Captain, a man named McGraw, saw the timbers

go over and rushed to see what had happened. He stopped short when he saw Kirov and his men pointing guns at his crew, then pushed forward to confront Kirov.

"Who the hell are you people? What do you want?"

"We're tax collectors," Kirov said. He waved his gun. "I'd like you to take me to your quarters, Captain, if you don't mind."

He lifted his gun and pointed it squarely at the captain's chest to make sure he understood what the consequence would be. The Captain decided to do as he was asked to protect his crew.

He alone knew they carried a secret cargo. A wealthy Maine ship builder had arranged to ship two cases of a Bordeaux wine dating back to Napoleon III that had been preserved in a cave in Normandy, a keg of hand-distilled Scotch from Balvenie, and a long, carefully sealed wooden box containing a precious hunting rifle with an ivory stock. The ship builder had put an emerald necklace in the box with the rifle. He knew there was a risk shipping valuable goods in this manner, but the ship's captain and her owner were both close friends of his, and promised to take special care of the cargo.

The cabin was cramped, but elegant, with wood paneled shelves and built-in closets. Kirov surveyed the space, then began to ransack it, turning over tables and ripping open doors. He tripped over what looked like a velvet-covered table in a corner. It was the whiskey keg. The wine cases were jammed into the captain's locker, covered with a cloak. Kirov grinned slyly at the captain. He had learned that ship captains often keep the most valuable goods they are transporting hidden in their cabin, safe from the hands of the other men, and he suspected there might be more. He raised his gun to the captain's temple. "Show me whatever else you've got stashed," he said to him calmly.

The captain seemed surprised at this, and hesitated. Kirov moved closer and cocked the pistol. The clicking sound resounded through the muffled cabin. The captain thought for an instant more, then nodded. He was not ready to die. He pulled back the mattress of his bunk and lifted out a lid. The long box was stashed inside. Kirov leaned over, and with a gleam in his eye, yelled for Tucker to come.

Tucker, on the deck, heard him and began to move away. One of the sailors lunged at him. William fired and the man fell to the deck, hit in the leg. William held his gun up and looked at the others. They stood as still as they could on the rocking ship.

Tucker carried each case and the keg one at a time across the deck and lowered them into the skiff, which banged precariously against the hull. Kirov took the long box under his arm, held the gun out and crossed the deck. The captain watched with seething eyes, but did nothing to stop him. William and Tucker lowered themselves into the skiff, Kirov handed Tucker the box, and jumped down after it. His foot missed the gunwale and he slipped, but he righted himself and got into place. He cut the line and the boat drifted swiftly away as the captain and his crew glared blackly at the robbers.

On shore, the Peaked Hill Bars Life-Savers reached the flare. The seven men, winded from dragging the lifeboat over the sluggish sand, looked at the ocean, at the beach, at the dunes. There was no sign of any disturbance. Pendleton and MacDonald huddled together.

"What do you think?" MacDonald asked.

"Damned strange, y'ask me," Pendleton replied.

They looked out over the water, straining to see.

"Don't see anything at all," MacDonald said. "Let's keep going."

"Aye, sir," Pendleton said.

Buddy saw them moving down the beach toward him, lanterns swinging, another on the cart. He remembered how heavy that damned thing was. He wasn't sorry at all not to be with them. What a terrible life they lived. Soon he would be away from all this. As they got closer he could make out Joshua at the front, pulling a heavy rope alongside Punchy. It was a prickly state of affairs, but so be it. Buddy remained hidden behind a low rise in the dune. He lit the signal lamp and held it so Kirov could see it, but the men on the beach couldn't. He flashed the message that the Life-Savers had arrived with a lifeboat.

Kirov saw the signal. "Shit," he muttered.

He could see the lanterns now. He hoped they couldn't see him.

MacDonald scanned the waters. He did not see the small boat rowing in the dark; it was hidden behind rising and falling breakers, and he was looking for a ship. He spotted it, foundering on the bar.

"There she is, men. Get the boat down."

Joshua and Punchy moved the lifeboat into the water as the others found their places. The water was damned cold, Joshua thought—but it didn't seem so severe now, and at least the storm was not too bad. Nothing like the triple header in December. He lifted himself over the gunwale. As he did, he glanced back toward the beach and his eye caught a movement. He stared for a moment. Was there a man perched on top of one of the dunes? He thought he could see someone moving around up there. Then he was struck by a disturbing notion: that it was Buddy.

Buddy watched as they launched. He felt as if he and Joshua were looking directly into each other's eyes, as if Joshua were somehow staring into his soul. But they were a hundred yards apart on a foggy night, neither sure what the other was seeing. Joshua couldn't possibly know who he was looking at. Someday, Buddy thought, someday we'll meet again, under better circumstances. I know we will.

Joshua and Punchy took their places and the men began to row, MacDonald at the helm. The lifeboat slid forward and crossed into the first line of breakers. They rowed hard and went over, hitting the other side with a slap. MacDonald could see the ship more clearly. She was twisting and turning, and he thought perhaps the captain was still trying to free her. Almost never works in this heavy sea, he thought, but it can be done, with luck.

Then he spotted the skiff. It was moving at a quick clip toward shore. He thought he could see the silhouettes of three men rowing. Who were they? Not Life-Savers—too small a boat. Did it come from the ship? As he pondered this, leaning hard against the long oar to keep them on course, they struck the first timber. Soon the water was filled with them, tossing precariously. The men rowed harder, and the lifeboat rammed its way through the logjam, smashing into timbers and nearly flipping. MacDonald focused on getting his men through this, and forgot temporarily about the skiff. They reached the ship.

The lifeboat was ten feet off. Punchy readied the heaving

stick and called to one of the sailors. The sailor stood with several others at the rail.

"Go to hell!" the first sailor yelled.

"We don't need no more a' your help," a second one cried.

Then the captain made his way to the rail. He looked at the men in the boat, their uniforms, the Keeper at the helm, the boat that was much larger than the previous one, and he knew these were real Life-Savers.

"Catch their line and make it fast, Mitchell."

"Aye, sir," the sailor responded.

Punchy threw the line and the sailor secured it. As the boat moved closer, Joshua and Pendleton boarded.

MacDonald called to the captain. "You all right?"

"Lost a mast, mainsail is gone, I'm trying to free her, but she's not going. Appreciate your help," he shouted back.

"What was that about, sir?" MacDonald demanded.

"We was robbed, sir. Three men on a long skiff."

"Life-Savers?"

"No sir," the Captain answered. "Three men with guns. Took some things from my cabin, cut free some lumber."

"Anyone hurt, captain?" Pendleton asked.

"One man shot in the leg. Otherwise no."

"Let's get you and your men off," MacDonald said.

"Take the wounded man and two others. I'll keep the rest with me."

MacDonald looked up at him. He was a tough old bird, weathered and strong like the ship. "Not a good idea, sir. Weather's pretty bad out here."

"Aye, that it is, sir. But I'll try to save my ship if I can. She's not stuck too bad. I may be able to get her off when it calms."

MacDonald nodded. "We'll take your three men now, then leave a man to watch from the beach."

"Thank you, sir," the captain said.

"Scotty, get those men down here."

"Aye, sir," Pendleton replied.

He turned to Joshua, and they began helping the man with the wounded leg over the railing.

Kirov and the others reached the beach and staggered out of the skiff. Kirov took the long box, and William and Tucker unloaded the liquor crates. Buddy drove the cart back down, horses in tow, and helped pull the skiff out of the water. A dozen or so large timbers had already floated in.

"Get those boards on the cart and let's get out of here," Kirov said. He was angry. "Fuckin' Life-Savers," he grumbled.

"You knew they'd show up, didn't you?" Buddy asked. "The flare brought them down this way."

"Who asked you?" Kirov snapped.

With the wood, the cases of wine and scotch, and Kirov's long box loaded on the wagon bed, they headed back to town, Kirov and William on horseback, Buddy and Tucker on the cart.

The Life-Savers rowed back, the lifeboat low and tippy with the extra passengers. Jurgen stayed behind to watch the ship. The others lugged the cart, with the wounded sailor riding on top adding more weight, back along the sand to the station.

Joshua had one more patrol that night. The storm was subsiding. As he walked he wondered about the indistinct figure on the dune. Could it possibly have been Buddy? He decided to find out for himself.

CHAPTER ELEVEN

Two days later, Jurgen went to town to retrieve the mail and Joshua went with him. There was a letter from his father. An actual letter, for once.

Dear Joshua,

I hope your Christmas was a pleasant one. Life must feel quite different for you out there on the desolate coast. I've been leading a secluded existence myself. The house is quiet and austere; I've let go all the help except one Negro woman who cares for me like a child. It is odd to think of the times when it was filled with voices. My work for the Navy consists of answering correspondence and reviewing reports, very dry stuff.

Your present calling is very noble and I am certain it feels like an important contribution. I'm hopeful you will emerge from the rigors of your assignment without serious injury, and that you shall come to your senses once your commitment is completed and rejoin the world into which you were born. It may not always be a sensible world, and Lord knows we have both witnessed its injustice. You have always been too much of a dreamer, something you got from your mother. But you have an obligation, to yourself, to the family from which you come, to make a place for yourself that suits your upbringing. I hope you will consider this.

I have been ill of late, something related to pneumonia, the doctors believe, but other than an obstinate cough, I am apparently recovering. No need for alarm. Be well.
   Your Father

Joshua sat on the edge of the wharf and looked at the sparkling harbor. Fishing boats were tied to the bigger wharves, though no one sailed them this time of year. The wind was sharp, the air cold, but Joshua didn't mind. He looked over the small town, charming, secluded, primitive, trash scattered on the beach, dogs and gulls picking at waste and dead fish, separate from the bigger world, yet its own microcosm, its own freestanding existence, the old Cape houses, piers and sheds gleaming in the sun, the smell of the sea so clear and fresh. Even with all its blemishes, in the dead of winter, it seemed to

Joshua a place of breathtaking beauty.

His father had been ill. What if something happened to him? It made Joshua tremble, the thought of losing another member of his family—a dreadful thought. He remembered the last time his father had sent him a letter.

It was only a few days after the protest march. There had been increased rumors about the war. The Harvard president held his own rally in support of it, and threatened to expel those who had so disrespectfully tarnished the university's reputation. This had worried Buddy, but in the end nothing came of it. Then Joshua received a letter from Gideon; the same letter had been sent to Lucy. Joshua read it at dinner, Buddy at his side as always, and tears came to his eyes.

> *Dear Lucy and Joshua,*
> *I am well aware of your feelings toward a poten-*
> *tial war, my dear. You have no need for worry.*
> *Our country is growing stronger. The new bat-*
> *tleships, including the one I now command, are*
> *among the most powerful and up-to-date in the*
> *world, and we have little to fear if the war does*
> *come. Adam is strong and has a good head on his*
> *shoulders, and I am not concerned for his safety.*
> *Besides, it is highly unlikely the war will extend*
> *beyond an initial naval confrontation.*
>
> *There is one concern I must share with you both,*
> *however. Joshua, you are a smart young fellow*
> *with a bright future ahead. This war, if it comes,*
> *will be a milestone for your generation and a*

turning point for the nation. It is my fervent belief—and I am certain I can picture your mother's expression as she reads this—that if war is declared, you, too, must enlist. It is your duty as a young man and a citizen, and an important opportunity, regardless of your later ambitions.

Take care, both of you. You are deep in my heart.
  Gideon

"Nice father you've got!" had been Buddy's comment—though his own father hadn't understood his son any better than Gideon did. Joshua didn't want to leave school to fight in the war, but he felt the sway of his father's unyielding invective and the pressure of the mounting public turbulence everywhere he turned. He and Buddy had sat up most of the night talking about it. Sam had already gone home to enlist. Buddy tried every way he could think of to convince Joshua he did not have to go. But in the morning, Joshua took the train back to New York. He'd wanted to tell Buddy, to say goodbye, but he had gone out and was nowhere to be found. So Joshua left and did not see Buddy again.

When he arrived home, Lucy greeted him in the parlor. He rushed to her and they hugged desperately, afraid at first to speak about their very real fears. She looked at him, her face wracked with the pain they both felt. She picked up her copy of Gideon's note from a nearby table and waved it at him.

"Oh, Joshua! Joshua…" She looked anxiously into his eyes. "Hear me well, Joshua. You do not have to listen to your father. Not in this instance."

Joshua felt more torn and bewildered than ever. "I don't

know, Mother, I don't know." He kissed her cheek and patted her shoulder, then went up to his room.

As the Navy cutter took him across the river to the Marine training facility, Joshua watched his mother's defeated figure grow ever smaller. He had kissed her tenderly. She had called out to him, "Take care of each other!" Despite his fears and misgivings, he felt a certain pride at being part of a group of Marines going off like so many before to fight for their country. But he was sure he didn't have his father's and brother's courage. Adam greeted him warmly and Joshua was impressed that his brother had already grown stronger and more physically confident. Joshua threw himself into training. They were all raw and a long way from becoming seasoned soldiers.

Three days later, word spread through the camp that the United States had declared war against Spain. The boys were to be part of the First Marine Battalion, commanded by Lieutenant Colonel Robert W. Huntington: five companies, six hundred twenty three men and twenty-three officers. On April 22, 1898, they boarded the USS Panther, a converted banana boat, headed for Hampton Roads. There was a dizzying excitement—this was the very first of the Marine Expeditionary Force. They were armed with the new Lee smokeless rifles and accompanied by an artillery unit with four three-inch landing guns. As the ship sailed out of New York harbor, crowds gathered to cheer them, fireworks exploded and bands played. It had been a grand farewell.

The last day of April, they sailed into Key West for a month of further training. The small island was lovely and temperate, the surrounding sea the color of pearls and robins' eggs. The swaying palm trees seemed idyllic and safe—but the young Marines, though overflowing with bluster, shared an unspoken feeling of dread. Not one of the enlisted men, and few of the officers, had any combat experience. One morning, a man's body was found severely mutilated outside a notorious watering hole known as the Last Chance Saloon. He was not an American, though there were rumors he was Cuban, might be one of the rebels, and that the Spanish had killed him. Key West was a wild place with a rocky coastline. There were few women to be seen and no settled areas, just cabins, supply stores and bars. They were told it was populated mostly by men in the shipwreck trade, who preyed upon ocean going freighters crashing on the rocks. The Naval authorities placed the entire island under martial law.

Their father's ship, the Indiana, appeared off Key West; she had taken part in the bombardment of San Juan. The boys had joined Gideon for supper at the officers club, an enormous privilege. Gideon and Adam toasted Joshua and teased him; they knew he didn't want to be there. Joshua could feel the ancient resentments, but now he was in the service and like it or not, things were different.

Gideon looked at his sons and his expression turned serious. "I'm proud of you boys," he said. "I know you'll do well, that you'll look out for each other, that if the time comes you shall comport yourselves bravely." He smiled stiffly. "I assure you things will be fine. The country shall win this war quickly and we shall all come out of this." He stood and put on his cap, bowing his shoulders at them ever so slightly. "I shall keep you in my thoughts, and I wish you Godspeed."

The Indiana left the next day to join the blockade of the Spanish fleet by Rear Admiral William T. Sampson. Sampson needed a nearby area for a coaling station and asked Huntington to send in his Marine battalion to secure the harbor at Guantanamo Bay, which was defended by a single decrepit gunboat and nine thousand Spanish soldiers. On the sixth of June, a day of effervescent splendor, the Panther sailed into Guantanamo harbor.

"It's beautiful here," Adam said.

Joshua nodded. He wondered when the firing would start. The transparent turquoise bay, the gently leaning palm trees, the very silence of the place seemed eerie. The boat dropped anchor. There were flies and mosquitos, the air remarkably hot. Joshua saw two sharks pass under the boat and hoped they wouldn't have to swim.

The Marines disembarked on steam cutters, their newly issued rifles and bayonets clanking awkwardly. Joshua wondered if his brother, sitting beside him, could hear the hollow thumping sound his heart was making. The boat slid onto the beach and they all jumped out and ran knee-deep through tepid water. There was no sign of the Spanish. They were to make their way up a hill and set up camp. On the way up, they were ordered to burn several huts and shacks. Joshua turned to another Marine and asked him why.

"To get rid of the vermin," he answered. "Yella fever, y'know."

They dug in near the top of the sandy hill as the sun set, long shadows catching the beach grass. After midnight, the Spanish opened fire. It was impossible in the darkness to tell where the barrage was coming from, but a lieutenant, himself untested, said it was from a hill farther inland. Joshua and Adam sat pressed tightly among the others in the darkness. Once the Spanish began shooting, they had little choice but to shoot back, beating off swarms of mosquitos, which viciously molested their necks and arms. Joshua looked toward his brother, but could barely see his face. The air was muggy and his shirt and pants felt sticky, but the sandy dirt on which they were perched was chilly and damp. The enemy, wherever they were, continued to fire and the battle raged all night—but it didn't feel to Joshua the way he imagined a real battle should feel. His fear subsided slightly as he pictured groups of men on both sides following orders and firing into the tropical night with little notion of why, although each time the sound of gunshot pierced the peculiar night, he and Adam both jumped. They got no sleep.

As dawn broke over the harbor in a surreal burst of color, the Spanish began to bombard the hill with artillery shells. In what seemed like seconds, several Marines were wounded. They cried out as they fell upon the pink-hued sand, and soon two medics rushed in. One, handsome and tall with a trimmed moustache, was shot in the chest while leaning over a downed Marine, suddenly bleeding profusely a dozen yards from where they were perched. Joshua watched in horror as two other medics dragged him out of the line of fire. Adam and Joshua looked at each other—they were pinned down, and Adam no longer looked so confident.

As Joshua sat there thinking of his brother, the light was fading. He stood, stiff from sitting in the cold, and walked into the little town. Since the night on the beach, he had been thinking about Buddy, wondering what he was doing, how he was feeling—and whether his crazy notion that it had been him on the hill in the dunes could possibly have any truth to it. He found Buddy playing cards at the Mermaid.

"I'd like to speak with you," he said leaning over Buddy's shoulder.

Buddy looked up, surprised to see him. He was ready to jump joyfully to his feet, but caught himself. Instead he just nodded. "Done soon."

Joshua waited at the bar. After ten minutes, Buddy sat next to him and ordered a glass of ale. Both pretended disinterest in seeing the other. Then they both spoke at once.

"How are you?" they blurted simultaneously. They both grinned at the gaff, looked at each other, giggling quietly—then faced forward and nursed their drinks.

After several awkward moments, Buddy turned to Joshua. "What's going on?"

"Nothing much," Joshua said. "You okay?"

"Sure," Buddy said. "Why wouldn't I be?"

"I don't know," Joshua said. He felt tension sweep over him, a tightness in his chest and throat, and his expression grew more severe. Suddenly he was angry. In a tightly controlled voice, he asked, "What the hell are you doing, Buddy?"

"What do you mean?"

"How could you just walk away like that? From the station, from the men, from me?"

Buddy turned, his own face as stern as Joshua had ever seen it. "I had no choice. You know that as well as I do. Those men didn't like me, and made it clear every minute of every day I was there. I didn't like them either. I didn't belong there."

Joshua knew this, of course, and did not disagree. But he began to protest.

Buddy cut him off. "I am sorry, Joshua. I'm sorry I listened to you and joined. I'm sorry I was not well-suited for that place, that I couldn't make it there, or whatever the reason was. I'm sorry I got in that fight with Punchy, and I'm more sorry I got in a fight with you. I mean you no harm—I think of you as my dearest friend. I think you could have done better by me there, with the others… but it doesn't matter now. I'm glad to see you and I wish we could somehow be friends again. But it's over. I'm planning to leave this lousy town. I'm sure you'll understand."

They sat there awkwardly. Then, remembering why he'd come, Joshua said, "There was a hijacking of a ship off Race Point last week."

"A hijacking?" Buddy asked.

"Yes. Several men rowed out to a ship foundering on the bar, took some valuable items at gun point and stole a stack of lumber ."

"That sounds more like a robbery than a hijacking," Buddy said.

"A man was shot," Joshua added.

Buddy looked surprised. "Did he die?"

"No. He was all right. The ship got off the bar, the captain couldn't identify the pirates, and he left town."

"Pirates. That's a strong word. Sounds pretty harmless, all in all," Buddy said.

"Were you part of it?"

Buddy slammed his glass on the bar, spilling half of its contents. "What?"

"Were you part of it?"

Buddy exploded. "You've got a lot of fuckin' nerve," he shouted. He caught his breath and looked at his friend with great earnestness. "Joshua, what on earth would make you ask me such a question?"

A sheepish smile crept over Joshua's face. "A hunch, I'd call it."

"A hunch? That's pretty stupid. Next time you have one, go

have a drink or something." Buddy's tone changed again. "This is what you wanted to talk to me about?"

Joshua didn't trust Buddy's response. He felt badly that this was indeed what he had wanted, but he stuck to his guns. "So you had nothing to do with it?"

"I don't know what you're talking about," Buddy insisted. Joshua placed a coin on the bar. "You look good. How long you sticking around?"

"I don't know. Not much longer."

"Well, so long, Buddy." Joshua turned to go. He was still angry, but also confused.

"See you again, sometime," Buddy called out as Joshua walked away.

Before he went to sleep that night, he wrote a letter to his father.

> *Dear Father,*
> *It was wonderful to hear from you. I'm sorry you have been feeling ill and am glad your health is improving.*
>
> *My life here is challenging. It is a difficult exis-tence by the ocean, and I have seen my share of tragedies. I am concerned over a recent incident involving what might be considered an act of piracy, an attack on a ship foundering on the bars. This is uncommon in these parts. Whilst all this offers its share of excitement for a young fellow like me, there are times I wonder if your advice is more sage than I might think.*

*You are in my thoughts. Please keep me apprised
of your health.*
Joshua

He sealed the letter, dropped it under his bunk, and lay
back. He felt ill at ease. It was a powerful feeling, but he could
not put his finger upon what, if anything, was wrong.

The next Tuesday, the men had lifeboat drill. It was a
gloomy day, not bitterly cold, but grey and clammy, the wind
gusting and tossing whitecaps at them as they grudgingly
pushed into the icy water, their minds still on the hot breakfast of oats and potatoes they'd eaten too quickly. Even after six
months, Joshua found it unpleasant to plunge into cold water
to wrestle with the boat. The men, already wet, were shivering
and in foul moods as they dipped their oars and rowed out
toward the breakers, Pendleton at the helm.

"Fuckin' cold," Silva complained.

"Heard Billy's brother Joey signed on a merchant ship,"
Peter Abbot said.

"Someplace warm, if the son of a bitch has any luck," Silva
said.

Pendleton guided the steering oar. They rose and fell with
the waves, as a few gulls swarmed curiously above their heads.
Punchy began to sing a song in Portuguese.

"What's that yer singin'?" Pendleton asked.

"Just somethin' my mother taught me."

Silva snickered, a bit too loudly. "Doubt it was yer mother."

Punchy began to stand up. "Fuck you!"

"Settle down," Pendleton said.

But it was too late. Punchy's precipitate motion rocked the boat, it listed to port, and a wave caught it and helped it over. The port gunwale dipped in the water, took on more, and the boat swamped. All the men were tossed into the sea. Pendleton, the last to hit the water, cursed loudly as he went over.

Since they had to end up in the water sooner or later as part of the drill, this turn of events didn't seem like much of a disaster. But Jurgen hit his head on the gunwale going over, a nasty gash, and as he thrashed he caught his sleeve and could not get free. He struggled and yelled until Punchy and Joshua got him loose. They had already been in the water longer than they were supposed to be. The men had to flip the boat back while Jurgen tread water. They got back in the boat. Jurgen had broken his wrist and couldn't row. He winced in pain when Punchy touched the head wound.

Pendleton turned the boat around. "That's enough. Let's go in. It's fuckin' freezin.'"

"You got that right," Punchy said.

Jurgen went to town to have his wrist set. The crew was short-handed again, but they managed to get through the week. On Friday it snowed. MacDonald set them all on day and night patrols, even Jurgen, but no ships found their way to the Peaked Hill bars.

After walking the beach round the clock for three days, the men were tired, the skies were clear, and MacDonald gave them a rare Monday off. Joshua went into town. He wanted to see Julia. He had not stopped thinking of her, and whenever he did, he felt plagued by an impalpable physical discomfort, something akin, he imagined, to food poisoning. A calmer voice in his head assured him this mood of hers would pass. They had something, that was clear enough. Whether it was true love he couldn't be sure, since he didn't really know what that was, but it felt powerful enough. Joshua forced himself to try to focus on his work.

Instead of going to see Julia, he went to the New Central House. Dinner and a drink, a game of billiards at the Mermaid, then home to the station—that was what he needed. He sat at the bar and ordered an ale and a plate of beef stew. It was quiet, a weeknight when the wintry weather kept most people home except a few hardcore barflies—fishermen waiting for spring. Joshua dug hungrily into the steaming plate of meat and vegetables. He ate quickly and took several long drinks of ale, happy to be away from the station and sitting someplace warm. The bony piano man played with less spunk than Joshua remembered.

A few people ambled in. In the corner of his eye, Joshua saw a couple approach a table near the window. It was Julia, with a man Joshua had never seen.

She didn't notice him sitting at the bar. She took off her warm cloak and a wool hat; the man pulled out her chair, and she settled into it, her back to Joshua. The man wore a cape and carried a beaver top hat. He was far shorter than Joshua, stockier and older by a decade or two. He had nicely trimmed mutton chops and mustache, and, overall, a refined appearance for this part of the world. The waiter came to their table and the man ordered a bottle of wine. Joshua couldn't help watching. The waiter returned with two glasses, opened the bottle with a flourish and poured them each some wine. The man held up his glass, Julia did the same and they clinked them together. Joshua heard her giggle.

"Anything else, sir?" the bartender asked Joshua.

Joshua turned back to face him. "No… no, thanks."

His head was spinning. He did not have to leave, but he couldn't think of any reason to stay, so he put some coins on the bar and walked out, looking once more at the couple by the window. As he did, the waiter brought their food; Julia turned and saw Joshua watching her at the edge of the hallway. She nodded slightly, then looked away.

In shock, his ears filled with explosions, Joshua left the hotel. He trudged down the middle of the misty road. The town seemed unreal—shadowy, damp, an empty vessel floating helplessly at the edge of the known universe. He turned and headed across the dark dunes; it seemed an extraordinarily long walk. That night he tossed in his narrow bed, awakening in the darkness bewildered and afraid, then recalling the source of his anguish. Yet he marveled at it. Why would seeing her at dinner with another man make him so crazy? He managed finally to sleep. When he was awakened by the other men getting dressed, he felt as though he hadn't slept at all.

The next two days, MacDonald seemed to be watching Joshua as he went through the drills. He was quite aware that he was distracted and of little use. MacDonald took him aside the following day after lunch.

"Are you all right, son?"

Joshua was surprised at the question. "Yes, sir. Of course."

"You seem upset by something."

Joshua paused. "Everything is fine, sir. Sorry if I seem..."

"Forgive my presumption, Mr. Duell," MacDonald said in a tone he only used when he was being fatherly, "but your current state of mind is contributing, I daresay, quite less than zero to the efficiency of the station or the safety of the greater populace. You would be doing everyone a favor if you would take steps to resolve whatever it is."

"Yes, sir," Joshua said.

"And quickly, son."

"Yes, sir."

Sunday was still several more days away and Joshua did the best he could, halfheartedly fulfilling his duties. He felt as if his muscles were on strike. Saturday night he remained at the station for patrol while several of the men went to town. Walking the beach, he looked up at the star-speckled sky and swore loudly at whoever was listening, demanding to know why life—and the women in it—had to be so goddamned capricious.

In the morning, he crossed the dunes. He had to see Julia, to confront her. He would insist on knowing what she was doing. How dare she behave so outrageously, after all they had… What nonsense, he thought. I have no rights here. Still, he had to go.

It was ten o'clock when he reached her door. The sun was shining, which Joshua found somehow ironic. He went through the little gate and knocked. After several minutes, Julia opened the door, dressed in nightclothes with a heavy sweater and a shawl wrapped around her. The fire was not lit. She had been sleeping.

"Joshua! What a nice surprise," she said, stepping aside and suppressing a yawn.

"Are you alone?" he asked.

She looked a little put off by the question. "Of course I am."

He walked to the sofa, removed his coat, and turned to face her. "I'd like to speak with you, Julia." He thought his voice sounded tentative.

"Of course. Sit down," she said. "Would you like some tea?"

"No thanks but go ahead if you like."

Joshua sat down. He felt nervous, and at the same time ridiculous for feeling so nervous. Julia put the kettle over the flame on the stove. Turning her back, she adjusted her night clothes and rewrapped the sweater and shawl. Then she walked over to him.

"I... I don't really understand," he said, looking up.

"What don't you understand, Joshua?"

"I saw you the other night..."

"I know you did. I saw you, too."

"But... how..."

Julia laughed. She didn't mean any harm by it—he was just so adorably befuddled. He looked at her rather sharply.

"I'm sorry, I'm not mocking you," she said. "I guess I'm a bit surprised you'd be shocked I might have dinner with another man."

"Yet you were."

She looked at him, wondering at his immaturity. "Joshua, I'm a good five years older than you, I've been married and divorced, I'm a professional woman and I've been living in this town for a number of years before you came here—"

"Who is he?"

She looked stunned by the question and the intensity with which he asked it. "What difference does it make?" She looked at him. "Oh, for God's sake... he's a banker."

"A banker?"

"Is that so odd? He provides financing for a number of shippers and fishermen around here. He's a very reputable man."

"So you're suggesting that I'm not?"

Julia shook her head. "I like you for who you are."

"But it's not enough for you..." he said.

"Oh, Joshua…"

"Well, that's what you said last time. I couldn't believe it, honestly. I thought we were… I thought there was something special between us."

"You are so young and sweet," Julia said. "My God, I do like you, I do, but I don't think—"

Suddenly, he reached for her skirt. She moved closer, unsure what to do. He wrapped his arms around her legs.

Joshua felt his mind bursting. He was afraid and embarrassed. Yet he pressed on.

"I think I love you, Julia. I… I've never felt like this before." She walked over to the stove and moved the kettle. Then she came and sat next to him. She took his hand.

"I'm sorry. I'm so sorry. I never meant to hurt—"

He reached over and wrapped his arms around her, pressing his lips to hers. The kiss was so desperate and passionate, she felt herself being drawn into it like water rushing out in a riptide. She kissed him hard. He held her closer. Their bodies pressed together. The shawl fell away, and she could feel him against her nakedness under her nightgown. He kissed her neck and the inside of her ear, then her lips again, holding her tighter until she thought she would burst. She pulled back and lifted her head, gasping for air like someone who's been underwater.

"Joshua! My God, what are you…?"

He looked into her eyes. The feeling was unstoppable now. He kissed her again. They slipped off the edge of the sofa and fell to the floor in front of the hearth. He was on top of her. She lifted her knee and felt him pressing against her. She gripped his back, ran her hands through his hair, kissing him wildly. She had never felt like this with any man. He was so driven and wild with his passion for her that she found it irresistible.

Julia tugged at Joshua's shirt. He stopped for a moment and practically tore it off. She caressed his back and shoulders, his hair, his face, his belly. He lowered the wispy silk of her night-gown and took her breast in his mouth. She closed her eyes and put her head back. He lifted her shoulders and pushed the sweater away. She watched him do this, surprised at the change that had come over him; he was gentle, but unwaver-ing. He pulled the other side of the gown down to her waist. She had no time to feel self-conscious about her nakedness. He kissed her breasts, her belly, then moved up again to her neck and lips. He was kneeling over her, caressing her hair. They looked at each other deeply but without thought, only the rushing feeling.

For an instant, she recalled the affair in medical school. But it had not been like this, not like this. She touched his heavy belt. Then she was holding it and pulling him down on her. He pushed against her, kissing her, touching her breasts, then moved back. She watched him undo the belt. She tugged at his pants. He scrambled frantically to get them off. Now he was naked above her. She looked at him. There was no turning back. He settled back down against her, and her gown rode up her thighs. She moved against him and could feel him. She was breathing hard. He slipped inside her. She groaned at the feeling. They moved faster and faster, then slowed and watched each other's eyes, then sped up again. He kissed her and touched her. It made her feel so good. Then, in a final rush that made them both cry out, it was done. He sank into her body and she wrapped her arms around him, staring, bewil-dered, at the ceiling of her cabin.

They rested that way for a long time. Perhaps they both

slept. Then Julia stirred, and became aware of his weight over her. When she tried to shift him, he opened his eyes. He wore a beatific expression, transcendent, as if he had undergone a metanoia.

Julia drew herself free and got up, holding her wrinkled gown at the waist. She put her arms through the straps, covered herself, and then put the sweater back on. He watched. Neither of them spoke. She went into her bedroom and closed the door.

She looked at herself in the small mirror over the dresser, wondering if this had been a terrible mistake. She had such mixed emotions—it wasn't like her to behave so impulsively. And yet her feelings for him were strong. Unable to decide what else to do, she got into bed and pulled the covers over her.

Joshua lay on the floor for what seemed a long time. He could barely believe what had just happened, that it could happen, in this way, with this woman. He felt contented, but plagued with the fear that it had somehow been wrong, that she would react badly afterward. He realized she'd been gone too long. He stood, fixed his pants and went to the bedroom door. He put his head against it and listened.

"Julia," he called softly.

There was no answer. He debated whether to knock again, open the door, or just leave. He stared at the door for a long moment. Finally he summoned the courage to open it. She was asleep in her bed. More confused than ever, Joshua returned to the living room, got dressed and left the cottage.

CHAPTER TWELVE

K irov's little raid had been an inspiration, really. No one had died—and better still, no witnesses remained who could identify them. McGraw, the ship's captain, did manage, with the help of the incoming tide and a shift in the wind, to maneuver off the bar. It was near dawn when the ship had finally limped with one working mast into Province-town. McGraw filed a complaint with the police, although the only person he thought he could identify was "a Negro feller". This didn't lead the investigation very far, and eventually the police dropped it. The captain collected his crew—the man who'd been shot had not been seriously hurt and recovered quickly—and sailed back into the lanes of commerce. Upon returning to Maine, he was promptly relieved of his commis-sion by the ship's owner, who placed a higher value on the lost necklace and rifle than on their friendship.

The night after the raid, Kirov drove the wagon thirty

miles south to the larger town of Hyannis and sold the keg of scotch, the cases of wine, and the lumber to a friend in the trade. The friend paid him two hundred dollars for the Napoleon wine. Kirov knew it would be worth far more than that in New York, but he didn't mind. The lumber fetched a very good price. Kirov kept the long box for himself, not revealing to William and Tucker what was inside. He stashed the necklace in a false panel in the wall of his cottage, and carefully wrapped the beautiful ivory-stocked carbine and hid it from view. Four days later, he paid Buddy two hundred seventy two dollars as his share of the take.

Buddy was relieved to actually be paid, but it wasn't enough to live on in Europe for the rest of the year. In retrospect, it didn't seem worth the risk he had taken, with other people's lives and with his own security. He had gone home afterward, drank half a bottle of whiskey and slept until late the following afternoon. By the time he ate dinner, he was feeling some remorse, which grew on him in the days that followed.

Eight days later, Kirov went to look for Buddy and found him again at the Mermaid. Buddy had had one too many drinks and was talking the ear off a fisherman named Raoul. Kirov sat at the bar next to Buddy and ordered two whiskeys. When they came, he downed one and passed the other to Buddy.

Buddy turned to Kirov. "What are you doing here?"

"Buying you a drink."

Buddy looked at the glass. This must have been what Eve felt like.

"Go on, take it. It's not poison."

"Maybe it is," Buddy said, picked up the glass, and drank the whiskey.

Raoul, like many people in town, thought it better to avoid any contact with Kirov. He excused himself. Buddy turned to the Russian.

"What do you want?" Buddy asked.

"Is that any way to treat a friend?" Kirov said.

"Now you're my friend again. What do I have to do for this friendship?"

"Same thing."

"You mean the beach?" Buddy asked skeptically.

"Yes, the beach," Kirov said. "It was good, the beach. Everyone made money, no one got hurt, everyone's happy."

"No… no, I don't think so. I'm happy enough now," Buddy said.

"You are a bad liar. You're not happy. You're still here."

"Maybe I like it here."

"That's not what you said before. I can pay you more."

"How much?"

"I'll give you one thousand," Kirov said.

"What if you don't make that much?"

The unrelenting smirk on Kirov's face made Buddy feel queasy. He figured the Russian counted on the fact that sooner or later he'd agree, that he needed the money and that he gave the impression he didn't care much about other people. Buddy hated the idea of someone like Kirov thinking he understood him—he knew his real feelings were far more complex than people assumed.

"I like you, so I pay you more. Simple." Kirov paused and looked at him. "Okay?"

Buddy shook his head. "I'll think about it."

"Don't think too long. End of the week the tides are just right."

Buddy wrestled over whether to join up again with Kirov. He didn't want anyone hurt. But he needed the money—it was his ticket out of this hellhole—and he also carried a growing resentment of nearly everyone he'd had any dealings with here: the Life-Savers, the police, Joshua. He slept and ate little and drank too much for two days. Finally, he decided to go along with the Russian one last time. After all, he was only the lookout.

Then the weather improved and there was little likelihood of any disasters. Kirov found Buddy at the bar and told him to keep himself available in case something came up. For the next five nights, Buddy sat at the Mermaid, which he would have done anyway, but he was more nervous and depressed than usual and drank more than he needed to.

The sixth night, it began to rain. Soon torrents poured off the rooftops and splattered the streets, which ran thick with mud. Buddy sat at the bar drinking beers. Suddenly Tucker rushed in, looking like a drenched sewer rat, and grabbed Buddy's collar. Buddy spun around angrily, and Tucker spit the information at him that a ship was foundering out past Race Point and they needed to go right now. Buddy thought he was stupid even to whisper such a thing in public, let alone make a spectacle of it, and he was not happy about going out in this weather. But he followed Tucker outside to the wagon, the handsome skiff resting on its bed.

They met Kirov and William out near the moors. Buddy and Tucker rode in the wagon to the beach, with Kirov and William on horses alongside. The rain continued to fall in buckets and the sand ran with rivers of rain, so the carriage kept getting stuck. The wind howled like an angry demon. On the beach, the wind blew even more wildly, stirring up the whitecaps and breakers.

"How the fuck we gonna row out in this?" Tucker asked.

"Same as before," Kirov said. "You afraid of some waves?"

"I ain't afraid, but it's fuckin' wet and cold!"

"Shut the fuck up," Kirov snapped at him.

They sat looking out at the bleak sea. When their eyes had adjusted, William let out a whoop.

"There she is, the ship, Gogol!"

Buddy could see her. She was limping along with two of her three masts broken, having great trouble keeping on course. Buddy thought it was a miracle she'd made it this far up the coast in that condition.

The ship struck the sandbar. It was closer in here and she couldn't have been more than seventy yards out. They could see the jolt as she hit, and heard the men aboard crying out in panic. The ship immediately tilted to port, taking on water amidships.

Kirov sprung into action. "Let's go!"

They dragged the skiff off the wagon and over to the water's edge. Kirov jumped into the boat while William and Tucker pushed it out. Kirov and Buddy locked eyes.

"You stay here and watch." Kirov reached into his belt and extracted what looked like a derringer brass pistol.

"What the hell is that?"

"It's a Very gun. Shoots a flare. Just squeeze the little trigger if you see them," Kirov said. Then he turned to the others. "Launch her!"

They pushed off into the waves, three ragged men rowing for all they were worth.

It was raining so hard Buddy worried if he hid behind the dune he wouldn't be able to see. He drove the wagon with the horses to the base of the dune, then squinted his eyes in the downpour and watched the ship flailing in the storm.

Buddy felt certain this was one of those moments he would come to deeply regret. What was he doing here in this bleak place, drenched to the bone, watching men about to drown? He thought about simply running away, this very instant, and going however far it might take until he was safe, truly safe.

Then he heard the sound of the ship's hull cracking. Kirov, William and Tucker heard it, too. They rowed near the ship and somehow managed to toss a line to one of the crew. There were five seamen aboard, plus the captain and two mates. Two sailors clung terrified to the ratline while the first mate tried to get them down. Just as the sailor made fast the line Kirov tossed him, one of the men on the ratline succumbed to fear and nature and fell into the sea. His head went under, a wave passed over, and he was gone.

Tucker remained in the boat while Kirov and William jumped aboard. The second mate helped them up. "Life-Savers?" he demanded. Kirov just nodded. He walked over to the captain, a wizened man with a plump face. When Kirov pulled his gun, the captain understood this was no rescue.

"Show me your cabin," Kirov demanded.

The captain nodded and led the way. William remained with his gun trained on the sailors. Kirov and the captain could barely keep their feet as they crossed the deck and made their way through a door, swinging in the wind and rain, into the aft deckhouse. The cabin was a mess, all of its contents flung onto the floor or flying through the air. The captain looked stricken, resigned to whatever fate awaited him; the devil himself was aboard. He pointed to a chest on a railed shelf over the bunk. Kirov reached over and took it.

There was a small silver key stuck in its engraved keyhole. Kirov turned it and opened the heavy top: inside were three necklaces of precious stones, a raw uncut diamond, and a small pouch filled with gold coins. A treasure. Kirov smiled and tucked the box under his arm, then signaled with his gun. They went back out to the wind and crashing waves.

Kirov moved quickly over the deck to where William stood. As they turned to go over the rail, the first mate appeared holding a pistol. He fired at them. A bullet smashed through Tucker's upper body below his right shoulder. William leaped to the skiff and Kirov tossed him the chest and jumped after him. Removing his dagger, he cut the line and the skiff moved quickly away. Kirov tucked the chest under the plank seat, anchored it firmly between his legs, and he and William began to row.

Buddy spotted the familiar lanterns of the Life-Savers moving down the beach, still a half mile away. For a moment he was overwhelmed with panic, afraid to be caught by his former mates, afraid to abandon Kirov and his crew, afraid to be there at all. He fired the flare gun. A sickly yellow light flooded the beach, illuminating the fiercely blowing rain. The flare shot in an arc and hit the water. He found himself praying Kirov and the men would move fast enough to flee the beach before the Life-Savers arrived.

His prayers were answered. The skiff appeared, riding over a wave and hitting the beach. Tucker, half hanging out of the boat, was gushing blood and howling. Kirov jumped out gripping the treasure chest tightly. He shouted to William.

"You drive the cart. Gotta get out of here now!"

Buddy drove the cart over and helped get Tucker in the back.

"What about the skiff?" Buddy asked.

"Forget the fuckin' skiff. Leave it! Go!" Kirov yelled. He grabbed his own horse and jumped up, the chest under his arm. With his other arm he reached down and grabbed the reins of William's horse, wrapped it around his saddle and took off down the beach.

Buddy and William looked at each other. The lanterns were not far off. They mounted the wagon, William grabbed the reins and they followed Kirov as fast as they could in the slushy sand. For a while, Tucker continued to moan, then fell quiet.

By the time the Life-Savers reached the spot, unloaded their boat and rowed out, the ship had split in two. The second mate and another sailor, caught in the rigging as the last mast teetered and fell, were dragged over with it and drowned. The captain, first mate, and two remaining sailors watched the real Life-Savers approach. The tide was going out and the water separating the ship from the shore was shallower and less violent than it had been. Pendleton, at the helm, called to the captain, who reported their condition. Pendleton decided to take them all. It was a close call, but they managed to get aboard the lifeboat. Punchy cut them free and the men rowed hard and reached the shore in one piece.

They made their way back to the station with the four staggering survivors. Joshua saw the captain stop in the beating rain, which ran off the visor of his cap over his hardened face, and watch his proud ship breaking to bits on the bar. He'd lost his home and his life of thirty years, and three men whose bodies would wash ashore in the morning or slip out to sea, never to see this world again.

At the station the seamen were given food and drink and sent to sleep upstairs. The captain stayed in the galley with MacDonald and Pendleton. He told them about the bizarre robbery of his ship. MacDonald nodded. He could see a pattern developing, and he didn't like it. Not one bit.

The day after the wreck, the sea was once again calm and a hazy sun spread over the beach like a malaise. As Joshua walked toward Race Point, he could see the remains of the ship. Half her hull rested askew in the sand, exposed by the falling tide. The remainder of the ship and all its debris drifted over the water and across the beach in a broad swath. Just a few townspeople sifted through the wreckage. One body had washed up and two men from town were loading it on a wagon. Kirov and his men were nowhere to be seen.

At breakfast, MacDonald and the other men discussed the wreck.

"Looks like the same bunch as did the last one. Same pattern as before. This time they left without their skiff," MacDonald said.

"I think we'll hang onto that one," Pendleton said. "It's a beauty."

"Not quite the same pattern," Joshua said. "There was no flare in the sand."

"True," MacDonald said. "One of the thieves got shot, according to the captain. The police are looking for traces of him."

"What about the missing sailors?" Jurgen asked.

"Found one body ashore. The others are probably gone."

Punchy looked at all of them. "Three men dead. Oughta do something about this, don't ya think, Cap'n?"

MacDonald nodded. "Aye, that we should."

"But it's not like these men caused the wreck," Peter Abbot said.

"No, but they robbed the ship," Joshua said.

"It's piracy," Pendleton observed. "Isn't it?"

"It's against the law, that's for sure," MacDonald said.

"And they did it on our fuckin' beach," said Punchy.

The men all grumbled in agreement.

"Who are these men? Anyone know?" MacDonald asked.

Joshua looked out the window and said nothing.

The escape from the beach had been hell for Buddy. He was terrified of being found out and angry beyond words with Kirov and his two idiot cronies who had so badly botched what should have been quick and simple. Above all, he again cursed himself for not foreseeing what might happen and for getting drawn in to another dangerous, hare-brained scheme. As they slogged through the sand, the rain still coming down, Tucker wailing and William yelling at him to stop, Buddy sat in the dreadful cart planning his escape. Whether or not Kirov paid him, he would leave town the next day and go as far away as he could manage. Then he could decide what to do next. He swore, like an alcoholic in the morning, that he would never do such a stupid thing again.

William drove the cart to Kirov's cabin. Kirov was not there. Buddy imagined he had run off with whatever had been in the chest he was clutching and abandoned his accomplices to their own fates. Buddy helped William get Tucker into the cabin. Then he went back out into the rain, removed his blood-stained shirt and buried it. He made his way to his hotel.

In the morning, the town was in an uproar. MacDonald went to Chief Nickerson and told him what had occurred. The police began to search for a wounded man. Suspicious, Nickerson sent two officers to look for Kirov. No one answered at his cabin and for some reason the policemen did not break in, or they would have found Tucker unconscious on the sofa and William behind the door with his gun drawn.

Tucker's wound was not fatal, though he was in pain; William had cleaned and bound it and plied his friend with liquor. After the police left, William decided they couldn't stay there and he went off to fetch a wagon. While he was gone, the policemen circled back to try again. This time they broke down the door and found Tucker. He was placed under arrest and hauled away. As the police wagon drove toward the center of town, William passed it going the other way in a buckboard he had just stolen. He could see Tucker's face as the police passed by. In a panic, William saddled his own horse and headed for Wellfleet, to a cabin Kirov sometimes used, and where he found the Russian.

When William told him what had happened, Kirov threw a chair at him. "Stupid fucking idiot!" he shouted. "How could you let them find him like that?"

William's face twisted with anxiety. "What are we gonna do, Gogol?"

"We'll get him out, of course."

With MacDonald's permission, Joshua went into town the next evening to look for Buddy. He could not put his finger on what exactly made him suspect that Buddy had something to do with the two piracy incidents, but though he tried to push it out of his mind, it nagged him persistently. He had not informed MacDonald or anyone else of his suspicions. He had seen no tangible evidence Buddy knew anything—but his instinct told him something funny was going on. His relationship with Buddy had always been peppered with emotional zigzags, but it had allowed him a window onto a complex and sometimes twisted mind. It was frankly what made Buddy charismatic and intriguing, but it left open the possibility he might do something dangerous. He was certainly capable of it.

He entered the New Central House, taken aback by the brightness and noise, the women in flowery gowns and men in suits and ties and bowlers, smoking cigars, waving beers in the air and shouting jovially, all carrying on as if nothing could be wrong with the world. He remembered the sense of giddiness he and Buddy had felt when they first came to this place, the freshness of it all, the endless possibilities of summer. He ordered a beer, and then took it outside to look at the harbor and clear his mind. The brisk air felt fresh, and he walked to the rail and looked out over the dark water. The dim glow emanating from the wintry town reflected off the low lying clouds.

"Hello, Joshua," said a voice in the darkness.

Joshua squinted and could see someone sitting on a chair in the shadow of the building. "Who is it?"

"It's me. Buddy." The steam of his breath puffed out into the cold.

"What are you doing out here?" Joshua asked.

"I felt like getting some air."

"You never do that." Joshua peered at him in the darkness.

"Maybe you're hiding."

"No!" Buddy insisted. "No, not at all. It was hot and noisy in there. I'm getting tired of this town." He smiled. "You always walk out here for a breath of air when you come to this place."

Joshua sighed and looked at his friend, if that's what he still was. "What's your connection with Kirov?"

"He's a slime. You know that."

"Yes," Joshua said. "I do know that. But I've heard tell you and he have been pretty friendly of late."

"Not true. We've never been friendly." Buddy paused, as if drawing distant facts from the ether. "We did have a beer or two together earlier in the year."

"Why was that?"

"He came over to me. Seemed to want something. He bought me a beer. I drank it." Buddy seemed pleased with his answer.

"You're being smug," Joshua said. "But you're not telling me anything."

"There's nothing to tell."

Not for the first time, Joshua felt the impulse to strangle Buddy. Yet at the same time he felt a tinge of regret—maybe he was looking for a reason to blame Buddy and be angry with him, maybe Buddy was right and Joshua was chronically unfair to him. But another thought overpowered that one: that Buddy was playing him, that somehow the mysterious robberies were something between him and Buddy—which of course was not possible.

Joshua walked over to where Buddy was sitting. "Get up," he demanded.

Buddy stood and faced him. Then in a gesture of defiance

he relaxed and leaned against the railing. "What?" he asked quietly.

Joshua moved closer and with a sudden, violent motion that shocked them both, he pushed Buddy hard against the railing, hard enough so Buddy's head hung over the edge.

"What are you doing?" Buddy shouted, more alarmed than angry and shoving back.

Joshua leaned his face close to Buddy's, his hand now around his neck. "Listen to me, my friend. We've had our differences. You left me at the station and went off on your own; no one made you go. There has been some funny business around here, and people are ending up dead. I think you know something about it. And you're going to tell me what you know." He said this through gritted teeth. "You understand me?"

Buddy pushed back, shoving Joshua's chest and driving him backwards. He straightened and brushed himself off. "I don't know what your problem is, but don't you ever do that to me again!"

"I know that tone in your voice, the one you get when you're cornered or pushed. 'I'm warning you, sir!'" Joshua said, mocking him. "But I'm not buying it." Joshua's voice grew yet darker. "You want to have it out right here and now?"

"Go to hell," Buddy shouted.

Joshua hauled back and swung his closed fist solidly at Buddy's jaw. Buddy's head spun back; he staggered against the rail, and then crumpled to the deck.

"I want to know what you know about this," Joshua demanded.

"What, are you crazy?" Buddy shouted. "I'm telling you, I don't know a thing."

"I think you're lying." That damned voice still nagged him, that voice of doubt—did he really believe this? But he reached down, grabbed Buddy up by his collar and hit him again, this time in the chest.

Buddy slumped, then struggled to pull himself up. Grabbing the rail to steady himself, he took a swing at Joshua, who pushed him so hard he fell back and his head hit the rail. He lay supine on the deck.

"Are you working with Kirov?"

"I know nothing about it!" Buddy yelled, his face twisting up toward Joshua. "Nothing!"

Joshua moved over him and slapped his face hard enough to pop blood vessels. He knew he was out of control, especially since he was only fishing and had no idea whether Buddy really knew anything. But this irrational anger took hold of him and he punched him again. Buddy's face was bleeding and he was half crying. Joshua set his fist to strike yet again—but someone grabbed his hand.

"That's enough now!" a stranger yelled, and pushed him violently away from Buddy.

The two of them sat sprawled on the cold floor of the deck, out of breath and looking at one another. Buddy spat out some blood. He had a long cut on his forehead. Joshua got up, grabbed his hat from the deck, and stormed through the door into the bar. People gaped at him, but he kept going, through the lobby and out into the night, his heart pounding. He walked back to the station. He knew he had overreacted, that his anger was based on more than just Buddy, no matter what mischief he had gotten himself into. Maybe it was Julia. Maybe it was his life here, in this empty place, surrounded by danger and death. Maybe it was him.

All week, he was tormented by images of Buddy's face, which somehow took on an innocence he knew, in truth, wasn't there. The next Sunday morning, he returned to town. Small groups of people walked along quietly, dressed in finery and headed to church. It had been a long time since Joshua had been to any service other than a funeral. He stopped at a Methodist Church in a small white clapboard building. The service had begun, and Joshua removed his cap, but stood at the back. The preacher had a pleasant, lyrical voice as he spoke about God and the sea. Joshua didn't pay much attention but looked at the earnest faces following the preacher's words. People's needs can be so basic, he thought: sanctuary in the face of an intimidating universe, love, friendship, a warm home to retreat to. The denizens of this place lived simple lives, yet they seemed more self-assured and less troubled in their lives than many more sophisticated people he'd known in New York.

After the service, Joshua walked to the other end of town and knocked on Julia's door. She answered promptly and appeared dressed to go out.

"Joshua!" she said. "What are you doing here?"

Joshua nodded in the direction of the interior. "Do you mind if we speak a moment?"

"I do mind," she said brusquely. "I've got nothing to say to you."

"What do you mean?"

"What has happened to you? I was awakened late in the evening with an emergency call. I had to give your friend Buddy three stitches in his forehead, for God's sake! He told me you attacked him. What could have possessed you to behave like that?"

"Perhaps I was possessed. I don't know."

"Is he your friend, or not?" Julia demanded.

"Well, yes, I thought so, but… I'm not really sure, to be honest."

"Then what…?"

"I am convinced Buddy knows something about these hijackings on the back shore."

Julia looked astonished. "What, pray tell, makes you think such a thing?"

"I was told he has been seen with Kirov."

"Kirov. The Russian hooligan?" Julia asked.

"The very same," Joshua said. "There's a suspicion Kirov and his men are behind it."

"My God, Joshua," she looked at him with a mixture of pity and disgust. "So you tried to beat it out of him?"

"I'm not saying it was rational. Nor would I say in the aftermath I feel terribly good about it."

"This is not you," Julia said. "I'm shocked." She looked deep into his eyes, as if reevaluating him.

"Listen, Julia, I came to see you about something else…"

"I'm sorry, Joshua. I must tell you. I've been seeing the banker again."

"What? But why?" Joshua felt his breath growing shorter, his heart beating faster. "I thought—"

"You thought what? That after we made love we would be together forever?"

"That's a rather callous question. Something like that, yes. Is that wrong?"

Julia smiled at him. "You're such a child."

"I don't see what is childish about loving someone."

"You see, my instincts are right. You're out at the beach,

risking your life, saving people from shipwrecks and pirates, you're brawling in the bars, you're sure, you're unsure, you're here, you're not… and now you love me?"

"I… I think so."

"My poor Joshua, it is too bad you're not older, or I'm not younger, but this is not going to work." She looked at him tenderly, and touched his cheek. "I do like you. Quite a bit. But I've got my own life to lead. I'm sorry."

"I don't really understand," Joshua said meekly.

"Well, perhaps you will one of these days. But you must excuse me, I'm late for an appointment."

Julia put on her cloak and looked at him one last time, then brushed past him, and walked down the street, leaving him to stand in her doorway watching her go.

Joshua walked along the sand flats. He felt lost, angry, mystified really—maybe his father had been right, maybe he didn't belong here.

CHAPTER THIRTEEN

All day long, they had returned fire, dug in on their steamy hill, bombarded by Spanish artillery. They had dried provisions, but Joshua was hungry and dehydrated, and felt slightly ill in the sticky heat. The wind died and no breeze arrived to relieve them, just the lingering smell of blood and flies.

In the late afternoon, a man fifty feet from where Adam and Joshua crouched let out a startling cry, his wrist shattered by a rifle shell. A medic rushed over and bandaged him, and he was taken back to the beach. The assault continued, neither side making the slightest progress against the other. Finally, suddenly, the smoke and cannon fire stopped. After a half hour of silence, during which they squirmed uncomfortably waiting for the next barrage, someone stood and moved toward the center of the little camp they had set up the night before and made a fire. Mumbling, fearful, filthy and soaked with sweat, the men slowly moved in and sat in a circle to eat their first meal of hardtack and coffee. Someone cut a long, narrow tree trunk and they raised the Stars and Stripes on their little hill, the first American flag planted on Cuban soil. The Spanish seemed to have vanished.

That night, sitting in the dampness and heat swarmed by mosquitoes and sand fleas beneath a glorious moon, the firing resumed. When a troop of Spanish soldiers rushed over the ridge, Joshua was surprised that a rush of energy and rage replaced his nagging fear. The men gave a massive shout, rallied and fought back, firing and reloading rapidly. Somehow they pushed the Spaniards back down the hill. Bullets were flying everywhere and Joshua's head spun. Mostly he fired into the darkness, but one Spanish soldier surprised him as he ran from behind a tree. Joshua fired his rifle and the man went down. A mere shadow, there and then not, a moment in time, simple and horrific. Two more men in their unit were wounded; the firing continued sporadically, and once again, no one slept.

Nearby was a place called Cuzco Well, and the Admiral had asked Huntington to destroy the Spaniards' water supply there. As the sun rose on the third day of firing the two companies of Marines were joined by sixty-five Cuban guerrillas, and they were ordered to take the well. They cowered behind palm trees and outcrops of rock, pummeled by Spanish artillery hidden in a nearby cemetery. Like most of the others, Joshua and Adam were tired and losing faith. Then two American cruisers steamed around a bend and began firing artillery shells at the Spanish positions. The Marines were caught in the middle of a firefight. A shell smashed into a tree just twenty feet from the boys and a large piece of shrapnel caught a nearby Marine in the side, ripping him open.

As the man screamed, the brothers turned. A Spanish soldier jumped from behind a tree fifty yards away and ran toward Adam, firing rapidly. Joshua watched this specter of death running at them. He pointed his rifle and fired. It jammed. He struggled with the bolt, but nothing happened. His bayonet was fixed on the end of his rifle. He leaped up, and with a piercing yell in a voice not his own, charged at the Spaniard, who continued firing. He heard Adam cry out. In a blind panic, Joshua plunged the blade into the man's chest. The blade seemed to quiver as it pierced the flesh between the soldier's ribs. The Spaniard's eyes peered deep into his as he fell to the ground and died. He ran over to his brother, who was bleeding heavily, then yelled for help. He had killed his brother's shooter, but he'd been too late.

Adam had been hit three times, in the shoulder, side and hip. He was in severe pain and shock from loss of blood. He grimaced frighteningly, but made barely a sound. Joshua sat by him, holding his hand as two medics examined him and taped his wounds. He prayed silently his brother wouldn't die there on a sun-drenched tropical beach so far from home. When they placed Adam on a stretcher to take him to the ship, Joshua tried to go, too. His sergeant, a big fellow named Koppelberger, stopped him. The Marines were in the middle of a serious battle and Joshua had to remain with the company. He watched as they carried Adam away, wiping muddy tears from his face with his sleeve.

After Adam had been shot on the beach in Cuba, Joshua's battalion had regrouped, taken the well and destroyed it. They'd won the battle. A dozen Americans had died, along with twice that many Spaniards. Joshua felt something slip away from him, the fear he had been fighting off, the fatigue and anger and confusion, and something else, some piece of his soul. Making sure none of his fellow soldiers could see, he slumped to the sand and wept.

This was not honor or glory or any of the grand things people mention when they talk about war—but two days later, several American and British journalists showed up to take pictures and post stories, among them the novelist and journalist Stephen Crane, whose story about them made its way to all the best papers. One Marine was given the Medal of Honor and the action made the Fleet Marine Expeditionary Force the stuff of legend. Joshua felt sick over the whole affair. His brother had been shot, perhaps fatally, and for what? To blow up a well, burn some shacks, stop a small bunch of tired Spanish soldiers anxious to get home without contracting a tropical disease or getting shot? It seemed to Joshua a mockery of honor.

Adam was sent by ship to New York, where Lucy met him and stayed by his side in the hospital. The vessel that carried Adam home was filled with wounded and sick men from the Cuba and Puerto Rico campaigns, a modern ship that stank of rot and blood and disease. Far more men died of typhoid and smallpox than of battle wounds. Against Lucy's vehement protests, Adam was sent with other sick and wounded to a facility at Montauk Point for rehabilitation.

Joshua's battalion saw no further action, but languished in Cuba all summer in the heat. He finally returned home in late September. The Americans had rained down destruction upon the Cuban villages and devastated the Philippines, and the war against Spain was won. His mother met him at the train station, hugging him tightly, sobbing on his shoulder, relieved to have him safely home. They went to the old house, which felt abandoned, then traveled by coach to Montauk to see Adam. Lucy arranged for rooms at a nearby boarding house.

When Joshua first saw Adam, he was shocked at the change in him. He was thin and weak, his skin pale; his eyes had lost the sparkle they once had. His voice was soft and raspy, and he coughed between sentences. The coughing was a deep, viscous rattle. Joshua tried to seem upbeat, but Adam patted his hand and smiled thinly at him.

"I know I don't look very good," he said.

"No, you look fine."

"You were always a crappy liar. How was the rest of the war?"

"Not nearly as much fun as when you were there," Joshua said, trying to be jovial.

Adam patted his hand again. "I know," he said, and closed his eyes.

The doctor told them Adam's wounds were healing, but he was not properly recovering. He seemed to be developing a respiratory problem, but they would watch him closely. Outside the building, Lucy leaned against a wall and wept, the only time Joshua could remember seeing her do that.

They spent the autumn there, on the eastern tip of Long Island, where Joshua would go for long solitary walks along the beach, watching the waves crash as winter gathered its forces, haunted by the faces of the two men he had killed. He watched his mother's growing anxiety as she prepared herself for the worst. She complained often that Gideon was not there, but he had remained in Cuba, where the Indiana played a key role in one of the most significant battles, helping to wipe out the Spanish fleet. Lucy telegraphed often that she was concerned for Adam's health, but Gideon was not one to shirk his responsibilities and didn't arrive in New York until late November. He requested reassignment and joined Lucy and Joshua in Montauk in time for a somber Thanksgiving.

The family celebrated the holiday with Adam at his bedside. Lucy had arranged for dinner to be brought for them and the other wounded soldiers, with turkey and stuffing, potatoes and cranberries, glasses of ale, candles scattered around the room—all the exquisite things they had always shared together on this day. Gideon was resolute in his effort to remain cheerful and supportive of his son. He kept referring to him as "the hero of Guantanamo", and Adam tried hard to smile. His infirmity was wearing on all of them, and when Gideon and Lucy went outside for some fresh air, Joshua sat next to his brother.

Adam took his hand. "Listen to me," he said. "I have something to say."

Joshua nodded. Adam's voice was even weaker and raspier than before.

"I know we haven't always seen eye to eye…"

"We're brothers," Joshua said. "We're not supposed to."

Adam nodded. "I know you thought I was stealing Father's attention, and you never liked all that military stuff."

Joshua appeared uncomfortable with his brother's tone. "Never mind," Adam said. "You did well in Cuba, and I was proud of you."

"I didn't," Joshua said, choking slightly.

"I was proud of you, and I want to ask something of you."

"Anything," Joshua said.

Adam nodded again. His face was strained; he was growing tired. "I want you to promise you'll look out for Mother and Father…"

"Don't talk like that!" Joshua shouted.

"I mean it," Adam continued. "If for some reason I'm not around, I'm expecting you to make sure Mother is all right. Particularly her. You've always been closer to her than I have, but I love her more than she knows. Father is a tough old bird, but I know this whole thing…" he paused and looked at the ceiling. "This whole thing with me, the war, it has been hard on her. I want you to make sure…"

"You know I will. You know I will," Joshua said. "But please, stop this way of talking, will you?"

"I'm going to sleep for a while now," Adam said, and he closed his eyes.

Sometimes Joshua would awaken in the middle of the night at the station, surrounded by sleeping men living and working at the edge of the sea, and remember that moment, the last real conversation he'd had with his brother. Adam had gone downhill after that, his condition deteriorating beyond hope. On the ninth of December, he finally succumbed to prolonged complications from pneumonia and died, quietly wheezing and ghostly pale, his mother, father and brother by his side.

The next day was one of utter emptiness, as Joshua remembered it, for all of them—although he later became aware that the Treaty of Paris was signed on that day, ending what would be known as the Spanish American War. In it, Spain recognized Cuba's independence, ceded Guam and Puerto Rico to the United States, and gave America the

Philippines for twenty million dollars. It was the last official American war of the nineteenth century, although it went on five more years as the Americans, turning against the Filipino rebels who had helped them defeat Spain, pursued an unacknowledged conflict deep in the jungle that meant the deaths of many Americans and native guerillas and was deeply criticized by many at home, including Mark Twain and Andrew Carnegie, who formed a group called the Anti-Imperialists.

The Duells went to Arlington Cemetery to bury their son. They traveled by train, in the gloom of a rainy December, to lay Adam to rest to the sound of fifes and drums as a hero of the Cuban campaign. Even Gideon, reading from the family bible and holding back tears, had trouble considering him as such. Though Gideon had witnessed the deaths of many young men, Joshua could see in his father's face the toll Adam's loss had taken on him. Joshua and his mother had wept openly.

Then the family took the train back home—but Lucy had decided to continue on and visit her sister in Boston.

CHAPTER FOURTEEN

S till reeling from his talk with Julia, Joshua went to the
Mermaid. It was mid-afternoon, but he got a beer and
watched a game of pocket billiards being played by
two sailors. They played well, but the older man, sporting a
short beard speckled with grey, had the keener eye and was
winning. As the game came to its end, Joshua stepped up. He
had played at Harvard and enjoyed the game.

The man racked the balls, leaving a perfect triangle
pointing toward the opposite end of the table. He set the cue
ball and with a look of hard concentration snapped the stick.
The ball flew across the table and hit the array with a loud
clack. They spread out in geometric patterns. The three and
six went in. Continuing his assault, he dropped the one and
five balls in the side pockets. Then he went for the four, which
sat in front of the twelve near the far right corner.

"Four ball right pocket," he called out.

He took his time lining up the cue. Then he took the shot. The ball moved the twelve forward, pushing the four, but the angle was off and the balls veered to the left. The man muttered under his breath.

Joshua took up his cue. He pocketed the nine ball, then the ten. He called each one as he saw it, executing each shot with precision. The fourteen required a bank shot. He leaned over and lined it up, his eyes peeled, then fired. But physics pulled the ball just a hair to the right and it missed. The other man had three balls remaining before the eight. He took his first shot, sinking the six. The four ball required the use of a bridge. He chalked his cue, set up the bridge, then aimed. He made the shot. The last, the seven, seemed ready to go. The man took a breath and fired confidently. Too confidently, for the cue ball skimmed past its mark, tapping it on the left, but too lightly to gain the pocket.

"Shit!" the man cried.

Joshua pocketed his last two balls, then called the eight in the center. It was partly blocked by the four ball. The shot would require a reverse angle, just tapping the eight on a cross shot that would send it gently in. It would have to be just right, not too quick, not too soft. Joshua straightened and chalked his cue. He walked once around the table.

"Come on, take the damn shot, will ya?" the man said impatiently.

Joshua ignored him, stepped closer, cradled the cue on his spread fingers and fired. The ball kissed the edge of the black eight with enough power to move it forward at a gentle roll. It lingered at the edge defiantly while the men around the table watched, muttering comments, then fell gently into the pocket. Several men cheered. The man placed his cue on the table and walked away. Joshua felt triumphant, momentarily forgetting his black mood.

One of the onlookers offered to buy him a drink and he accepted. He went to the bar and had a whiskey. This led to another. He was feeling elated and reckless—never a good combination when whiskey is freely at hand. He ordered a third as his ill temper began to reassert itself. He looked around the room at the throng and felt suddenly alone.

Then, like a ghastly specter, there was Kirov, grinning like a canary-gorged cat. "Nice game ya played before. I admired yer skill."

Was it really the Russian standing there gloating at him? Or a delirium fueled by liquor? Joshua looked at Kirov. "You're trying to get out of this thing you've done. Think you're pretty smart…"

Kirov looked at him without changing his expression.

"Well, Mr. Kirov, you're not going to win."

Kirov grinned even more broadly. "We'll see, young sprite, we'll see." And he drifted away across the room.

Compelled by some inexpressible force, Joshua followed Kirov out of the bar and into the street, where he caught up with him and grabbed his shoulder.

"No," Joshua heard himself say, too loudly. "You won't."

He took a swing and hit Kirov in the cheek. The Russian staggered a bit, then looked back at Joshua with a foul grimace.

"You're gonna be sorry for that, young sprite."

Joshua was too drunk to know what he was angry about, but he swung again as Kirov got closer, and hit him again in the face. Kirov fell to his knees and rubbed his face, stunned.

Then Joshua saw the glitter of silver. The brooch, the one

his mother had worn. Kirov still had it on his vest.

"Where did you get that?" Joshua demanded, pointing at the brooch.

But Kirov's fist found its mark, hitting Joshua in the gut and knocking him down. He felt a warm sickness spread quickly over the middle of his body. He vomited, then got himself to his feet.

"I want to know where you got that brooch," he demanded again.

"Fuck you!" Kirov shouted, hitting Joshua in the jaw.

He fell again and once more got to his feet.

"That belonged to my mother. Where'd you get it?"

"I said go fuck yerself!" Kirov swung, hitting Joshua's shoulder. "Fuck you and fuck yer mother, wherever she is."

Joshua felt rage fill his eyes and ears like a red storm, and he flailed blindly at Kirov, who hit him over and over until Joshua lay face down in the muddy sand road. Then Kirov took his dagger from his belt and pressed the blade into the space between his shoulders.

"I took the fuckin' thing from a woman what died in a wreck." He pressed the blade down, breaking the surface of the skin. "I took other things, too, and I had my way with her, then I cast her aside."

Joshua groaned and tried to get up.

"Ah, fuck it," Kirov said. "You ain't worth the trouble."

He reversed the hand that held the blade, and with the knife's grip hit Joshua hard in the back of his head.

"Fuck you, little Life-Saver, fuck you," Kirov said, and tottered away into the night.

Joshua lay in the dirt, his head spinning with pain and uncertainty. Had he really heard those words from the Russian's foul mouth? Could any of what he'd said be true? He might never know. He lay there until the cold shook him awake and he stumbled to his feet and began to walk, tripping and staggering, toward the west end. He had no goal, no more thoughts in his brain. He simply followed one foot behind the other, until he found himself near the darkened moors at the end of town.

There was no moon, though the sky was clear and bright with stars. It was mid-tide and a prickly wind blew across the moors. He walked through the knee deep water, feeling his way to the edge of the marsh and up the small dunes there. He descended to the beach, where the land turns sharply to form the last crooked limb at the tip of the Cape, and continued northwest until he reached the tidal flats. The water churned with the incoming tide. Just up from the tide basin was a series of dunes known as Snake Hills. Joshua had never walked here. There was something magnificent about such a barren corner of the earth, exposed, weather beaten, a place of solitude and nature. Few humans came to this place—the Life-Saver patrols, the fishermen of Helltown. Helltown was gone, though it was said a few men still came to fish in the coldest months. The whales passed in spring and fall; dolphins, sharks and seals plied the waters; sea birds thrived, free of predators. Joshua walked into the low hills and climbed to the top of a dune. Turning away from the sea, he saw a dim flickering light from a hollow a good distance away and walked toward it.

The sand hills surrounded a canyon created by a series of small basins. A half mile in, a long, low cabin was nestled against a dune, like a Quonset hut but with a pointed roof of old wood shakes and a rickety iron chimney. The dim light came from an opening, a window with no glass. Inside, light flickered from a burning fire. Joshua approached. At one end was a doorway covered with animal skins. He peered in at a room the length of the hut, its spaces hidden in shadows. On one side in the middle was a fireplace fashioned from a large cast iron box perched on stones. The floor was sand. In spite of the chilly outside wind, the room felt warm from the fire.

Before the flames sat an old man wizened by time. In the dim light it was difficult to make out his features; he had dark stringy hair with streaks of silver and gray that hung to his shoulders and his chiseled cheekbones suggested the features of an Indian.

Joshua called out, "Hello. May I come in?"

The Indian glanced in his direction, not the least disturbed by the appearance of another human. Joshua walked toward the fire. The man sat cross-legged, poking at the logs with a long stick. Joshua sat next to him. Neither said a word, but sat watching the flames. After maybe a quarter of an hour, the man walked to one wall, retrieved three pieces of driftwood, placed them on the fire and sat back down.

Joshua turned and looked at him. In the firelight, his face was more visible: an old face, decades of lines and ridges, toughened by outdoor living, as if impervious to the ravages of the sea or of any other obstacle that might come at him. Yet it was an exceedingly handsome face with all its ridges and crevices: a long and regal nose that hooked slightly at the tip, high cheekbones and a rich mouth with ruby lips that pushed outward like fruit. Up close, his hair was an astonishing helmet of thick woven strands in many shades of black and grey, parted in the center and resting on the man's strong shoulders. He wore an old chamois shirt and faded canvas pants, his feet bare.

The Indian pulled a tobacco pouch from inside his shirt and rolled a cigarette. He handed it to Joshua, and then rolled himself one. He put the stick in the fire until it flamed, then lit both their cigarettes, still without uttering a word. Joshua never smoked cigarettes, but this was an offering without choice, a gesture between two men in the night, and he puffed the harsh tobacco and continued to stare into the fire.

The man spoke, a rich, deep voice that cracked slightly. "It's a dark night. Why are you here?"

"I felt like walking," Joshua replied.

"Many men would stay home a night like this."

"Yes, I suppose so. I like the beach at night. The cold doesn't bother me."

The man nodded in agreement, uttering a brief grunt. "What do you want?"

"I want nothing," Joshua said.

The man studied him for a few moments. He lifted Joshua's hand and examined it.

"Fisherman?"

"No," said Joshua. "I'm not."

"Life-Saver?"

Joshua nodded, though he felt a lump in his throat. It occurred to him suddenly that he should have reported back to the station long ago. He pushed the thought aside. "And you, how long have you lived here?"

"I live here when I am here, but it's been a long time."

"Where do you live when you're not here?"

The man looked at him. "When I was younger I traveled the wide world, hunting whale."

"And now?"

"Now I am at this place much of the time. In summer I fish further south, but in winter I fish here."

"You fish out here?" Joshua repeated.

"Fishing is good in winter. It has always been good."

"Always?"

"Yes. Helltown was here, or close."

"I've heard of it," Joshua said.

The Indian's cracked face broke into a kind of grin. "Helltown was a special place. Men came to live in the cold months when the sea became too wild for the big ships to go out. They lived in shacks and fished from dories. It is hard work to fish from a dory."

They stared at the flames for a while. The Indian got up and went to an area that resembled a kitchen. He grabbed a whiskey bottle and two glasses. He returned to where he'd been sitting, folded his legs again, then poured whiskey into the glasses. He handed one to Joshua.

"Thank you," Joshua said. It tasted good. The room was smoky and dark. The wind howled outside. "I've heard they called it Helltown because men were wild, there were whores, lots of drinking."

"That is one story," the Indian said. "But it was not that way. Life was not easy. Many men with little comfort. Men who worked hard."

Joshua nodded.

"Whaling was harder."

Joshua nodded again. "What are you called?" he asked the man.

"Shep."

"Why Shep?"

The man stirred the fire. "White man gets confused. Often, I'd say. My people called me Chepewessin. Means the northeast wind. I have always liked the storms." His expression grew warm again. "And the storms have liked me. I was a boy when I went on my first ship. Two years, a New Bedford whaler. We hunted off Chile and sailed around the horn. Many bad storms. First mate learned the meaning of my name, threw me off the ship in Montevideo. Men on the ship couldn't pronounce my name anyway, only part they could get was Shep. Next ship I sailed on that was my name."

Joshua liked the man. "You enjoyed whale hunting?"

Shep nodded. "Hard work, but amazing animals. Smart as men, smarter than some men, that's for sure."

He rolled another cigarette, offered it to Joshua. He shook his head.

"You fish?" Shep asked.

"I worked on a boat once, and fished with my father. Long ago."

"You want to fish with me?"

"I don't know," Joshua said. "I'm not sure what the hell I'm doing, to be honest."

"Fishing is good for making a man think straight." He filled Joshua's glass, then his own. He tossed back the shot. "You stay here tonight. Sleep by the fire, stay warm. In the morning you decide what to do next."

"Thank you. I think I'll do that."

They sat for another hour. It was the middle of the night, Joshua had drunk too much, yet he was awake, his mind whirled with thoughts, doubts, images. He stared at the fire, listening to the sea outside, the crackling wood inside. He stretched out on the sand, feeling the fire's warmth, the cold of the night, the dampness of the ocean. After a while, he closed his eyes.

He awoke a few hours later. It was early morning; he could hear sea birds. The Indian was cutting pieces of fish. The fire had been revived and a dented coffee pot sat on the edge of a log. The smell of burnt coffee was comforting. Joshua sat up. Shep saw him and nodded. The room was still filled with shadows, but the open window let in some light and there were two small cracked glass windows at the far end. In the muted daylight, Joshua could see Shep more clearly. He was very tall, and looked older than Joshua had first thought. His teeth and complexion were bad, yet his face seemed majestic.

"Coffee," said Shep.

"Thank you," Joshua said. He found a tin cup, then went to the fire for the pot and poured himself a cup.

"I fish today. Weather is good. You gonna come?"

Joshua looked at him. He had green eyes. "All right."

They ate pieces of fish cooked on sticks they held in the flames. The crispy pieces glistened with oil and were delicious. They went outside and walked through the hollows to the beach. The Indian carried a wooden mast and a folded boom wrapped with a canvas sail and two long oars over his shoulder. Joshua followed with two fishing poles and a box of bait. An old wooden dinghy lay upside down in the sand, and Shep turned it over. There was a wooden tiller underneath; Shep placed the tiller, sail and oars inside. Joshua put in the fishing gear and together they carried the boat to the water's edge. The Indian wore a heavy pea coat, canvas trousers and a wool cap, much like what Joshua was wearing. He knew they would feel the cold. They pushed the boat into the water. Shep gestured for Joshua to sit, then walked the boat out and hoisted himself over the gunwales.

The surf was not high. The dinghy was small, about fourteen feet, made of heavy, weathered oak with three seats, a ribbed floor and a block for the mast. The boat drifted as Shep locked the oars in place. Joshua began to row and Shep stepped the small mast with its gaff-rigged sail. When they got past the surf line, Shep raised the sail, caught the wind, and they headed out to sea. The sky was overcast, though swathes of blue and white shone through. The air was cold and the wind came up as they sailed away from the land. The little boat moved sprightly through the rolling sea. Whitecaps came and went, sea birds passed and sometimes settled on a wave for a few moments before moving on. Two dolphins swam quickly by, breaking the surface.

The Indian nodded at Joshua. "It is a good day."

Joshua was not so sure the weather would hold, but he was enjoying the freedom of the open water. "Where do we fish?"

"A few more miles. Fishing is better out there. Maybe get a few cod."

Joshua nodded. He had unshipped his oars and rested them under the seats. The little boat heeled slightly in the wind. Shep held the tiller and the sheet, keeping the sail close-hauled. From time to time, they would sail into a trough and hit with a splash, spraying them with seawater.

After an hour, Shep headed the boat into the wind and folded the sail, wrapping it around the boom. "We will fish here."

He sat and picked up one of the poles, which had a heavy reel and a large hook at the end of the line. He took a herring from the tangle of seaweed in the bottom of the bait box and ran the hook through its mouth and gill. He tossed the baitfish over the side and let out the line. Joshua took the other pole and copied the Indian's steps as best he could. The men fished off opposite sides of the boat, which drifted along, riding the long waves.

For thirty minutes, the men fished in silence. Then Shep got a strike. It seemed like a good-sized fish from the way it pulled the pole, although the Indian had no trouble reeling it in. When the fish came alongside, Shep hauled it into the boat and held it up. It was spotted, with a strange hair-like extension below its chin, five fins, three on top, two on bottom, about thirty inches long and hefty in girth.

"Yep, it's a cod," Shep said. "Good cod fishing here." He carefully removed the hook from the fish's mouth, and then tossed it in the bottom of the boat. He reached for another herring and cast his line out again.

Shep caught three more cod, none quite as large as the first, and Joshua, disappointed, caught nothing. After a while he changed his bait and tried again. The sky was getting darker and the air colder. The waves grew in size, forming great rolling hills. Then a fish struck on Joshua's line. It was powerful and Joshua fought to pull it in, tugging and reeling until they could see it running with the line twenty yards off. The fish dived and the line strained against the reel.

"Loosen the drag," Shep warned.

Joshua did and the reel clicked as the fish ran. Joshua was feeling colder and more vexed, and finally stood and reeled in as fast as he could.

"Good, good," Shep said.

The fish came to the side of the boat and Joshua reeled him

up. Shep reached for the line just above the hook and lifted the fish inside, thrashing and struggling. It was even larger than the first. Shep grasped it securely in his strong right hand, and with his left jiggered the hook from its mouth, tearing it. He tossed it next to the other fish, rinsed his hands in the sea, and then put his own line back in the water.

The wind was quite strong now, the boat tossed about. Heavy clouds filled the sky.

"The weather doesn't look good," Joshua said. "Maybe we should go back."

Shep looked at the sky and sniffed the wind. Joshua thought he looked slightly crazy. "Soon," he answered.

Joshua shook his head, unsure about this. But he put his line back in. He caught no more fish. Shep caught a small one. Rain pelted them, a drizzle at first that turned into a downpour. The temperature dropped. The rain became sleet, icy needles that blew into their faces, the boat tossed. Finally, Shep gave up. They pulled in their lines and stowed the rods and reels. Shep raised the gaff sail and took the tiller. He seemed to know instinctively which direction to go toward home. At least, Joshua hoped so.

Within twenty minutes, they were riding a winter storm. The waves grew larger until they could not see from the trough they were in to the next wave's crest. The small craft was little more than a scrap tossing in the maelstrom; powerful wind gusts made the boat heel over so the sail nearly touched the water. Yet the Indian, his jaw set and eyes hard under frosted eyelashes, held on to the tiller and kept the bow pointed up, and they moved forward. Ice formed on the lines and Shep's hands were crusted with frost. All Joshua could do was hold on. It occurred to him this was how his mother had died, and so many others, and perhaps it was as good a way as any to go. But he was not ready. If he could have rowed them out of there, he would have, but he could accomplish nothing with oars in this sea.

Then he heard the Indian chanting. It was a deep, mournful song, the notes barely changing from one to the next. He sang in a monotone, but with great determination and passion, punctuating his song with grunts and screeches. The sounds filtered through the whistling wind and thundering waves—as if they were in a tunnel and the man were singing his way out of it. Perhaps he's praying, Joshua thought.

They rode up the face of a long wave and found themselves in a space where the troughs and crests were less extreme. The boat was encrusted with ice. Then a strong gust nearly blew the boat over. The sail dipped into the sea but came back up. The wind shifted and another gust hit them. This time the boat jibed and flung the boom at the Indian's head. He ducked, the boat heeled, and he went overboard. Joshua leaped to the stern and grabbed the tiller. Shep was still close by, his arms flailing as he tried to swim toward the moving boat. Joshua pushed the tiller as hard as he could to bring the boat into the wind. Thinking quickly, he grabbed the sheet from the sail and tied a hitch around a cleat, then wrapped it around the tiller. He tied a bowline and put his wrist through it, then jumped over the side. If he could reach Shep before he and the boat drifted too far apart, he could get him back aboard, but already he was slipping away.

Joshua reached out his arm. "Take my hand! Quick! I can't hold like this!" He couldn't tell if Shep could hear him.

For a moment, suspended in time and the history of men lost at sea, the two of them tried desperately to reach one another. The boat loomed over them, bobbing dangerously. Joshua felt Shep's hand grip his, and he pulled the Indian toward him until their bodies were touching. Joshua could see the fear in the man's eyes, and wondered how his own looked. They reached the side of the boat.

The Indian grasped at the gunwales with his frozen hands. With Joshua giving support from below, Shep lifted himself upward until his long upper body flopped over the side, then dragged his legs behind him and collapsed on the floor. Joshua climbed in, removed the rope from his wrist and untied it from the tiller. The sail was flailing and tearing at the edges, the tiller flipping back and forth. Joshua grabbed hold of it and pulled in on the sheet until they were moving forward again.

Shep sat up. He looked surprised to still be alive. They nodded to one another. Then the Indian moved toward the stern and motioned to Joshua to let him take his place at the helm. Joshua moved out of his way and they sailed on.

Their clothes were caked with ice. Joshua was so cold, he felt he had moved into a new realm of consciousness. The Indian's eyes bulged from his head, but again, he set his jaw and piloted the little craft through the wild waves and howling wind.

As if by some miracle, the grayness lightened and Joshua could see the beach through the sleet. Joshua thought how astonishing it was that Shep had found his beach in the storm. They passed over a line of small breakers and the Indian glided the boat onto the sand. They both jumped out and dragged it up the beach, running and panting with the daunting weight. They dropped the boat past the line of beach grass at the base of a small dune. The Indian reached in and lifted the mast from its support, then laid the boom and mast, the sail still flapping, on the sand next to the boat.

"We'll leave it," he said. "Home now."

Joshua needed no convincing. The two men ran and stumbled and ran again, supporting each other as they trudged up the dune and across the little valley until they saw Shep's long house. Inside they collapsed on the sand floor by the fireplace. After several minutes, Shep got up and started the fire. As the flames jumped and the light flared, Joshua felt a pulsing weakness wash through his bones and his veins, coming at him like a flood.

A while later, Shep brought him a cup of hot soup and a tea. He wrapped Joshua in an old blanket.

"You have a chill," he said.

Joshua felt giddy. The warm drink and the food gave him a little strength, but still he felt overcome by weakness and a profound cold.

Shep hovered over him, shaking his head. He knelt and touched Joshua's forehead. He went to the cupboard, brought the whiskey bottle and poured Joshua a glass. "Drink this," he said. "Then you must sleep."

The whiskey felt like fire going down Joshua's throat. He choked slightly, but finished the glass. He wrapped the blanket tighter and laid his head on the sand. The fire flickered. The wind blew through cracks in the long house. He closed his eyes.

When he awoke the room was filtered through a light grey glow. His ears were ringing and he thought he could see his own body from a distance wrapped in the blanket on the sand floor. The fire still burned. A sharp pain flashed across his temple, but when he touched his forehead, he found no blood or cut, just heat. He was hot and cold at the same time, his body shivering uncontrollably, but the heat under the blanket was unbearable. He lifted his head slightly and looked around. He could see no one. He lay back down and drifted off, somewhere between sleep and wakefulness.

When Joshua opened his eyes again, it was daytime. He was still on the floor. The fire burned and he could smell smoke and fish cooking. It turned his stomach. Shep must have gotten the fish from the boat, he thought. With great difficulty, he sat up. He immediately felt dizzy. And cold. He pulled the blanket around him.

"Another blanket?"

Shep stood before him holding a plaid blanket. Joshua took hold of its edge but he was too weak to lift it around his shoulders. The Indian helped him.

"Thank you," Joshua said. He looked up at the Indian's rugged face. "You have green eyes."

"Yes."

"Why?" Joshua's voice was quavering.

"My mother was Irish. My father was a Wampanoag chief."

Joshua nodded and smiled. He slipped back onto the floor. "Very green."

A while later, Shep propped him up with one arm and held a plate in his other hand. There was a fork on the plate and some fish and potatoes.

"Eat," Shep said.

The smell of the fish nauseated him. "How long have I been here?" Joshua asked.

"Three days," said the Indian.

"Long time."

"Yes. You haven't eaten. You need food."

"All right," Joshua said. "I'll try."

Joshua took the plate in his lap. He could barely lift the fork. He managed to take two bites of fish, then dropped his arm and the fork flew to the ground. Shep picked it up. He put some fish and potato on the fork, and lifted it to Joshua's mouth.

"Here," he said.

Joshua opened his mouth like a child and took the food. Shep gave him another bite, then a third.

"Good," Joshua said, then slipped back down and slept.

He began to dream. He is back in Cuba, on the beach next to Adam. The Spanish are attacking, bullets and shells flying. Joshua crouches behind a tree, shaking with fear. The noise is so loud it fills the entire world. Time itself is suspended, men and bullets moving at first slowly, then too quickly, then slowly again. The enemy soldier appears, charging from behind the tree trunk. Adam stands proudly firing his rifle. Joshua watches himself as if a stranger, frozen in time while the Spaniard's bullets fly through the air as in a ballet, streaks of light slowed to visible. He is behind the tree and hears his own thoughts, palpable, as if spoken aloud. I am afraid. I cannot move. I must help Adam, but I can't. I will die, not Adam. I don't want to die here. The light has dimmed, the air a different color. The bullets keep coming, the noise builds, deafening, terrifying. The Spaniard moves closer, like a ghost in another dimension—how is it even possible? Joshua is behind the tree, waiting, not moving. Then, as if a bubble has burst, the sound grows still louder but the light returns to normal. There he is, running toward me. Joshua raises his gun to fire, afraid to kill someone this close, afraid of the blood. The gun jams, it will not fire, Joshua is in a panic, he screams, he tries again to fire, but the rifle is jammed. What will he do? He must protect himself and Adam… Adam and himself… himself. The fucking rifle… the bayonet glistens in the light, catching the sun. That's it! He lowers the rifle, straight ahead of him now, a javelin, a spear, he rushes forward, toward the man rushing at him, no idea what he will do. He is aware he is screaming madly, though he cannot hear his own voice, only bullets and explosions. Then the man is down, the spear is in him, blood spurting from his chest, his body in its now bloodstained white uniform twitching on the ground as he dies, peering into Joshua's eyes as if he could read the mind of his slayer. Joshua looks around. The beach sparkles, the sky a bright cloudless blue, the air warm and heavy. And there, by the tree where Joshua had hidden from the bullets, lies his brother Adam, blood all over him, too. Joshua moves toward him. And suddenly Lucy is there on the beach, watching her sons, one fighting, and the other dying. A deep, resonant sound emits from her throat. "NOOOOOOO!" In the swirling obscurity of the pitch black night, there is the stern face of his father. You let him die, Joshua, you did not protect your only brother…

Joshua's absence from the station caused great concern. Pendleton was angry, MacDonald was worried, and the other men were nervous. It was unlike Joshua to shirk his responsibilities even slightly. Something must surely be wrong.

Word that Joshua was missing reached Julia through Doc Meads. She was worried, too. Joshua had been acting oddly of late, and he was obviously upset. But to run off from his duties at the station? She thought this unlikely. She went looking for Buddy in the bars. Eventually someone pointed her to his hotel. She mounted the steps of the Union House.

It was early evening and already dark when she knocked on the door of Buddy's room. He opened it, surprised to see her. He'd only met Julia once, when she'd stitched him up after his fight with Joshua, although he knew of Joshua's interest in her. He smiled his seductive smile and welcomed her in.

"Do you know where Joshua is?" she asked.

Buddy shook his head. "I haven't seen him."

"He seems to be missing. No one has seen him for four days. I'm worried."

"He's strong. I'm sure he's fine."

"I know he's strong. You don't have to tell me that." She looked at Buddy with some annoyance. "He's been acting strangely lately. The fight with you, but also… well, strangely. He seems concerned about the hijackings."

"I'm concerned about that, too," Buddy said.

"Did Joshua ever apologize to you for your last fight?"

"Apologize? No, I wish he had. He hit me pretty hard."

Julia nodded. "It was wrong. The whole thing is wrong. I don't understand it."

"Doesn't make much sense to me, either, the way he's been. Like a different person."

"He thinks you know something about the wreck," she said.

"I don't."

"Are you sure?"

"Am I sure? Of course I'm sure. What is it with everybody?"

Julia stood just inside the door. She had on her cloak, but she removed her hat. If anyone could find Joshua, it was Buddy. Joshua had told her how difficult he could be, how mistrustful he was of everyone. She needed to get him to open up to her somehow.

She looked at him. "Everybody is persecuting poor little Buddy."

"Don't make fun of me."

"I can see why people do," she said.

"Do what?" Buddy asked.

"Make fun of you."

"You're mocking me."

"And what if I am?"

"I don't like it," Buddy said.

"And what are you going to do about it?" she demanded.

Buddy had been sitting on the edge of the bed. It was a cramped room, with too much furniture and little space to stand. Julia removed her coat.

He walked over to her. "I don't like being made fun of."

She smiled. "Are you threatening me?"

He stepped back. "No, of course not. I don't like it, is all."

"I'd like you to go out and ask around, see if anyone knows where Joshua is. Can you do that?"

Buddy seemed to grow physically uncomfortable. "Why should I?"

"He's your friend. Has that changed?"

"I don't know," Buddy said. "Ask him."

"I'd like to. Will you help me?"

"Well, I guess I can ask a few people…" Buddy grumbled.

"Thank you, Buddy. I appreciate that." Julia picked up her coat and hat. She opened the door.

"Do you like me at all?" Buddy asked.

She turned back. "I don't know you, Buddy. You seem charming enough. I suspect you're nicer than you'd like to imagine yourself."

"I don't know what you've heard, but you've got me all wrong," he said. "I'm not a bad person."

"I've no reason to think you are," Julia said. "Perhaps just a bit confused."

"Well, I'm young, you know!"

Julia laughed out loud at the precocity of this statement.

"I believe I am generally misunderstood by people."

"Aren't we all?" Julia asked.

"I don't mean to harm others," he said carefully. "It's just that… I find myself preoccupied with my own predilections…"

Julia began to laugh again. Suddenly there was an explosion. Not far off. It rocked the hotel, shook the floors and walls and rattled the lamps. They looked at each other.

"Jesus," Buddy said, "what the hell was that?"

Julia rushed down the stairs and Buddy followed.

Outside, they could see flames and smell smoke coming from the direction of the Town Hall two blocks away. People were rushing in that direction, while others seemed to be fleeing. When they reached the little square in front of the building, flames were shooting from the lower floor windows and thick, black smoke billowed from the upper floors. People were still staggering out, their clothes blackened. Julia spotted the fire chief, Joseph Perano.

"What's happening, Joe?" she asked.

"Explosion in the basement," he said, then ran off to help his men.

Within minutes, every fire engine in town had arrived. Commercial and Ryder Streets were jammed with volunteer firemen, policemen and ordinary citizens hauling water to save the building. Horses and carts blocked the streets. Julia saw Doc Meads and went to see if she could help. Buddy felt suddenly exposed and slinked back to his hotel.

The Town Hall housed the police station in its basement, with the jail set at the back. A single barred window at street level provided meager ventilation to the cells. Tucker was the jail's only inhabitant. He had been treated by Doc Meads, kept two nights in an infirmary under guard, and now awaited arraignment. Kirov had started the fire as a distraction, using a stick of dynamite—the drama of it appealed to his thespian instincts. He and William drove a heavy wagon up to the single window. He tied a heavy rope from the wagon tongue to the window bars, clucked and whipped at the mules, and in a few moments the bars came off. Nobody saw or heard anything because of the commotion out front. William kicked in the glass window and Kirov climbed in, holding the same rope. Tucker looked at the Russian and grinned, shaking his head in disbelief. Kirov tied the rope to the bars of the cell door, and then moved back to the window to signal William to move the mules.

Kirov climbed back out the window. The mules strained against the load until the rope snapped and went slack. Tucker soon came scrambling out the window and jumped in the back of the wagon. Kirov took the reins, whipping the mules as they drove away from the center of town.

They abandoned the wagon by a stable near Kirov's cottage. The stable owner was a fireman and Kirov knew he'd be busy with the fire. They broke in and stole three horses, saddled them hurriedly and rode twenty miles to the cabin in Wellfleet.

In the morning, Provincetown was in disarray. The fire had been put out quickly enough to save the building, but it had sustained damage to the front and sides and to several structural beams in the basement. Chief Nickerson was fit to be tied. He called every police chief on the Cape and asked for their help, then sent every man he had to search the town and question anyone who might have a lead on where the criminals had gone.

A sliver of sunlight woke Joshua. His head felt a little clearer, and he sat up. The Indian was stirring the fire. He nodded at Joshua, then brought him a cup of coffee. The heat of the coffee and its stimulating effect felt good.

"How do you feel?" Shep asked.

"Better, I think."

"I'll go out now. Be back this afternoon."

Shep went out and Joshua got up and began to explore the hut. It was filled with salvage from the beach: half-soaked paintings, kegs of nails, signal flags, a dress sword, two military tunics, a rug unraveled at one end. The sun shone through the cracked windows, creating twisted shadows in the long, dusty room. There were two old dressers in a corner. Joshua walked over and began absently poking through the things on top. He opened a drawer and found a pile of old socks. The adjacent drawer was stuck and would not open. In a third he found wrinkled shirts rolled into a ball. He took one out, shook it, and held it in front of him. Then he noticed a brown leather folder that had been tucked under the shirt.

He lifted it out. Its cover was cracked and dry. When he tried to open the folio the front and back covers stuck together at first. Inside was a single cracked piece of paper that looked as if it had been wet and then dried. Joshua saw handwriting on it, faded and smudged. It looked vaguely familiar. He lifted it up and started to read. Suddenly he dropped the portfolio to the floor and sank to his knees as if his very breath had been sucked away.

This was his mother's writing. How could it be? Was this another feverish dream? But no, it wasn't. Still kneeling in the sand, he picked up the folio and began to read.

> *My Dearest Joshua,*
> *The seas grow rough, but at least we are finally underway and I shall be with you soon. The sea has kept your father from me often, but I grew up by it and love its deep mysteries. I miss you both terribly and am so sorry to have missed spending Easter with you.*
>
> *It feels silly to write a letter to someone I shall see a day or two hence. But my darling boy, there are some things, important things, that are easier to write than to say face-to-face. I have wanted to tell you this, and my heart won't let me stay silent any longer. I know you blame yourself for Adam's death, but you should not, you must not. You're a good boy, the very best, you are strong—in your own way as strong as your father and brother, perhaps more so—and I am and forever shall be enormously proud of you.*
> *With deepest love,*
> *Mother*

Joshua sat on the floor for an eternity, stunned—as if the sand on which he rested would be frozen in time forever. The light turned from sharp white to a dimmer grey, then filled with a yellow hue. The air grew colder.

Finally, Shep returned. He held two fish tied together. He was surprised to see Joshua sitting on the floor, but he smiled, glad to see him up.

"Where did you get this?" Joshua demanded hoarsely. He held the portfolio.

"What?"

"This," he said more loudly, brandishing it higher.

"Oh, that," Shep said. "I found it."

"You found it?"

Shep nodded.

Suddenly Joshua was on his feet. He turned and ran wildly at Shep, screaming at him, out of control. His face inches from the Indian's, he shouted, "Liar! Where did you find it? Tell me!"

Shep, who made no connection between Joshua and the portfolio, stood immobile before him, shocked. Joshua seemed desperate and crazed, tears forming in his eyes.

"We will sit and talk," Shep said.

He went to get the whiskey bottle and two glasses, then returned and the two men sat in the sand. He poured Joshua a glass. Joshua took a sip. It made him feel dizzy.

"I was on a salvage crew," Shep began. "A thing I do in the winter. The ship owners hire crews to go to the wrecks. It pays well. It is cold work, wet work. There are men who do only this."

"Is one of them a Russian?"

Shep nodded. "Yes, he is one. He came here from off Cape, working for a big crew." He took a sip of whiskey. "It was a bad storm. We got there in the evening, off the beach in Wellfleet where the big bluffs are. Lonely place. Light was almost gone. Ship was barely afloat. Not much left of her, foc'sle broke clean away."

Joshua stared ahead, listening intently, yet floating among the words.

"There were bodies in the water, on the beach. We rowed out. Boarded. The Russian wanted to look for booty, he said. But we found this woman. Her body was twisted, something broken, wore a heavy coat."

Shep watched Joshua cringe.

"She was still alive…"

Joshua looked up.

"The Russian starts to rummage through the poor woman's clothes. Takes off her coat. She seems to be moaning. I…" Shep paused as if fighting off a painful memory. "I tell him to let her be, but he pushes me away. She's got a pretty face, but it's blue." He looked again at Joshua, his face unmoving, his expression dark.

"Then what?" Joshua asked.

"The Russian took a silver brooch from the woman's dress."

Joshua nodded again. His heart was pounding wildly. "I've seen it. Go on."

"The Russian strips her bare. Son of a bitch is smiling. Takes his dagger—"

Joshua gasped.

"Takes his dagger and runs it through her breast. It was pretty dark but we could all see. Then drags her to the edge and throws her over the side… the man's a fuckin' animal."

"But you didn't stop him."

"Happened too quick. We was all shocked. Russian says

anyone says what they saw he'll kill him. He says let's go and we go. As we climb over I see that"— he nodded at the portfolio—"and I take it. That's all."

There was utter silence.

Shep looked deep into Joshua's eyes. "Who was this woman?"

Joshua could barely speak the words. He choked, trying to keep from crying, and said in a near whisper, "She was my mother…"

Shep fell to his knees in front of Joshua, and bowed his head, his cheeks more sunken than ever. "Good Jesus, no."

Joshua looked at the big man. He understood all at once that Shep was experiencing Joshua's own pain. As if their souls had intertwined.

"I never knew what happened. Only that she drowned in a wreck. On Easter, it was."

Shep nodded. "Yes, that was the day. I am…" His voice was soft, like a whimper. "I am sorry, my friend."

"Someone should have stopped him…" Joshua clutched the portfolio against his chest, slipped to the sand floor and curled up.

Shep put his arm over Joshua's shoulder. Joshua didn't move. The Indian picked Joshua up, like a baby, and carried him to the sand in front of the fire. Then he fell to his knees once more and, tilting his head to the sky, began to moan. He moaned loudly, a mournful wordless song, and continued for what seemed an eternity. Joshua said nothing, just stared blankly, until finally sometime in the night he slept.

Morning came. Joshua opened his eyes. He lay watching dust float through the air around him, the stillness surrounding him. There was something familiar about the feeling—he realized it was like some moment deep in his past, when he was a young child, before real memory. The peace and silence of a world not yet tainted, a world protected and safe, his own little space peopled by no one else, except when his mother's face would appear, her brilliant smile that warmed and comforted him. She would appear and he would eat, or laugh. She would clean him, kiss him, stroke his forehead, the sound of the room in that distant memory filled with unknowable echoes. His brother was there, somewhere, his father, others—but no, it was only him and his mother's benign aura. We all have such memories, he thought absently, yet each one is unique to us alone, a series of moments when our lives were first forming, when all we would later learn had yet to be discovered and there was only this floating silence.

Much later, he got to his feet and went outside. The sun seemed piercingly bright. He mounted a dune and looked out over the perfect blue ocean. Gentle waves close to shore gave way to low wind-whipped whitecaps, seagulls riding the swells. The wind, ever present, like a deity, never ceasing, never backing down, a pillar, a missive, heaven-sent, whatever that might mean. He didn't know. What he knew, what he now understood, was that somehow the world, Joshua's world, cratered and ravaged, had been returned to him. He went back to the hut.

"I must go," he said to Shep.

Shep nodded but did not move, staring silently at Joshua. He stared back. This place was an island, a mist, incorporeal and illusory, one he would never encounter again. An aching thought, despite the pain it had caused him.

Shep sensed this, as if it were born in his own blood. "Yes, it is time." He made an attempt to smile, though the weight of Joshua's emotion prevented him. "It's good to see you up again."

"Thank you for keeping me going."

Suddenly Shep laughed, breaking the tension. "You did that yourself. I just made soup."

Joshua nodded warmly. "I shall always remember your soup. And the fishing."

The Indian smiled and tossed his head, as if crowing to the stars. "The fishing! For sure!" He looked into Joshua's eyes, as if fixing them in some compartment of his soul. He held his hand out to Joshua. "You saved my life. I hope you will be well." Shep handed him the leather portfolio. "I'm sorry for your loss and my part in it."

Joshua took it, then nodded. "Be well." He walked out of the long house and down the little valley to the beach.

CHAPTER FIFTEEN

Very early, the same day that Joshua left the Indian's hut, Buddy was awakened in his hotel room by Kirov, who gave him a rough shove.

"Get up," he demanded.

Buddy could barely focus. "What's going on? How'd you get in here?"

"I want to talk to you. Get up."

Buddy forced himself to sit and looked at the Russian groggily. "What do you want?" He hadn't seen Kirov since the night of the hijacking, and now that he was awake, he remembered how angry he still was. "I thought you'd disappeared. What do you want?"

Kirov glared.

Buddy continued. "I'll tell you one thing. I'm getting out of here. I'm not sticking around for the next disaster. You and your friends are amateurs—"

Kirov slapped Buddy hard across the face. Buddy heard bells and saw stars. He shook his head to clear it, and Kirov whipped his dagger out and held it under Buddy's chin.

"Now you listen to me, young fellow, and listen good. I like you. You're smart and I could use a man like you. We can make good money together if you watch yourself and do as I say. But you ain't going anywhere, not now." Suddenly Kirov smiled. It was almost a warm smile. He slipped his dagger back in its sheath. "Besides, my friend, I owe you some money. Don't you want it?"

Buddy was speechless. Tentatively, he replied. "Yes, sure, I'd like to get my money. Do you have it?"

"Do I have it? Ha! Of course I have it."

He took a roll of bills from his pocket and counted out five of them, then handed them to Buddy. Buddy spread them in his fingers.

"This is only five hundred," Buddy said. "You told me a thousand."

Kirov laughed again, his most serpentine laugh. "Of course I did, my friend, and you shall have it. But first, I want your help with one more job."

"No," Buddy said. "No more. I'm done."

"This will be a very big job. I will do nicely from it, and so shall you," Kirov said. He paused, as if thinking. "I'll tell you what. For the next one, which will be my last, I will give you the five hundred I owe you, and another thousand."

Buddy felt frightened. But he asked, "What is the job?"

"You see, my friend, that's why I like you. You are a man of principle. I admire that. A man of principle who is willing to ignore his principles if he can make some money. This is what makes America the great nation it is."

"But, what—"

Kirov interrupted him. "This will be very special. A little trick that was done in other places, but never here, never here." He looked at Buddy and pronounced with great pride, "We are going to make one of them ships to wreck."

"What?"

"Shhh. Please, young friend, don't shout. Yes, why wait for some accident? We will cause the accident! With a light to confuse the ship's captain, a light on the beach."

Buddy looked at him. "That's crazy."

"Why?" Kirov asked. "It's a simple trick, and we will do it when the tide is low enough so we can get in and out quickly. This time no one will get hurt."

Buddy shook his head. "You know that's impossible to say. No. No, I won't—"

Kirov's smile made Buddy shake inside.

"I'll tell you what," Kirov said. He removed a large paper from inside his shirt. "I'll do something special for you. You see this?" He opened the paper. It was a government bill of some sort.

"What is it?" Buddy asked.

"It's a gold certificate for one thousand dollars, 1882 series. It is payable to the bearer. Anyone can cash it. I give it to you. A bonus."

Buddy examined the bill. It was much larger than normal currency, on a heavy paper marked with symbols and the United States seal. The number 1000 was in one corner. Buddy had to admit it had a certain striking quality about it. Then Kirov took both ends of the bill and tore it neatly in half.

"Are you nuts?" Buddy demanded. "What the hell are you doing?"

"I give you half now, the other half plus the five hundred the night of the job. I promise." And he handed half of the torn bill to Buddy.

Buddy took it and held it between his fingers. It was heavy and felt real enough. Kirov walked toward the door. Then he stopped and turned back.

"One more little thing, my friend. If you leave before I say so, I'll find you. I'll track you down and I'll gut-slit you, I swear I will." Kirov laughed and walked out the door.

Buddy fell back on his bed. A new nightmare had descended upon him.

Joshua made his way along the beach to the station. As he walked, he reflected on all that had happened. He had failed to return to the station, a punishable offense, and then disappeared for nearly a week. He had saved a man and nearly died himself. He had learned how his mother died. He'd lost Julia; he'd attacked Buddy and probably ended their friendship. But he had also, in his own mind, determined that it was his duty—to himself, his family, the town and the Service—to bring Kirov to justice. One way or another, he would stop that man.

He moved briskly over the sand and watched the ocean rising and falling, the whitecaps, the seals and gulls, the endless miles of solitary beach. The sublime magnificence of it all. He pictured his mother in a different world, a different time, a progression of random moments, in her fine dresses and her sleeping gown, on horseback in Central Park, in the bustling kitchen planning a meal with the cook. He remembered her playing Mozart at the piano, the room filled with ethereal sound. He thought of her love for life, and the terrible way hers had ended. Just before she died she had written to him. To him! It was not fair. She deserved a better ending. No matter what he did, where he went, what deeds he accomplished, he would never be able to give that to her.

He came around a bend and saw the weathered red tower of the station. He felt anxious about his reception, but immensely happy to be back. It was lunch time when he walked into the galley. The men looked up, surprised to see him, and several applauded his return. But Pendleton's scowl made it clear how he felt about anyone who abandoned his station. Captain MacDonald was breaking a piece of bread. He looked at Joshua and a broad smile came over his face.

"Hey, Joshua," Jurgen called out.

Punchy jumped up and threw his heavy arms around him. "I've been doin' double shifts for ya, ya sloucher. You owe me plenty."

Joshua laughed. "I'm in your debt."

Peter Abbot came over and hugged him. "You look a bit pale, Joshua."

"I know," Joshua said. "I feel a bit pale."

MacDonald gestured to Joshua to join them. When the meal was finished, he asked him to come to his room. Joshua explained everything that had happened to him.

MacDonald listened patiently, nodding at certain points in the story. "We were worried about you, you know. I confess I was losing hope. What got into you that night?"

"I was angry, sir. About a lot of things."

"Doesn't seem like you," MacDonald said. But he understood. Joshua could see it in his eyes.

"I apologize. It was not right what I did."

They left it at that.

It was Thursday, so after lunch the men had beach apparatus practice. The early spring afternoon was chilly, but glorious, the beach swept by the long winter's winds and littered with debris but teeming with birds newly arrived from the south. The wind held a glint of tropical promise in its currents, as if the birds had carried it northward.

They hauled the equipment cart down the ramp and over the sand. The wreck pole waited in the distance. The men unpacked the cart, lifted out the heavy Lyle gun, arranged the faking box, buried the sand anchor, set the fall and raised the crotch pole, everything in the same precise order. There was something consoling about the stringency of the regimen. In this place what came next was entirely predictable. The only unpredictable thing was the weather and the action of providence upon ships passing in the night.

The powder was placed in the gun, then the projectile. Pendleton aimed and fired. The projectile carried its passenger through the air, passed above the cross tree and wrapped around it. The shot line hung in the breeze over the beach and the men cheered, as if this were the first time Pendleton had made the shot successfully. Joshua ran to the wreck pole, clambered up and pulled in the hawser, and the men sent the breeches buoy to him. He stepped into the ring, signaled and was carried over the sand to his mates. A vision flashed into his mind: a lonely, frightened woman, drenched to the bone and dangling above the cold ocean on a dark, snowy night. He felt certain he would see such things again.

Pendleton looked at his stop watch. "Four minutes, twenty two seconds! Not bad for a bunch a' lubbers!"

As they recoiled the ropes, repacked the equipment and placed it on the cart, Peter Abbot called out, "Whale!"

345

They all stopped and looked at the sea: a deep blue punctuated by rolling waves on which crowns of wind-whipped foam appeared briefly then petered out. Birds circled, dove down, then flew up again. Suddenly, a narrow spout of water shot six feet in the air and dissipated into mist. The birds screeched and spiraled wildly. The surface broke and a large, dark shape emerged, extending partly out of the water with great bulk and deliberate speed, although where the creature began and ended was difficult to discern. The bulbous head plowed through the surf then submerged as the whale descended, its giant split tail flipping up, then vanishing. The surface smoothed as if nothing had disturbed it at all.

"A young one," Punchy said. "Must be a mother somewhere near. They're heading north to feed for the summer."

Peter Abbot said softly, "Billy would've been the first to see it."

The other men all muttered their assent.

"And the last to stop talkin' about it, too," Punchy said.

Everyone laughed.

There had been a letter from his father. He was recovered from his illness and was feeling better, he said, keeping occupied with his work and looking forward to summer. He expressed his hope that Joshua would come home to see him. Joshua wrote back that he, too, was feeling better and would come to see Gideon in June. In spite of all that had gone before, Joshua was looking forward to it.

Several days later in the fading afternoon, Julia was walking on Commercial Street, returning from the apothecary with a sack full of medicines. The days were longer now, and she enjoyed the warmer air and the lengthening rays of sunlight, when a month or two earlier the street would have been dark and empty. She saw Buddy on the other side, moving quickly and furtively.

When he caught sight of her he called out, "Julia!"

She was surprised he used her first name. He hurried across the street.

"How are you feeling, Buddy?" she asked.

"Oh, me? I'm… fine," he answered. He seemed very distracted. "You know Joshua is back at the station…" He had heard this news at the Mermaid.

Julia nodded. "Yes, I was told. Is he all right?"

"I've no idea," Buddy said. "I haven't seen him."

"I see. Well, if you do, please give him my regards."

"Um, yes, I will…" Buddy said.

"You seem upset, Buddy. Are you sure you're—"

He cut her off. "No. I'm fine. Fine." And he hurried off.

Buddy was terrified. He knew sooner or later Kirov would come and ask him to do some new, horrendous act. He had to find the courage to go far enough away that Kirov would never find him, or to stand up to him and refuse whatever he might ask. Either strategy was fraught with risk. The money was enticing—but he had tempted fate twice now, and his instinct told him a third time would turn out very badly for him.

Late that night, his fate caught up with him. There was no moon, though the skies were clear. Past midnight there was a knock on the door. Buddy had remained in his room all evening, drinking whiskey until he fell asleep. It took a few knocks before he heard. He went groggily to the door.

"Who's there?" he called out quietly.

"It's me. Open up."

Kirov. Buddy opened the door with a sense of dread. The crazy Russian had also been drinking.

"What do you want?" Buddy demanded.

"I am here to offer you a chance to become rich."

"Oh, great," Buddy said.

"I told you last time there would be another job. I gave you half the big bill. I give you the other half now," Kirov said. He took the paper from his coat and handed it to Buddy.

Buddy took it reluctantly, turning it over in this hand.

"It is pretty, isn't it?" Kirov asked. "Well, there's more. I will give you one fourth of whatever I get, minus my usual ten percent, if you come along tomorrow night. You ask no questions, you tell no one, you help me get this done. I pay you and you go on your way."

The Russian looked terrifically pleased with himself. Buddy's heart was pounding.

"No," Buddy said.

Kirov laughed. "What? No? You're joking!"

"I said no. I'm not going to help you."

The Russian laughed again, the snake laugh. "But of course you are. You just don't know it yet."

"No, I'm not. I'm through. I don't care about the money, I'm—"

Kirov hit him so hard in the stomach that Buddy sink to his knees. Nausea swept over him.

"I don't care what you do. I'm finished, I tell you."

"Look, Mister Buddy," Kirov said in a deeply sardonic tone, "you and I both know that you need the money and you don't have the balls to stand up to me. You want to die or you want to help me?"

Buddy felt a lump in his throat. "Die," he said.

"Suit yourself," Kirov said. He casually lifted the big dagger from his belt. "Let's get it over with."

A thought occurred to Buddy: if he agreed to the Russian's demands, he might live through the night and buy some time. By tomorrow, he would figure a way out of this mess. Buddy watched the blade move toward his throat. He was sick of this game.

"All right, you son of a bitch," Buddy said, heaving a sigh for extra effect. "Tell me what I have to do."

"You are such a smart young man after all," Kirov said. He sheathed his dagger. "This is simple. You meet us at Snail Road at six, just before dark. We will go to the beach. You ride in the wagon. You will be finished by morning. It will be cold, so wear your coat." Kirov nodded, pleased with himself. He turned to go out the door. Then he turned back. "Okay, one other thing. You're not thinking of running away, are you?"

Buddy shook his head.

Kirov slowly stepped back, and with a motion almost too quick to notice, he whipped out the knife and slashed Buddy's left cheek. At first Buddy felt nothing, but in a moment his cheek began to sting as blood ran from the crescent cut.

"I know you will not. Because you cannot get far enough away in one day, not even in two or three days, that I will not find you." Kirov leaned in, his face close to Buddy's. "Look in my eyes. What do you see?"

Buddy stared at the man. He was seething with hatred, the most powerful he had ever felt. But he was also afraid.

"I tell you what you see. It is truth. You know I am right. I will find you." He stood and went to the door. As he walked out, he said without turning around, "You will be there."

At Peaked Hill Bars Station, the afternoon was cloudy, with a chilly north wind. By late afternoon, a fog blew in. Joshua and Peter Abbot were stowing gear in the big room, its wide doors open to the sea.

"Think there'll be a storm?" Joshua asked.

Peter Abbot looked out at the grey sky. "Nah. No storm. A dark night, maybe a little rain. That's all."

At supper, the men talked excitedly about the bass they had seen. Punchy had caught two just past sunrise that morning. It was early in the season, but he saw it as a good sign. Everyone seemed relaxed. The long season of storms was nearly over, and soon they would leave the station for their two months of freedom.

Punchy got up to refill his glass of ale, and as he passed by Joshua he ruffled his hair. "Young fresh fish here has done all right for himself."

Pendleton looked up at them. "Yeah, 'cept for his little disappearing act."

"Ah, leave him alone, will ya?" Punchy said. "He's a good kid."

"He just needed a little vacation, right?" Jurgen said.

Joshua was uncomfortable with the talk. He was glad to be back and sorry he'd gone missing. After supper, he stood on the porch watching as a couple of the others went down to the beach for a smoke. He noticed a light on in the Keeper's room, went in and found MacDonald writing at his desk. Joshua stood at the threshold and knocked.

MacDonald looked up. "Ah, Joshua! How are you, lad?"

"I'm fine, sir, thank you. Happy to be back."

"You seem to have survived whatever happened to you and come through unscathed."

Joshua paused, then said, "Yes, sir. I imagine I have."

"What's wrong then?"

"Do you know an Indian named Shep?"

MacDonald looked at him, reflecting on his answer. "Yes, I know that man. I thought he left these parts long ago. Not a terribly good man."

"Sir, he was the one who cared for me while I was ill. He lives in an old Quonset hut in the hills near Hatches Harbor."

"Out by Helltown, that is."

"Yes, sir." Joshua told him about their fishing trip, the storm, and his illness.

"You're lucky you survived."

"Yes, sir, I was lucky. But I learned some things in that place."

MacDonald leaned back, curious.

"Well, first I learned what happened to my mother after the shipwreck." His voice quavering, he recounted all that Shep had told him.

MacDonald shook his head and said grimly, "This Kirov fellow is bad news. He will need to be stopped."

"I agree, sir. That was the second thing I came to realize. That man is a danger and I—maybe we—have an obligation to put a stop to him. Once and for all. Whatever it takes."

MacDonald smiled. "I admire your zeal, though it may be harder than you think. Perhaps the police might be better…"

"I came to another realization there, about myself. It was not a pleasant one."

"What was that, Joshua?"

"I believe, sir, that I acted in a cowardly way during the battle against the Spanish when my brother was wounded."

MacDonald appeared shocked. "Cowardly? You? I doubt

that, son."

"It's true, sir. I never realized before. You see, if I could have stopped the Spaniard who shot my brother, he would still be alive."

"Yes, but…"

"And if my brother hadn't died," Joshua said, his voice choking and tears coming to his eyes, "my mother would not have been grieving, would not have gone to her sister in Boston, and would not have died on her way home to us."

MacDonald was shaking his head. "You cannot carry the burden of all that. No man can."

"But Captain, when the Spanish soldier ran at us I was behind a tree, and I was afraid."

"You were afraid."

"Yes, sir. I was hiding."

"How long?" MacDonald demanded.

"I don't know, sir. It seemed like a lifetime. "

"Yes, but how long?" MacDonald insisted, rather firmly.

"I don't know. A few minutes? Maybe not… less than a minute? Many, many seconds, I'd guess, but if I hadn't…"

MacDonald stood up and came close. He spoke deliberately, his grizzled face close to Joshua's. "Now listen to me, son, and listen well. I have been to war, and I've been to sea, and I've been a keeper. I've seen a lot of men die. I've seen men put themselves in harm's way under a great many circumstances." He sighed. "Too many." He put his hand on Joshua's shoulder. "You must believe what I tell you now. The history books are filled with tales of brave heroes and glorious battles. But it is never that way. Men do heroic things, but when they do them, they do not feel like heroes. They feel afraid, they feel small and they want to run away or hide, they want to die, they shit in their pants and sweat and cry, and then some—many, really, in my experience—do what they have to do. To survive, to save their fellow soldiers or sailors, their family or friends. They do what they can and they hope to endure. Afterward some are called heroes, some cowards, some live, some die, some suffer terrible wounds from which they never recover. This is the truth about war—and about the Navy and the Marines and the Life-Savers, firemen, police, ordinary men who struggle every day with the forces and demons that pursue them."

"Thank you, sir, but…"

"You could not have saved your brother's life. He was shot during a terrible battle. Whether the battle was fought for glory or for the good of man or because someone decided that group of men should be in that place at that time for whatever reason, it doesn't matter. He was shot, you fought by his side, you killed the man who attacked him, you lived and your brother died. It's a terrible story. It was terrible for your mother—and terrible for your father, I assure you. And, by God, it was terrible for you. But it was not your fault. The only way you can live your life, the kind of life your mother would have wanted you to live, is if you believe that is true. You must promise me you will try to believe that."

Joshua stood in the doorway, looking at the old man whom he had come to love like his own father. "Thank you, sir, I shall try," he said, although he really wasn't sure. He did not feel any better. But he turned and walked back outside.

Buddy walked along Commercial Street, feeling the fog and gloom descending, the grey light fading to darkness. He was frightened and angry to the point of utter distraction. The sidewalk boards creaked beneath his feet. Afraid the sound would somehow betray his presence, he moved into the sandy street. He was heading toward the rendezvous, but every fiber of him told him not to go there. He stepped behind a grove of low pine bushes. Hidden, he let out his breath. He had to think. There was precious little time.

Then, suddenly, he decided what he must do. He crossed the street, headed north between two storage sheds, cut through to Bradford Street, and went into the woods. He had to cross the dunes ahead of Kirov and his men. He began to run through the scrub pines until he reached the first steep hill of sand.

Joshua was still on the porch, looking over the ocean. The wind was building, hardly a storm but plenty of white caps and blowing sand, the temperature dropping. Jurgen and Sonny Silva were on patrol, the others had gone inside; when Jurgen returned, Joshua would go out. A few stars were visible, but he could see the dark shadows of clouds blowing rapidly across the sky. He heard a sound, caught a movement in the corner of his eye, and suddenly Buddy stood there below him.

"Buddy!"

"Shhh!" Buddy hissed.

"What are you doing here?"

"I came to warn you."

"To warn me?"

"Shhh!" Buddy hissed again. He half-whispered. "It's Kirov. He has a plan. Tonight!"

"Okay, okay, slow down. What are you talking about?"

Peter Abbot and Punchy, hearing the commotion, came out to the porch. Punchy saw Buddy and ran at him.

"What the fuck is he doin' here?" he asked.

Buddy looked frightened. Punchy took a swing at him and hit his shoulder, reeling him backwards.

"Take it easy, Punchy," Joshua snapped. "He's trying to tell me something." He thought a moment. "Maybe we should go talk to the Keeper."

Buddy nodded. He mounted the steps to the porch, holding his shoulder and feeling Punchy's fury like the breath of a dragon on his neck. He followed Joshua into the station. MacDonald was still at his desk.

He looked up to see Joshua with Buddy, disheveled and out of breath, his face and cap wet with fog. "What in the hell are you doing here?"

Buddy stepped backward, intimidated by MacDonald's harsh tone. "I... I... sorry, sir, I..." he stammered.

"Goddamn it, boy!" MacDonald bellowed. "What are you doing out here?"

Buddy caught his breath, removed his cap and looked at MacDonald. "Sir, I came to warn you, to warn all of you."

"Warn us... about what?"

Buddy seemed unsure of himself, but pressed on. "It's Kirov, sir."

"The Russian fellow?"

"Yes, sir. He has a plan, a terrible plan. He wanted me to help, but I refused. It's tonight! It's..."

"It's what, son, for God's sake?" MacDonald bellowed again.

"He's planning to set a false light on the beach and cause a ship to wreck, then rob its cargo."

MacDonald nodded and went to the phone. "I'm going to call all the stations and warn them."

He called High Head's keeper and told him, then the keepers at Race Point and Highland, the latter promising to notify the police. While he was on the phone Pendleton came in the room. He glowered when he saw Buddy.

"What's going on?" he demanded.

MacDonald hung up the phone and looked gravely at Pendleton. "We have a bad situation, Scotty, 'least it could be one, very bad. Kirov and his men are on their way out here to try to get a ship to wreck so's they can rob it." He looked at Buddy. "Any idea where on the beach they'll try this?"

"I'm not sure, sir. I was to meet them at Snail Road. I overheard him and William once, talking about surveying the stretch to the east, behind East Harbor." Buddy paused, and then added, "The other times we met at the west end and was on the other side of you."

"The other times…" MacDonald nodded. He thought for a moment. "Toward Race Point. Yes." He looked at Pendleton. "Get the men and the lifeboat cart and let's head toward High Head. It's a gamble, but send Silva the other way in case I'm wrong. He can signal if he sees something."

"Aye, sir," Pendleton said, and turned to go.

"And Scotty," MacDonald said.

Pendleton turned back.

"Issue rifles to Punchy, Jurgen, Joshua, and one for yourself."

"Aye, sir."

MacDonald turned to Buddy. "You coming with us?"

Buddy looked like a lost boy. "Yes, sir, if you'll have me."

MacDonald opened a drawer and removed two long barreled Colt pistols. "Know how to use one of these?"

"I think so, yes, sir."

MacDonald handed him one of the pistols. Punchy, still in the room, was shocked.

"Sir..." he said.

"Let's get a move on, Mr. Costa. No time to lose."

"Aye, sir," Punchy said, and ran out of the room.

MacDonald looked at Buddy, not without sympathy. "You're a very confused young man," he said. "But you've done the right thing by coming out here. Now let's go out and put an end to this nonsense."

Buddy looked straight in his eye. "Yes, sir."

A ship was moving north up the coast from Chatham, a small steam freighter with a steadying sail and a tall smokestack. She had a crew of six and three passengers. The night had turned colder, with a blustery wind and wisps of damp fog, though visibility was still reasonably good. The captain stood on deck near the helm. He thought he could see the shadows of the dunes along the coast, though he couldn't be sure just how far off they were. He pushed up the collar of his pea coat.

The Life-Savers set out down the beach toward High Head. It was an eerie night, fog wafting over the water's edge in slivers and slices. Buddy walked in front with Pendleton and MacDonald; following closely behind, Joshua, Punchy, Jurgen and Peter Abbott pulled the lifeboat cart. Buddy felt out of place. Pendleton kept shooting him dirty looks and he could sense Punchy still breathing down the back of his neck. But he liked the feel of the Colt in his belt and was convinced that by giving him the gun, the Keeper had bestowed some special stature upon him in spite of the past.

The men moved along the sand as quickly as they could; at least there was neither snow nor heavy wind. They could see the white of the breakers stretching a short way out. It seemed odd to rush toward a rescue when none seemed imminent. Then the freighter's deep foghorn shattered the silence. The sound filled Joshua with dread.

They came around a bend in the beach and there, beneath a wall of high dunes, they could see a dim light. It seemed to be moving up and down and around.

"Looks like a ship's light on the water," Jurgen said.

Joshua squinted and thought he could see the hulk of the ship. Now he could see the steadying sail, maybe a half mile out.

"Jesus," Joshua whispered. "That ship's going to get too close in a few minutes."

"She sees the light on the beach," MacDonald said.

The ship's captain mistook the erratic beam for another ship. He thought it meant he had plenty of distance between him and the bars. He signaled the helmsman to edge closer to the shore where there was less fog.

As the Life-Savers drew nearer to the dancing light, they could see Tucker driving a long wagon slowly in their direction along the beach, a brightly glowing lantern rigged from a wooden trestle across the wagon's rear. The slow bobbing motion made the light swing back and forth.

Captain MacDonald turned to Jurgen. "Give me your rifle. I'm going to stop that son of a bitch."

Jurgen handed it to him. The others came to a halt. MacDonald held up the rifle and sighted it. It occurred to Joshua he had never seen the Keeper do such a thing. The next instant, he fired. The shot rang out like a thunderclap. They watched as the bullet struck Tucker in the middle of his chest. He slumped in his seat, and then fell completely out of the wagon. The mule kept walking, the lantern jiggling on the back.

"Light a flare!" MacDonald shouted. He fired the rifle again, extinguishing the lantern.

Punchy took a Coston flare from his belt, pulled the striker and ignited it. He held the flare in his hand, red light and smoke instantly brightening up the night. Now, by the light of the flare, they could see Kirov, William and two men Joshua did not recognize, clustered around a new skiff some twenty yards off near the water's edge.

Kirov drew a pistol from his belt and fired at the Life-Savers. His first shot hit the sand next to them. The men froze. He fired again and hit Jurgen in the side of his neck. Then he signaled to William and the others and they pushed off in the skiff.

Onboard the ship, the captain heard what sounded like gunshots. The lantern was extinguished and he wondered why he could no longer see the other ship's light. A few moments later, the flare lit up the beach and he saw the men. The next instant, the freighter hit the sandbar. The engine screeched as the hull twisted against the sand. MacDonald's shot had come too late.

Kirov stood at the helm of the skiff, a Napoleonic figure, exhorting the rowers to pull harder. MacDonald saw them and ordered Pendleton to launch the lifeboat. The Life-Savers scrambled to drag the boat from the cart to the water's edge. Joshua knelt by Jurgen. The bullet had skimmed his neck at the base, just above the shoulder. The wound was bleeding steadily, but had not cut an artery or a vein.

"Leave him be, lad," MacDonald called, running toward the boat. "We'll be back soon enough with any luck."

Joshua looked in a panic, worried to leave Jurgen. He removed his scarf and wrapped it as best he could around Jurgen's neck. "Press on this."

Jurgen nodded weakly. "Go now," he said.

Joshua ran to the lifeboat.

The ship had been under full steam and she struck the bar with terrific force. Two of her crew were thrown into the sea. Feeling the impact, the three passengers ran to the deck. The freighter was now in pandemonium, debris and rigging flying about, waves crashing over the rail and across the skewed deck, the captain shouting to be heard over the roaring breakers and screeching timbers. One sailor had scrambled up the steadying mast. Now the mast cracked in the middle and he was flung, tangled in sails and rigging, into the waiting ocean.

The Life-Savers heard the screams. They knew the sound all too well. Kirov heard them, too, aware he had to move fast. The ship's captain saw Kirov's skiff approaching. At first his heart leapt with joy at being rescued so quickly. When the skiff was close to the ship's port midsection, a sailor ran over and Kirov threw him a line. His motley crew of pirates scrambled aboard. They all held guns and knives and the captain knew instantly they were not Life-Savers. One of the passengers, seeming to understand, ran toward them from the aft deck in a wild rage. Kirov drew his dagger and caught the man in his gut, wrenching his arm upward to cut the fellow wide open. Kirov turned and ran toward the captain, his blade still dripping and his gun in the other hand aimed at the captain's temple.

"What do you want?" the captain cried, almost hysterically, over the wind.

"Take me to your cabin," Kirov demanded. He moved the pistol closer to the captain's head. "Now!"

Knowing he was defeated, the captain turned and led Kirov and one of the new men to the cabin, while William and the other man held the passengers and crew at bay.

The Life-Savers rowed hard. Snow began to blow in bursts like icy grapeshot biting at the men's faces. Joshua's rifle was slung by a leather strap across his chest. Buddy sat in front of him, sternward, also rowing.

Inside the cabin, Kirov snarled at the captain. "Show me what you've got, and be quick."

The captain opened a cupboard built into a table. He extracted a heavy wood chest and opened it. Inside were sheaves of paper and a bar of gold.

"What are these?" Kirov demanded, holding up the papers.

"Bearer bonds," the captain said. "If you can keep them dry—"

Kirov smacked the man on the side of his face with the butt of his gun. "What else ya got?"

The captain looked around in a panic. "That's all there is. That and the cargo in the hold. Lumber, leather skins, barrels of kerosene—"

Kirov struck the man again. "I think you're lying. What else?"

The captain, a tough man who had endured much danger and hardship, appeared on the verge of breaking down. His ship was nearly lost and he was faced with a madman who held him captive as the ship foundered.

"Please, sir, let me tend to my men."

Kirov hit the man a third time. "What else you got?"

The captain said no more, but glanced for a fleeting

moment toward an alcove on the starboard side of the cabin. Kirov followed his gaze. A looking glass was set into the alcove above a porcelain bowl; the surrounding wood was paneled. Kirov walked to the mirror, turned his dagger handle outward, and smashed the glass. Behind it was a small compartment.

"No!" the captain yelled, and ran at Kirov.

The Russian pushed him away and hammered at the door. The wood splintered. He reached his hand inside and came out with a small knife, forged in gold, its handle encrusted with emeralds.

"Now we've got something..."

"Don't touch that, you bastard," the captain said. The room rolled and tossed.

Kirov turned and shot the captain point blank in his chest. Kirov's accomplice jumped at the blast. The captain slipped to the floor.

"It was my daughter's dowry," he said, choking.

"Not no more it isn't," Kirov said. He shoved the bejeweled knife into his shirt, sheaved his dagger, and holding the gold brick in one hand and his gun in the other, he turned to the other man. "Let's get back!"

They moved outside, leaving the captain dying on the floor.

The Life-Savers approached the ship. The burgeoning surf pounded her wildly. With no one at the helm, her bow wedged in the sand, she kept shifting direction, the engine screeching, the remains of her rigging whipping in the wind. As they came closer, a sailor saw them and understood who they were. He ran to the rail to help them aboard. William saw this and fired, but the boat shifted, the sailor slipped, and the bullet only nicked his shoulder. Then the entire ship tilted further over on its starboard side. First one, then another, then a third man slid toward the rail, howling as they went. They hit the railing and piled up against each other, but did not go over.

Joshua called to MacDonald, "Can you get any closer?"

MacDonald pushed hard on the long steering oar. Joshua saw his chance and leaped for the railing. He caught it with one hand and scrambled to grab hold with the other before he fell into the waves. He lifted himself over the rail.

"Throw me a line," he shouted. Punchy threw him one, missed, threw again and Joshua caught it. The lifeboat rose and fell dangerously close to the ship. Joshua wrapped the line around the stanchion and pulled until the boat was about four feet out. Then, one by one, the other men jumped, helping each other across the gap. Buddy followed Peter Abbot. Only Pendleton stayed with the boat.

When Kirov reached William, he saw through the fog and spray the Life-Savers scrambling aboard. "What the fuck you doing?" he shouted at William, pointing at them. He drew his gun and began to fire.

The Life-Savers tried to get their bearings. The deck of the ship, now at a steep angle, was twenty feet across. Kirov, William and the other two would-be pirates were gathered near the stern on the raised port side. The Life-Savers had come aboard near the starboard bow. The two groups were separated by some forty-five feet of drenched, sloping, reeling deck. Between them, at the stern, holding on for dear life, were the two passengers and three sailors. Visibility was getting worse by the second as the storm grew more intense and the waves fiercer. A plume of steam shot upward from the foredeck.

MacDonald held onto a stanchion and assessed the situation. He gestured to Joshua to stick with him while Punchy and Peter Abbot tried to circle around the deckhouse to get closer to Kirov and his men without being seen. Buddy came up alongside Joshua and his face twitched in a half-grin; it occurred to Joshua that in Buddy's twisted mind this was some kind of adventure. The truth was Buddy felt terrified, that all this was somehow his fault.

William spotted Buddy and called to Kirov, "Gogol, look! It's him! Fuckin' traitor!"

Kirov looked up and saw Buddy. He lifted his gun and fired, but the tossing boat threw off his aim. William, like some mad banshee, let out a howl and ran straight at Buddy, knife drawn, firing a pistol with his other hand. Punchy, struggling to keep his balance, aimed his rifle and fired. He hit William in the shoulder but didn't stop him. William fired back then lost his balance. The errant bullet hit Joshua in his side. He felt the sharp sting; for a moment, it took his breath away.

When he saw his friend hit and stumbling, Buddy screamed, "Joshua!" Losing all sense of fear, Buddy ran at William, firing his pistol over and over. The wraith fell to the deck, fatally wounded, but still shrieking. He slid down the deck and over the side, his phantom screams following him into the waves.

Two of the sailors moved in on one of Kirov's new men, who held two pistols and shot one of them dead. The gunshots sounded like distant firecrackers in the roar of the sea. For an instant, Joshua and Buddy looked at each other; Joshua could see the dread in his friend's eyes. Peter Abbot rushed over and jumped on the man shooting at the two sailors. They fell to the floor, tearing at each other's faces and throats, slipping across the deck. Kirov's other man took aim at MacDonald with a pistol and shot him in the leg. MacDonald fell, and Punchy rushed to his rescue, firing the rifle, then turning it and beating the man, who had taken a bullet in his chest, until he was near dead.

Buddy spotted Kirov, engulfed in fog and foam like some crazed Ahab cursing and firing his gun at anyone he could see. Buddy rushed at him.

"Oh. It's you!" Kirov yelled. "You're a fuckin' traitor, a fuckin' traitor!" The metal of his long dagger glistened in the night like a mythical sword.

Buddy pointed his Colt at Kirov. "I'm not afraid of you. You're a scourge on the earth. I know that now..."

"Scourge on the earth, is it?" Kirov shouted.

He lunged at Buddy with the dagger. Buddy fired, but the boat slipped again and the shot went low. The bullet only grazed Kirov's leg and he kept coming.

Joshua saw what was happening. Trying desperately to make his way across, he screamed, "Buddy, get out of there!"

But Buddy moved forward and aimed again. Kirov side-stepped him, turned, and plunged the knife into Buddy's ribcage. Buddy cried out.

Joshua shouted, "Buddy! No!"

Buddy fell to his knees and found himself sliding. Some-how, he got to his feet. Kirov, himself wounded, seemed to be laughing at him. Buddy stepped toward him again, grim-faced.

Kirov lunged. He sank the dagger into Buddy's gut and twisted the blade, again and again. Buddy went down for good, sliding on the slanting deck, leaving behind a bloody smear. Peter Abbot caught his arm just before he went into the waves.

Joshua, barely able to breathe, lifted his rifle to fire at Kirov. At that moment the ship's boiler exploded. The boat shook to its core and rolled even further on its side. The kerosene in the hold burst into flame, and in moments the deck split apart. Flames shot through the gap and the air was engulfed by thick, acrid smoke. Both men were thrown by the blast and Joshua's shot diverted. Kirov's face twisted into a deathly leer. He lunged at Joshua. Joshua tried to get the rifle up again, but Kirov was too close. Joshua swung the rifle barrel hard against the Russian's shoulder. Kirov staggered, but found his feet and moved in. Despite the wildly pitching deck, the knife in Kirov's hand seemed to float in a graceful arc through the air. Punchy and MacDonald, rushing to help Joshua, stood frozen, watching the dagger, certain it would find its mark. Kirov's face seemed to light up, as the malevolent blade moved toward Joshua's chest.

Holding the rifle by its barrel, Joshua swung again. The blow hit Kirov in the side of the head, and he fell. Joshua dropped the gun and jumped on him. Half blinded, Kirov swung the knife wildly. It caught Joshua in the shoulder—razor sharp, it cut through the heavy clothes and parted the skin—then arced downward and cut his upper thigh. Joshua did not feel the cuts. Kirov's knife arm came up again and Joshua grabbed it above the wrist with both hands. The men wrestled, cursing and grunting, sliding down the water-soaked deck. Joshua had never felt such anger at another human being. With all of his soul, the one thing he desired was to kill the man beneath him.

MacDonald tried to take aim at Kirov, but the two men were so intertwined he couldn't be sure he would hit the right one. Joshua gripped the Russian's arm for all he was worth, and raised his knee to smash Kirov in the chest.

Kirov laughed like an insane man and spit at him. "You're gonna die, man! You're gonna die!"

"No, I'm not, not today!"

Summoning whatever strength he had left in him, Joshua turned the knife slowly toward Kirov, pushing the knife arm down toward the man's chest. Both men's faces were bright red, their muscles bulging.

Joshua pushed until the tip of the blade pressed into Kirov's shirt. He leaned on his own arm and kept pushing. The blade went in further, finding its path between the upper ribs. Kirov watched his blood bubble up through the shirt. His strength surged and he pushed their arms back up, but Joshua strained harder and the blade resumed its descent. Deeper and deeper, harder and harder, until abruptly the blade plunged all the way in, the carved handle pressed against the bone. Blood gurgled out. Kirov held on a moment more, and then expired. In death, Joshua thought, his rage and strength gone, he became just an ordinary man.

The flames were spreading over the boat. The entire battle had taken only moments, but to Joshua, to all aboard still alive, it had been an eternity. Joshua twisted free of Kirov's body, got to his feet, then fell again. He allowed himself to slide down the deck to where Buddy lay.

MacDonald managed to get himself up. He and Punchy and Peter Abbot helped the others across the deck. The ship, on her last legs, charred and bent, pitched again in the surf. MacDonald grasped the rail near where Joshua knelt over Buddy, who lay pressed against the bulwark, his body twisted, blood on his chest and clothes. His eyes were open. Joshua turned. He and MacDonald looked at each other.

Joshua leaned his head very close to Buddy's.

"Joshua? Ol' sport?" Buddy murmured faintly.

Joshua held up Buddy's head. Buddy looked up at him. His eyes still seemed to have their sparkle. "Always tol' you…"

Joshua strained to hear him. "Told me what?"

"It was a beautiful place…"

Joshua choked up and shook his head. "It was never your kind of place. You only came for the girls."

Buddy lifted his head and seemed to smile. Joshua was certain he smiled. He nodded at Joshua, then rested his head back on the deck. His eyes closed. Then they reopened.

"Joshua," he gasped, his words slurred. "I was… was on your side. Always…"

Joshua's eyes filled with tears. Buddy's eyes closed. He was gone. For a moment they remained there, then Joshua began to drag Buddy's body over to the lifeboat. Punchy came back and helped him, and with Peter Abbot they got him over the stanchion and into the rocking boat where the others waited. Joshua stepped over and lowered himself into place. The cut in his side and the one on his shoulder both were bleeding and sore, made worse by the wind and cold and sorrow. But he took up his oar, and they all did the same, and they rowed back, through the impossible surf and over the breakers to the beach.

CHAPTER SIXTEEN

W hen the Life-Savers reached shore, the crews from High Head and Race Point were there, along with two policemen on horseback. Jurgen had already been taken into town and was said to be in good condition. Joshua staggered out of the lifeboat and spoke to one of the policemen to make sure Buddy's body would be taken to Nickerson's funeral parlor and properly cared for. Then he collapsed in the sand.

He awoke in the station's guest room. He had no idea what time it was, and he felt disoriented. He lay in bed, bandages wrapped around his ribs and side, over his shoulder and one arm, and his thigh. Before he opened his eyes, he became aware of the brightness of the light and an odd stiffness all over his body. He looked up. A light seemed to shine over him. There, towering above him like some reverent angel, as if despite the bedclothes and bandages he had died of his wounds and gone to heaven, was the radiant face of Julia. She smiled, happy to see him awake.

"Joshua," she said, in that indelibly calm and confident doctor's voice of hers, "we were worried about you."

He smiled weakly and closed his eyes, warmed by her luminescence.

He awoke early, his brain still fogged. Peter Abbot came in and told him crews from town had removed the bodies of the murdered captain, Kirov and his two men, and that William's body and the slain sailor had floated ashore. Joshua fell back asleep. Later a crew hired by the ship's owner showed up to salvage what they could. As far as Joshua could ever discover, the gold ingot and emerald knife were never found.

In late afternoon, when he awoke again, his wounds hurt terribly and he remembered everything. Julia was gone. The sun was going down and the warm glow reflecting on the sand and beach grass seemed somehow incongruous. Joshua forced himself out of bed and with great difficulty made his way down the stairs. Pendleton warned him he should not be up, but Joshua ignored him and sat at the big table. The others gathered round and they ate dinner and drank whiskey and ale, relieved to have each other's company, plagued by the weight of the tragic events they had faced together, by Buddy's horrific death and by all the deaths they had seen over the long year.

The following day, they held a burial for Buddy on the dunes. Joshua had no idea if any of Buddy's family were still alive and had no way to contact them. Buddy had few friends in this place at the continent's edge. But the Life-Savers came to see him one last time, despite all that had happened.

A bright sun was shining, with fast-moving cirrus clouds

casting deep shadows. Buddy's body, which Peter Abbot and Punchy had wrapped in linen, was placed inside a large hole dug in the sand, whose loose sides were already slipping. The priest from the Sailor's Episcopal Church had been brought out to perform the service. Julia came, along with a few people from town who knew Buddy, and Life-Savers from the nearby stations. The priest recited funeral prayers and the Life-Savers mumbled amen to all he said. They hadn't loved Buddy, nor shown him much sympathy in life, but he had been one of them for a short time, and as MacDonald said in a brief but solemn speech, Buddy had saved quite a few lives and had done a noble thing in coming to warn them. He had died in their service after all. Even Punchy let a tear or two form on his cheek at those words.

Joshua listened and watched, leaning on a cane Mac-Donald had given him, feeling the stubbornly cold ocean breeze. It blew his hair, and Julia's, who stood next to him. He was in pain and struggled to keep his feet. Julia kept looking over at him, concerned. But whatever pain he felt seemed beside the point. There had been too much death. Granted, the world has not seen a single day since its inception when death failed to take its toll upon the races of man, the young and old, men and women, fairly or not, gently and with great violence, an inexorable tide of death that would forever sweep over the human condition like icy waves over a sinking ship. The cherished ones gone forever. Humanity ever replenished by a persistent renewal of life, an inimitable cycle that held a certain irony at moments such as these. Joshua, young as he may have been, felt seared to his deepest recesses by the tragedies he had seen and felt, as a Life-Saver and as a man.

He looked around at the people assembled there to bid

goodbye to someone they hardly knew, someone no one really knew, except Joshua. All were silent, knowing he would speak of his friend. He looked at them, one to the next, as if seeing these people and this place for the first time, the wind burning his eyes and reddening his cheeks. Twisting his cap in his hands, he began to speak, then looked up suddenly at the crowd, and, remarkably, smiled.

"Look at you all," he said. "My God, Buddy would have been amazed. All these people, here for him."

He looked over at Julia, and she nodded. The men laughed nervously.

"He would have been thrilled," Joshua said. He felt a warmth pass through him, even as he spoke with near-trembling lips, horrified to find himself actually in this moment. "But it's sad. That he's gone, that we're here. Without him." Joshua took a deep breath. "You know, there are people in the world who are driven by a need to be right, or to do good, to please others, to win something big. But there are a few who are driven overwhelmingly by their curiosity, a basic thirst for life that must be quenched. Buddy was one of those. He was one of the smartest people I've ever known, and what he wanted, really, most of all, was to experience things, and people, and places. I think he was scared of people, too, of what they thought of him, of whether they might get the best of him—and I think it made him do bad things because he was frightened of what might become of him. But he was a good boy, if you knew him. He thought about things no one I ever knew thought about, he read philosophers and poets and talked about things like freedom and loyalty... and he wanted to see the entire world. Every inch of it. Every person in it. Often he was disappointed, and it hurt him when he disappointed others, though he'd never admit it. But he held the world to a higher standard than it's capable of living up to. He believed, against all evidence, that people are good and should be treated fairly, should live free, should be able to trust each other. What wonderful things to aspire to. I admired him for all of that, and for his friendship, his loyalty. I won't ever forget him. We were lucky to have known him." He looked out at all of them again. He caught MacDonald's eye. And he felt the heavy weight of the moment on his heart. "That's all I've got to say."

All the Life-Savers mumbled in unison, "Hear, hear."

Joshua turned from the gravesite on that windswept dune and began to walk shakily toward the station, leaning heavily on the cane, Julia next to him, occasionally holding his arm when he stumbled. He worried that his words had been inadequate, but it had been the best he could do.

Poor Buddy, he thought, his heart wrenched with sadness and fatigue, poor Buddy.

When they reached the station the wagon Julia had hired stood waiting. She turned and looked at Joshua. There was sadness in her eyes, and she still looked concerned for him, but he had no idea if anything else remained between them.

"You are hurt, Joshua," she said softly. "You need medical care."

He wasn't sure what she meant.

"You should go to a hospital in Boston," she said. "We can arrange to put you on the train."

He shook his head. He didn't want to leave.

"Then at least spend a couple of days at Dr. Meads' office. There's a care room there, and we can watch over you and keep you comfortable."

Joshua began to shake his head, but MacDonald, standing near them, took his arm.

"She's right, son," he said. "You need more help than we can give you here. Go with Dr. Masefield; let them take care of you. Just a few days until you're stronger."

Joshua was too tired to argue and it was better than a train ride all the way to Boston. Julia mounted the wagon and gestured to Joshua. He looked at MacDonald, then laboriously placed one foot on the step of the wagon, grasped the rail and pulled himself up next to her. As they began to move through the rough sand, he grimaced at the wagon's jittery motion.

Julia and Dr. Meads installed him in one of the small rooms off the main medical office. He felt terribly awkward undressing, struggling to put on a linen robe and climbing into the crisp white sheets. He fell asleep almost instantly.

For the next two days, Julia took care of him. She brought him food and changed his dressings, gave him medicine to thwart the pain, and sat at his bedside. They didn't speak much. He could see in her face she was worried; when they did speak, she tried to be encouraging. But he was too tired, too sore, and too sad to do much more than simply accept her care. Still, he found it terribly comforting to have her so near to him. He felt sure somehow he loved this woman, though what that might mean for the future he had no idea.

The third day he was there, Julia came into his room just after lunchtime. She carried a tray with a teapot and cup, as she had done before. Joshua struggled to sit up.

"Feeling better?" she asked.

He nodded, but his face twisted as a bolt of pain shot through his ribs. "I'm fine."

"Well, no, you're not," Julia said. She was shaking her head as if about to pronounce a death sentence against her will. "But you are very stubborn, despite your deceptively sweet countenance, and I suspect you will come out of this just fine." She was looking deep into his eyes.

"What is it, Julia?"

"The banker."

Joshua felt an irrational thud in his chest, as if he'd been hit by a spar. He looked at her questioningly.

"He has asked me to marry him," Julia said solemnly.

The air in the room filled rapidly with the silence between them. Joshua just looked at her.

"I'm sorry, Joshua. I don't know what to say. I know the timing is rotten, but…"

"What did you say?"

"That I would think about it."

She gave him a weak smile, turned and left the room.

Joshua was aware there were tears forming in the corners of his eyes. He felt somewhat nauseated. He turned his head to face the wall. It was all too much. He slept.

The next morning, Joshua's fourth in this strangely quiet retreat, Julia knocked on Joshua's door and opened it. Joshua was finishing a light breakfast. A man came in, one he'd never seen before, a local Portuguese. The man stood uncomfortably in front of the bed.

"I'm very much sorry to be the one what unfortunately must bring you this news," the man said in faltering English, "but the Keeper out to Peaked Hill called this morning and asked me to come see you and to tell you right away, if you don't mind…"

Joshua tried to clear his head. "For God's sake, what is it?"

he demanded.

"Sir, yer father is ill. In hospital. Cap'n MacDonald said to tell ya. Sorry, very sorry to say this news but..."

Joshua closed his eyes. "Thank you," he said. The man turned and went out, and Julia closed the door. After a little while he called for her.

"I've got to leave," he said. "Got to get my things from the station."

"You're not well enough to travel," Julia said.

Joshua just looked at her. She could see that he was determined, and in her heart she knew he probably had the strength to manage it—and, anyway, he would go no matter what she said. Julia nodded. "I'll arrange it," she said.

Someone was sent to the station for his things, and Julia had a man with a carriage come and take Joshua to the train. She went with him. Before he stepped up on the platform, she put her hand on his shoulder and kissed his cheek.

"Goodbye, Joshua. Be well." That was all she said.

He stood in the doorway, his duffel by his side, as they moved slowly down the wharf. It was April, still cold and windy. He held onto the railing as the train made its way past the vessels tied to the pier, across Commercial Street and Bradford Street and out past the dunes. He caught a glimpse of the harbor with its little lighthouse. He had asked Julia to tell the men at the station he would return as soon as he could, but he wondered, would he see this place ever again?

With his fresh wounds and bandages, it had been an exceedingly uncomfortable trip. He had changed trains twice. But his memory of it would be of the time passing slowly, his mind numb, tormented by the fear of losing the last member of his family, and thinking of Buddy. Joshua pictured him sitting there by his side, embarking on long diatribes as the fields and tunnels flew by, about girls he'd known, about goddamned politicians, the power mongers and capitalists of the world, some poet or philosopher he'd just read. Buddy's presence on that train would have cheered him and driven him to distraction. He wished it could be so. It was nearly dawn when the train got close to the city, slowing as it crawled past rail yards and tenements, and Joshua was exhausted. He had not slept. He could see the buildings of the great city, his family's city, stretching ahead in the early daylight. They reached Grand Central and he took his bag and stumbled over the grey platform, the thick urban smell surrounding him like a shroud. Part of the old station was being demolished. He asked a Negro porter in a white jacket about it. The porter said there would be a new and far grander terminal built there but it would likely take some time. "Welcome to New York, suh," the man had added.

His father had been admitted to the German Hospital at Park Avenue and Seventy Seventh Street, the closest one to the family's house, with an infection in his lungs related to the pneumonia of earlier that year. Joshua arrived by hansom cab at the entrance, covered by a long green awning, which bisected the tranquil old street. Joshua left his bag with the receptionist and took a creaky elevator to the third floor. The place smelled of carbolic acid and cigarette smoke. It was a warm day and all the windows were open, the cries of children echoing from below.

His father lay in a narrow bed by a window; he looked pale and diminished. He stirred from a light sleep when Joshua came in leaning on his cane. Gideon opened his eyes, and when they focused he looked alarmed.

"Joshua! You're here. What's the matter?" Gideon said, his voice crackly from disuse.

Joshua hobbled over to the bed. "Of course I'm here, father. I came as soon as I heard you were ill. Why didn't you send for me?"

Gideon stared at him, as if unsure to whom he was speaking. Then he sharpened. "What's the matter?" he repeated.

Joshua smiled. "I'm fine. Really, I am. Ran into a little trouble up there."

"I see," Gideon said, leaning back on his pillow. "You're not seriously wounded?"

Joshua smiled again at his father. "No, I'm afraid I'll survive."

Gideon closed his eyes. "Thank God." He fell back asleep.

Joshua sat watching his father. He appeared older. Joshua thought of MacDonald, who would someday, not too far off, lose his own potency. In time it would come to all of us who survive mortal peril, Joshua thought. After a while, he grew tired himself and took a carriage to the house on Sixty-Third Street.

An old Polish woman opened the door. Joshua didn't know her, but explained who he was. With tears in her eyes she said how fond she was of his father, and asked if the "Admiral" were all right? Joshua smiled at this; his father had never wanted to be an admiral. He carried his bag upstairs to his old room, and then walked around the house, from room to room, dogged by fatigue and a kind of hazy gloom that seemed to fill the old house like smoke. His father's office was dusty, piled with books and papers, a robe draped over the big chair behind the desk. A captain's hat with shiny buttons sat on the desk, and a photograph of the family in Central

Park in better times. Joshua went to his room and fell asleep in his clothes.

He slept until the middle of the next morning and awoke with a sense of banishment, unsure who or where he was. He sat up and looked around the unfamiliar room, hearing the alien city sounds outside the window. He went downstairs; the Polish lady must have been elsewhere in the house. The kitchen was a long galley with wide planked floors, at its center an enormous white-enameled cast iron stove of sixteen burners and three ovens. Joshua had always thought of the stove as the heart of the house, glimmering and hardworking. When he was a child, the family would come down for breakfast in the dining room, where a buffet would be set by the servants with copper trestles to warm the sausages, eggs and potatoes and baskets of freshly baked biscuits. But Joshua always preferred to eat in the kitchen. He liked the scurrying servants, the clanking pots, the tittering of silver place settings. He did his homework here and sat before the warmth of the mighty stove, reading his favorite books, Kipling, Twain, Emerson, and tales of the Wild West. Lucy had teased him for hiding among the servants.

There were freshly baked muffins on the kitchen table and a pitcher of milk. He drank and ate, then went back to his room, cleaned up and dressed. He left the house to go see his father, but decided first to walk up to Fifth Avenue. He passed elaborate stone mansions, well dressed strollers and graceful carriages. The city was bustling with vitality, as always. Joshua felt out of place after so long amid the beach and sea and weathered clapboard structures, after all that had transpired. He made his way to the hospital. His father was once again asleep, but Joshua met his doctor, who said

Gideon was improving greatly and could return home in a day or two.

The next two days, Joshua visited his father every afternoon, but otherwise never left the house. He was pleased to see Gideon growing stronger; they did not speak much, but his father did seem glad to see him. In truth, Joshua couldn't wait to get back to the house. He explored each room, rediscovering forgotten details: books, paintings, small sculptures and ceramics his mother had collected, his father's military decorations and West Point textbooks, the books and toys that belonged to Adam and him. He, too, was feeling stronger and could now walk without the cane, though he still felt pain from the wound in his side.

He returned to his father's study. He looked through books and papers on the shelves. His father had always been an avid reader, but he was surprised to find books on philosophy and religion, on Christianity, Judaism, Islam, and Hinduism. He found a poorly printed pamphlet of Friedrich Nietzsche's writings stuffed between two larger volumes and laughed aloud, thinking of Buddy, trying to imagine what had gone through Gideon's mind as he'd sat there.

The house was lovely, quiet, serene, dusty, and lonely. All it lacked was people. Joshua felt as if he had walked through some portal, in time or space or he knew not which, memories following him from room to room as if in an echo chamber, impossible to pinpoint clearly but nonetheless audible or if not audible then corporeal. He felt a sense of sorrow and loss, as he thought about the family and friends and servants who had populated this space—here he was, as if in some reverie, wandering the house alone, able to look at everything, touch and feel everything—yet none of it seemed real. He wondered if he had lost his mind and slipped into some delusional version of the past. But no, he was here. He had somehow to make sense of it all and chart a course—like a captain, avoiding the storms and bars. But how?

He went to the parlor, where the Christmas tree once stood, and sat in one of the winged leather armchairs his mother so adored. At one end of the room was a piano; Joshua closed his eyes and could hear someone playing Chopin, his mother looking on, her head bobbing with the cadence of the music, when he was young.

On the third day, Joshua walked to the hospital. He felt better, more alive than he could remember feeling for some time now, enjoying the early New York spring. When he arrived Gideon was dressed and speaking to the doctor. Joshua felt a sense of joyous relief—and some trepidation, that his silent reverie at the house would end. Still, he happily helped his father, who was in a wheelchair, down the corridor, out of the hospital, and into a waiting carriage. At home, his father was installed in his bed by two nurses, and one remained to help care for him. The Polish woman made dinner and Joshua ate with his father by his bedside. Afterward, Gideon seemed to perk up.

"Go get me some cognac in the parlor, will you?" he asked. He looked at Joshua, who seemed surprised. "And bring a glass for yourself."

His father had never before suggested such a thing. Joshua did as he was asked and returned with a decanter and two snifters. He sat next to his father and poured them each a drink. His father raised his glass.

"To our health!" he said with a laugh. "Good to see you, my boy."

Joshua lifted his glass, then drank. It was a very fine cognac and tasted delicious. He looked at Gideon, uncertain what to expect.

"Don't look so nervous, son," Gideon said. "It really is good to see you."

"Is it?"

"Don't be foolish. Of course it is. You seem to be feeling better. You've lost the cane."

"Yes, sir," Joshua said, pleased he had noticed.

"In a day or two, I expect to be up and about myself," Gideon said. "Perhaps we can go for a walk together."

"That would be very nice," Joshua said.

In the morning, Joshua went to check on his father, but he was not in his bed. He found him at the breakfast table, drinking coffee and reading the morning paper. For a moment it was as if they had been transported two years into the past, as if none of the terrible things that had happened really had at all. Gideon looked up when Joshua entered.

"Some coffee?"

Later, Joshua found his father sitting at his desk, reading over a document.

"Oh, Joshua. Sit down, will you?"

Joshua hesitated a moment.

His father looked up at him. "Please. I want to talk with you."

Joshua sat in a leather chair facing his father's desk. He had sat here as a boy, watching Gideon work, imagining what it would be like to be a grown man, so busy and filled with responsibilities. His father had rarely spoken to him at such times.

Now as he began, it sounded almost as if it were a speech

he had practiced, and Joshua listened with trepidation.

"You realize of course you have an obligation."

"To do what?" Joshua asked.

"Well, to become the man you are meant to be."

Joshua sighed. Here we go, he thought. "Meaning what, father?"

"Meaning a man worthy of your family, of your brother, your mother." Gideon paused, as if out of breath.

"And of you?" Joshua asked.

"Yes, of me, too." Gideon said, nodding.

"But I'm not?"

"You're not what?"

Joshua smiled, feeling a bit frustrated. "Doing that. Being worthy of my brother, of you…"

Gideon's face was stern, the proud skull turned slightly, as if he would shake his head "no." But instead his head held still and Joshua saw dampness creeping into the corners of his father's eyes. It was astonishing. His cheeks became flushed, and tears were forming, the skin of his face quivering almost imperceptibly. Gideon turned then and looked right into Joshua's eyes.

"I know I've been less than enthusiastic about your joining the Life-Savers. I have been alone in this house since you left, alone with the memories of all of you, of all that has passed. I miss your mother terribly, and Adam." Joshua could hear a slight choking sound in his voice. "And you, Joshua. I have had a good deal of time to think about many things in the past months, and my illness has changed my perspective of things, I imagine. I was afraid, to be blunt, I would die alone in this house. I was frightened, to be honest."

Joshua looked at his father, somewhat bewildered. He had

never heard him speak this way.

"Your mother loved you deeply. She loved you both, but somehow you were special to her, the blessed creature fashioned from her very ribs, so to speak. Like many men, I had little enough time for my children, which, I imagine like many men do, I regret as I've grown older. Perhaps I spent more time with Adam, expected more of him, that somehow he would be more like me. A silly idea, really, for our children are an amalgam of their parents and the world in which they are raised. But I have always loved you, my boy, and I am proud of you."

Again, Joshua looked surprised and realized he was fidgeting in his seat.

"Please, hear me out. I think I was a good Naval man, a good captain, as was expected of me. I was well-trained and tried to live up to the traditions with which my fellow students and I were endowed. I even believe I was respected by my men. But I've come to understand that in truth I never felt I was giving very much to the world. I worked diligently and demanded the same from those under my command, but lately I've come to wonder: to what end? Through all those years, I never questioned myself, or my service. My great passion for the war turned out to be misguided, and I lost a son to it. You seemed a bit lost when you left for the war, especially when I saw you in Florida, overshadowed by your older brother, whose assumed destiny was to become a hero. But the other day I lay in that hospital bed, before you arrived, having no idea if I would ever see you again, alone, my family gone, and I suddenly thought to myself that you had your mother's heart and that, in the end, you are the one who has accomplished something of value, by engaging in the saving of men's lives rather than the taking of them. At that moment I prayed for the courage to someday tell you how much I respect you for that."

Joshua sat stunned, silent, uncertain how to respond. He felt tears come to his eyes, and quickly wiped them away. He and his father looked at each other, but Gideon said no more. After a few long, awkward minutes, Joshua cleared his throat and stood.

"Thank you, father," he said. "I think I need to excuse myself. I, uh… should think about what you've just said."

Gideon simply nodded, and picked up the paper he had been reading. Joshua left the room.

He decided to go out. Once again, he walked to Fifth Avenue. The onslaught of spring was overpowering in its fullness and beauty, and the street bustled with life: people walking and riding in carriages, vendors selling dry goods and souvenirs and sweets along the sidewalk, children rushing, dogs barking. Central Park exploded with color, with blooming trees and flowers. As he walked, he thought about his father. He had always been strong, tough and worldly, unafraid of responsibility and unable to escape his sense of duty and honor even when he might have benefited from a less formal relationship with his family and friends. Yet it seemed he was a complex person, more than Joshua had ever imagined, filled with passions and interests, who in his solitary moments pondered the purpose of life and the failings of his fellow men. This was a gratifying revelation—but what did it mean for Joshua? What should he do now? He was still so young. Should he return to college, look for a job, travel? He hadn't thought about these things since before the war, and the quandary now suddenly rushed at him. He felt a momentary flush of panic.

And what of his life in Provincetown? He was expected to

return. But should he? Julia had said she doubted he would spend his life as a Life-Saver, nor had he ever really considered it seriously. His father had thought it unsuitable. But if not that, then what should he do? He thought of Julia, her loveliness, her strength, the touch of her body, her kisses, and her toughness and the determination with which she had driven him away. She had cared for him after the battle on the ship, but then told him of the banker's proposal. There was no reason to believe a future might lay ahead for them, that she would want him any more than before. He felt caught between his life as it had been until now and some unforeseeable future.

He came to the magnificent Metropolitan Museum building at Eighty Second Street and decided to go in. He'd come here often with his mother and her friends, and the massive building with its classical interior held a special place in his heart. Maybe it would distract him from the confusion that seemed to plague him.

Inside, a short line of well-dressed New Yorkers waited to view a recent show entitled 'American Contemporaries.' Intrigued, Joshua joined them. The gallery contained canvases and drawings of living artists, much of the work in tribute to or imitation of popular European styles, particularly French Impressionism. He walked slowly along, following the line of elegant browsers who shuffled and whispered through the muted rooms, until he came around a corner and stopped before a painting that seemed to be attracting attention.

The painting was entitled 'The Life Line', by a New England painter named Winslow Homer. When he looked at it closely, it took his breath away. It was a dark canvas, depicting a raging sea along a rocky coastline. A house perched upon high cliffs was at the right, a foundering clipper ship to the left. The centerpiece of the painting was a woman suspended on a breeches buoy from a heavy line, stretched unconscious over a sailor or perhaps a Life-Saver in heavy boots sitting in the buoy, whose arm held her firmly in place. She wore a drenched gray dress with no coat, a red scarf flying over her rescuer's face. Joshua stood transfixed for an hour or more, as people shuffled past. He simply could not believe the image before him—for it was a scene he had witnessed himself only months earlier.

It was an incongruous, unsettling sensation, to be in New York amid finery and sophistication, culture and urbanity at its height, he a son of wealthy New Yorkers—who had been to war and spent a year at the edge of the sea witnessing scenes just like this one, scenes of anguish and fear and death, so different from here. Perhaps in the history of the world it was always so, the shocking contrast between civilization and frontier, between home and the battlefield.

He closed his eyes and it was as if he were there, back on that beach, the ocean roaring like a thousand cannon, the wild white foam of the crashing surf, the Life-Savers in their wool pants and oil slickers and cork vests, drenched, freezing, shouting above the impossible din. The lifeboat, its smell, the feel of its damp wood, the hardness of the seat as they bounced over the breakers, the amazing heaviness of the oar as he pulled, and the helmsman—the Keeper or Pendleton—guiding them, leaning on the long steering oar, shouting encouragement. It had been a life apart. For these moments, he was back on that beach. And suddenly it was as if a curtain had parted, a wall fallen away. The truth was clear, the only truth there could be. Whatever his father might once have thought or expected, he should follow his own heart now. This was what he had learned from his father's words, his mother's letter. Her days had ended too soon. His father, in his old age, regretted not having accomplished enough. Joshua did not want to feel that way. His destiny was laid out before him and he had no choice but to go and find it.

When he returned home his father was asleep. Joshua sat in his room half the night, thinking of these things. In the morning, he went down to breakfast. Gideon was there, reading the paper. Joshua told him he had decided to return and finish what remained of his contracted time with the Life-Savers. Then he would see. Gideon was sorry to see him go, but he understood. For the first time in his life, Joshua felt he and his father understood each other. This was an excellent start.

CHAPTER SEVENTEEN

W hen the train passed East Harbor, Joshua could
see the bay off to the left glistening before him,
its vast openness, the tall sails capturing glints
of the sun upon their whiteness, the steam trawlers making
their way back to port. It was a port like no other and it had
called him back, too. Finally, the train pulled along the wharf,
its bells clanging, and came to a stop in a cloud of steam. The
conductor swung down from the front car and called out
loudly, "PROVINCETOWN! END OF THE LINE!"

Joshua stepped down, holding his duffel. He hoisted it over
his shoulder and walked stiffly back along the pier. It was a year
since he'd first come to this place. He knew he had changed, in
ways he had yet to fully understand. The place itself had not
changed a bit. It was itself, an outpost at the edge of the continent. The sun was bright, white clouds dotting the sky, the
sharp wind rattling the rigging on sailboats tied to the pier.

It was early in the season, but the streets of the little town were already full of people—tourists, merchants, sailors. He walked down Snail Road to the base of the dunes. His duffel felt heavy and carrying it hurt his side. He was sorry he hadn't arranged for a ride to the station, but he took a breath, threw the duffel onto his shoulder, and began to climb. The air was warm and the heat reflected off the sand as he struggled upward. A family of gulls and their chicks perched at the top watching the human slip in the sand. He walked slowly and stopped frequently to rest, but though he was winded, he had to admit it felt astonishingly good to be out here, surrounded by a stark sea of sand, the light reflected across its vast stretches, the stunning silence of the place.

When he reached the station, it was just before lunch. The morning's drills were finished. MacDonald stood by the edge of the water, smoking his pipe while Punchy fished. He tossed his line far out into the waves, then reeled it back in, over and over, without a bite. He grew grumpier at each toss of the line. MacDonald offered occasional sardonic comments. Joshua watched them.

Punchy reeled in the line again to find a clump of seaweed. "Damn fish!" he cried.

"No fish there, Punchy," MacDonald pointed out.

"With all respect, sir, that ain't a nice thing to be sayin'," Punchy said. Then he looked up and saw Joshua. He ran over and hugged him so hard Joshua thought the man might suffocate him.

"Good to see you, lad," MacDonald said. "Are you back now?"

Joshua smiled. "Yes, sir."

"And your father?"

"He's fine, sir, thank you. Had everyone worried, but he seems to have fully recovered. I'm glad I went to see him. And, honestly, sir, it's good to be back."

"Big city's too much for you now?"

Joshua looked around the empty beach and laughed. "I guess that must be it, sir. How are you doing?"

"A bit creaky in the bones but I'm fine, thank you, son. Ready to go back to work?"

"Yes, sir, I am."

"Good. We'll be rowing out after lunch."

"I can't wait, sir," Joshua said.

He went to the sleeping room and stored his gear. He looked at Buddy's empty mattress and remembered the day they'd first arrived. So much had happened… and yet, he was barely much older. He took a deep breath of ocean air. It would be summer soon. He had his life ahead of him. That seemed, for now, like a good thing. He went down to join the men for lunch. Once again, they welcomed him back.

After the capsize drills were done, Joshua joined a few of the men who were roasting potatoes over a fire on the beach. The sun was still strong, the late afternoon light refracted into a warm yellow-orange. Joshua walked to the water's edge. MacDonald walked down and stood next to him.

"Any plans for the summer?" he asked Joshua.

Joshua stared out silently for a while. He did not have a good answer. "I've come back here, sir."

"I see that, son, and we're glad to have you. Was it a hard decision?"

"I wouldn't say so. I realized this is where I belong, at least for now."

MacDonald nodded. He held his pipe unlit between his

teeth. He removed it and turned to Joshua. "And what about the young doctor?"

Joshua didn't answer for a while. "I don't know, sir," he finally said.

"Well, it's none of my business, but it seems to me there was something there between the two of you."

"Yes, sir, I believe you're right."

"Then what are you going to do about it?" MacDonald asked.

Joshua looked at the man who'd become his surrogate father in so many ways, yet with whom he'd barely ever had an intimate conversation. "There was something there, sir, that's for sure. But she pushed me away. She was going with some banker. I wasn't sure what to make of the whole thing. Not like I'm much of an expert. What would you do, sir?"

MacDonald laughed heartily. "Well, son, it would be presumptuous of me to hold myself out as much of an expert either, considering my own marriage, but there are times when a man asks himself if this is it, if she's the one."

"Well, how do you know?"

MacDonald laughed again. "It's impossible to know and no one can tell you. You might be wrong even if you think you know." He smiled. "But I'll tell you this much. If you let the moment pass, if you don't act when your inner voice is saying you should, you'll regret it bitterly for a long time to come."

"Hmmm," Joshua said.

Saturday late in the afternoon he crossed the dunes and turned onto Commercial Street. He headed west to find Julia. He knocked on the door of her cottage. There was no answer. He tried again, but she wasn't there. He leaned against the picket fence to wait for her, trying to keep his beating heart calm.

Nearly an hour went by. Joshua felt increasingly restless, not sure what to do. He thought about what MacDonald had said. Perhaps there would be other chances—but he felt a pesky urgency that wouldn't let him walk away. Then, suddenly, she appeared. She stopped when she saw him, her face slowly registering surprise, then what seemed like joy, then a neutral retreat.

"Joshua," she said softly. "You're back."

"Yes."

"Are you all right, Joshua?" she asked.

She was still beautiful, still enigmatic, a puzzle he did not yet know how to unlock.

"Yes," he answered. "I am. What about you?"

"Me? Oh, I'm the same. Fine. What about your father?"

"He's all right, actually." He paused, then added, "Thank God."

Her hair was blowing in the breeze. Her face, he realized, was far more than beautiful—it reflected a complex set of emotions he might never fully decipher.

"Why don't you come inside, Joshua?"

They sat together on her sofa and filled each other in on the week gone by. He told her about his father's illness, his time at the house in New York. She said there had been a wreck, at High Head, two days after he'd left, and she'd been called to the station. A young mother had been traveling south with her husband and daughter. The husband was drowned. The woman was bereft. Her child was all right, but the woman came unhinged for a few days. Then, miraculously, she recovered.

"I think she came to understand, despite her grief, that the child needed her to be strong, to be both its parents, and she accepted the responsibility and rebounded."

Joshua told her about the amazing painting he had seen, how he'd felt standing before it. "I've come back because I came to a realization. An important one, at least for me." He looked expectantly into her eyes, but she was waiting for him to finish.

"This is where I belong. For now, maybe forever, I can't say for certain. I'm young, as you've so often told me, but I want to be here. This life I've... built, if that's the right word—is what I want, what I must do."

She nodded, seeming to be considering. After a few moments, he spoke again. "I realized something else, or let's say I'm discovering it."

She looked at him, aware of a difference in his voice. "What is that?"

Joshua moved closer, touching her hair lightly. "You are the one I want."

She seemed to pause, to reflect. "It must have been hard for you. I mean, wounded as you were. Going back home."

He felt an odd, twisting feeling in his chest. "You're right. It was hard. But I discovered something else."

"What's that, Joshua?"

"I discovered I'm an adult. That I have a way forward."

Julia smiled. "That's good."

He felt an awkwardness subsuming him. The question foremost on his mind, fighting to come out. "What about the banker? Will you marry him?"

Julia laughed. Joshua looked at her, surprised. Almost angry.

"What's so funny?" he demanded.

"Would you like me to make you some dinner?" Julia asked. He felt confused. "Yes, I guess that would be nice."

She stood and suddenly began moving quickly. She went to the little kitchen and began taking food from the cupboards. She lit a fire in the stove. She unwrapped a roasted lamb leg she'd made for herself and placed it in a Dutch oven over the flame. She poured wine from a flask into two cut stem glasses and placed them on the little table. She set down dishes and lit candles. Joshua watched her, somewhat amazed. As she worked, she chatted about people in town, a wedding engagement, a child with a broken leg, a fisherman who got in a fight. Finally, she served the dinner and they sat down, facing each other. She lifted her glass and smiled warmly.

"I am glad you're here, Joshua." She took a sip of wine.

He drank, too. "Are you really? Honestly, Julia, I'm never sure…"

She laughed. "I believe I owe you an explanation."

He nodded, feeling a stirring in his gut he couldn't quite identify.

"It may sound funny to you, but since before you left, since long before that, I've been having an internal debate over you. I know I made you suffer, and I didn't mean to. But I was beginning to care for you, to like you in perhaps a more serious way. We had… some serious moments together." She looked at him and smiled. "But then, what in the world was I doing? What could I have been thinking? I'm the town's doctor, one of two, expected to have people's respect and trust at all times. It was hard enough to gain that respect. You have no idea what it means not to be taken seriously."

She paused and drank a large swallow of wine, then continued.

"What would people think of a woman, a doctor, responsible for saving their husbands and birthing their children, running around with a twenty year old boy? It was madness, no matter how good it felt to be doing it. So I stopped."

He was watching her closely now. She had his attention.

"I put an end to it. But it was hard for me and I knew it was hard for you. Then you were in that dreadful battle with Kirov, you were seriously hurt, your friend was killed. I took care of you, but there was really nothing I could do. Then you got word of your father. So I watched you go." She drank more wine. "You know, I really had no idea if I would ever see you again."

He nodded. "I know. I felt the same way."

He began to eat. The food and wine were delicious. The room was imbued with a kind of glow. She watched him in the flickering light.

"But I haven't been able to stop thinking about you," Julia continued. "I thought of you when I was caring for that woman I told you about."

"The one who lost her husband?"

"Yes. I thought about how level-headed you can be, despite your youth, how generous and loving. I began to question myself and my decision regarding you."

No one had ever spoken to him so intimately or so directly. Joshua imagined viewing the two of them from a distant point, there in the small cottage, having this conversation which might be with them a long time—or vanish like a wisp into nothingness.

"But still," Julia continued, "I wondered which way of looking at it was right. You are young, you are in a time of great flux in your life, you could go anywhere, do anything.

Why would you want to be with me? And why would I want to entrust my future to someone like you? Would it be right—or fair—for either of us?"

Joshua couldn't contain himself. "But... why the hell not, Julia?" he said, louder than intended.

"Well, that's been my dilemma," she said calmly. "Honestly it's rather exhausting and sometimes I grow annoyed at myself for thinking about it." She laughed.

Julia picked up her fork and began to eat ravenously. Joshua watched her, somewhat in awe. He didn't know what to think, either, but it felt like it might be good.

She put down her fork again and looked deeply into his eyes. "Do you love me, Joshua?"

This time it was he who laughed. "Yes. I believe I do."

She nodded, as if gauging something. "You see, the night before last I came to a realization, in the middle of the night. I couldn't sleep. See? You actually keep me awake." She giggled. "And it's this. If I was not afraid to become a doctor, or to marry, or divorce, or come to a small fishing village to care for people who couldn't possibly trust me, then why would I be afraid to find out the truth about you and me?"

She tossed her hair and smiled at him. It was a warm smile, a lovely smile. He felt almost overcome with warmth, in his heart, his head, filling the room.

"Oh, Joshua," she said warmly, "I do love that silly expression you get on your face."

He reached over and touched his hand to her cheek. So ravishing, he thought. He looked in her eyes. The complexities remained, but there was the same warmth in her face as in his. He stood and took her hand and pulled her close to him. She wrapped herself in his arms and they kissed. For a long time.

Then he looked at her, wanting to absorb this moment. She stepped back, too.

They stood looking at one another, the quiet room spinning around them like a time machine, so many unknowable futures.

She spoke again. "So we are agreed, then?"

He nodded, not sure to what.

"We will find out the truth. About us."

She extended her arm, took his hand and shook it, as if concluding a business transaction. Joshua could not hold back another second. He burst into laughter, and the two of them just laughed and laughed, and drank their wine. They laughed at the silliness of it all, the absurdity of life, the astounding weight of the moment. After a while, not sure what exactly was the right thing to do in this situation, Joshua stood and walked to the door. He kissed her again.

"Good night, Julia," he said with a twinkle in his eye.

She was smiling as he walked away. Maybe it's impossible to ever know the future, he thought. But it felt right and he would let Julia take her time, and they would see.

There was one more incident at the station. A fishing boat loaded with cod was returning from Georges Bank in a deep fog and struck the bar. Joshua, on patrol, saw the ship and heard the cries of the men. It was no longer cold and it was not a fierce storm. Still, the breakers were strong enough and they would need to be rescued. Joshua removed the Coston flare from his belt and struck it. The heavy red smoke enveloped the fresh sea air, and the smell of it, the color of the sand and the reflected sea, brought him back to that night, still fresh in his memory, when Buddy was killed.

The others arrived with the surfboat. Joshua and Punchy plunged into the water to launch her, and they all rowed out to the foundering ship. It was as if he were dreaming it, a replay of other nights, darker and colder, perhaps of more such nights to come. They removed the fishermen and got them safely ashore, and no one died that night.

One morning, MacDonald announced they would be free to leave for the summer at the end of the following day. The season of the Life-Savers would be coming to an end. There was much to be done: all the equipment needed to be properly cleaned and stored, the station house washed down, the food storage emptied, the linens and blankets washed and folded. The Keeper arranged for two long wagons to carry the men and their belongings into town. Some would stay there with their families, some would head elsewhere. They would all be due back in August.

MacDonald would of course remain behind. Joshua went to see him just before the wagons were ready to move out. He sat rocking on his chair on the porch, smoking his pipe and looking over the ocean.

"It's going to be quiet here," Joshua said.

"It sure is," MacDonald said. "I can't wait." He laughed, then turned and looked at Joshua. "So, young lad, you've done well for yourself here. It hasn't been easy, and you've seen some troubling things."

"Aye, sir, I guess I have at that."

"But you'll be coming back?"

"If you'll have me, sir."

"It will be my pleasure to have you, Joshua." He puffed at his pipe. "You know, I'll have to wander into town in a month or so and look for a new recruit. We could use another hand out here. You'll keep your eyes open, won't you?"

"I will, sir."

"Might think about getting a horse out here one of these days, too, if I can spring the money from the home office."

"That would be a good thing, sir. Pulling those heavy carts can be a chore."

"Yes it can," the Keeper said. "You take care of yourself, son. I'll see you soon."

"Thank you, sir. You take care, too."

Joshua turned and walked past the station to the waiting wagon, hopped in and rode over the dunes to Provincetown. He was let off at the pier, said goodbye to the others, and made his way to the east end. He liked it down there. He found a couple of rooms to let in an old cottage perched on a pier overlooking the harbor. It looked like a good place to spend the summer.

THE KEEPER

EPILOGUE

I have seen them riding seaward on the waves
Combing the white hair of the waves blown back
When the wind blows the water white and black.

We have lingered in the chambers of the sea
By sea-girls wreathed with seaweed red and brown
Til human voices wake us, and we drown.

—T.S. Eliot, *The Love Song of J. Alfred Prufrock*

CHAPTER EIGHTEEN

One day in mid-July, they let horses from the same stable as before and rode out to the beach. The day was very warm and the sun shone brightly. The horses were sweating long before they reached the dune at the far edge of the moors. They stopped and looked out over the sparkling blue ocean. A few gentle waves rolled in. They rode along the water's edge to the dilapidated cabin, and tied the horses to a piece of driftwood.

Julia had packed a basket with lunch. They kicked off their shoes and sat in the sand barefoot not far from the water and ate. Julia untied the ribbon holding her hair and let the warm breeze blow it. Joshua leaned over and kissed her cheek, then rose and walked toward the water. He stopped to remove his shirt, then his pants, and when he was naked he ran into the waves. He howled when his body hit the cold, but in a moment he was swimming comfortably. He swam vigorously for a few moments, then turned back and stood in the water. Julia was watching him.

She began to untie the bows that ran down the front of her dress. Then she let the dress fall. She removed her petticoat and various undergarments, and stood naked feeling the warm breeze on her skin. She ran forward and dove in. She, too, screeched at the initial coldness, but soon she was swimming beside him. They swam for a long time, up and down along the edge of the beach. There was no one else to be seen.

They came out of the water and sat in the hot sand. It felt good.

Joshua turned and looked at her. "You are very beautiful. Do you know that?"

She smiled. "I've been told from time to time. I don't pay it much mind, though."

"Truly beautiful."

"You're trying to turn my head, Mr. Duell."

"I confess."

"You should be more careful," she said, touching his hair.

"Why?"

"A woman like me is hard to find."

"That's the truth," Joshua said.

He kissed her on the lips, his eyes closed, feeling the sun beating down. He offered her his hand, she stood up next to him and they walked across the sand to the little cabin.

It was many years later. He sat at his desk, writing in his journal, picturing that long ago day, and others like it. He was old, his long hair and beard white, his body thin but still strong. For as long as he could remember, people around him had referred to him as the Keeper. To Joshua it could never truly be so, though he had been one a long time. He put down his pen, the fine fountain pen—with a cartridge of ink, of all things—Julia had bought him years ago, and looked out across the harbor.

Joshua had returned to the Life-Savers that August. A new young fellow named John Oliver, a Portuguese from New Bedford who later was given the nickname of Smoky, had joined the station, and he and Joshua became close friends. Smoky became somewhat of an expert on whales, and later joined the Woods Hole Oceanographic Institute when it was formed in 1930 as captain of its biggest sailing ship. Joshua sailed with him on research expeditions from time to time. Pendleton left after Joshua's third year in the Service, and Joshua was made Number One. MacDonald stayed on for another five years, although he was the oldest keeper on the east coast when he finally retired. There was a great celebration when he did. A temporary keeper was named, but no one liked him much and the following year, at the age of thirty, Joshua was named Keeper at Peaked Hill Bars.

In 1915, the Life-Saving Service was merged with the Revenue Cutter Service to form the United States Coast Guard. Joshua became an officer in the new service and remained there until he retired. In the First World War he commanded a patrol boat off the coast of Massachusetts. After the war, he returned to Provincetown as captain of a patrol unit that helped develop new advanced methods for rescuing sailors from ships, which continued to wreck along the dangerous outer beach. In 1914, the original Cape Cod Canal was opened; it had been a dream since the Pilgrims' time and one of its intended benefits was to allow ships to avoid passing the bars of the Outer Cape. The first canal was privately owned, charged a huge toll and was a failure. But by 1940, the Army Corps of Engineers had built a new, bigger canal, owned by the government, which saved thousands of ships from the fate of those earlier vessels along the Cape beaches.

In the Coast Guard between the wars, Joshua and his crew rescued fishing boats, passenger ships and other craft that ran into danger in the waters from the Cape all the way up to Cape Ann north of Boston, and from the shallow coastal waters out two hundred miles at sea. He was well-respected by his crew, other Coast Guard officers, and his superiors in Boston and Washington. In the Second World War, Joshua served as a senior officer on a Coast Guard Cutter off the coast of England. After the war, he came back to the Cape and his family and served for nearly a decade more before he finally left the service. They held a big party for him at a place called the Flagship Restaurant. Afterwards he and Julia walked hand in hand along the flats under a full moon, its light sparkling on the water.

Julia and Joshua were married in 1901. She had invited him to live with her at Christmastime, a year after they had visited the Sousas, which led him to believe she had finally accepted him. He moved in, but lived much of the year out at the station, though they saw each other every weekend. They bought a house together on Commercial Street in the east end that many years later became known as the Keeper's House. It sat on a broad bulkhead overlooking the harbor. They raised their three children there, two boys and a girl, and taught them to swim, fish, sail, dig for clams and take mussels from the rocks and how to walk the dunes at night and how to read and write and sing and dance and all the joyous and difficult things the members of a close-knit family learn together. Before he died, Gideon came to visit from time to time, and in his stoic fashion rejoiced at being a grandfather.

Joshua and Julia lost their older son Robert, a Marine Major, in World War II. The other son moved to New York and became a famous journalist. He lived in the upper half of the old house on Park Avenue, which Joshua had kept at Julia's urging after Gideon passed. The bottom floors had been converted in the twenties to a separate apartment. When Adam, as he was called, made enough money, he bought his own place and Joshua decided to sell the family house to a developer who tore it down and built a large and stylish apartment tower that still stands there today. Their daughter Susan graduated from Barnard College and went to art school, lived in Europe for many years, and returned to Provincetown in the late thirties, where she became part of a growing colony of artists that grew in influence and importance over the years—until much of the busy art world that had swarmed over the narrow streets and through the galleries that sprung up along Commercial Street moved on to other places. But Susan had stayed and married a sculptor. When they had children, Julia and Joshua enjoyed their grandchildren nearly as much as they had their children, and taught them to swim and fish and sail and hunt for clams and pick mussels and walk the dunes at night and all the other joyous and difficult things.

Julia never stopped practicing medicine. By the time she was old, she had delivered thousands of babies and treated their measles and mumps and sewn up fishermen and set broken arms and given so much advice to so many men and women and children that long before she retired, they had built a little memorial to her in a park near the pier.

Joshua took up photography and could often be found walking the outer beach, in any kind of weather, of which he never tired; his knowledge of the tides and dunes and storms, of the creatures and plants by the ocean's edge, became well known. When he walked along the vast stretches of sand where few humans went and marveled at the infinite, unstoppable power of the sea, he thought back to the first days, when he learned the skills of a Life-Saver and became a man. For the rest of his life, Joshua felt the scars of the wounds he had received during that fateful battle aboard the ship, of Kirov's dagger and of the bullet wound in his side, which always made him think of Buddy. He thought of him often, of the man he might have been had he lived, of the odd prism of beliefs about which he fantasized, ideas that would come to dominate, for better or for worse, the history of the twentieth century. He kept his mother's letter, the one he'd found at the Indian's hut, in a frame near his desk, the paper yellowed and frayed, the once familiar handwriting now barely recognizable.

On a warm summer night in the year 1969, Julia sat with Joshua on the front porch that looked out on Commercial Street. They watched people walk by, heading into town to eat and drink, go to parties, dance at the clubs or gather at the bars where people liked to sing along to an old player piano. The world had changed so much it was barely recognizable from the one that existed when they'd first come here. People behaved and looked differently and everything in this new world seemed to move so fast and in such a chaotic and irrational manner that even the craziest things they remembered from their youth seemed tame by comparison. Joshua held her hand with his left hand and smoked his ever-present pipe with his right. Somehow, miraculously, they had grown old, together, and their place in the world was both secure and no longer important.

" I do love you," he said.

She turned her wizened old head to him and let down her thick silvery hair. She smiled. "I know," she said.

THE END

ACKNOWLEDGEMENTS

The idea for this novel was born many years ago, when my brother, Jim Ives, sent me a little book called The Life Savers of Cape Cod and said it would make a good story. He was right, though getting there was a longer process than either of us suspected. My love for Provincetown and the sea were born when I first came here, at ten, in 1959, and I have cherished the local stories my entire life. Yet, considerable research went into this project, including at the Provincetown, Truro and Wellfleet Public Libraries, the Hull Life-Saving Museum, the Old Harbor Life-Saving Station at Race Point, and the Cape Cod National Seashore Visitor's Center. I am particularly grateful to Robert Finch, whose scholarship and collections were terrifically inspiring.

I am extremely thankful to many people who read part or all of various drafts, including Tony DePaul, Brooke Newman, Brenda Wineapple, Kathy Shorr, Rosa Empis Plummer, and the late artist, the magnificent Arthur Cohen. And Kathryn Winder, who read and proofed the manuscript. I worked with three editors at different times: first, Nancy Doherty; second, Jean Garnett—the talented assistant to my original agent, Leigh Feldman at Writer's House, whose early belief in the book was magical; and Blythe Frank, film producer and great friend, who talked me back from the brink and helped me incalculably to achieve the final draft. I had support and counsel all along from my friend Will Balliett, editor and publisher extraordinaire, with whom I've shared a relationship over thirty years based on writing and literature. I also received valuable support from Christopher Busa, Founder and Editor of Provincetown Arts Magazine, who encouraged me to find an editor, to re-write, and to keep the faith.

I am grateful to Catherine Wood at the Norman B. Leventhal Map Center of the Boston Public Library for the use of the 1909 Map of Cape Cod and Vicinity found in the endpapers. I'd also like to acknowledge the excellent work of the U.S. Life-Saving Service Heritage Association, and the United States Coast Guard online history resources.

Most of all, I want to thank my incredible daughters, Camille and Justine, who have read the manuscript and supported my efforts from the start. Justine's beautiful cover art, illustrations and book design—and her enthusiasm for launching a publishing venture with her crazy, old Papa— have made this project a reality. And my wife Kina of thirty two years, who has ridden the rails with me and stopped at strange and inspirational stations along the way, and whose belief in this book, and her patience and support for its creation, make her truly eligible for sainthood.

BIBLIOGRAPHY

J. W. Dalton, *The Life Savers of Cape Cod*, On Cape Publications, 1991

Robert H. Farson, *Twelve Men Down: Massachusetts Sea Rescues*, Cape Cod Historical Publications, 2000

Ralph C. Shanks, Wick York & Lisa Woo Shanks, *U.S. Life-Saving Service: Heroes, Rescues and Architecture of the Early Coast Guard*, Costano Books, 1996

David Wright & David Zoby, *Fire On The Beach: Recovering the Lost Story of Richard Etheridge and the Pea Island Lifesavers*, New York: Scribner, 2000

Robert Finch, Ed., *A Place Apart: A Cape Cod Reader,* New York: W.W. Norton & Company, 1993

Henry C. Kittredge, *Cape Cod: Its People and Their History*, New York: Houghton Mifflin Company ed. 1930, 1968

Mary Heaton Vorse, *Time and the Town: a Provincetown Chronicle*, Dial Press, 1942

Richard F. Whalen, *Truro: The Story of a Cape Cod Town*, Xlibris Corporation, 2002

Asa Cobb Paine Lombard, Jr., *East of Cape Cod,* Cuttyhunk Island, Massachusetts, 1976

Irma Ruckstuhl, *Old Provincetown in Early Photographs*, Dover Publications, 1987

Henry David Thoreau, *Cape Cod*, New York: W.W. Norton & Company, 1951

Richard G. Ryder, *Seashore Sentinel: The Old Harbor Lifesaving Station on Cape Cod*, West Barnstable Press, 2009

Annual Report of the United States Life-Saving Service U.S. Government Printing Office, 1900, 1914

United States Life-Saving Service, Beach-Apparatus Drill, by Lieut. C.H. McLellan, U.S.R.M., 1873